THE GATHERING STORM

Against the clouds of war, the characters in *Axis* play their parts: the nervous young Scot, Lord Dunsinnan, taking ever-more-frequent trips to Germany; Ruth Dexter, the American beauty torn between Dunsinnan's alluring charm and the old-fashioned fascination of Captain Seton; Lady Margery Taverner, who has lost her fortune but not her figure; the shadowy Admiral Canaris, Hitler's head of intelligence; and his game-legged agent, von Klagen, who comes to England on a mysterious mission that he insists is for the good of Germany. Winston Churchill, out of power and out of favor, sounds his Cassandra-like warnings; King Edward VIII abdicates to be with the woman he loves; Neville Chamberlain flies to Munich . . . and the novel *Axis* sweeps toward its thrilling climax.

AXIS

A Novel by
Clive Irving

AXIS

Clive Irving

BANTAM BOOKS · LONDON · TORONTO · NEW YORK

AXIS
A Bantam Book

PRINTING HISTORY
Atheneum edition published June 1980
3 printings through October 1980
Bantam edition / June 1981

ISBN 0-553-14590-8

Published simultaneously in the United States and Canada

*Bantam Books are published by Bantam Books, Inc. Its trade-
mark, consisting of the words "Bantam Books" and the por-
trayal of a bantam, is Registered in U.S. Patent and Trademark
Office and in other countries. Marca Registrada. Bantam
Books, Inc., 666 Fifth Avenue, New York, New York 10103.*

PRINTED IN THE UNITED STATES OF AMERICA

0 9 8 7 6 5 4 3 2 1

Foreword

Nobody in this story could know at the time who would win the Second World War. In the early summer of 1940, when the story ends, Britain's chances of survival seemed slender—even to Winston Churchill. Five days after becoming prime minister, Churchill warned Roosevelt that the threat of imminent defeat could force him from office, leaving the way open to those ready to sue for peace. For years before this, the will to take on Hitler had been undermined by influential men on both sides of the Atlantic who feared Nazi Germany less than they did Communist Russia, whatever the outrages being carried out by the Hitler regime.

Although the principal characters in *Axis* are fictitious, they live out their lives among real people and real events. No historical figure is made to say or do anything contrary to his known beliefs, and, as often as possible, they speak in their own words.

*"It should never have happened.
It could have been stopped.
It should have been stopped."*

WINSTON CHURCHILL,
September 1939

I

Whispers

1

Buckinghamshire, England, July 1936

The Rolls was being driven too fast into the bends of the meandering lane, but the only flaw in its deportment was a slight tilt. The front-seat passenger discreetly reached for and held a door handle, otherwise feigning calm. The driver carried on talking, oblivious to the stresses—human and mechanical—which her speed was causing, talking as though having to drive the car was a barely tolerable distraction.

"Roosevelt is such an *intemperate* man," she said, looking at her passenger and not the road.

"Intemperate?"

"Intemperate in language, intemperate in life," she said with the flatness of moral censure. The Rolls pitched a little more violently, and her passenger's knuckles turned white. Looking at his inquisitor was preferable to looking ahead.

"Malefactors of great wealth! Is *that* any way to talk of capitalism?" she persisted. "More like *communist* talk!" She looked suspiciously at her passenger: "Do *you* think he's good for America, Sir Alex?"

The answer came from a tongue trained by years of framing unrevealing replies: "America has great powers of recuperation, Nancy."

The Rolls navigated another bend by taking to the wrong side of the road, observing the laws of geometry rather than those of driving.

"No. It's *capitalism* that's good for America, and Roose-

3

elt is *bad* for capitalism." Her tone was final. She turned at last to look ahead, for the first time comprehending the contours of the road.

"There's a corner coming up," she said, surprised. "I'm going to slow down."

"I *do* hope so," he said. The Rolls and he regained their composure in the same second. Beyond the bend he saw the gates of the great house.

From a second-floor window Edward Seton watched the Rolls pull up the drive and stop below him at the steps. The woman getting out bore little resemblance to the portrait Seton had first seen only half an hour earlier in the main hall—a Victorian vision of ethereal beauty. But the reality, Lady Nancy Astor, was more vigorous and more impressive, considering the passing of years. The man behind her strained to keep pace; he was smaller than she, his large head out of kilter with his body, more cautious and deliberate. Seton recognized Sir Alexander Cadogan, deputy head of the Foreign Office.

Cadogan's presence was just one indicator of the world embraced in this house called Cliveden, a house of increasingly controversial reputation, and Seton was still unsure why he had been invited to it. His experience of English country-house weekends was occasional, not regular. The attentions of the servants unnerved him; he remembered once finding the paste already squeezed on his toothbrush, and always felt that some deficiency of toilet or manners might show his unfitness for such pampering. And no house had been as awesome as this.

There was a light knock on the door. Seton turned from the window and went across the room.

"Your bath, sir. Would you like me to draw it now?"

The butler's eyes came to a social judgment in a splinter of time.

"Yes, thank you," said Seton, moving to one side.

"A lovely room, sir."

"Yes—yes, it is."

"It's called the Sutherland Room, sir, after the Duchess of Sutherland."

The butler had paused on his progress to the bathroom, seeing Seton's open case on the bed. He was an old man with a veined bloom on his cheeks.

"Your evening suit, sir. I could have it sponged and

pressed while you take your bath." There was no trace of indictment, just an even fastidiousness.

"Thank you, yes."

The bathroom was lined with marble, the tub set into the floor and reached, Roman style, by a small flight of marble steps. Seton heard the motions of ancient plumbing, and in a minute or so the butler reappeared in the bedroom, his face more florid, condensing steam on his brow.

"Yes, sir, this room was left as it was, when the new house was built last century. When the Duchess of Sutherland lived here, it was just a small country house. The fireplace, sir—it's rather magnificent, don't you think?"

"It's Charles the First, isn't it?" Seton indicated a portrait set into white marble: The fireplace went from floor to ceiling, and the portrait was above the higher of two mantels.

"That's correct, sir." Seton's stature had risen. The butler took his evening suit and went out.

Seton was disappointed to find that the bath was not filled with asses' milk. He sat with a sponge in the steam and had a surrealist thought: Suppose, at that moment, the roof of the house could be pried off. What would be exposed?

The truth was: women before mirrors; men, half-dressed and sipping the first whisky of the evening, one of them straining into a corset; a great literary lion, gray-bearded, lying quite naked on his bed and thinking of nymphs; a small but vigorous politician copulating with the secretary who for years had been the rejuvenation of him; an austere couple standing at a window while marvelling at the vastness of the property and bristling at the ideological offense; a captain of industry, choleric and harsh, trading on the telephone; another politician, alone with his medicines, knowing the creep of death; a bishop and a Christian Scientist, in doctrinal conflict, drinking sherry; a young girl writing in her diary and concealing from it what she really felt.

Seton's fantasy evaporated with the steam. Why was he here? The invitation had been indirect—from a friend, Peter Endmere. It had seemed casual enough, but Endmere was a journalist and Seton could never quite be off guard with him. Endmere had said that somebody was keen to talk to him here, that in spite of Cliveden's reputation it was a congenial place, that a great mixture of people came and went, that he shouldn't believe everything he heard about it. But Seton already knew enough to be sure that this house was used for a peculiar interchange of political and social lives, and of course

he had wanted to judge it for himself. Out of his view on the
other side of the house two men walked in conclave on a lawn
below the terrace. One was tall, the other short. The tall man
bent to catch every word from the short man's mouth, a
mouth long respected for its Delphic advice uttered in the lo-
quacious style and seductive rhythms of the Welsh. The short-
ness of the one exaggerated the tallness of the other, but these
extremes were made compatible by a common interest: the
nature of Adolf Hitler.

"We should find out what it is that he really wants, and
give it him. *That* would be the best way of disarming him."
The pun pleased both but noticeably its Welsh author.

"It would be simpler, much simpler, if only Baldwin
would show enough interest to talk to him, to *go* there," said
the tall man with impatience.

"Baldwin has never flown and does not much like the
sea, I'm afraid. What he really needs is a rest. Three months,
at the very least. Nothing seriously wrong, just exhaustion."

"It's the strain of this business with the King." The tall
man nodded as he spoke, his ambition kindling. "If he's *that*
tired, perhaps he should get out."

They stopped and looked up to the house. People were
starting to gather on the terrace.

"Yes . . ." said the Welshman thoughtfully (and a little
artfully, "but who to replace him. *That's* the puzzle."

On the terrace the Maharajah of Mysore sppeared in evening dress and a turban, his accents more English than the
English. A group formed around him, waiters providing
champagne.

Someone laughed: ". . . So they took the villa at Antibes at a *thousand* a month, only to find out that the King
had changed his mind and was going off with her on the
yacht instead. That's *dished* them, the rotten climbers. . . ."

A waspish female voice took up the laugh: "Of course,
the war in Spain gave him a good excuse for skipping France
this year, and a yacht has much to be said for it as an alternative. More *private*, as a love nest. . . ."

"We have to choose between Russia and Germany, and
choose soon . . ."—this from another corner, a lubricated
voice. ". . . Hitler can't tackle Russia on his own. We may as
well go in with him. Let Germany be the bulwark, that's what
Halifax says." Heads nodded in unison.

Arriving at the terrace, Seton looked anxiously for a
known face and saw Endmere slumped on a divan, at his feet

an ice bucket holding champagne, and his head buried in *The Times.*

As Seton's shadow fell across the paper Endmere looked up. "Ahhh, Edward, sorry I wasn't around when you came. Fixed up all right?"

"Rather unusual room. Apricot damask, a crown over the bed, a bath fit for Nero."

"Ah, yes, so they've put you *there?* You *must* be thought a catch." Endmere pulled the bottle from the bucket. "Here, have a glass. You look as though you need it."

Seton sank into the divan and took the drink. They watched the tall and short walkers come up the steps to the terrace. Endmere motioned his glass toward them, the drink spilling.

"Know him—the little chap with the big conk?"

Seton shook his head.

"Ubiquitous little bugger. Something of an *éminence grise*—or, more like it, *éminence* grease." The pun amused Endmere more than it should have. "Supposed to have retired from the civil service long ago, but still pops in and out of Downing Street—doing God knows what. Very thick with Baldwin—and Lloyd George. What's *more* interesting, though, he's been over to Berchtesgaden, to see Hitler." Endmere finished the surviving champagne in his glass and leaned down to the bucket again, refilling. "A lot of mischief, there."

"What's his name?"

"Thomas Jones."

"Of *course*," said Seton, with a glimmer of memory.

In the still clarity of the evening air the sound of distant voices, of people from an excluded world, carried up from the Thames. Beyond the river, on the horizon, the turrets of Windsor Castle were held in a crimson light.

Seton looked around the diverse groups on the terrace. "You know, I wonder . . . how can one woman keep track of *so many* people. What do they really have in common? I can't see it."

Endmere laughed. "Knowing Nancy, that's all."

"But she has causes, doesn't she?"

"Christian Science?"

"And Hitler."

"Yes, that too," said Endmere. "But she doesn't preach, at least not *all* the time." He put down his glass and lay back on the divan, his dinner jacket riding up clear of his waist, the

shirt popping. "No, old chap, Lady Astor's power is often
made too much of. She has the ears of the mighty, but most of
them don't take a lot of notice. The point about this place is
not what *she* says. It's what they say to each other."

Thomas Jones, for once, was listening—to a tanned
young man with black slicked hair who punctuated points by
pushing down his right palm.

"Who's that with Jones?" Seton asked.

Slightly the worse for drink, Endmere looked across without raising himself, through lidded eyes. "Oh, *him?* That's
Dunsinnan. The dashing Lord Dunsinnan. Just succeeded to
the title. You must have read about it. All that oil money, all
those Scottish acres? Interesting case, that. Educated at Oxford and Göttingen, *very* hot for Hitler." He relapsed into
thought, then said, "Got a lot in common with Jones, I should
think." People were beginning to go into the house. Fighting
lethargy, Endmere got up. "Time for dinner. Your audition."

The dining room was French, eighteenth-century panel-
ling on the walls and an authentic Louis XV ceiling. The main
table and chairs had been made for Mme de Pompadour. It
was the first time all the weekend guests had come together.
Endmere took Seton to their hostess. As he walked across the
room Seton thought of the portrait again, trying to see what
remained of the girl, Nancy Langhorne, the Virginia beauty
who had married into the landed aristocracy of England. The
older woman, erratic but luminous in the center of this con-
stellation, had the eyes of the portrait, intense blue.

As Endmere introduced Seton she put out a gloved hand.
"How nice. . . . Welcome to Cliveden, Group Captain. Been
hearin' about you." The Virginia voice was undimmed. "You
must meet Colonel Lindbergh."

But there were more than thirty people at Lady Astor's
table. When Lindbergh and his wife arrived, they went
straight to the head, one on each side of their hostess. Seton
was placed halfway down the table; on his left was a member
of the government of Stanley Baldwin, known to him only by
sight, and on his right, the wife of a surgeon. They settled into
small talk, each of them more interested in the upper reaches
of the table. Seton noticed that Lady Astor's teetotalism did
not bring prohibition: The table was well provided with hock
and claret. He saw the young Dunsinnan settle at a far corner
with a deeply tanned girl.

Gradually conversations interlaced into one theme: the
king and Mrs. Simpson.

Lady Astor turned to Lindbergh: "Have you *seen* the stories in the American papers, Colonel—the scandal of the yacht?"

It was a tactless question for the Lindberghs, fugitives from the American tabloids. Lindbergh was terse: "No, I have not. But Anne and I found the King a really charming man."

"Too charming by half," muttered the politician to Seton, confiding: "He's infatuated. The cabinet spends half its time talking about it. God knows what they can do. Baldwin thinks of nothing else. Poor chap, he's so decent he hopes God will intervene."

Across the table an old man dissected a grouse. He spoke downwards, addressing the carcass. "It's a deplorable royal line—these German parvenus. They wrecked Europe with a family squabble. Now they'll finish off our monarchy in the bedroom." A piece of grouse adhered to his lower lip, unheeded.

"There speaks a quarter of a million acres and eight centuries," whispered the politician. "The *real* voice of England."

The more Seton drank, the clearer headed he felt; conversations subsided into the background, leaving him above them, engrossed in morbid reflections on power in England and those who exercised it. The people of England were well beyond these panelled walls, but the power was here. He noticed that Lindbergh had become a listener, brooding in silence. At the end of dinner the gentlemen separated from the ladies. The men were directed to a large drawing room with two great fireplaces and scattered leather sofas—the most overtly masculine room Seton had yet seen, lacking even flowers. He took a large brandy from a waiter and turned to find Lindbergh bearing down on him.

From the distance across the table Lindbergh had seemed the same gangling, socially maladroit man Seton had first met in his days in Washington, but now, emerging in close-up, there was a change. Lindbergh's face was passing from prolonged adolescence to premature middle age, without an intervening stage. Around his eyes the freshness had already gone, replaced by a look that seemed to Seton to mingle zeal with suspicion.

Lindbergh thrust his hand forward. "Wanted to see you, Group Captain, and Nancy said she could arrange it. Want to have a talk." His head was rolling slightly with animation. He steered Seton to a sofa in a corner. "You're just the kind of person who might understand."

Seton had a feeling of having been importuned. Lindbergh sat down and waved a hand to embrace the great drawing room. "These people, they only want to talk about one subject, the King and that woman." Making no attempt at discretion, Lindbergh glared at them. "They are supposed to be running this country, but I'm damned if I can get them to think straight." He sighed and turned back to Seton, dropping his voice. "Now see here, Group Captain. I've just come back from Berlin. *Those* people are thinking straight all right. They have no nonsense with socialism or communism. *They* know who the enemy is."

A manic note was apparent in Lindbergh's voice. Seton had the uncomfortable feeling of facing a man suddenly irrational: "Do they?"

That response was too equivocal for Lindbergh. "Yes sir, they do. The Soviets."

"You were impressed—with Germany?"

"I certainly was. That country is achieving miracles."

"At some cost to democracy, surely?"

Lindbergh was disconcerted but aggressive: "Democracy? What does *that* mean?"

"Freedom to oppose, a free press . . ."

"A *free press?*" Lindbergh seemed on the verge of hysteria; other heads turned. "That's the beginning of decadence, the newspapers. *I* know that. . . ." His voice fell again. "I look at Germany, and I see a new power. I look at England, and I see an old power, too many tired men. How are you going to get people to face facts?"

"What are the facts—as you see them?"

Lindbergh shifted his ground in the face of Seton's coolness. "See here, Group Captain. You and I have one thing we both understand, whatever the politicians. We *know* the future. We've seen it, we see it every day. *Airplanes* are the future. That's the only kind of power that counts. That's why I wanted to see you, to tell you. The Germans showed me everything, anything I asked to see, nothing was kept back. *Astonishing.* As of this moment the Luftwaffe is the most powerful air force in the world." Lindbergh's right hand sliced through the air in a chopping motion. "That man Messerschmitt, what a designer."

"You saw hiw new pursuit plane?"

"There's nothing to come even near it." Lindbergh leaned forward. "At least, nothing that *I* know of."

Seton let the implied question pass. "And from what you have seen, what conclusions do you draw?"

"If you can't lick 'em, join 'em."

"For what purpose, exactly?"

This was altogether too obtuse for Lindbergh, who became openly exasperated. "For what purpose? To deal with the Bolsheviks, dammit. Isn't that what we all want?" He stopped, assessing Seton again, his disillusion transparent. "I figured you, of all people, would get the point. *You* must know how defenseless this country is against air attack. I'm trying to persuade these people, but they don't understand. You, however, have influence."

"Ah," said Seton slowly, "that's a fine point." As he shaped his words Seton deliberately continued the style of effete evasion. "What *kind* of influence? In technical matters, perhaps some. But you're jumping beyond that, I'm afraid. You seem to have a political point. Does a technical problem—*if* we have it, and I'm not admitting to it—does a technical problem require a political answer? If it does, that's outside my field."

As Seton intended, Lindbergh ran out of patience. His long legs unwound and he stood up, minatory: "You don't have a choice. It's gone too far for that."

Lindbergh wandered away across the room with that peculiar self-consciousness of those who know that for the rest of their lives they can never be anonymous, and Seton found himself feeling sorry for the man. Remembering the ghoulish treatment of the kidnapping and murder of the Lindberghs' son in the American press, he wondered what those strains were doing to the state of mind of this man who had come to England for refuge.

"You look as though you've been run over by a bus." Endmere appeared at Seton's right shoulder, settling into the seat where Lindbergh had been.

"Something worse, I think," Seton replied.

"He's getting people rattled."

"That seems to be the idea."

That night Seton slept fitfully in the apricot room. Voices overlapped and recurred, faces came and went, and with them images of gluttony. A woman's hand, heavy with rings, tapped a wineglass nervously to the rhythm of a song and this delirium fused with wakening: From somewhere below the bedroom he could hear a guitar and a young girl singing:

". . . has anybody seen my Sal?
She's so tall and shy and stately,
If you see her passing by
Tell her I'm the same old pal . . .
Although she drinks an awful lot
      with other men
She's a darned fine gal . . ."

The butler came in carrying a tray with tea and drew open the heavy silk curtains to reveal another crystal day. The branch of a cypress hung across one of the windows. The butler saw Seton's evening suit lying in a chair. He folded it, then put it away.

Experimenting with democracy, Seton said, "Was it my imagination, or did I hear someone playing the guitar?"

"Her Ladyship's sister, sir, playing to the children." There was enough familiarity in the butler's voice to encourage Seton.

"How long have you served here?" Judging it finely, Seton substituted *served* for *worked* at the last second.

The butler closed the wardrobe. "I'm not on the staff of the house, sir. I belong to a party—waiters, butlers, maids, footmen—we go all over the country, hunt balls and county balls, that kind of thing. I've been coming down to Cliveden for the past twenty-two years whenever they have a house party or a ball." He stopped, suddenly unsure of the intimacy and looking to Seton for signs of complicity in the breach of etiquette.

Seton said, "You must have seen many famous people, passing through this house. . . ."

It was too much of a leading question. The butler retreated from it. "It is very busy here, sir." He poured Seton's tea. "Breakfast is on the terrace, sir, it's such a fine day."

When he dressed, Seton was drawn to the lawns. The house could swallow people with ease, and few of them were yet at large. Cliveden covered an entire hill overlooking a curve in the Thames. Its style reflected the period of the nineteenth century when English country houses turned to Italy for a veneer of grace. Its massiveness—three floors on the huge terrace platform—was masked by Italianate proportions and flourishes, like a heavy man in a cunningly cut suit. Several sculpted tiers of garden swept down to the river from the terrace. The sun was already warm, and Seton wandered into a small walled garden. Passing from grass to gravel, he heard light steps behind him and turned.

"You don't *know* me, do you? I tried to catch your eye last night, but you ignored me." It was the dark girl who had sat with Dunsinnan at the table. She was both accusatory and teasing.

It was her voice that saved Seton's perplexity.

"My God! Can it be? I don't believe it . . . *Ruth*—Ruth Dexter? The little girl I remember in Washington, with braces and pigtails?"

She laughed and reached out, kissing him decorously on a cheek. "The same!"

Seton stood back, making a deliberate, studied appraisal, slightly embarrassed. *"Well,"* he said, trying to see the vestigial girl in the emerging woman, "of all the surprises— *pleasant* surprises. What on earth brings *you* to Cliveden?"

"I'm doing Europe for a year. I'm staying with a friend, Lady Dunsinnan, at her house in London."

"Doing Europe?" Seton took her arm tentatively, and they walked on through the garden.

"Postgraduate studies, at least that's what *I'm* calling it." She laughed. "Medieval art—my subject at Radcliffe."

"I remember now, your father couldn't understand how medieval art could interest a Dexter."

"That's the trouble with the Dexters—a father and three brothers with nothing on their minds but airplanes."

Her voice had the springlike tensions of the Boston Irish, but her looks were molded by a Californian mother with a trace of Indian blood. Seton felt uncomfortably middle-aged; Ruth Dexter, whom he had known almost from the cradle, had flowered into this self-possessed beauty.

"You should have told me you were coming to England."

"I know. Father said that. It all happened so fast, when I made up my mind . . ."

"How is your father?"

"Absolutely the same," she said with a mixture of pride and exasperation. "Somehow he gets twenty-eight hours into twenty-four, you know, you know him. The airmail business isn't enough. He's going into flying people now—from *Miami.* They should call it Alligator Airways."

"Airlines are a good thing to be in," said Seton, implicitly defending her father.

"I know . . . I know," she conceded, looking at him mischievously. "You and he have a lot in common, don't you?"

"Not any longer, I'm afraid." Seton tapped the frame of his glasses. "Those days are over, I'm afraid. I fly a desk now."

The glasses had confused her the night before, when she was trying to identify him. She thought they flattered him. "You must miss flying."

Before Seton could answer, they heard other feet walking across the gravel. A tanned young man in gray flannels and a tennis shirt approached them, too energetically for Seton's comfort.

"Aha!" said Alastair Dunsinnan, "discovered in the rose garden!" His heartiness was forced. He looked inquiringly from Ruth Dexter to Seton.

"Alastair, this is a very old friend of father's, Edward Seton."

Seton winced at the "very old."

Dunsinnan studied Seton as he put out his hand. "Dunsinnan, Alastair Dunsinnan. Nice to meet you." He paused, still taking stock. "Friend of Patrick Dexter's? Not in the same line of business?"

"Not exactly."

"Edward and father flew together in the war," said Ruth, curious about Seton's evasion, "they were rather deadly."

"Oh, *really?*" said Dunsinnan. "Like Richthofen?"

"No," she said, "they survived."

Mother's looks, father's wit, thought Seton with satisfaction. He said, "I think it's time for breakfast. Will you two join me?" He knew that Dunsinnan was still trying to relate the idea of a wartime pilot to his present dissimilar appearance, but did nothing to enlighten him.

The serenity of breakfast was ended with the arrival on the terrace of their hostess, dressed for golf. She came on the tables like a whirlwind, crying, "Why don't you all go *out?* Why do you want to sit around *here,* talking? Go out! Look at the lovely day! GO OUT!"

The cry became a command intimidating even the most fragile guests. Those who didn't seem capable of vigorous movement slunk into corners of the house to hide.

Possessively, Dunsinnan took Ruth Dexter away to the tennis courts, leaving Seton exposed to the rallying call. He was saved by Endmere, who suggested as the least damaging exercise a walk to the stables.

By the early evening all energy was spent; the golfers,

riders, tennis players recuperated on the terrace. The air was heavy. There were one or two new faces, afternoon arrivals, visibly more strained than the others. Seton recognized among them the Chancellor of the Exchequer, Neville Chamberlain.

The weekend culminated in the ballroom. A small orchestra, a strange mixture of strings and saxophones, played a repertoire that was no less strange: Viennese waltzes that were too brisk alternated with swing that was too slow.

"This is where we go back to the nursery," warned Endmere, who had fortified himself generously. "It begins with the charades and goes downhill."

But the charades were better than expected: a series of self-mocking sketches delivered by an angular young woman with rampant teeth—caricatures of preppy English women in tea shops and virginal innocence in a girls'-school dormitory, suggestive, without being vulgar, safe humor expressing good breeding and the self-assurance of an indomitable class.

Ruth Dexter's dark shoulders heaved with the pain of her laughter, and her head came to rest on Dunsinnan's left shoulder. Between the laughter and the music the mosaic of transactions continued, registering in fragments of conversation: ". . . The trouble is, don't you think, the Jews are too *strident* about it . . ."; a disappointed voice: "You can never go on form at Ascot"; "I'm afraid more goes into Stanley Baldwin than ever comes out"; "I thought Göring a *very* striking man"; from a woman: "Eden is soft." Seton saw Dunsinnan move away, leaving Ruth Dexter alone by the orchestra. He crossed the floor to her.

"You've been deserted."

She offered him the seat left by Dunsinnan. "Alastair's mother is unwell. She's been upstairs the whole weekend, such a pity. He's just gone to see that she's okay."

"How well do you know them, the Dunsinnans?"

"Hardly at all. Father knew Lady Dunsinnan back in the war. Didn't you know that? When he was wounded. She worked at a hospital in London, and she gave her home to men for convalescence."

"I see . . . I stayed in France when he was wounded and came back. What do you think of this place?"

"Cliveden? You know, I thought it was *I've-den* and only just found out it was *iv.* What *can* you say? I've never seen anything like it. I discovered they have fifty gardeners. *Fifty.*"

The music stopped, leaving Ruth's *fifty* salient in the air. Their hostess came onto the floor, another commanding glint in her eyes. "And *now,*" she announced, looking at her victims, *"musical chairs!"*

Footmen took the chairs from the side of the ballroom floor and placed them back-to-back in two lines down the center.

"Ladies to the left, gentlemen to the right," she cried, and they obeyed, making two snaking lines.

The orchestra began playing snatches of "St. Louis Blues." Seton, trapped between two semi-senile aristocrats, could only shuffle as the line moved around the room waiting for the first abrupt break in the music, when the first scramble to find a chair would come. He watched Ruth Dexter in the other line and resolved to lose as soon as it was decently possible. After each descent to the chairs the footmen took four chairs away, the unseated having to move away to the side while the survivors vied for the remaining seats. The orchestra ran through more jazz, switched to swing, and then, with one chair and two men remaining, struck up "Here We Go Round the Mulberry Bush." The music died in midbar, and Neville Chamberlain moved with surprising agility into the chair, leaving his rival in midstride.

Over the applause Endmere said to Seton, "Do you believe in omens?"

Later, slipping away to his room, Seton saw Dunsinnan, Lindbergh, and Thomas Jones in an alcove behind a potted palm.

2

Lady Margery Taverner's clothes were lying where they had been thrown on the wicker chair. They were creased, and that irritated her now, not from any concern for neatness, but because her maid would notice. Nothing would be said, but it was still a form of mute blackmail. There was no real danger, just the slight inexplicit clue, but she believed that adventures were best made untraceable when they were impulsive, and this had been almost too impulsive. They had not even bothered to draw the curtains.

Lady Margery sat on the end of the bed and pulled on her stockings, wondering about the indecent haste of it. Her legs were not quite dry from the shower, so the silk twisted. Endmere lay in the bed on his back, his mouth slightly open and the breath coming easily. There was, she thought, no convincing reason why she should have consented to his maneuver. She had done so partly because of his reputation and partly because she was bored. Now she had to concede that his reputation was deserved—at least that part of it that she had enjoyed. She even had the fleeting impulse, which dismayed her, to pull off the stockings and get back into his bed. But there wasn't time. His eyes opened. For a second or two he seemed disoriented, and then he saw her.

"So soon?" he asked.

"It's been *three* hours."

"There's a curfew?"

She was pulling at her hair with a brush. "I have a timetable. If I depart from it, there would have to be explanations."

"Dunsinnan?"

She bristled. "No."

Pleased with the provocation, Endmere raised himself on his elbows and took a cigarette from a pack by the bed. Neither of them spoke for a minute. He saw that her nipples were erect again. He marveled at the passionless face, a face that contradicted her body so completely, yet also marked her rank and left him with an uneasy feeling of being patronized.

She was half decided that it shouldn't happen again; she knew this instinct, trusted it, and usually abided by it. But something in this case blurred the resolve. Dunsinnan was away, and Endmere was, after all, a transient. In Spain last week, where next?

Endmere got up and slipped on a silk dressing gown. "Didn't you sleep at all?" he said.

"About five minutes. There's a draft from your window."

"I never noticed."

Dressed now, she held her head slightly back, in the swanlike way that he had often noticed, and she looked at him carefully and critically. "How often can *you* spend your days like this?"

"It isn't a way of life."

"And *The Times* is?"

Endmere liked this edge in her voice; it had been part of what had drawn him in the first place. He still wanted to get behind that voice, almost as much as he had wanted to see that exquisite body. The body had proved easier. "You going to Berlin for the Olympics?" he asked, turning away to light another cigarette.

"Probably."

"It's like watching a gangster clean himself up, putting on a new suit to go to a wedding. They're desperate to look respectable. Half of London seems to have free tickets."

She looked at her watch.

"So where's the next slot in your busy calendar for today?" he said, his tone a little too sarcastic.

"Tea. With Emerald Cunard."

"I'd better get you a taxi, then."

"In your dressing gown?"

She walked out, went round the corner into Elizabeth Street, and found herself a cab.

Endmere decided that she would be back, although nothing had been said.

Hardened Londoners, the starlings occupying the roof of the Foreign Office remained in place as Big Ben struck 10 A.M. From his Whitehall office Seton shared their perspective, if not their composure. His skyline was one of towers, some authentic and ancient and some, like the Foreign Office itself, mock imperial. To the west of Parliament and Westminster Abbey he could see the newer granite of emerging business empires like the headquarters of Imperial Chemical Industries.

In the architectural pecking order of the Foreign Office, rank diminished as you approached the roof. Seton had been cast into the upper reaches, partly to mask his importance, partly to keep him clear of the hierarchy—and partly to appease those who had resisted the creation of such an unorthodox role. He shared this part of the building with the young resident clerks whose job was to watch the telegrams while their masters dined, slept, or followed their other passions. The arrangement suited Seton. His only apparent connection with the great Foreign Office machine was a nest of vacuum tubes in his outer office. Color-coded canisters hissed up the tubes from varied and arcane sources, supervised by Seton's assistant, a fleshy pink-faced young man whom Seton suspected of virginity.

"Morning, Pickles," said Seton, throwing his trilby with one practiced movement to a bamboo coatrack. The oriental coatrack was one of a number of deviations from the official norm: Another was a glass-fronted Georgian bookcase holding a twenty-four-volume set of Voltaire in French, with red leather bindings. There was a stuffed peregrine falcon on top of a filing cabinet, and a print of the Suez Canal on one wall.

Seton closed the door, shutting himself off from Pickles and the vacuum tubes. He stood by the window, pensive, looking over the cobbled courtyard below. He pushed his glasses to the tip of his nose, a new implication of pedantry, of looking at too much paper. Creeping shortsightedness, the mildest of debilities, had been enough to end his flying career, and the glasses were an irritating token of going to seed. He picked up one of the two phones.

The connection, though barely three hundred yards away, took time.

"Yes. That would be fine," said Seton, "eleven, by the bridge." He turned again to look out the window. "No, I think the rain will hold off." The voice on the other end had no view of the sky.

Little under an hour later he left the Foreign Office by a back staircase, came out within the shadow of the statue of Clive of India, and crossed into St. James's Park. A cool wind came off the lake. A few people threw scraps to the ducks. Screened by trees, the noise of traffic in the Mall diminished. Seton went to a small stone bridge across the lake and looked back, down the length of the lake to Horse Guards and the rooftops of Admiralty House. Whitehall, he knew, was a village, a career apex—or a dead end. He could now see no career beyond it. The thought depressed him further.

"Good morning, Edward."

Sudden materialization was this man's gift; born of a life of deference, his habit of easing in and out of shadow persisted even here in the park, where corridors gave way to an open-air conspiracy of government, of power brokering, of traded alliances.

"I wonder," said the newcomer, "if you are not feeling, perhaps, a little caged?"

Not for the first time had he successfully read Seton's mind.

"Wings clipped?" said Seton, conceding the point with a flicker of a grin.

"It can be tedious, I grant that. I thought you might become restless when we embarked upon this experiment."

"There's a deluge of paper."

The other man was shaped by a life of sedentary duty: bulkier than Seton, in a thick blue serge suit, wearing a homburg. He tapped the parapet of the bridge with a silver-tipped umbrella. "Yes, as a substitute for action," he said, then turned to face Seton more directly. "Now. What's on your mind?"

"I told you I was invited to Cliveden."

"And?"

"Well, it was everything I expected, of course. Plenty of casual comment, quite a bit of the Astor line. But—I don't really know—I had the feeling of having disappointed someone's expectations. It was Lindbergh, he had somehow got them to get me there."

"Ah, yes, Lindbergh. Newly converted to the great German dream."

"He could be a nuisance. He seems determined to have us collapse into Hitler's arms. The trouble is, people are going to listen to him. Because of *who* he is, they think he knows what he's talking about."

"What do *you* think, Edward?"

Seton hesitated, trying to be strictly fair. "He's been through a lot of stress. I don't think he's unhinged—nothing like that. But the Germans have been very clever, caught him in a receptive mood and—well, he's obviously sold on their way of running things, *and* on the Luftwaffe."

"Yes. *Somebody* knows what they're doing." He suddenly sounded weary, turning from Seton to look down at the water, talking quietly. "This kind of thing is catching. One conversation at Cliveden and by the end of the week it becomes the conventional wisdom, infects Whitehall, gets enshrined in policy. There are many ready to listen to that particular drift."

The dipped face rose and gave Seton a measuring look. Then the man spun on his heels and marched over the bridge to the grass, the umbrella moving like a soldier's pacemaker. Seton, taken unawares by the decisiveness and by the unfamiliar energy, hurried to catch up.

"Look, Edward, I'll be frank. When I asked you to take up this work, the need was legitimate enough. We needed someone with your background, independent of the departments. I improvised a little, bent the system. But I have to be careful. Allegiances are rather confused." His gaze was fixed on Buckingham Palace. "You may think this Simpson woman is causing enough trouble, but there's something else. The fact is, he's taking too much of an interest in one aspect of affairs, more than is the custom. More than is healthy." He turned to Seton. "There are family ties with Germany. Some effort is being made from that quarter to play on his sympathies."

Seton could not conceal his surprise.

"The fact is, we've even had to prune the papers that go to him. It's never happened before."

Seton realized the effort the man had had to make to share the confidence.

"What you've been saying about Cliveden simply underlines the dangers. There's far too much traffic between Germany and high places here. It's difficult to keep track of it all. I'd like you to help. As a natural extension of what you're already doing, of course."

"I still don't quite see," said Seton.

"Did you run across a young man called Dunsinnan at Cliveden?"

"Yes."

"We've been watching him. Whatever is going on, he's in it somewhere."

"I have a way to keep tabs on him."

"Yes. I thought you might."

There was already such a babble inside the flat that Seton had to ring the bell twice. When the door opened, he was overwhelmed by the smell of Turkish cigarettes.

"Oh, Edward. Do come up. Cool night, is it not?"

Over the voices he picked out a song, Roy Fox singing "A Pretty Girl Is Like a Melody." It brought back memories of America. There were about a score of men in the room and perhaps a dozen women. He always felt out of place here and had come only because the party's excuse this time was the birthday of an old friend, a friend whose wayward social habits were in strange contrast to his brilliant scientific mind— Seton suffered the one for the stimulus of the other; but it was already clear that his host was lost to pleasure.

"Whisky, isn't it? Straight?"

"Soda—quite a lot."

A young woman nosed up to him trancelike, trilling.

"How *are* you, you old stiff?"

Recognition unnerved Seton. He smiled weakly.

She came up only to his shoulders. Her face was flushed, and she breathed juniper. "I know I shouldn't ask," she said, fluttering long artificial lashes, "but do you think we shall have an American queen?"

"I think," said Seton, feeling pompous but not checking it, "that I would leave that kind of speculation to the newspapers."

She drew back from him in elaborate reproof: *"Hah!* We *are* being discreet." She laughed. "But then we all need to be, don't we?" Her eyes swept the room.

Seton saw a lifeline, Endmere in a corner, and wondered how to reach him. An ivory cigarette holder came between him and the woman, making an arc in the air. "Surely, Edward," said his host, "you don't expect us to depend on the newspapers for news of our future queen?"

The woman broke in: "You're *right.* Everybody knows they've been gagged. It's all been fixed, with the Palace."

Seton ducked out from between the two of them as they closed on each other.

Endmere had watched Seton's escape. "She has a one-track mind," he said, leaning on the wall.

"Like most." Seton took up his own position at the wall, watching and feeling more a voyeur than participant. Without looking at Endmere, he said, "Your prediction on Spain is looking right."

"Franco? Yes, it may look a long shot now, but he's got powerful friends."

"Mussolini?"

"Not just Mussolini."

"I don't see the Germans risking involvement."

Endmere drew on his cigarette and put his drink on top of a discarded woman's glove, staining it with spilling whisky. "Oh, you don't? I think it'll be too much of a temptation." He looked at Seton. "Have you got over Cliveden yet?"

"I can see where your paper gets its ideas."

"You don't approve?"

"It's what you don't print that worries me."

Endmere picked up his glass and emptied it in one gulp. "Well, *look* who's here."

A new figure had appeared at the door, an Apollo: flaxen-haired, more than six feet tall, broad shouldered, and narrow hipped.

"Always tell a German aristo from a British one," said Endmere. "Theirs don't have bums. Ours do."

This one didn't. The man's jacket fell to his thighs without diversion.

"Saxe-Coburg-Gotha," said Endmere, waving his empty glass. "Duke of. Bit of a split personality. Grandson of Queen

Victoria. Old Etonian, now a devoted apostle of Herr Hitler. Been seeing rather a lot of the King, rather too much, I gather, for the taste of *some* of the cabinet."

The small room was now full of people and the scent of Turkish tobacco. Endmere was feeling slightly sick. "Want to join me in a cab?" he asked.

Seton nodded. He had already had enough. They pushed through the crush. Seton discovered in passing that the Nazi Duke had a feminine fragrance—the woman with the juniper breath was addressing his midriff. Seton and Endmere left their host with his cigarette holder describing an arc as though to ward off spirits.

In the taxi Endmere sat slumped in a corner. There was a smell of damp canvas. The streets were wet. He coughed. "You think we're suppressing things, is that it?"

"You must know what's happening there."

"Yes. We know. And we're not the only ones. But as long as it's the Jews who are on the receiving end—well, you don't expect anyone to make much of a fuss, do you?"

Endmere left the taxi first, at Chester Square. As he came through the door he heard the phone ringing.

Although it was warm, Lady Dunsinnan lay wrapped in a tartan blanket in the conservatory of her London home in Eaton Square, the chill developed at Cliveden in slow retreat. Ruth Dexter sat by her, ministering unrelished potions.

"Why must medicines always taste so *foul?*" said the patient. When Ruth did not answer, Lady Dunsinnan went on: "Maybe it's because most doctors are Scots. Like Calvin, they equate cure with suffering." She pushed the bottle aside. "There's only one real cure—and they don't prescribe that." She reached under the sofa and produced a small flask bound in leather. "When a country is endowed with a gift as rare as this, I can't think why we should bother with *that* rubbish." She uncorked the flask and took a devoted swig. "Ahhh . . . the tears of the gods." The Scottish accent rhapsodized the phrase.

Ruth pretended to frown. "That's very wicked of you!"

But the conspiracy between them was already secure. Lady Dunsinnan winked. "My dear, until you've acquired a taste for Scotch whisky your education won't be complete. We'll take care of that." She put out a hand. "Alastair must take you to our distillery when we're in Scotland."

Ruth took the flask and sniffed it. "I guess I'll need time to acquire the taste."

By the time Dunsinnan joined them, the flask was safely concealed and an air of genteel innocence pervaded the conservatory, helped by the scent of violets. But Dunsinnan knew better, and his eyes narrowed as he looked at his mother. "You're looking more *bonny*, mother, in fact, *very* bonny. Too bad you can't join us at the Hamiltons for lunch." He turned to Ruth. "Isn't it a pity, your having to come without a chaperone?"

"I think I can handle it."

"Yes . . . I'm sure you can," said Lady Dunsinnan, glancing up at her son. Ruth Dexter was proving to be a tantalizing stimulus in both their lives.

They walked across Hyde Park to the house in Hyde Park Gardens, Dunsinnan once taking her hand to cross a street and then releasing it. There was something faintly gauche in his manner that she considered with amusement; it contradicted his aspiration.

The lunch produced a tone of voice that she was already beginning to find familiar, political intercourse interwoven with social banalities. Ruth was placed at the table next to a young woman in a black dress and a small black hat. Her lips were carelessly made up, their thinness masked by thick strokes, and her eyebrows pencilled into thin, arching curves. On the collar of the dress she wore a small swastika in gold. She spoke in a series of assertive bursts, in the manner of someone used to attention.

"Where are *you* from?" she said, hearing Ruth speak across the table to Dunsinnan.

"Boston."

"Never been to America." Her attention turned instantly on to a pale young man moving down the table to a seat two places from Dunsinnan. She whispered obliquely to Ruth, "That's Jimmy. His thing is incest. You've no *idea* how much is going on." It was as though she were describing a commonplace. "Is there much of it going on in America?"

"Much of what?"

"Incest."

"It's not something I've studied."

"Really?" The eyebrows arched even higher. "I know a frightfully clever young man, a scientist. He says incest is prevalent in royal families and among the Welsh."

"I don't think the news has reached Boston."

"No, I expect not." She gave Ruth a speculative look.

An older woman intervened. "How is the Führer, Unity?"

"He's quite marvellous, absolutely heavenly."

Pale-faced Jimmy said, summoning a surprising belligerence, "You wouldn't say that if you were a Jew."

"Oh, Jimmy, *really!* He's only doing what we should do, if we had any sense. You should have been with me a few weeks ago, we had supper with Julius Streicher in Munich. Now, *there's* a man who knows how to treat the Jews. He keeps them in his cellar, you know, then asks them up after dinner and lets them eat grass. Absolutely terrific."

A man on Ruth's left, ear bent to this conversation, grunted. "I say, that's going a bit far, what?"

The swastika leaned across Ruth. "Not too far for me." She laughed. "Let them eat grass."

Outraged, Jimmy stood up and threw down his napkin. "I won't listen to any more of this. Unity, you're a disgrace, an absolute d—disgrace." He departed without more than a fleeting disturbance. Ruth noticed that the swastika woman's fingers were like sausages, the nails bitten blunt.

At the end of lunch Dunsinnan went to the woman's side. "Will I see you—at Bayreuth?"

"You will. We'll be staying with Frau Wagner."

Ruth overheard the exchange and, walking back to Eaton Square, said, "Is that woman quite sane?"

Dunsinnan was bland. "Unity Mitford? You mustn't mind her, she gets a bit carried away, but she's really quite harmless. She's got a crush on Hitler, a sort of schoolgirl thing. Easy to understand—he does have a mesmerizing charm." He looked at Ruth. "It's a little embarrassing for him when these maidens throw themselves at his feet."

"Have you met him?"

"Not actually *met* him, not yet. I've been quite close, friend of friends, that kind of occasion."

"You admire him?"

"A great man. A truly great man, not enough people realize that, *yet.* Where is there another as great?" He frowned and answered his own rhetoric: "Not *here*, unfortunately."

3

Germany, July 1936

For hours nothing and no one had held still in a clear
light. Places and people overlapped in a succession of changes
from plane to car to plane again and then another car through
the night: the darkness of open country, occasionally punctured by oncoming headlights; the streetlights of a town; finally searchlights playing on a building and flashlights directed at their faces by black-uniformed S.S. guards. It
seemed a conspiracy of lights designed to keep everything indistinct: a world of stark contrasts rather than of definition,
highlighted features not faces, shadows not identities, and always one more turning before the final door opened—if ever
it would.

They had travelled for four days, two of the men in civilian clothes and one in uniform. In Berlin there had been
barely time to wash before they were flown to Nuremberg.
There they were given a dark-blue Mercedes with a driver,
and another Mercedes followed, carrying three Nazi officials.
Now at Bayreuth an S.S. officer questioned their driver and
turned them back, pointing to a spur road on the side of the
hill. Behind them they left a strange building picked out in
the searchlights: the Festival Theatre, shrine of Richard Wagner. It was a semicircular domed auditorium with a colonnade
at its base, curiously improvised in appearance, a tower with a
pitched roof behind it and four smaller towers, each flying
Nazi banners.

The cars' headlights illuminated a graveled driveway divided by a small oval lawn framed by low hooped railings. In
the center of the grass was a small pedestal topped by a marble bust of Wagner. Beyond the lawn the cars drew up to the
steps of an ugly two-storeyed house of stone. The three men
were led into the house. As the car engines died they heard
the music from the distant auditorium reaching its climax.

26

One of the three, familiar with Wagner's music, recognized the tumult of *Die Meistersinger*.

Inside the auditorium, taking its cue from the music, the audience rose and turned away from the stage toward a gallery. *Die Meistersinger* got to its point:

> *"Beware! Evil deeds are threatening us.*
> *Once the German people and kingdom*
> *have been submerged by false French majesty,*
> *soon no Prince will understand his people,*
> *and they will plant ephemeral French*
> *taste and French vanity in German soil."*

In his box in the gallery Adolf Hitler rose to meet the climax and to return the salute. He was flanked by Hermann Göring and Joseph Goebbels. The final bars of the opera were drowned out by waves of applause for the Führer. Built to contain the resonance of Wagner, the fan-shaped Festival Theatre embraced the idolatry as it had the music, the one flowing from the other as an anthem to Holy German Art and resurrected German power. Among the many services they had rendered their leader, Göring and Goebbels had survived nearly forty performances of *Die Meistersinger*. For Goebbels the consummation of opera and loyal ovation was one more opus in his own orchestration of Nazi devotions; for Göring it was a paralyzing lapse into histrionic vulgarity. Hitler's eyes glistened with emotion. But in formal evening suit with stiffly starched white shirt and white tie he looked out of character, too much of a masquerade.

A row behind Hitler sat a severe matron in black and two younger women in crimson, their colors breaking the sober convention of Bayreuth. The woman in black was Winifred Wagner, Welsh-born wife of Wagner's son Siegfried. The crimson women were Diana Mitford, a classic English beauty, and her sister Unity.

As the music and applause slipped away Hitler's enraptured face turned to Frau Wagner in gratitude. An oblique glance fell on the Mitford sisters, registering but not acknowledging. They stood in reverence. Behind them, in the shadows of the gallery, Alastair Dunsinnan felt on the fringe of a magnetic field, seeing the orbiting bodies in their ordained places and wanting to be drawn closer himself but knowing that his moment had not yet come.

Then there was a slight disturbance of this settled order.

A uniformed adjutant pushed through the box and whispered to Göring, and Göring turned to Hitler, making his leave of Frau Wagner. The box emptied, leaving Göring, Goebbels, and Hitler in deep communion. After several minutes Hitler turned away, picking up a white silk scarf and leaving the final command: "Find von Blomberg and tell him to come." He walked down toward his car, draping the scarf over his shoulder.

The three fatigued men who had come from Tetuán in Spanish Morocco still waited at the other side of the final door. They were Johannes Bernhardt, a German businessman; Group Leader Adolf Langenheim, the head of the Nazi organization in Morocco; and, in uniform, Captain Francisco Arranz of the Spanish Nationalist Army. Hearing voices in the next room, they fell silent, able to pick out the one clearly dominant voice and trying to judge its mood. Then the door opened. An adjutant beckoned them to softer lights.

Bernhardt went in first, arm raised and heels snapping noiselessly into a carpet, muting the gesture and putting him off balance as he uttered the *Heil Hitler*. Hitler waved the men to a sofa and remained standing over them, arms folded across his chest, rocking slightly on his feet as Göring spoke.

Of the three men it was Arranz who emerged as the most insistent. After Göring and Bernhardt reached the brink of disagreement, Hitler turned to the Spaniard and waved Göring to silence. "We should hear them out." Arranz's determination was clear. He spoke directly to Hitler and explained that unless the Germans provided his army with transport planes they would be unable to resist the Communist takeover in Spain. The Spanish Civil War was nine days old. Hitler listened without revealing any sentiment. Again Göring intervened to protest that his air force did not want to be drawn into the war.

Hitler sat down, waving Göring and Field Marshal Wernher von Blomberg, the war minister, to armchairs beside him, resigned to a conference lasting into the early hours. He watched Arranz's reaction as Göring continued to resist. Then Hitler intervened decisively:

"Isn't this what the Luftwaffe needs—operational experience? A chance to bloody our young men in war?" He stopped, glancing at Arranz and indicating to Bernhardt, the translator, not to complete the thought: "Better still, if it can be somebody else's war."

Langenheim began to press the virtues of the unknown

general leading the Spaniards against the Communists, Francisco Franco. Hitler, openly disenchanted by Göring's resistance, slapped his right palm on his knee. "Before I decide to
help Franco, I must know more about him—what kind of a
man he is, what his beliefs are. Who can tell us that?"

Stirring from a prolonged silence, von Blomberg said,
"Canaris—he knows Franco personally."

"Of course," said Hitler, "bring him here."

Like the slow onset of an eclipse the great shadow moved
noiselessly across the Unter den Linden. Heads turned upward, disconcerted, and saw the airship Hindenburg—flying
so low that they could pick out the faces of people peering
down from the windows of the gondolas slung under its belly.
Berlin was sultry and dusty. The streets were lined with vertical crimson banners, each punctured by the white disc with
black swastika, each flagstaff topped by the Nazi eagle. All
public buildings had a new coat of paint. Loudspeakers strung
among the trees gave results from the distant Olympic stadium. Brown-shirted storm troopers patrolled in pairs, and
traffic was frequently swept to the curbs to make way for
official cars in headlong cavalcade.

On the Wilhelmstrasse Endmere found his way blocked
on one side of the street by S.S. guards and on the other by a
cluster of gaping tourists. The attraction, he realized, was Hitler's house. He turned off the Wilhelmstrasse and went down
a small back street to his rendezvous, a bar called the Dragon's Head. At a gingham-topped table in a corner Guy Burgess was already draining a bottle of Italian Stock brandy,
undiluted. Endmere couldn't remember ever seeing Burgess
without a glass in his hand. Sometimes useful and sometimes a
liability, Burgess's most mysterious talent was to appear in a
place at crucial moments—a gift that Endmere knew to be
common to only two professions: journalism and espionage.
Which of these was Burgess's real calling remained—for Endmere—in doubt.

Burgess looked up, eyes veined red. "Peter, I do hope
you don't mind, I've started . . ."

"You must have fled the stadium early."

"Absolute hell, old chap. A hundred thousand fanatics.
Not *just* 'Deutschland über alles,' but the bloody 'Horst Wessel
Song' as well." Burgess's nails were dark and broken and his
shirt collar was soiled.

"Isn't there a stink being raised about the Negro?"

Burgess lightened. "I'd say. They hadn't reckoned on that, a blow to their racial theories. Whenever Jesse Owens appears, Hitler disappears. He equates the Negro with the ape. This particular ape runs fucking fast."

Endmere added soda to his brandy. "I'm sorry your trial at *The Times* didn't last."

Burgess shrugged. "Something told me I didn't belong." He grinned.

"I *did* try. Really quite hard, even a clean shirt every day. Somehow, though . . ."

"So how did you manage this trip?"

"Dame Fortune—Mrs. Rothschild, actually. Share-punting, on my inspired advice. She gives me a hundred a month. I got free tickets to the Olympics from a Tory M.P. Very keen on Hitler, it seems. So you see, it all fell into my lap."

"It doesn't sound like real work."

Burgess pushed his chair away from the table and up against the wall; he loosened his tie. *"Real work?* Now, there I have some news. Where *The Times* failed to perceive talent, the B.B.C. has been more alert. I start in October. The Talks Department."

"The B.B.C.?"

"No need to sound so surprised, old chap."

"How'd you manage that?"

Endmere's incredulity annoyed Burgess. "Manage it? I was recommended on the very highest academic authority. Wheels within wheels, you might say." Burgess drew back to the table again and leaned over to Endmere, breathing fumes. "I hear your chap here, Ebbutt, he's getting the cold shoulder."

"It's a tough post, Berlin."

"Tough if you work for *The Times* and don't care for Hitler." Burgess drained the last of the Stock. "If you ask me, we've lost the last chance to stop him. It was a hell of a risk he took, going into the Rhineland. If the French had moved then, he would have had to back away. Then, *kaputt* Adolf! There was only one vote in it, in the French cabinet—I have that on *very* good authority. Just imagine if it had gone the other way."

There was a sudden commotion. Two storm troopers got on their feet and began shouting at a middle-aged man in a beret who was asking for a drink at the bar.

"I think he's a Jew," said Burgess.

The storm troopers banged their glasses up and down on the table, shouting. The barman shrugged and pulled the mug of beer away from the other man just as he reached for it. He turned and walked out.

"The meek won't inherit the earth—not here," said Burgess.

The Olympiad's social climax was orgiastic, a series of parties given by Ribbentrop, Göring, and Goebbels. Crowned heads came from the Balkans, and more practical friends: business leaders, newspaper proprietors, politicians, broadcasters, all avid in their celebration of the risen Nazi princes. Dunsinnan stood in line with Margery Taverner in the gardens of Göring's *Ministerium*. The Anglophile Göring had taken care to invite the most impressionable British visitors, but his welcome to Dunsinnan was a little too mechanical, his eyes diverted by Dunsinnan's companion.

As they walked away she said, "Fishy hands, urrgh! I don't take to that man. He's too *gross*."

Dunsinnan protested, "It's not what you think. Not his appetite, but his glands."

"His eyes!" she persisted, "his *eyes*. It must be true that he's on drugs."

The banquet engulfed the gardens. Eight hundred people sat down to dinner, and a corps de ballet danced on the lawns. In his white uniform hung with medals Göring moved from table to table.

"He should be wearing a toga," she said, annoying Dunsinnan with her sniping. His adulation of Göring was too unguarded; she had noticed a change in him, his supplication was overzealous. She, unlike him, had found an unspoken tension in Berlin: The people seemed unsure of the juggernaut they were now riding, relieved to be rid of their past but unnerved by their future.

The ballerinas evaporated into the shadows, and another section of the gardens was floodlit, revealing a medieval village with a beer house, cafes, a parade of horses, and welcoming parties of girls in peasant costume carrying fruit, pretzels, and steins of beer.

"I think Ribbentrop has just been upstaged," Dunsinnan said. They were both slightly drunk. The lights of the roundabout blurred, the brassy music swept away the *hauteur* of the banquet, and the bacchanalia assumed the coarse gusto of its host's character. Stepping uncertainly from the beer house, they came face to face with Endmere.

She froze for a second and then summoned Dunsinnan's fading concentration.

"Alastair, this is Peter Endmere. He's with *The Times*."

Dunsinnan's fluid eyes came to rest on a pretzel in Endmere's hand. *"The Times?* We haven't met? Sound paper, *The Times*, very sensible." His eyes moved up. "Dunsinnan—Alastair Dunsinnan. Very glad . . ."

Endmere had to intercept the wavering hand, but he looked at her. "Amazing, isn't it—this show?"

"Yes, it is." She looked at him steadily.

Dunsinnan pulled at her arm. "Come along, Margery . . . interesting to see you, Mr. . . ."

"Endmere," she said, glancing back grimly as they were sucked into the revelry. Endmere bowed gravely.

4

Scotland, August 1936

Once the car crossed the River Forth, Lady Dunsinnan's Scottish accent seemed to broaden. The Bentley now passed through the shadows from a pine forest to the left of the road, and in the sudden chill the tartan warmers across their laps were welcome. Then, gradually, the pines thinned out, and through the sparser tree line Ruth saw the reflection of water. "That's the loch," said Lady Dunsinnan, following her eyes. "The castle is beyond, on the hill. We can't see it yet." A quarter of a mile further the car turned left to a gravel track that ran over a small bridge. "The Tummel—a whisky river," said Lady Dunsinnan. "The distilleries are upriver, between here and the loch."

From the river the track ran up a gradual incline, and at its crest the view suddenly opened up: The narrow loch was about two miles long, and on its far side moorland rose to a tree line of conifers. The trees stopped short of the summit, and on the summit stood Dunsinnan Castle.

"The trouble with castles, my dear, is that they make a good defensive position, but they're hell to keep warm."

The Bentley coasted down to the loch, then took another track threading up through the trees to a gate house in the castle wall. As they rolled to a stop a huge man in tweeds and leather gaiters bowed to them. Lady Dunsinnan wound down the window. The air was like the first bite of a cold shower.

"Welcome home, Your Ladyship." The man had a melodic accent. Though in late middle age, he was muscular and quick in his movements. His right hand rested on the rim of the lowered window; tufts of red hair showed above the nails.

"McCabe," said Lady Dunsinnan, "this is Miss Dexter, from the United States. Ruth, this is Hestall McCabe." The man bowed again. Lady Dunsinnan tapped the partition, and the Bentley moved through the gate and down a curving drive to the castle. "The McCabes have been here forever . . . long before the castle." Ruth caught the chauffeur's glowering face in the rearview mirror, realizing that he was watching McCabe who walked up the drive behind them.

At first glance she found the castle hideous. It had a squat central block and two turreted wings. At the second storey the turrets canted outward, giving the building the appearance of being ready to topple. A large wooden main door was framed in a vaulted arch flanked by pillars, each pillar topped by gargoyles, and similar gargoyles adorned the turrets, Victorian embellishments added when the castle's defensive role had past. Over the main door the Dunsinnan coat of arms was fashioned in a painted plaster shield—an arrow held in a mailed fist.

But inside, there was a different hand. Only flagstone floors covered in tapestried rugs echoed the Gothic style; otherwise there were armchairs covered in floral chintz and chesterfields in buttoned leather. This style of furnishing, coupled with scores of vases filled with fresh cut flowers, softened the harshness. But to Ruth the dominant impression became one of sounds: feet on flagstones; spitting logs in deep fireplaces; a yelping distant dog; inexplicable creaking like the beams of a ship; and wind trapped in stone crevices tapping out low rhythms at the windows. There was a long twilight, a crimson sky with herringbone clouds tinged mauve, the colors cast from below by a sun wedged between hill and sky.

The scale of this life seemed alien. At breakfast the next morning Ruth sat alone, served by a silent mousey girl. She tried to make small talk, but the girl shrank away. The protocols ran against Ruth's nature. The Dunsinnans did not flaunt their wealth but *assumed* it; Lady Dunsinnan, for all her plain ease and directness, presided firmly at the center. She remained late in her bed, recovering from the journey—a night on the train and half a day in the car from Edinburgh.

Dogs barked at the door. Ruth found McCabe holding three retrievers on the leash. His eyes smiled, his deference was obligatory: "Good morning."

"Yes, it is," she said truthfully, observing the flawless sky.

"Do you ride, Miss Dexter?"

"Sure, but I haven't any riding clothes."

"I don't think that's a problem." He pulled back the dogs from her shoes. "My wife will arrange it. She'll bring you to the stables afterwards."

She was given a beautiful white Arab. McCabe measured the pace at first, waiting to see how surely she handled the horse. They took a narrow path through the trees; the air was scented with pine. When they broke from the trees, McCabe increased the pace, and she drew alongside him, now confident of the horse and already knowing its strength. In twenty minutes they were at the edge of the loch, running along a bridle track in a meadow where cattle nosed into wiry grass. Over the loch clusters of birds wheeled and swooped above two small boats. There was a whitewashed cottage by a wooden jetty. McCabe rode up to the cottage and dismounted. He went to help Ruth down, but she jumped, unassisted, her face red from the wind.

"You ride well, Miss Dexter."

"It's a wonderful horse."

"Lord Dunsinnan's." He took both sets of reins and tied them to the cottage gate. "I think we can beg some refreshment," he said, and knocked on the door.

A large, harassed woman in a stained apron ushered them inside, where a kettle hung over a peat fire. McCabe introduced her as the wife of the warden of the loch. The woman seemed nervous in McCabe's presence. The tea she served was more like soup, but Ruth gulped it down gladly; the chill of the ride had penetrated her jacket and cashmere sweater.

"You'll be having a full house again before long?" asked the woman.

"Aye," said McCabe, "and you can tell John that we'll want some salmon."

Outside, McCabe said, "Did you smell anything in there?"

"Only the peat."

McCabe grinned. "Not fish?"

Ruth shook her head.

"I've a nose for salmon," he said.

This time McCabe put a hand on her calf to help her on the horse. "And if there was—a salmon?" she said.

"He can only fish with my permission. But there's a man in Pitlochry who trades whisky for salmon."

As they returned Lady Dunsinnan watched from her bedroom window. The white horse seemed already an extension of Ruth, the two of them moving with easy grace. The girl arched her back and brushed hair from her brow, turning back to McCabe and laughing. She was an exotic thing, new life in a dour landscape.

A sepia photograph hung on a wall of Seton's flat in London. It showed a group of a score or so of seated figures in flying suits and was captioned "70 Squadron, 1917." Seton was in the center of the front row, at twenty-five years old the hardened senior. The dominant quality in the faces around him was duty—a duty worn, like the uniforms, by obligation, in a fatalistic way. There was one other photograph in the flat, on a small table by his bed: Seton with a dark-haired woman, strong in character, a little younger than Seton himself. The background, though blurred, was unmistakably an English garden, and the woman was looking down slightly to shield her eyes from the light.

Seton pulled himself from the bed and looked out across the Bayswater Road to Hyde Park. It was dry enough to walk to Whitehall. The flat was becoming noisy from the increasing traffic, but it was the possibility of walking to work through three parks that kept him in the place. Picking up the newspaper, he saw more headlines on Spain. And when he threw his trilby at the coatrack that morning, it was Spain that consumed Pickles.

"Just in, sir," he said, giving the telegram to Seton. Walking to his desk, Seton pushed the glasses to the end of his nose. The telegram, marked "MOST SECRET" read:

JULY TWENTY-EIGHT LUFTHANSA PILOT FLUGKAPI-
TAN HANKE REACHED CADIZ FLYING JUNKERS JU 52
FROM TETUAN MOROCCO. AUGUST THREE S.S. URSANO

DOCKED CADIZ CARRYING SIX LARGE CRATES ABOVE DECK. EACH BELIEVED TO CONTAIN HEINKEL 15 FIGHTERS. MORE JU 52s BELIEVED DUE. INDICATIONS ARE THIS PRESENCE MORE THAN TRANSIENT. ARMY TRANSFER FROM MOROCCO COMPLETE. GERMAN TECHNICIANS INCOGNITO BUT OBVIOUS. ENDS MESSAGE OLOROSO.

Seton swung onto the desk and picked up a phone. As usual, there was a delay, and then the inimitable voice came on. Seton's voice was more urgent:

"The Luftwaffe are going into Spain."

There was a pause, and Seton said, "Yes, I'm certain. No doubt anymore."

In the glen beyond Dunsinnan Castle the view was foreshortened by the pall of thin rain. It was a windless day, and the rain was warm, a reminder of the blessing of the Gulf Stream, which alone made Scotland habitable. Hestall McCabe had been sitting on a bench inside the inn for half an hour. One wooden table stood outside the window. A metal tray left out there gradually accumulated rain, and McCabe measured his waiting time by its rising level. No traffic passed. The landlord, a fleshy, stunted man, dozed behind the bar. McCabe could not see how such a place could provide a living, since the new road had left this route a backwater . . . which was why he had chosen it for the rendezvous.

The car, a small Austin, had its lights on. It was open at the sides, with a canvas canopy. The driver wore a raincoat, scarf, and leather cap. The right shoulder of the raincoat was stained dark with rain. As he came into the inn he took off the coat and shook it. There was a smell of damp tweeds.

"I'm sorry," he said to McCabe, "the wipers packed up . . . I've had to go slowly. This road is not in much repair, is it?"

The landlord stirred and leaned forward over the bar.

"You'll need a dram," said McCabe. "What'll it be?"

"Oh," said the newcomer, his diffident English voice too conspicuous, "I don't mind. Whatever you're having."

McCabe called for two more malts.

The man sat down, smiling awkwardly. "It's certainly quiet here," he said.

They waited for the drinks and for the landlord to return

behind the bar. He didn't sit down again but fussed around with bottles.

"Are you going straight back to Edinburgh?" asked McCabe.

The man nodded. "And London tomorrow."

"They go to a lot of trouble," said McCabe.

The man sipped the drink and nearly choked on it, turning pink in the face. McCabe grinned.

The man cleared his throat. "I think I'd better take water with it. It's got a distinct flavor, hasn't it?"

"That's the peat," said McCabe, wondering where they found people like this. He poured more water into the man's whisky. Then he produced a slip of paper from his pocket and passed it to the man, who looked at it silently for a minute and then said:

"The usual people. No surprises."

"Aye," said McCabe, "all good guns." He looked at the man's face slowly returning to its normal paleness.

"Of course," said the man, "they would have to be. You'll keep your ears open—as usual? We'll be in touch again."

Within ten mintues the Austin had gone from whence it came, and McCabe was driving, slightly too fast, back toward Pitlochry. As he came round a bend there was a woman on a cycle in the middle of the road. Pulling over with a jerk he hit the grass verge, ran off the road, and only just regained control. The woman had not wavered. The people on these roads retained a stoical contempt for cars. McCabe cursed and knew that the mud on the side of the Bentley would intensify the chill between him and Drummond, the chauffeur.

In Pitlochry he had little time for the groceries, but luckily the order was ready and the boxes were soon loaded. The grocer's boy noticed the mud and looked questioningly at McCabe, who merely glowered.

The rain was easing. As he came up through the wood there was a lighter gray in the sky from the west.

Ruth and Dunsinnan crested the hill behind the castle just as the Bentley emerged below them from the trees. She still rode the white Arab; he had gallantly deferred to a chestnut, equally fleet but less elegant. Their faces glowed with rain streaked across them, and the rain had brought out the full smell of the moors, peat, heather, and nameless wild herbs.

Dunsinnan, hanging a length behind as they came up the hill, was aroused by the way her thighs gripped the horse, and the unison of her haunch and that of the Arab. Her vitality stirred him in a way that was new, not only her physical zest, but her keenness of spirit, which he was not quite sure how to handle.

In the stable yard she slid to the ground and cupped the Arab's muzzle in her hands. "Oh, I *love* this horse!"

Taking off his cap in spite of the rain, Dunsinnan joined her, his dark hair matted over his brow. "He knows that," he said, slapping the horse's flank. "And if he has any sense, he'll feel the same way about you."

A stable boy took the horses, and she threw her head back to catch the thinning rain. "Isn't it great—riding in the rain? Don't you think so? And the air—it was like breathing incense."

He put a hand lightly on her shoulder. "You're getting carried away."

As they walked back into the castle Dunsinnan saw the streak of mud on the doors of the Bentley just as McCabe came down the steps. Dunsinnan tapped a door of the car with his stock and glared at McCabe. "That was careless, wasn't it? I'd get the boy to clean it before Drummond gets back from Edinburgh—if you don't want another of those scraps of yours."

McCabe nodded ruefully but didn't answer. He watched Dunsinnan's guiding hand reach Ruth's waist. In the hall she sat down, and Dunsinnan pulled her boots off, taking one sock with them. The toes of the naked foot curled. He noticed that the top of the foot was as dark as the rest of her, but that the sole was as pink as a Negro's palm.

"Drinks in half an hour," he said.

She lay for longer than that in the bath, occasionally reaching forward to the tap to top it up. The exhilaration of the ride merged into a deeper inner satisfaction. The longer she remained with the Dunsinnans, the less inclined she felt to turn her mind to more serious intentions; this pervasive hedonism was like an opiate, but energizing rather than enervating. From the bath she went to the fire blazing in her bedroom and rubbed herself down. Before she was dressed, she heard cars and then, echoing from the flagstones, new voices. Maids' feet went by her door, carried luggage dragging their tread, followed by the lighter step of a woman issuing commands in accented English.

In the drawing room Ruth found two men with Dunsinnan. Their conversation stopped in mid-sentence. Even Dunsinnan was for a moment mesmerized: She wore a long blue velvet gown, backless to the waist, and she had pulled her hair into a high bun, emphasizing the arching neck. Finding his voice again, Dunsinnan introduced her.

One man, olive-skinned and compact, was an Italian count; the other, a huge bucolic-looking figure wearing flecked tweeds and a tartan tie, had a heavy German accent but was named Bell. The count, introduced by Dunsinnan as Alfredo Albinoni, greeted her with a courtly bow. Bell simply nodded.

"It was worth waiting for," said Dunsinnan. "We're having whisky—would you . . . ?"

"I haven't acquired the taste, not yet. Can you manage a martini?"

While Dunsinnan mixed the cocktail the count said, "Not to drink whisky in this house is like refusing pasta in mine. You should adapt." His English was perfect.

"When in Rome?" she said.

"Rapallo. In my case, Rapallo. You must come, sometime."

Dunsinnan caught the invitation as he brought the drink. "Be careful," he said, winking. "Alfredo has a reputation. And the contessa. She's upstairs, you'll meet her at dinner."

The contessa came in layers of orange silk. She was pale and willowy, with long ruby nails. They ate the first of the season's grouse, hung for a fortnight to reach its prime and simmered in a sauce betraying the tang of the Dunsinnan whisky. No cloth was put on the mahogany, and with the men tearing at the grouse and drinking beer from pewter mugs, the atmosphere was almost medieval. Lady Dunsinnan, at the head of the table, drank whisky. Ruth and the contessa shared a bottle of claret.

"I think Scotland agrees with Ruth, don't you, Alastair?" Lady Dunsinnan nodded across the table.

"Yes," he said, "she's blooming."

Ruth flushed. "Sometime, I'm going to have to think about my work."

"*Work?*" said the contessa with alarm. "Why ever would someone as beautiful as you have to *work?*"

Ruth laughed. "Don't misunderstand. Not *manual* work. Just my studies."

"Ruth is here to study medieval art," explained Dunsinnan.

"So?" said Bell, suddenly interested. "You must come to Munich. We have much fine medieval art . . ."

"*Munich*," said the contessa disparagingly. "Too much beer, too much politics."

Bell wiped sauce from his mouth. "A political renaissance. What is wrong with that?"

The contessa's brows rose in silent dismissal.

The castle's acoustics were as eccentric as its shape: Victorian plumbers had driven through thick stone to install baths, and the copper pipes radiating from the furnace below also conducted sound. That night Ruth was awakened in the small hours by raised voices. Eavesdropping was inescapable.

One voice was Dunsinnan's: "I don't think you *quite* understand, Alfredo. . . ."

The count was vehement. "The Germans are a race of carnivorous sheep . . . you will be bitten by them."

His voice rising, Dunsinnan said, "There's enough for you *and* the Germans. It's in our interest to keep both happy. You are allies, after all. . . ."

A frail complaining sound came from the contessa.

"I'm sorry," said Dunsinnan, "we'll talk about it tomorrow, when the others are here."

Ruth subsided again into sleep.

5

Southern Bavaria, September 1936

From its peak at 6,400 feet the mountain swept down to a highland valley at 2,000 feet. A few years earlier the pine forests on the mountain had been intersected only by rough tracks, and dairy herds had grazed the valley alongside farmhouses, inns, and chapels. Now most of the buildings had been cleared from the valley, and paved roads cut into the mountain, looping up through the pines to a complex of plain-plastered buildings. Around the complex was a fortified wall, nearly nine miles long, topped with barbed wire. Nearer the summit another wall enclosed an area of nearly three square miles. From this higher plateau there was an unobstructed view over the valley to a mountain *massif*. At this time of year, after mornings of crystal skies, warm moist air rose from the valley and evaporated in the colder air at the peaks, gradually building into storm clouds through the afternoon.

The nearest of the great peaks across the valley from the fortified eyrie had a mythic appeal as well as its physical quality. This was the Untersberg, where the Emperor Charlemagne was said still to sleep, ultimately to reappear and restore the German Empire to its legendary place.

The three official Mercedes limousines had left Munich at 3:00 P.M. and driven the sixty kilometers along the new autobahn. To some of the British passengers in the cars, the autobahn network was yet another token of a future world unfolding under inspired direction. Just after 6:00 the cars reached the checkpoint at the larger of the perimeter fences manned by the black-uniformed S. S. guards who waved them on. The cars labored on up the mountain. By 6:30 P.M. they were at the hotel, a new building that from the outside looked like a marriage of barrack and mountain inn, with square-cut concrete walls and an Alpine roof to take the heavy winter snows. There was no snow in September, but the evening storm was forming.

Joachim von Ribbentrop and his wife gave dinner to their British guests; thunder and lightning punctuated their conversation. At Ribbentrop's side Baron Geyr von Schweppenburg tried to assess the outcome of all the trouble he had taken to bring these people here, particularly the value of the pilgrimage of David Lloyd George, the victorious prime minister of the First World War, now, at age seventy-three, eager for reconciliation.

After dinner, with the guests gone, the baron bared his misgivings to Ribbentrop: "They seem too concerned about the state of the churches!"

Ribbentrop shrugged, sharing the despair: "They're Welsh, what do you expect? Hypocrites, of course. You know Lloyd George's reputation with women?"

"It doesn't seem to stop him worrying about why our chapels are empty."

They considered the coming meeting.

"What use can he be to the Führer?" asked the baron.

"We can play on his guilt, for one thing. He feels responsible for the Versailles Treaty, as he should. The Führer is very clever on that point, you know the speech—Britain,

France, and the United States vengeful, draining the last drop of German blood. Remorse can be a powerful weapon on an old man. Lloyd George wants to put himself right with his Maker."

The baron remained skeptical. "Even so, who will take notice of him, in England?"

The question amplified one of Ribbentrop's recurrent problems, divining the British state of mind. He spoke as a man whose own overtures had been too often unrequited. "I don't know." He saw the outline of the Untersberg in the glare of sheet lightning. "If the King's opinion counts, then Lloyd George will find a powerful ally—the King needs no more persuasion himself. The problem is, the King has enemies, and this affair with the American woman offers a pretext. . . ."

The guests had to wait until the following afternoon to make the final ascent. The last bend in the narrow road was too sharp for the cars to make it in one turn; they had to reverse at the edge of a precipice and swing around again. Now, on a small ridge above them, they saw Hitler's favorite retreat, the Berghof. An S.S. guard of honor was lined up at the foot of a flight of steps. Hitler waited at the top of the steps, wearing a light-gray suit, a soft-white shirt, and a swastika band on his left arm. The light reflecting from the concrete was so strong that he shaded his eyes with his right hand until Lloyd George reached him. Schmidt, the interpreter, stood a pace behind. Lloyd George's thick white mane of hair was as effective against the sun as a hat. He clasped Hitler's hand with both of his own and turned obliquely to the mountains, exclaiming, "You know, I came here forty years ago, Herr Hitler, before there were any buildings. It was cloudy, I remember, we couldn't see anything."

Hitler waited for the translation and then waved his arm toward the valley. "Well now, today, we have the whole view for you."

Adjutants circled nervously. Hitler turned and led the way across a broad terrace to a narrow door with two short steps. None of this prepared the visitors for the scale of the room inside. Its northern end, facing across the valley, was open to the sky: A floor-to-ceiling window was lowered out of sight, leaving an uninterrupted view. Just visible through a gap in the mountains was the city of Salzburg.

Hitler led them to the window. "You see the Untersberg? It is no accident that I chose this spot."

They left the panorama for a more modest alcove, Lloyd

George taking a place on a soft sofa; the cushions were so broad that so short a man could have no back support, and he sat awkwardly. Cakes, sandwiches, and tea were served on a low circular table. Hitler took a deep armchair, leaned forward, and began questioning Lloyd George.

Schmidt translated rapidly. "I have always been interested in promoting good relations between our two countries," said Lloyd George.

"I agree with all my heart," said Hitler. "We come of a common racial stock, and understanding between us is essential."

They talked for two hours. Toward the end Hitler turned to Thomas Jones, seated beside Lloyd George, and asked him about Baldwin. Jones explained that the British prime minister was really a shy and modest man who had never got over his astonishment at finding himself in power.

Hitler grinned. "I also."

They agreed that Bolshevism was the greatest menace to the future of civilization. Hitler reflected on Lloyd George's role in the Great War: "It was you who galvanized the people of Great Britain into the will for victory. If any single individual won the war for the Allies, it was you, and I am glad to be able to tell you so in person."

Lloyd George glowed. "And I am glad to have such a compliment from the greatest German of his age—the greatest since Bismarck."

As the meeting ended one of the British party, Lord Dawson, the King's doctor, produced a portrait of Hitler, which he asked him to autograph.

"A new beginning!" said Hitler, walking toward the open window again. He lifted his eyes and looked into the distance. "One day, the British prime-minister will come here. Then he will understand my view of the world."

6

On the grouse moor Count Alfredo Albinoni was made distinctive by his plumage. From the boots to the waist he was conventional enough: boots, leather gaiters, and tweed plus fours. But then the Scottish idiom gave way to the Tyrolean: a loose light-brown chamois hunting jacket crossed, bandolier fashion, by black leather cartridge belts, the brass caps of the cartridges reminiscent of studs on medieval armor. Round his neck was a white silk scarf, on his head an Alpine hat with feather. He presented the ammunitioned chest to the wind, pressed the butt of the rifle into his right shoulder, tracked the soaring bird, and fired. The gun, made to fit by a venerable firm in St. James's, was as true as his aim, and the grouse ended its life in midbeat.

Behind the count his loader, prepared for farce, adjusted his reaction. Visibly impressed, he took the fired gun and handed the count its twin.

Of the shooting party gathered at Dunsinnan Castle only Ruth and Lady Dunsinnan, among the women, went up to the moor on the first day. The contessa remained behind with two other wives, playing cards. At first Ruth stayed with Lady Dunsinnan in the horse-drawn shooting brake, watching the line of beaters marshalled by McCabe go into the heather with their sticks, advancing in line.

With Dunsinnan and the count were a Scottish politician, a financier from London, an Irish peer, a solicitor and doctor, both from Edinburgh, and George Bell. In vintage years as many as thirty people had come, Lady Dunsinnan told Ruth, "But now Alastair confines it to those he has a use for." There was a clear hint of criticism.

After the first sweep of the guns Dunsinnan came back to the brake and looked up at Ruth. "Come along. I'll show you how it's done." In his dilapidated tweeds he looked convincingly the laird, and she liked him this way. She took his hand and jumped into the mud. He explained the role of the loader, with his leather pouch of cartridges, showed her how to stand so that the gun could have as wide a sweep as possible to follow the capricious course of the birds, and then gave her one of his guns, a vintage Purdey. He stood behind her right shoulder and placed the butt on the seam of her jacket, leaning forward to guide the left arm under the stock. "Just get the feel of it . . . try sighting." She was surprised by her own relish for the sport. The beaters went into the heather again, sticks flailing. A cloud of birds rose, all at once, careening through the air. Ruth moved the gun upwards, selected a bird, and aimed just ahead of it. She hit a wing, and the grouse turned over on its back and zigzagged into the heather.

The count applauded.

"Not at all bad," said Dunsinnan, taking the gun and handing it to the loader. The other men carried on shooting.

A beater came to Dunsinnan with a bird. "This was the lady's, My Lord."

Dunsinnan held the bird by its one intact wing; its neck swung uselessly. "We'll keep it for you, Ruth, so you can taste your own spoils."

By the end of the morning the game cart, an open wagon with semi-circular hoops mounted across it, was festooned with dead birds. McCabe produced a large wicker bag and went down the line of beaters, each man taking from it a sandwich.

Dunsinnan sat with Ruth and his mother in the brake. "A fine bag," he said, and looked at Ruth. "I thought that first shot of yours was novice's luck, to be truthful, until I saw the others. You've handled a gun before."

She grinned. "I have to confess, I guess—but it was nothing like this. Just some light hunting in the Adirondacks. My brothers taught me."

He wondered what other virtues lay concealed.

Lady Dunsinnan was watching the count preening on a hillock. "It's a pity those cartridges on his belly don't go off. What an absurd outfit." She looked up at the slate sky. "I think maybe we should get back. It'll be pouring down in half an hour."

Dunsinnan got down from the brake and went to McCabe to close the shoot.

"He's different up here," said Ruth, watching him go.

"You've noticed that, have you?" said Lady Dunsinnan. "Yes . . . it's true. But it won't last. He has no talent for relaxing. These men, they're all up to something, up half the night." Pointing to Bell, in his ulster coat and tartan cap, she continued, "That one, for example. He seems a bit of a joke, claiming his Scottish ancestry, but he's a thoroughgoing Nazi. Have you heard of Deterding—Sir Henri Deterding, the oil magnate?"

"Vaguely."

"Bell's an agent for him. Deterding regards Hitler as good for business. He's just married a Nazi woman. No, Bell's not here just for the sport." She pulled out her flask and fortified herself. "Ask Alastair to go through those pictures in the hall with you some time. You'll see a connection."

Dunsinnan came back to the brake and sat next to Ruth, his thigh pushing against hers. "Right. It's all arranged. We'll keep our appetites sharp for a really good dinner."

The contessa welcomed Ruth back with the enthusiasm of someone finding rescue from a desert island. She steered her away from the rest of the party to a smaller drawing room, then sent for tea.

"What do I do, my dear? I cannot stand shooting and I cannot stand bridge. What I like is *fun*—how can such a place be fun?" She gestured toward the windows already opaque with rain. "It gets into my bones, this damp. No wonder everybody drinks so much. You must have noticed, my darling, Lady Dunsinnan, she is never without the whisky." Then she became conspiratorial: "Tell me, how do you like Alastair?"

"He grows on you."

"Ah, I thought so!" She paused, deciding what tone to strike. "Yes . . . he has his charms. But be careful. He has a reputation."

"Reputation?"

"A philanderer—I think that is the word, yes? A ladies' man."

"Really?" said Ruth. "Tell me more."

"That would be indiscreet. Under this roof. Perhaps some other time— The idea doesn't dismay you, though?" She looked at Ruth archly. "No. Young women today . . ." Her voice trailed off as the maid entered with tea and a pyramid of sandwiches.

When they were alone again, the contessa had more to confide. But first she peeled open a sandwich and grimaced at its contents. "They call this paste—fish paste. They do terrible things with food, these people. My dear, have you any idea what these men are doing?"

For the second time in an hour Ruth received broad hints of curious transactions.

"Alfredo, he is not so foolish as he may seem. We have done well with Mussolini. Now, the stakes are bigger. You know who is the cleverest of them? Alastair. He will be important, one day. Unless they are backing the wrong side. But that is not like Alastair."

Before dinner Dunsinnan came into the hall with two retrievers. The dogs, slipped from their leashes, romped and skidded across the rugs, leaving mud on the flagstones. Dunsinnan pulled off his Burberry. His hair was wringing wet. The dogs sought out Ruth as she came into the hall, leaping at her legs.

Dunsinnan stilled them with one command. *"Why* is it that all the animals in this place have taken to you so much?" he said, taking her arm. "Could it be that they share my enthusiasm?"

She thought of the contessa's warning and realized that instead of diminishing her interest it had heightened it. "It helps me feel at home," she said, steering him to the photographs. "Now, you can tell me about these." She pointed out a maharajah of great girth with his retinue. "Your father seems to have kept exotic company."

"Yes, he did," he said, straightening his hair. "That was Prince Duleep Singh. A great gun."

"Now, this one," she said, moving on, "this isn't Dunsinnan Castle, is it?"

"That's clever of you, to spot that. No, that's Achnacarry Castle, 1928. Do you recognize those men?" He pointed to a solemn, camera-conscious trio.

"No."

"The one in the center, that's the owner of Achnacarry, Sir Henri Deterding. Royal Dutch Shell." He glanced at her to see if the name registered.

"An awful lot of oil," she said.

"More than you realize. The chap on the left is Walter Teagle—"

"Standard Oil, New Jersey," she interrupted.

"Well now, you keep surprising me."

She laughed. "Father runs airplanes, airplanes use gas. Simple as that."

"Of course." He sounded unsure.

"And the other guy, on the right?"

"Ah, one of ours. Sir John Cadman, Anglo-Persian Oil.

Very clever. It's been said of him that he's more Persian than the Persians."

"And that's a compliment?"

Dunsinnan laughed and squeezed her arm.

"Don't tell me," she said, "they just happened to be in Scotland shooting birds."

He guided her from the pictures to the fire in the main reception room. "Well, they were all carrying guns, weren't they?"

"So do your guests."

He leaned against the mantel and looked at her through lowered lids. "It *is* the season." The innuendo had become a sexual game. She knew it and responded with an amused, bold stare.

This dinner, like the others since the shooting party began, was masculine and boisterous. Ruth felt that under the high spirits the men were impatient to see the women disappear, to remain with the whisky and cigars in conclave. She decided on provocation and raised the subject of Berlin and the Olympics:

"It seems to have had the desired result, to make Hitler respectable in the eyes of the world." She looked across the table to Dunsinnan. "That *was* the idea, wasn't it?"

Bell saw her intention and stopped drinking, his eyes on Dunsinnan.

"There was more to it than that," said Dunsinnan. "It was to prove to the Germans themselves that they are great again."

"And are they?" She had the attention of the whole table now.

"What takes weeks or months to achieve here, they seem able to do at the stroke of a pen."

"You mean the trains run on time?"

Becoming irritated, he glared back. "We have to encourage them, to become strong. It's in our own interest. Many people have quite the wrong idea." He looked down the table to his mother. "People here don't realize, they should go and see for themselves." His eyes moved away to Ruth, his irritation now subsumed in other feelings.

At night the castle remained restless, still plucking the various noises, mechanical and human, from their sources and deflecting them through the walls. Ruth slept fitfully, sometimes unable to distinguish dreams from these other incoherent intrusions. Neither Dunsinnan nor the other men appeared

for breakfast, nor did Lady Dunsinnan. Ruth found McCabe
in the drive.

"Would you like a ride, Miss Dexter? It's a fine morning
for it."

"Of course. Give me five minutes."

McCabe—and occasionally his wife—had been her one
bridge to the world belowstairs; McCabe himself, as the most
senior of the estate staff, carefully—too carefully for Ruth—
observed the rules of caste, deferring to his superiors and regi-
menting all the servants except the sour chauffeur, Drummond. McCabe's companionship when riding was governed by
this version of courtliness, of being the escort but not the
equal. It annoyed Ruth the more because she had grown to
like him, to find a kind of trust in him that overcame the
avuncular barrier. As they rode down again to the loch she
sensed that he had something on his mind—but it would take
an effort to unburden him.

They cantered along the reedy fringe of the water.

"Do you realize how deep it is?" he said, looking over to
the dark center of the loch.

"I know the legend about Loch Ness—that it's bottom-
less."

"Oh, *that* nonsense, the monster! I don't care for that,
just a stunt to attract witless tourists. No—but they do say this
loch goes down for miles. Nobody has been able to find bottom."

"Very deep, like the people," she said, glancing at him
sideways.

On a less tanned man his flush would have shown. He
patted the neck of his horse, avoiding her face. "You've
brought pleasure to us here, Miss Dexter. I hope you'll be
back."

"Ruth. *Please* call me Ruth."

He was uneasy with the idea. "Thank you," he said, and
then looked back toward the castle. "Will you be coming
back?"

"That's not up to me."

"No . . . Lord Dunsinnan has many things on his mind.
I think your presence here has been good for him." It was an
effort to break the discretion of service. "He needs taking out
of himself."

"I know."

"Well—" he could not quite bring himself to say Ruth—
"it would be good for us all, up here, if he had fewer of these

outside interests." He searched for the right nuance. "I'd not like for to see you drawn too far into those things, yourself. . . ."

"What do you mean?"

Her directness disturbed him. "Some of the people are a bad influence."

She met his eyes: "Thank you."

They broke into a canter again, following the line of the loch to the whitewashed cottage.

The cars were being loaded in the drive, and the servants had assembled to say farewell when Lady Dunsinnan summoned her son to her drawing room on the first floor of the castle. She had agonized over the need for the encounter, and she knew her only remaining influence on him was tenuous, emotional.

He came into the room in haste, as though deflected from other priorities.

It was hard to see the similarities in them: she, small and broad, with swept-back silver hair and eyes of an unusual metal gray; he, of medium height, compact, blue-eyed. Seated in a high-backed chintz armchair that all but swallowed her, she set her eyes resolutely on her son.

"Alastair . . . you'll forgive me for saying so, but your father always knew how to divide his work and his pleasure. You don't seem to know the one from the other anymore. This house party, it's been quite the most dreary I can ever recall."

He was annoyed but attempted a halfhearted conciliation. "I'm sorry you see it like that, Mother. But these aren't the old days, for lavish parties. The world is changing. There's business to do."

"Aye"—she lapsed into her native accent—"and what *kind* of business?"

"I wouldn't want to bother *you* with it, Mother."

"I'm grateful for that." Her sarcasm was pointed. "Just look at you, the bags under your eyes." Transparently cunning, she added, "Why not take a holiday, a *real* holiday? Take the girl with you."

"Ruth?" He appeared to be scandalized. "You're not suggesting . . . ?"

"It's time you settled down."

He laughed and leaned on the wall by a window. "It's a bit soon for that, isn't it?" His tone was insolent.

"You know what I mean. You were with that woman

again in Germany—you needn't bother to deny it. It was all over your face."

"Was it? *Really?* How interesting." It was sarcasm traded for sarcasm now. "She's a good friend."

Her laugh was hard. *"A good friend?* You mean, a friend of the family? I've had to put up with that woman for twenty years. Do you not think you could do better?"

She stood up slowly and walked across to stand next to him by the window. "Ruth is a very . . . *energic* lass—and clever. I've watched you together. It's not all that fanciful." She switched to a tone of calculated connivance: "You could do a lot worse." The size of the landscape beyond the window seemed to weigh on her. "After all, this place is going to need an heir—from a respectable source."

7

There was a ripping sound and then the smell of scorched acetate. The light on the screen lost its form, flared, and then went out.

"Damnation," said Seton.

Pickles, flustered, switched on the room light. "It's this machine," he said, touching the tin casing of the projector and then quickly withdrawing his finger, licking its tip as he spoke. "Don't know *where* they found it."

"The East India Office, I shouldn't be surprised," said Seton. "It looks old enough."

Smoke began to seep out from within the bowels of the machine. The small room lacked ventilation. Pickles went to the door and pulled it back and forth to draw out the fumes.

Seton stood up, took off his spectacles, and wiped them clear. "When you've assessed the damage, I'll need you again, in the office," he said. Pickles nodded glumly. Seton picked up a note pad and walked out.

There was a warren of passages under the Foreign Office, with vaulted galleries leading off, smelling of rotting documents. The detritus of several centuries of imperial adventure lay in boxes, bales, and trunks. The passages reached under much of Whitehall, linking Downing Street and the other departments. Seton knew—he had been shown it—one passage that surfaced eventually into a Victorian flat overlooking the Thames, the retreat of a War Office spymaster. The game had obviously begun long ago, perhaps with the Crimean War. Since then the underground mentality had proliferated, lending credence to suspicions of "shadow" bureauracies and malicious forces never exposed to daylight. Seton treated such stories with knowledgeable skepticism: He already knew what intrigues were compounded above, in the respectable world. He came out from the basement, passed between two sets of filing cabinets in a Foreign Office corridor —as though emerging from a bathroom—and took the ceremonial staircase to his floor.

Pickles arrived ten minutes later.

"No use, I'm afraid, sir," he said.

"That's obvious. You had better go out and buy one— having first filled in the appropriate form, of course." He consulted his notes. "But first, if you will, let's run through it again, as far as we got, shall we?"

Pickles sat down, a large reference book on his lap.

"So," said Seton, "this is what we have. First, the Gibraltar surveillance—good stuff, that, I thought. Up to twenty Ju Fifty-twos, by August 28. Correct?"

Pickles nodded.

"Now, the agent in Jerez, Oloroso. He reports a name. It was?"

"Oberstleutnant Rudolf Freiherr von Moreau—"

"You've checked him out in the Luftwaffe List?"

"Yes, trained with Lufthansa, very experienced for his rank."

"Quite so," said Seton thoughtfully. "Now, what we could see from the film. We have the legend, which they conveniently painted on the aircraft for us." He consulted his notes. *Pedros y Pablos Escuadrilla*—if they go on in this style, they'll be writing flamencos for them. So, as far as we can make out, that means a single bomber *Staffel*, around six planes. The Ju Fifty-twos converted for bombing. What do we know about them—bomb load, et cetera?"

"Not enough," said Pickles. "We've asked for more."

Seton's unstable chair creaked. He spun cautiously round to look out the window. "The trouble, my dear Pickles, is that we know pitifully little. And here we are, with the Luftwaffe obligingly laying on a full rehearsal for us in Spain, and we're scratching for information. Now, if we wanted to know the state of the German battle fleet, that would be different. But when it comes to the air force, what do we have? On the one hand, grandiose claims, echoed by people like Lindbergh. On the other hand, precious little hard facts."

"Have you ever wondered, sir, how much they know about us?"

Seton grimaced. "I hate to think. Officially, of course, we converse politely. They come here, we show them things—"

"Not too much?"

"The dilemma is this, Pickles. Do you do what they do, select a few of the best things and then scare the pants off people with them, *or* do you do as we do, show them the antiques? If you do the latter, don't you end up making them feel more cocky than ever?"

"It depends what you have up your sleeve, I suppose," Pickles replied.

Seton pondered the point, sucking his spectacles. "We have a bit up our sleeves, thank God. But is it enough—when the day comes?"

The last phrase was out before he even realized it himself. Pickles raised his eyebrows but said nothing.

Sometimes Seton felt more like a spinster than a widower. Making tea in a china pot small enough for one; dipping the spoon into a tin of Lapsang Souchong, one for the pot, one for him, letting it brew for five minutes, then stirring it once before pouring—all the fussy pedantry seemed feminine, but he was a creature of habit and was beyond helping it.

The woody flavor of the tea soothed him; its scent induced memories of the spiced foods he loved, and the gallons of Lapsang Souchong he had consumed in rooms kept barely tolerable by large ceiling fans and feeble circulations of air through lattice walls. Taste and smell were the agonies of memory, as personal as a touch.

He was on the brink of dozing when the phone rang. He cursed—and picked it up.

"Ah, Edward . . . glad I caught you. Do you have a dinner jacket handy?" The limpid voice betrayed some urgency, even anxiety.

"As it happens, yes . . ."

"Good. Covent Garden, there's just time for you to get here. Box F. Have you got that, F? Rossini, I'm afraid, not your cup of tea, I know. Half an hour, then?"

Covent Garden was pronounced Cuvent, something Seton always found too precious. "Er . . . yes." The phone went dead.

He reached the opera house in Bow Street with seconds to spare before *The Barber of Seville* leapt into life. There was no time for conversation, just a motion of the program indicating the empty seat. During the first act his companion was motionless, apparently immune to vivacity. From boxes around them, in the baroque tiers of galleries, jewels glinted occasionally in movement, reflecting the light from the stage. The place stifled with its luxury.

In the interval Seton was led to the street, opposite Bow Street police court, and then toward the vegetable market, still shuttered, the pavements pungent with decaying cabbage. His companion drew a white scarf round his throat, though it was not cold. Reading Seton's mind, he said, "I do apologize for these measures, I realize they may seem excessive, but I could take no chances, *this time*." They came to a great hall, glass held in a spidery frame of cast iron, a Victorian flight of fancy. One shutter was half raised, and the man bent to look inside, then withdrew, and they stood where they were in the street, by a lamp. Producing a folded sheet of paper from under the silk scarf, he said, "Can you see to read it?"

Seton squinted in the yellow light and read slowly, with growing incredulity.

"Whenever anybody from the German embassy here speaks to the King, they send a report to the Foreign Ministry in Berlin. We picked this one up there, not here. Don't ask how—even I prefer not to know that."

Seton looked up, moving his spectacles back up his nose. "How much weight do you put on it?"

The man took the paper, folded it, and slipped it back into his breast pocket. "Perhaps Mrs. Simpson is more of a blessing than we first realized. If she takes him from us, it would clearly save much trouble. . . ."

"Why are you showing this to me?"

The face looked even more jaundiced under the street lamp. "A burden shared. . . ." The trite maxim seemed inadequate. "It is irregular, of course. But one has to be *very* selective about whom one turns to *these* days. Especially at my level." He began walking back toward the opera house, the overture of the second act already audible in the market.

"Edward, I recall you saw Thomas Jones, the Welsh seer, at Cliveden?"

Seton grunted, wondering more who had been watching whom.

"Jones has just returned from a second encounter at Berchtesgaden with Hitler. This time he took Lloyd George. They seem only one step away from Downing Street. It may all be a part of something bigger, I can't be sure. There is the case of young Dunsinnan, he's been entertaining some interesting people in Scotland. I have a feeling that all these movements relate in some way. This connection of yours. It could become important."

The extremes of British landscape and society were compacted into one window frame by the rail journey from Edinburgh to London. Ruth sat in upholstered privacy with Dunsinnan and his mother, their compartment lined with varnished veneers and framed watercolors of Scottish castles—but not quite sealed from the smell of coal smoke. At first it seemed a journey through a pastoral past, but when they stopped at Newcastle, Ruth saw the ravaged landscape of the first industrial society. In the foreground, servicing the train, were pinched, pale men apparently docile in their acceptance of the contrast between their world and that of the passengers in first class. Ruth remembered a more defiant proletariat in the news pictures of the Memorial Day massacre at the gates of the Republic Steel plant in south Chicago, and she wondered silently about the respective merits of submission and resistance.

Offering smoked salmon sandwiches from a hamper, Dunsinnan caught her mood. "Grim, isn't it?"

The train began to move, with a lurch. "An awful place," Ruth said as the station receded through a film of soot.

"We need regeneration." Dunsinnan took his own sandwich with a curious, almost epicene gesture. "This is the penalty for having been first." He pointed the sandwich at the pall. "Pioneering ends up as a museum. Hitler knows that. He's pulled Germany clear of its past."

Lady Dunsinnan, wakened by the talk, looked dreamily at Ruth. "What are you going to do, my dear, in London?"

"Fix my apartment. I hate the idea, but I can't live on your hospitality forever."

"You have a flat?" asked Dunsinnan.

"Father arranged it. It's in Davies Street, Mayfair—you know it?"

"Davies Street?" His interest increased. "That must be near Westminster's house."

Lady Dunsinnan snorted.

"He owns half of London," Dunsinnan continued, ignoring his mother's reaction. "Probably owns your building, too. Dicky Grosvenor, second Duke of Westminster—what a character." Then, more thoughtfully: "Eminently sensible. Very great fan of the King's. . . ."

"*And* of Herr Hitler," said Lady Dunsinnan. She reached for the hamper. "Open the champagne, Alastair. It's getting warm."

By the time the train reached London, the bathos of leisure had made Ruth restless, and the pampering by servants turned the restlessness into a guilt that had Bostonian roots, the Puritan work ethic.

At Eaton Square she found a note from Seton among her accumulated mail, and also a letter from California, in a familiar hand that renewed a forgotten pain; they had agreed to avoid contact for a year, and barely three months had passed. She folded the letter without opening it and stuffed it into a pocket.

The note from Seton was, she realized, surprisingly welcome. When she called him, he invited her to the theater. They saw *The Country Wife*, with Ruth Gordon, whose American cadences were as incongruous in Restoration comedy as Count Albinoni's clothes on the Scottish moor; but, playing the foolish wife, she walked away with the show in spite of her accent.

Afterwards Seton took Ruth to dinner in Soho, the best meal she had eaten since leaving home. Happy and uninhibited, she talked of Scotland and the gathering at the castle. Seton was casual, quietly attempting to select the significant from the insignificant. She capped her anecdotes with a royal scandal:

"The King was supposed to open a hospital in Aberdeen but cried off—his brother had to do it. The same day he went to Ballater station and collected Mrs. Simpson to take her to Balmoral. Quite openly. She sat in the front of the car."

"That will have gone down well, with those Calvinists."

"There's a joke, now—what's the opposite of moral?"

Seton shook his head.

"Balmoral!" She giggled and then leaned forward, more serious. "Edward, this might seem naive. But how much longer can it go on? How do they manage to keep it out of the papers? I get the *New York Times* from home, and it's all over that. *Everybody* in the world knows, except the British."

"No," corrected Seton, leaning back. *"Some* of the British know, those who don't depend on newspapers. It's self-censorship on the part of the newspaper owners—with a little encouragement from on high. That's the English way."

She frowned. "Incredible."

"You could say the same kind of thing is going on over Nazi Germany. Most of the papers are playing that down, too. In a way, that's more serious, more self-deluding. You know, if we don't talk about it, perhaps it will go away. . . ."

"That bothers you, doesn't it?"

He thought she looked even more beautiful when, as now, she passed from frivolity to concern and showed her intelligence.

"Yes—a bit."

The understatement, she was beginning to realize, was a curious English signal of gravity. She took another sip of the wine.

"How's your flat?" he asked.

"A mess. A *real* mess." She screwed up her napkin. "I really have to get down to it. Then, when it's fixed, you'll have to come to dinner. I'm really quite a good cook."

"Your mother used to make a marvellous thing, a Mexican chili—"

"The skull raiser, you mean? Well, if I can get the right things here, I'll even do that for you, if you promise to come. It's been *really* nice, this evening . . ." She embarrassed him with a touch of the hand. "Tomorrow I'm off on another of these country weekends. What a life."

"Where, this time?"

"Not far from London, apparently. Near a place called Tring, in the hills someplace."

"Yes, that would be in the Chilterns." He hesitated, then asked, "Whose house would that be?"

She ran a finger around the rim of the empty wineglass, and moistened, it found the pitch of resonance. "I've forgotten . . . another of Alastair's many connections."

"You like him—Alastair?"

The glass was sending out a higher pitch. She considered the question. "Yes. He's fun . . . when he wants to be."

"And when he doesn't?"

She looked up from the glass. "Moody. But we don't want to talk about him, do we?"

* * *

The stags came down from the higher slopes around October. They passed through the forest and, sometimes, strayed onto the moor. That morning McCabe had seen a buck, superbly horned, dipping his head into the heather and then, all his instincts finely tuned, looking carefully around. His haunches were tight and rippling. Those muscles could spring the beast from standing to thirty miles an hour, in a few seconds. McCabe inched forward, keeping the glasses just below the line of the grass. He was about as close as he dared to get. As a boy, he had learned to stalk, to slip through the undergrowth like a snake. In those days the guns had decimated the herds, and they had only now been gradually restored by limited hunting and protection. It was still the case that parties came up from the cities and tried to shoot them. Only a month ago the Dunsinnan constable had stopped a car on the bridge and found a butchered young stag in the trunk.

McCabe tried to check his breath, but he was having to drag his gun with his left arm while holding the glasses in the right, and he was not as easy in movement as he had once been. There was more exhilaration in shadowing a buck than in shooting it, at least as far as he was concerned.

Luckily, the buck was upwind from him, which helped keep his scent from it. The problem was birds: If he smashed into a nest, which was easy to do, or if he moved too quickly, the birds would rise and consort and mark his presence for the buck. There was no doubt who was the alien here; no matter how well he had learned to track, how many years he had spent in this careful balance of lives on the moor, he could not but feel the hunter, even, as today, when he was merely the spectator.

The seeds of the heather were beginning to fall, and there was no warmth left in the sun now, but the sky was clear in the weak watercolor blue of autumn. Suddenly a cock red grouse leapt out of the heather, as though beaten from it, spread its wings, and soared away, startling him. It made the almost human barking call *ko-bak, ko-bak*, as grouse do when staking out their territory, but it was acting strangely, rising and then diving with its neck extended and fanning its tail. Other birds came out of the heather, and the buck turned toward them, and McCabe, more alert. For half a minute it stood, nose twitching, antlers still, then lowered its head and cantered off, its hoofbeats vibrating under where McCabe lay. He cursed the birds. But what had disturbed them?

In a flash he saw it. Above him, out of his vision as long as he lay prone in the heather, a great bird circled. Its wings were at least six feet across, possibly more: a golden eagle, one of a pair from the nearby peaks. He knew what was coming. Its wings hardly moved, there was just a flexing of the tip feathers. Its head curved down. The eagle was measuring the distance, picking out its prey. It banked, then half closed its wings and fell. These birds dived at up to ninety miles per hour—with deadly precision. There was a rush of air, a squawking, a beating of wings, a cloud of heather seed, and the eagle was up again, a hen grouse in its claws—a taste they shared with man.

The deadly spectacle gave McCabe some consolation for losing the buck. The eagles were rare now. The surviving grouse settled into the heather again, and the barking died out. McCabe walked back, down a slope toward the glen, coming into a copse. An instinct caused him to stop and listen; he fancied he heard a step, a breaking twig. But there was nothing—how could there be, out here? He walked on, but something barely tangible disturbed him—birds rising, a shifting sound on the ground. So attuned to hunting, he also had the senses of the hunted.

He came out of the copse and into the bowl of the glen. He had a clear view around him. There was no sign of anything. His horse was tied to a tree at the end of a rough trail that ran up the other side of the glen, through a small wood. As he reached the wood he looked back. Over the copse, a good quarter of a mile away, the birds were still circling nervously. A small stream ran down through the wood, near the trail. The sound of the water obscured his keenest sense, screening out anything but the occasional cries of the birds. Halfway up the trail he stopped and sat on a small knoll. He put down the gun and took a swig of the whiskey from the flask he carried with him.

All this was deliberate. Looking unhurried, he was really growing wary, though still without knowing why. To the west, the blue wash of the sky now had an evening tint of salmon pink, and the wind was chill. The whisky helped. After resting for five minutes, he picked up his gun and walked on, up toward the horse, which had heard his approach and was pawing at the ground with a front foot, anxious to be off.

He was within twenty feet of the horse when his right foot broke through a depression in the track. As he lost his balance the foot sank down and then, in an instant, an acute pain shot up the leg. Steel closed around the foot and crushed the ankle, smashing the bone. He felt a surge of warm blood up his calf, his muscles contracted from thigh to knee so that as he fell he could not bend the leg but toppled, stiffly, face-down into the dirt, the gun flying into the ground. It felt as though his eyes were filling with blood, but it was pain—and the shock in his brain. The horse reared and cried out. McCabe lay, mouth in the dirt, only half-conscious but dimly knowing that what was embedded in his leg was a mole trap, spring loaded.

The horse calmed down and looked down the track, the way that McCabe had come. McCabe was losing a lot of blood, but the pain had ceased, and in its place a dim serenity, a form of stupidity, had overtaken his senses. He was unaware of the man's shadow falling across him. The horse reared again at the sound of the shot. A side of McCabe's face was blown away, and his good leg, the left one, twitched in a spasm. A gloved hand raised McCabe's body high enough to slide his gun, butt down, under it.

8

The innocent lullaby "Falling in Love Again" acquired a carnal appeal in the throat of Marlene Dietrich. Couples moved across the parquet floor in its spell, but the setting lacked the easy promiscuity of *The Blue Angel*; the phonograph was no substitute for the sight of those carefully arranged thighs, the garter, and its hint of vagrancy. Ruth's head rested on Dunsinnan's shoulder. His slicked hair smelled of musk. His jawline, foundation of his profile, ended beneath his ear in a pronounced bone, which she brushed as, in the last beat of the music, she pulled away to look him in the eyes. "Mmmmmmmm," she said, "what a sexy lady. . . ."

"You think so?" His right hand lingered on the small of her spine. "She was—once." His lids drooped. "I saw her the other night, at the Savoy. I thought she had a cruel face. And her *arms* were hideous."

The end of the music left people in unresolved embraces—some ardent, some jaded. Dunsinnan was reluctant to release her. She made two steps to a nonexistent beat and pulled him from the floor. "I'm *ravenous*," she said.

In the next room a buffet extended along the length of one wall. The food was composed in elaborate patterns, the centerpiece a boar's head surrounded by pâtés and mousses, glazed and studded with olives and diced vegetables in geometric designs. Ruth found a sensuous delight in puncturing these surfaces, the glaze fracturing like thin glass, releasing the salmon fragrance of the soft pink mousse as she scooped it out. Dunsinnan, less rapacious at the table, marvelled at her sweep of the food and grimaced at the clash of textures.

Small circular wicker tables were scattered about the room; more were on the terrace beyond. Dunsinnan responded to a wave from the terrace. A middle-aged man with a pink face half rose, napkin in hand. Ruth's heaped plate tilted, and she just managed to retrieve its balance as they reached the table.

"Bill, this is Ruth, Ruth Dexter. Ruth, this is Bill de Ropp—*Baron* de Ropp, actually." He delivered the title with mocking ceremony.

"Call me Bill." De Ropp countered Dunsinnan's pomp. Then turning to the woman sitting silently at his side: "My wife . . ."

A waiter brought champagne. De Ropp toasted Dunsinnan, including Ruth in the gesture. "You've neglected us lately, Alastair—but I can see you have charming distractions."

Dunsinnan looked smug, and sipped the champagne with a sidelong glance at Ruth. "Yes . . . Ruth is the daughter of an old family friend, from America."

"Ah—that is so?" De Ropp's interest increased. "Tell me, Miss Dexter, Roosevelt will be returned, you think?"

"Against Landon? It's no contest."

"As certain as that?"

"A landslide, you'll see."

Dunsinnan's hand closed on hers. "But do you *like* him?"

"Yes, I do. He's picked up the pieces, put us together."

De Ropp nodded. "I can see that. But there are influences around him, the Jews in particular, men like Baruch. Doesn't that worry you?"

"I don't think about it much," she said, deflecting the thought. She noticed the prolonged silence of de Ropp's wife. "It's quite a party, this."

Unsatisfied by the hors d'oeuvre, she led Dunsinnan back to the buffet, returning to the terrace with lamb cutlets, each capped by a white frilled paper collar. De Ropp's English wife finally came to life while Dunsinnan and the baron found common cause. The woman explained that their Baltic estates had been taken by the Russians after the revolution. "Now"—she nodded toward the unhearing baron—"our whole life revolves around stopping the communists." The effort seemed to weary her.

Beyond the terrace the landscape, emerald by day, had turned bluish in the night. There was no moon, and a low layer of cloud had trapped the warmth of the afternoon. Ruth interrupted a monologue from Dunsinnan: "Alastair, can we go for a walk? I'm feeling a bit fuzzed."

For a second Dunsinnan showed irritation, then relented. "Of course."

They went across a wide lawn, cropped and springy underfoot. She kicked off her shoes. "I've never had so much champagne."

"Nor so much food, I should think."

"You noticed."

His arm came around her waist. "I don't know where it goes, but it doesn't show."

"I'm lucky that way."

The hand moved up her spine to the back of her neck. She moved closer, but they kept walking. They came to a line of poplars dividing the lawn from a smaller enclosure framed on its other three sides by a low wall. Through the trees she saw several Grecian statues on pedestals.

"Oh, *my!*" She broke away from him and ran between the trees, seeing the glint of water. "A pool! You never told me! *And the style!*"

The pool was semicircular. A tier of marble steps flanked by goddesses ran the entire length of the straight side, nearest to them. Ruth reached up and followed the line of a thigh with her hand; the figures were plaster. Her fingers found a seam, the mating of two molds. "What a *pity*," she said, but Dinsinnan was uncomprehending, his mind elsewhere.

She stood on the first step, her feet in the water. "It's heated."

"How sad we don't have swimsuits," he said.

"*Skinny-dips!*"

"Sorry?"

"Skinny-dips—swimming in the buff. Have you never . . . ?"

"Not in mixed company." He hovered between primness and excitement.

"Okay, if you want to be discreet . . . stay here and strip off. I'll go down the other end. When I call, you can come in." She ran along the curve of the pool, past spouting Neptunes, pulling off her dress as she went. He watched until she was lost in the shadows. In a minute he heard a splash.

His own clothes lying on the grass, he took a run from the side of the pool and dived headlong, arms outstretched. He surfaced in the center of the pool and shook his head violently, for a second both blind and deaf. Her head came up directly ahead of him.

"There," she said, treading water, "it's the *only* way, once you've done it." As she dipped in and out of the water, her hair fallen across each side of her face, he saw the darker discs of nipples and the curve of her breasts.

"Yes," he said. "It does have its appeal."

She arched her back and went over in a backward somersault, disappearing in a bubbly wake. He went like a torpedo after her but found only the edge of the pool. While he recovered his breath, his hands gripping a rococo plaster lip, she surfaced behind him, laughing. She locked her arms around his waist, palms pressing so that he felt her breasts in his back.

"I'm not giving you any fight," he said.

She kept her grip for a few more seconds and then lay back on the water, floating with arms akimbo. He turned and saw the dark body made more voluptuous by the distortions of the water, her knees rising discreetly as she pushed slowly backwards through the water, her head framed between the two breasts which made separate wakes. She tilted her head back, looking at the sky.

"It's strange—I feel levitated."

"That's the champagne, not the water." He made a lazy stroke beside her. The water covered all but the peaks of her face and the nipples. His right hand closed on her upturned right hand. She raised her head slightly and turned to him, then slipped free and struck out in a powerful crawl, giving him clear sight of the arc of an arm and one glistening breast. They swam in a game of passing light touches, she moving faster than he and not tiring. Seeing his fatigue, she wallowed and then nosed toward him.

There was a sound from the trees and a spaniel appeared at the top of the steps, tail wagging. It dipped its nose into the water, then began barking.

"Damn!" he said.

The spaniel launched itself from the steps and paddled toward them, its nose held clear of the water.

"Nice dog . . . nice dog," she said, enjoying Dunsinnan's confusion. The spaniel came to her and put a paw on her shoulder. She drifted to the side and pulled herself out of the pool, turning to look down to him as the spaniel paddled away to the steps.

"You'll find some towels in the cabin," he said. "Can you get one for me?" He looked at the most perfect body he had ever seen.

She came back wearing a towel like a toga. "Here," she said, holding out another like a robe, covering him as he came out. "You're *very* hairy."

He wrapped the towel round his waist and leaned forward, giving her a light kiss on the mouth. "Don't tease," he said.

"Be paitent," she said. The spaniel was licking at her ankles.

McCabe's death had brought Lady Dunsinnan back to Scotland. Weary from the journey, she sat in her room with shaded windows. The constable had labored up the hill on his bicycle, and he, too, was fatigued. The mutual exhaustion lowered the social barriers, striking some chord in their folk memory: the plain, open man and the woman whose own roots, like his, went back centuries to a time free of English manners.

The constable had his hat on his lap; his brow was still wet from the exertion. "There'll need to be a post-mortem, I'm afraid." He fingered the peak of the hat.

"Yes—I expect so." She fell silent for a few seconds. "Who'll give evidence?"

"The doctor. And Drummond—it was Drummond who found him."

"Yes." It still bothered her that Drummond had been up here, when it happened, instead of in London with Alastair. "Yes, it was lucky Drummond was riding up there. Otherwise we might not have found the body for days." She sounded speculative. "It's a strange thing—he was always so careful with guns. And why should there have been a trap, in *that* place?"

"Aye, that *was* careless, Your Ladyship. There was whisky in his stomach, though—and the flask was by the body. Had he been drinking heavily?"

"Och, *no!*" The broadness of her accent came out again in her determination to refute the implication. "No more, no less, than anyone up here." She gave the constable a withering look, knowing his own taste for the malt.

"No, right you are." He shifted uneasily in his seat. "I'm much obliged, Your Ladyship, for your coming up at such short notice." He hesitated as he got up. "I don't suppose His Lordship will be coming?"

"I'm afraid not, Constable."

After he had left, she remained in the room, brooding uneasily. Then she remembered McCabe's family. She would make sure that they were taken care of.

Seton put down the paper, angry. "If this kind of thing goes on it could become infectious. Quite deplorable, and that man Mosley—to think, only a few years ago people were talking of him as a potential prime minister."

"Odd that, isn't it, sir?" said Pickles, looking at the picture of the man in the black shirt with arm raised, and the scenes of street riots. "He seems to have run the whole political distance, from left to right."

"Yes,'" said Seton, spinning in the chair. "Yet in spite of that he's still regarded as a reputable man, in the eyes of many. A reputable man is more dangerous when he gets hold of a disreputable idea. That's the point: Mosley has kept fascism *respectable* to many people, because of *who* he is, his background. If you look at the kind of people behind him, though"—Seton jabbed a hand at the mob in the pictures—"those thugs would be nowhere without him—*he* raises them from dirt."

Pickles had always kept his place with Seton, in awe of his reputation rather than in deference to any assertion of rank, but the more he worked with him, the more he realized his personal loyalty, even though he couldn't articulate it. Seton's self-reliance was not an easy shell to crack, but his passion this morning over the Fascist attacks on Jews in London's East End had—momentarily at least—made him more approachable. And another reason for speculation arose at lunchtime, while Seton was out of the office. The phone rang, and a woman's voice said—precipitately—"Edward?"

"No," said Pickles, "the group captain is at lunch."

"Oh—I see."

Pickles divined the American accent. "Can I help?"

"Thank you, yes. Would you ask him to call Ruth when he has a moment."

Pickles made his curiosity too transparent to Seton when he returned. "There was a young lady asking after you, sir— an American. She said could you call—er, her name was Ruth."

Seton was far too casual. "Ruth? Ah, yes, of course. I think I have that number." He looked steadily at Pickles. "Was there anything else?"

He waited for Pickles to retreat, then dialed her number. "Ruth?"

"Oh, Edward. Thanks for calling back so soon." He could sense her agitation. "Something has happened. I'd like to talk to you."

"I could call by on the way home. Will you be there this evening—at the flat?"

"Yes. Thank you. I'll see you then."

When Seton asked for her later, in the small lobby of the building in Davies Street, he could tell that the janitor, a one-armed veteran in the uniform of the Corps of Commission-aires, had already adopted a guardian role with Ruth. He scrutinized Seton cautiously.

"Miss Dexter? Who shall I say is calling?" He was uncer-tain with the *who*, considering *whom* but not taking the risk.

"Group Captain Seton."

As he knew it would, the title brought a reflex action, the janitor returning in a second to the parade ground. "Yes, *sir!* Very good, sir!"

"Thank you, Fraser," Ruth said to the janitor, now stand-ing behind Seton at the door of the elevator. As she closed the door behind Seton, she confided, "Nice man, Fraser. Treats me as though he's my uncle."

"That's good to know." Seton smiled, taking in the flat. "I see you're not quite settled in." He took off his trilby and put it on a low table.

"No," she said a little guiltily. "Coffee? I *can* at least fix you the best cup of coffee in London—not that that's much of a contest."

He waited on a sofa, looking through an old American

paper, noting the coverage given to the amours of the King.

"*Now*," he said, taking the coffee, "what is it?"

"You remember, when I told you about Scotland, my talking of a man called McCabe, the estate manager?"

"The chap you liked?"

"You've got it." She was pleased that he remembered. "Well, he's dead. An accident with a shotgun." She brushed a strand of hair from her eyes, looking solemn and nervous. "I only heard about it today. Lady Dunsinnan called and told me."

"That's very sad—but—?"

"I know this might sound silly—I suppose it is. Well, it's just that on the last day there, when we were out riding, he seemed bothered—bothered enough to try to warn *me* of something—"

"Warning?"

"Not explicitly. They're not very explicit about anything up there. I'm not sure, it seemed about the people around Alastair. Of course, I might be making too much of it. But McCabe's dying like this . . ."

"An accident, shooting?"

"Apparently he stepped into a mole trap, carrying the gun, and it went off. But he wasn't that kind of man—he knew every inch of the estate and was *very* fussy with the guns."

Seton decided that the best way of calming her was to lie convincingly. "I don't see anything sinister in that at all." He put down his cup. "There are accidents like that all the time, even with the most experienced people."

"You *really* think so?" She was visibly relaxing.

Seton had the odd sensation of becoming the counselling father to her, the dependent daughter. It unsettled him. "What have you been up to? How did that weekend party go?"

"I think we should have something stronger to drink, don't you?" She got up. "I've just acquired that essential accessory of civilized life, a cocktail shaker. Would you like to be a guinea pig—let me try out something on you?"

"What exactly?"

"See if you can tell." She laughed, disappearing into the kitchen. In five minutes she came back with two frosted glasses.

"I'm glad you haven't put a cherry on it," he said, "can't stand cherries in drinks." He sipped the cocktail with exaggerated caution. It tasted bittersweet. He took a second, keener sip.

"It's a Prince Charlie."

"What's in it?"

"One third Drambuie, one third cognac, one third fresh lemon."

Seton looked astonished.

She sat opposite, with a decorous and self-conscious arrangement of her skirt. "Tell me, Edward, do you think I'm on the road to dissipation?"

Endmere spent a lot of his life in clubs, usually of the oak-panelled variety. The Gargoyle Club was of another world, underground. The dance floor was illuminated from beneath, which, when the other lights were turned down, created a lurid effect on a clientele already quite bizarre. Their faces were cast in exaggerated relief, as though shaped in a plaster not quite hardened, eye sockets in the imprint of a great thumb, mouths too plastic. Genders were not always certain: youths like clowns in a ballet, girls in black tails and ties, one huge man swathed in silks held around his gut by a silver cummerbund—a blend of fakir and maharajah. His hands were jewelled, and his black eyes, from the recesses of shadow, seemed sightless. The music, too, was bogus oriental, including a large bronze gong stroked by a blackamoor. The underfloor lighting, inexpertly installed, made the floor too warm. The club was permeated by the smell of scorching inadequately countered by incense.

Guy Burgess looked across the dance floor to a table on the other side, straining to see. Under the table a man was crouched, licking a girl's painted legs. The girl continued to talk impassively to her neighbor, a man with heavily greased hair and a monocle.

Endmere followed Burgess's eyes. "Is that an erotic act, do you think?"

"Good God, no," said Burgess, turning his watery eyes on Endmere. "Flannery believes himself to be a dog. I have actually seen him on a lead, being walked in the park."

"I trust he is house-trained," said Endmere.

There was a quiet laugh from a third man at their table. Dark, more sober-looking, he wore a check woollen shirt and a flecked tweed jacket, the rustic wear out of place even in such catholic company. He had a wide, full mouth and sucked a pipe.

Endmere, much the senior of the three, turned to him. "You're married, Kim?"

"Mmmm," the man said through the pipe, almost absently.

Burgess became mocking. "Oh, Philby is a gallant, he took his wife in Austria, because she was a Red and needed to get out."

"Noble," Endmere retorted, half-serious. "Not *your* kind of generosity, Guy."

"Oh, don't misjudge me, old chap." Burgess's cigarette had accumulated a stem of ash, which fell into his glass. "Damn." He looked around for an exchange of glass. "No, I'm quite prepared to marry someone in that position—so long as I don't have to go to bed with her." He filled another glass from a bottle. "This really is the most filthy whisky—if whisky it is at all. Marinated elephant's piss, I should think." Sneering, he showed a scarlet lip. "So—Kim, you're hoping to get to Spain?"

Philby removed the pipe. "They seem likely to send me."

"Kim's made quite a mark at *The Times*, already," said Endmere.

Burgess laughed and then coughed. "I couldn't quite manage that trick."

9

Berlin, November 1936

There was a wholesomeness, almost an innocence, in the girl's face that seemed out of place, suggesting a domestic quality rather than the arctic bureaucrat he expected. As she brought him coffee this incongruity bothered him more: Given the time to study his surroundings, *they* seemed wrong, too. Few people seemed to wear uniform, or anything remotely conformist. The more he looked around him, the more it seemed a mistake. Perhaps it was a hostel, or a boarding-house of some kind, not an office at all. And yet this was the right address, and there had been guards on the door—

although they, too, were remarkably casual. Watching him drink the coffee, the girl understood his perplexity; she stopped typing and smiled.

"You haven't been here before?"

"No," he said, openly uneasy.

"We don't get many from the Luftwaffe in here." She studied his uniform. "What do you fly?"

"Did—I *did* fly until I collected this bent leg."

"Oh—yes"—she recalled the limp she noticed as he entered. "A crash?"

He nodded. "And now—this."

"You find the Abwehr strange? Most people do, if they come from the military." Her eyes hung on his uniform. "The admiral doesn't usually bring in people from the Luftwaffe."

"So I've heard." He lapsed into silence, sipping the coffee.

Still curious, she said, "He must have a reason—in your case."

The door beyond her opened, and a lean middle-aged man appeared wearing the uniform of a Wehrmacht major. The sudden affinity of recognizable ranks was reassuring.

"Von Klagen . . . ? Oberstleutnant von Klagen?"

He got up and, in the same movement, raised his right arm. "*Heil. . . .*"

He got no further. The major's expression was suddenly frigid. "Not here, Oberstleutnant—*never* here." He waited for the arm to collapse and then extended a handshake. "Piekenbrock. Hans Piekenbrock." The hands gripped. "You will find many things different at first, Oberstleutnant. Welcome to the Abwehr. The admiral is waiting."

They passed through another anteroom where two older women were submerged in paperwork, and went through another door. The linoleum floor was scuffed and stained, the furnishings austere. There was the inimitable smell of dogs. Beyond the second door was a larger, lighter office with deep windows opening to a balcony. Seated at a desk, with the light behind him, was a man with a thick head of white hair and heavy white eyebrows; his other features were indistinct because of the light. He nodded without rising: "Sit, please."

From the chair, as his eyes adjusted, von Klagen saw a model battleship and a bronze casting of the three oriental monkeys who saw nothing, heard nothing, and said nothing, and behind them an equally inscrutable face. Von Klagen had been warned that Admiral Wilhelm Canaris followed the oriental virtues symbolized in the figures on the desk, and he could understand their usefulness in running Hitler's spy network. Canaris was said to be politically as well as professionally inscrutable; there were murmurs that the Abwehr was not as pliant to the Nazi will as some wanted. His own gaffe with the Nazi salute seemed to bear this out. The admiral's eyes were on his leg.

"You're a casualty of Spain?"

"I was lucky. The Spanish doctors wanted to keep my leg as a trophy."

"The Spanish hospitals are not up to our standards, so?"

"Like many other things."

Piekenbrock thought von Klagen's readiness to damn the Spaniards might be too unwary, but Canaris remained sympathetic: "Yes, things must be very hard. You must remember that Spain is not Germany; it is a poor country, still medieval in many ways. They need all the help we can give them." He stopped and picked up a sheet of brown paper. "I think you have seen this report, already—von Winterfeld's crash—the flight from Spain?"

Von Klagen nodded.

"It is embarrasing. I instructed them to carry the extra fuel, to avoid landing in France. Now the plane has fallen into French hands anyway. Only a few kilometers short of Switzerland. I think he was trying to get over the border before he crashed."

"One of our best pilots," von Klagen said.

"Just so." Canaris got up and walked to the corner of the desk, looking down on von Klagen. "We need someone with your kind of background. Aviation is not our strong point. And since your flying days are unfortunately over . . ."

From behind the desk two dachshunds appeared, skating over the linoleum. They gathered at von Klagen's feet, sniffing. Von Klagen then realized how small Canaris was: He could not have been more than five feet four. He wore a thick dark-blue sweater and blue serge trousers.

"Don't mind them, they appear to like you. You speak English—how well?" Canaris delivered the question in English, breaking from the German without pause.

"I lived for two years in London, working for a wine merchant—Moselles, hocks." Von Klagen's English was the equal of Canaris's.

"Good. Yes, they know more about our wine than we, the English." Canaris reverted to German. "The documents on von Winterfeld's plane were a serious loss. A gift for the French and British intelligence revealing the strength of our Condor Legion—your former colleagues. I want to know who took that material from the wreck and what use they are making of it."

"We have the credentials prepared," said Piekenbrock. "You are going to acquire a new profession, magazine photographer. Properly accredited, of course, to the *Illustrierte Zeitung.*"

"You use a Leica, yes?" Canaris asked.

When von Klagen had gone, Canaris detained Piekenbrock. The dachshunds settled in front of the desk, Canaris behind it.

"Well?" said Piekenbrock.

"I'm not sure. Very confident—perhaps *too* confident. Too quick with his opinions. Snap judgments are no good in this kind of work. Normally, not the type of man I would want. But . . . he has the right knowledge, and his English is good—*very* good. We'll see what he can produce."

"He's not a party man."

"Strange that. I would have said, at first sight, he was ideal material for them." Canaris brooded, the thick white brows knitting. "You think he might be a plant?"

"I wondered about that. We checked him out very thoroughly. There's no sign of it." Piekenbrock got up and walked to the balcony window. Without looking back at Canaris, he said, "You've kept Heydrich at bay for two years now."

"I'm afraid that makes him more eager than ever to undermine us. Sometimes, when he's at my home, eating roast boar, I can see that he wishes it was my head on the platter."

Piekenbrock laughed uncertainly. "It would take a good hunter to manage that, my Admiral."

Canaris joined Piekenbrock at the window. Snow was driving across a canal on the other side of the street. "I'm going to try to settle things with Heydrich, while I can. Get an absolute understanding about our respective territory. He's coming to dinner tonight."

Reinhard Heydrich and his wife, Lena, lived on the same block as Canaris and his wife, Erika, in the suburb of Zehlendorf in southwest Berlin. Erika Canaris had watched Heydrich's rise since he was a naval cadet serving under Canaris. Now she knew him as one of the most feared men in the Third Reich—directing the Sicherheitsdienst, or S.D., the

Nazi party's own intelligence service, including the Gestapo, which was now ever more ambitious to compete with Canaris's Abwehr. She knew that behind Heydrich stood one of her husband's most persistent critics, Heinrich Himmler. While Canaris and Heydrich persisted with a facade of domestic comradeship their evenings and dinners together—Heydrich listening to Mozart, Canaris talking to the navy—also had the tension of professional struggle. On this evening Heydrich had hardly settled at the table before he began sniping:

"It's unfortunate, the loss of Winterfeld—and his pouch."

"He was a brave man, a good pilot."

"How much can it tell them, the pouch?"

"Numbers, mainly. We couldn't conceal it much longer anyway."

Heydrich's thin, feminine fingers drummed the table. "There was a letter, from Franco to you?"

"Only courtesies."

"Our military adviser there, Faupel—he does not think much of Franco."

"Faupel is a Prussian." Canaris used the word as a pejorative. "A long way from the Spanish mentality."

Heydrich's tight lips flexed at the corners. "The Führer served under Faupel in the war. *He* thinks highly of him."

"Perhaps. But he is not the right type for handling the Spaniards."

Erika Canaris looked across the table to Lena Heydrich. The women interceded to head off the collision. But by the end of the meal they were ready, tactfully, to leave the two men alone.

When Canaris came to bed, hours later, he took a dose of Phanodorm, his only reliable refuge. Heydrich's ambition to swallow the Abwehr within his own empire had become nakedly visible. The only constraint was the prestige Canaris enjoyed with Hitler. And they both knew how perishable that advantage could be.

It was too early for the season to be in full swing in Saint Moritz: The fashionable wave did not reach there until after Christmas, and Dunsinnan was feeling uncomfortably out of fashion, an *arriviste*, mistiming his appearance. But there was no choice: He had even been instructed to move from Saint Moritz itself up to the Suvretta House Hotel, a rambling Victorian building where skating waiters glided across the hotel's own vast rink delivering trays of drinks. His only consolation was Margery Taverner.

They sat in a huge tearoom, with vaulted windows overlooking the ice.

"You should learn to ski, since you're here," he said. "Drummond could teach you."

"I hate that man. There's something very *coarse* in him."

"Crutches have a certain appeal, don't you think?" said Dunsinnan, watching a Nordic beauty hobble across the room.

"A matter of taste." She disliked his mood. "What are you doing here, *really?*"

"I thought you understood—it's a diversion, and a little business to conduct." His eyes were still on the blonde.

"Who is this American girl who was up at the castle?"

He turned back slowly and looked at her. "Oh. You heard about that, did you?" She waited for elaboration. He drank the chocolate and then said: "It's Mother's interest, really, not mine. She's a daughter of a friend of the family, no more than a distant acquaintance."

"I hear it wasn't so distant at Tring."

In self-defense he became facetious: "My, *my*—the walls have eyes."

"I'm told she's just your type."

"I don't much care for being gossiped about. It's not even that I've touched the girl. I've had to make a gesture, to please Mother."

She laughed mockingly. "A *gesture!*" She moved a booted leg upwards under the table. "And how about pleasing me?"

He flushed. "Not *here*, for God's sake."

"We'd better get to bed, then—before you boil over."

In the morning he was among the first skiers to take the funicular car to the Chantorella slopes. At Chantorella he kept to the main track for about a mile, bent almost double in a finely balanced fast run, and then broke away to follow an oblique line over a lower slope, cutting into virgin snow. On his left was a long ravine, perhaps five hundred feet deep. Only a confident skier would have gone so close. At the end of the ravine he dipped into a steeper run and dropped completely out of sight of Chantorella. Below him, on a spur of the mountain, one passable road descended in a series of loops and ended on a plateau where three large chalets overlooked the glacier, which, in the early sun, looked like spilled cream.

His run ended at the foot of the first and largest of the chalets, a sprawling building inside a fenced compound. He pulled off the skis and walked to a gate in the fence. A dog came to the other side and began yelping. A small man in a black leather coat and woollen cap left the chalet and walked to the gate with a mincing step, kicking at the dog as he let Dunsinnan in. The dog persisted in its affections, running at the smaller man's heels.

As they went into the chalet the man said, "You must understand, this is a very unusual step. Only a decision at the very highest level could arrange it. I hope you appreciate that."

The chalet was too hot. Dunsinnan took off his skiing coat but still felt overdressed in the sweater. He disliked Max Lutze but had learned to suffer him. They spoke in German, which irritated Lutze because Dunsinnan's clear Junker diction contrasted with Lutze's rough Bavarian. Dunsinnan sat in shadow to one side of a window while Lutze scanned the glacier. After ten minutes they heard the plane.

It appeared at the far end of the glacier, flying low and extraordinarily slowly, skis in place of wheels. It came toward the chalets, banked slightly to check the surface of the glacier, and then made a short landing run, throwing up a cloud of fine snow and ice behind it. Except for a small German civilian registration, it was unmarked. Two men emerged. The first was tall with fair hair, the second of medium height and dark. Both wore leather flying coats with fur linings. The taller man had the step of an athlete, leaving the smaller trailing in the snow. Lutze went out to admit them.

Something about the men's suits suggested standard issue, identical in their bad fit. Each had a small swastika pin on his lapel. The taller man's face had a sharpness near to emaciation, as though his parchment skin had been pulled down over the skull to meet the chin, with nothing to spare. His eyes were clear blue. His first glance made Dunsinnan nervous. Lutze brought him forward first:

"Lord Dunsinnan, this is Reinhard Heydrich."

Heydrich took Dunsinnan's hand in a testing clasp.

"And this is Walther Schellenberg," Lutze said, as the shorter man stepped forward. There was a duelling scar on Schellenberg's left chin.

Almost genuflecting, Lutze led Heydrich to a seat, and they settled in a group, Dunsinnan trapped in sunlight, adding perspiration to his discomforts.

Heydrich waited for Dunsinnan to speak.

"I am very grateful that you were able to come," Dunsinnan began. "As you know, my group has tried to help the Reich in several ways . . . the supply of tungsten from Spain, the oil. . . ."

Heydrich nodded impatiently.

Dunsinnan's mouth was turning dry. He went on: "We now intend to give more *political* support."

Heydrich's voice was disconcertingly high-pitched: "Political?"

"We believe we can now have considerable influence on British policy toward Germany, a process of careful contacts, nothing too *public*. There is considerable sympathy—in the right quarters."

"Not Mosley, I hope," said Heydrich.

"No . . . he is, of course, too *vulgar*. He has limited appeal." Dunsinnan found his confidence. "Of course, the Blackshirts do have one useful purpose. They draw so much attention to themselves that it becomes easier for more serious contacts to be made without attracting notice."

Heydrich thawed by a few degrees. "I see the use of that. . . ." His hands, on his lap, disengaged slowly, and he leaned forward. "You will forgive me, Lord Dunsinnan, but we have had our hopes raised before. The Führer has been very patient. He has listened to many people: Lord Rothermere, his newspaper is very helpful; Lord Beaverbrook—less predictable, it seems; Lord Londonderry; lately Mr. Lloyd George. But there is little to show for it in British policy."

"That is precisely my point." Dunsinnan spoke more urgently. "It's all too *public*. The Lloyd George articles, for example, they were unwise. No, we have more *subtle* ideas." He met Heydrich's eyes unflinchingly. "I have three objectives. The first, that a British prime minister—there is a change coming—*must* talk directly to the Führer. Until then there will only be misunderstandings. Second, our ambassador in Berlin. Phipps will be got rid of. In fact, Baldwin has already been persuaded of that by Mr. Thomas Jones, who you know has seen the Führer twice. The new man in Berlin will be *much* more sympathetic."

"And your third objective?"

"Eden. He must also be removed."

Heydrich was openly skeptical: "How can you hope to do that? Eden has powerful friends."

Dunsinnan was careful. "At the moment, yes. But with a change of prime minister . . ."

"And who will that be?" asked Schellenberg.

"We cannot yet be sure, but the most likely contenders, all three of them, should prove more *constructive* in their attitude."

"Hoare, Simon, or Chamberlain?" said Heydrich with a precision that surprised Dunsinnan.

Dunsinnan knew the power invested in Heydrich, his intimacy with Hitler's mind and court, and now he knew that his own ambitions rested on convincing Heydrich that where others had failed he could succeed.

"It is essential," he said, "if we are to achieve our objectives, that I have the closest contact with your organization—the S.D. Only by very careful collaboration can we work effectively."

Heydrich looked to his colleague. "I am making that Schellenberg's responsibility. As my deputy, he will keep in direct contact with you."

Heydrich looked at his watch, and Lutze, anxious to anticipate command, began to rise. "Very well," said Heydrich, and then, going to the door, he turned to Dunsinnan again. "How will all this be affected if there is a change of King?"

"It will not be quite so easy, perhaps. But I see no reason to be discouraged."

"He is a good friend of Germany, the King." He looked at Dunsinnan coolly, then went out to the plane with Schellenberg. The pilot had been walking on the glacier, beating his arms occasionally across his chest, his breath hanging white in the air. The Feisler Storch left the ground as nimbly as it had come, and turned away to the north.

At the hotel Dunsinnan found a message asking him to call his mother in Scotland. It took him more than an hour to make the connection. Afterwards he called Drummond to his room.

"I told you—you were overreacting. It wasn't necessary to go that far." Dunsinnan was quiet in his anger.

Drummond approached insolence. "Nothing less would have solved the problem. McCabe was too much of a risk."

"You're a fool—it will just make them more curious than ever, if they realize what happened. Now, it turns out, they're not happy with the inquest. Your evidence—something doesn't square with the postmortem. You're lucky that I can get it hushed up."

Drummond refused to be penitent. "He was informing. I told you about the meeting with the man in the pub. In any case, they'll never be sure it wasn't an accident."

Dunsinnan could smell the perfume from the bathroom and saw Drummond's eyes diverted by it. He took him firmly by the arm and directed him to the door, talking even more quietly now, directly into his ear. "When *I* want extreme measures taken, I'll tell you. There is far too much at stake here to make another mistake of that kind. You had better be *very* careful."

10

At this time of the year the cold in the Abbey reached into the marrow. The building's origins were Norman; it had been preserved out of reverence for a time when the Taverners had been the Taverniers, the first Tavernier, as the French conqueror, having noted the number of cows, bulls, sheep, and people—in that order of value—within his new domain so that they should appear as his tally in the Domesday Book. Much later Tavernier became Taverner to survive the whims of the Tudors; it was said that the great master of Tudor church music, John Taverner, was a distant relative, and his skill in escaping execution as a Lutheran heretic had been matched by this branch of the family as they survived and prospered under each successive dynasty, however fickle. This success brought further wings and ramparts: a substantial Tudor house and another during the Regency, when textiles enlarged the family fortunes.

This good run went disastrously wrong only in the 1920s. Rash speculation in New York and bad luck at the casino in Monte Carlo were simultaneous and brought the family to the brink of penury. Such suffering was, however, relative. Not everything was liquidated: The Abbey remained, though stripped of many treasures and secretly mortgaged, and self-esteem endured.

As Margery Taverner walked the flagstones of the Norman crypt, noting the recent departure of some sacred vessels, there was a bitterness in her that might have issued from the voices of generations speaking from the walls. When would those stained-glass windows go, windows that had miraculously survived the madmen who had smashed the best windows of Canterbury? She shivered, but at least she shivered in silk.

In one large room of the Tudor wing there was a fire, a great fire of spitting elm with space almost to sit alongside the flames. The Dowager Lady Taverner was sitting in a high-winged chair of faded tapestry facing the fire, so that when Margery came into the room her mother was invisible. Only the prone Labrador drooling at the feet of the chair confirmed her presence. And only when she got to the chair was Margery able to share the warmth of the fire.

Her mother was dressed practically, if curiously. She wore a long velvet dress of faded green, woollen stockings, high laced-up boots, and a man's Harris tweed hacking jacket with leather-patched elbows. The masculinity of the garb was denied by the appearance of her face: Though now deeply lined, it had the kind of bone structure that, in youth, would have produced one of those bewitching Holbein faces, character with the lightest of molding. The daughter had this fineness too.

Each time Margery saw her mother, there was the unmistakable competitive glint in her eye: It had always been so. The Taverner women were as competitive as they were highly sexed. This drive of the blood had made *them* the family's real survivors and manipulators; Taverner weakness had always been in the men.

A meeting with her mother, as now, was in the nature of an audit. Mixed with the material assessment was the one of physical assets and political gain. Her mother looked at her with those clear unveined eyes—"pools of crystal" a Prince of Wales had once called them, in a vulnerable moment.

Margery smiled.

"You're tired, my dear," said her mother.

"Cold," said Margery. Over the silk she wore a mohair sweater and a Chanel suit. She slipped off her trench coat and sat in a winged chair opposite her mother. The one thing her mother envied in Margery was the breasts: Positive and firm, they moved with the rest of her, whereas the mother had the classic flat chest of the Taverners, a once valued quality that later in her life had come to be a flaw. Nubile was not a word that the Dowager Lady Taverner thought polite, but her daughter could claim it, and there were, of course, the legs. For her age, they were remarkable.

"You must have been used to cold," said her mother.

"Switzerland? Oh, surely you remember, Mother. It's not *this* kind of cold. It's dry and *very* healthy. *This* kind of cold, this house—it gnaws into you."

"The house is quite warm enough" was her mother's tart reply. "I won't have the place like a greenhouse."

Margery knew that even the greenhouses were now unheated.

Her mother put aside a book and looked at her critically: "The strain is showing."

"Life is precarious, Mother." She looked around the room, then leaned nearer the fire, drawn to the flames.

"You know very well what I mean. You won't keep your looks forever. You seem to believe yourself to be a Dunsinnan property in perpetuity . . . you know my views on that. As long as Lady Dunsinnan is alive, Alastair will have to treat you like a chattel." She sighed. "And she's one of those Scottish women who go on forever."

"I don't *want* another marriage, you know that."

"If it's a choice between being a courtesan and being a wife, the latter seems preferable to me." On the word *courtesan* she curled her mouth.

Margery held up her head—the defiant flick of the chin, which had been there since childhood—and said, "I would have thought I followed a great family tradition. " Her mother's hypocrisy was checkmated.

"It was different then. Money was never a problem; it didn't matter if one was dropped."

The mention of money struck home. She looked down at her lap and struck a contemplative pose. "Well—things are getting a little tight, that's true."

"Is there no one else?"

"A vagabond or two."

They laughed together, a note of mutual taste struck. It was as near as they ever came to intimacy.

Seton crossed Hyde Park Corner and walked down alongside Buckingham Palace toward St. James's Park. The King had gone in the night: The shock of his abdication, the suddenness of the crisis, the escalation from whispers to disclosure, the final broadcast—"I want you to know that the decision I have made has been mine and mine alone"—had now burst on the country in a cascade of headlines. Outside the palace a crowd was pressing to the gates hoping to see the second son now called to the throne. Seton thought of the ancient chant "The King Is Dead, Long Live the King" and realized that with modified meaning it was being said again on this bleak December morning with the departure of Edward VIII. At two in the morning, as the Duke of Windsor, he had sailed out of Portsmouth on a Royal Navy destroyer to exile, to limbo. *Abdication.* The ambiguous word was as novel as it was universal that morning, but it was too simple a term for what had really happened.

A sharp, salutary wind cut across the park as Seton reached the bridge over the lake, and he had to hold his trilby down over his brow. From across the other side of the bridge another figure appeared, more solid, moving briskly, his homburg seemingly cemented into place, defying the wind. At first nothing was said between them as they met. Seton's head, still bowed in the effort to secure the hat, gave the impression of a man straining to keep up with the martial pace of his companion's silver-tipped umbrella. They heard the distant crowd calling for the King. In one direction, through the leafless trees, they could see the dull facade of the palace; at the other end of the park were the towers of Westminster, one political and the other ecclesiastical—the forces that had united to remove the King, as they had done before. Seton reflected that English institutions outlived their human cargo—and that in some indefinable way the man beside him was a messenger of that power.

"You heard his broadcast?" They had reached the path before he spoke, looking sidelong at Seton but keeping up the pace.

"Yes. Surprising dignity."

There was only a grunt in reply, an inference of disagreement.

"Nothing so much made the man as the manner of his going," said Seton, deliberately persisting, to know the man's mind.

They walked another ten yards before there was an answer, and then the man stopped, spearing a cluster of leaves with his umbrella and pivoting to confront Seton: "You remember what I showed you that night in Covent Garden?"

Seton nodded.

"Things had gone a lot further." He stabbed again at the leaves. "A lot further." He looked around to reassure himself of privacy. Only a pair of huddled rooks overlooked them from an oak. "You know, Edward, it will be one of the abiding ironies of one's memory that that young man should have gained a reputation for being the people's king. The visit to the miners in Wales—as though *he* understood! But given that kind of reputation, who knows where it might have led?"

A funnel of leaves spiralled across the path making a brittle chorus. Seton's companion began walking again, still talking: "Another six months and the crisis would have been of a different magnitude. The Germans have been very deft."

"You mean—he was . . . ?"

"We may not be able to stop the whole of Mayfair from rushing Hitler-wards, but a King is another matter. Given time, I'm convinced he would have gone to Berlin, making the grand gesture. You can imagine the kind of speech—ties of kinship, common stock, binding the wounds of the past . . ."

"But that's appalling," said Seton.

There were clearer chants from the crowd at the palace. Seton's companion nodded toward them. "It seems we chose altogether safer ground on which to remove him." He paused and turned his back to the wind, speaking quietly: "There are, of course, many of a similar mind, about whom we can do nothing. Young Dunsinnan, for one. I fear we may have underestimated the rigor of *his* convictions. You raised the death of the man in Scotland—what was the name . . . ?"

"McCabe."

"Yes. McCabe. I've made inquiries. It seems that our colleagues—those of the nether world—have been involved. It's typical of course, this kind of muddle. Someone was using McCabe as an informer. Low-level stuff, as it turns out. However . . . there seems a distinct possibility that the death was no accident. Nothing that can be proved, mind you—rather derelict postmortem, I gather, and other problems of a local kind. But it does rather cast things in a new light." He sighed. "It makes it increasingly important for us to know what is really going on amongst those people . . . without, of course, any further mishaps. You have my meaning?"

"Is it hot enough?" Ruth looked anxiously across the table. Seton felt the slow burn of paprika and chili in his throat, appeased by the juices of the meat.

"I would say—*very*. The equal of your mother's." He

took a first draft of iced lager. "And you *never* get beer cold like this in England." He leaned back with a ruminative look. "It certainly brings back memories. . . . How is your mother?"

"I can't really tell from her letters—they're all interrogation about the King and Mrs. Simpson."

Seton took another mouthful of chili, salivating: "Yes— well, thank God *that* distraction has gone, at last."

"You're *sure* it's all right?" She watched the color rising from his neck to his cheeks.

"Lovely." He took another drink of lager.

"It was perfectly clear to anyone who's read Freud—or Havelock Ellis, for that matter."

"Pardon?"

She smiled. "The infatuation—why it was that the King succumbed. I know it's not something you people talk about much—but I could see it. For the first time the man had found sexual fulfillment. You could *see* it in the photographs. The way he looked at her."

"You think so?" Seton was dubious.

"I *know* so."

"Well, we didn't have much of a chance to study the photographs—that is, not until this week."

"Funny. Three years of history in one morning's papers, *and no one asks why*."

He swallowed another time bomb. "It's called controlling the public composure." The flavors of meat and garlic were now mingling with the spices in a series of sensations. He felt pampered and domesticated in a way that disarmed his old paternalism toward her. Her shoulders were one shade darker than the coffee-toned velvet dress, low cut and moving with her body. Round her neck was a thin cord of gold with an Indian figure of painted bone.

"I remember that." He indicated the figure. "Your mother wore it, the first time we saw her."

The *we* was something she let pass, still wary of trespass. "Yes, it's at least two hundred years old."

It was when, much later, that he lay on the sofa with his tie loose, still trying to recover his normal body temperature, that she said something that reminded him of unwelcome concerns. His question was almost absentminded:

"And how is the young Scottish lord? Have you seen him?"

"He's been away a lot. And I'm really getting down to

my studies now—there's a life's work in the British Museum alone. He's just got back, as it happens. From Switzerland. His mother's asked me to join them for Christmas. In Scotland."

Finding it hard to be casual, he said, "Really? That might be nice."

"I don't know." She dangled an arm over the side of the sofa, drink in hand, and looked at him. "It can be a grim place. Still, I guess the snow will help."

Von Klagen returned to the Abwehr's rambling building on the Tirpitzufer, already feeling more a part of its freebooting style. Shedding his uniform and being thrown on his own resources seemed to be a kind of personal release. Canaris believed in giving his agents a loose rein—another reason, perhaps, why the Gestapo looked on the place with such suspicion. For von Klagen the chain of command was obligingly short. He reported to Piekenbrock, head of Branch I, which ran all the spies. Canaris, he had been told, confided in Piekenbrock as he did in no one else. And it was to Piekenbrock that von Klagen now came.

They were looking at a series of photographs of street scenes, one set from Paris, the other from London.

"It's difficult to pick them out," complained Piekenbrock, holding up a print and squinting at it. One face was circled with a grease pencil. "This is Martel, Louis Martel, of the Deuxième Bureau . . . ?"

"I couldn't get closer, not without a risk."

Piekenbrock exchanged the print for another. "And this—this is Seton—the one carrying the newspaper?"

"He never appears in uniform. He went over to Paris and picked up Martel there. Then they went to the Alps, to the von Winterfeld crash together. It was our contact in Paris who identified them. Martel was easy enough, but Seton is more careful."

Piekenbrock rubbed his thinning hair. "What do you know about *him*?"

"Not much more than is in the R.A.F. List, his postings. Hong Kong, Cairo, Malta, then the spell in Washington. That's when he seems to have moved across to intelligence. Von Boetticher remembers him there, rates him highly. The Foreign Office thing is a transparent cover. But our military attaché in London, Baron Geyr—he was of no use. In fact, he made it clear that he thinks this kind of work is beneath him. You know the type—champagne soldier."

Piekenbrock felt himself warming to von Klagen at last. "Yes." He shuffled through more prints. "Officially, of course, England is still supposed to be off limits for spying. Still . . . this is a beginning. It will take time. Seton interests me. You should try the Registry, they might have a trace. In any case, you'll be going back to London."

Dunsinnan gave her the white Arab again, and the thin layer of snow deadened the hooves, giving the ride an almost ethereal quality. The landscape now had only two colors: white and the darkness of trees. They rode the horses to the limit and reached the great Forest of Atholl, coming to a stop by the spectacular Falls of Bruar. The sides of the rock were encrusted with ice, and in the hardness of this place Ruth saw Scotland's peculiar beauty in a way she hadn't before—and in the wildness, something in Dunsinnan, too: a tie that he had tried to repress, under the urbane sheen. He turned his head back toward the sound of the falls as they ran down to Pitlochry, one fugitive glance, the head cast back and his hair split by the wind. They were wordless until they reached the stables, and then putting a strong hand to her waist as she dismounted, he said, "You and the horse—you belong."

The contessa, a moody member of the Christmas party at the castle, watched the riders come in. When she could get Ruth to herself, she quickly became confidential:

"Lady Dunsinnan, she likes you very much. It is a pity that there is not more of her in Alastair. There is something else in him." She tapped her brow. "Some *frigio* up here, in the head—whatever may be in his heart. I think, perhaps, the German education. Why did he have to go to Göttingen?"

"Mathematics," volunteered Ruth.

"*Poufff!* And who is this new German who is coming here tonight— I ask you, as if Bell is not enough, another comes, *on Christmas Eve!*"

"I think he's already here," said Ruth. The voices in the hall had been joined by another.

When they went into the hall, Dunsinnan introduced the newcomer. He was dark, of medium height, and had a duelling scar on his left chin.

"This is Herr Dahlberg—Heinrich Dahlberg. I'm afraid he doesn't speak very much English."

Schellenberg, alias Dahlberg, looked warmly at Ruth and bowed. The contessa had slipped away.

The Christmas Eve dinner was the most lavish that Ruth had seen at the castle. A whole side of venison had been roasted on a spit, and they all went to the kitchen to watch it being basted. The count, a little the worse for drink, cornered Ruth. His gold teeth flashed in the light of the flames. "It is a barbaric way of cooking, this," he said.

"I guess so—but there's plenty of barbarism left in the world."

Dunsinnan rescued her, and they went into the dining room together. Lady Dunsinnan was already seated. She looked from them to the contessa and smiled.

Dunsinnan's present to her was a note inside a small velvet box. It said simply, "Consider the Arab yours."

On Christmas morning she rode alone, skirting the loch. She remembered McCabe's last conversation with her and she rode to the cottage where McCabe's widow now lived with her children.

When she got back, the castle was already heavy with cigar smoke. Dunsinnan came into the hall. She kissed him lightly on the mouth.

"It was a wonderful gift."

"I had no argument from the horse." He laughed, then took her by the arm. "Come. We want to talk to you—if you don't mind a moment of more serious talk."

The men were standing around the room; she had an impression of having interrupted something. Dunsinnan gave her a sherry.

"Herr Dahlberg wants to know about America, and I thought you might explain," he said. "I'll translate, of course."

"What about America?"

"What Roosevelt's view is likely to be on Germany now he has such an overwhelming mandate."

Bell spoke: "It's the Jews. Don't you think he pays too much attention to them?"

"I really don't know about that," she said, not wanting to be drawn.

Bell persisted: "Nine tenths of the land in New York City is owned by Jews—ah, but I forgot Miss Dexter, you come from Boston."

"There aren't many Jews in Boston," she said, but the irony was lost on them. She turned to Dunsinnan. "I don't get it—all this concern with the Jews. You can't explain every problem as their doing."

"Really?" He lodged himself against the mantel. "Did you know that when President Wilson went to Versailles, he took a hundred and fifty advisers—and a hundred and seventeen of them were Jews? The Zionists were behind the Versailles Treaty, and that was the greatest wrong done to any nation in our time, and it's a wrong we have to put right."

Ruth had the impression that Dahlberg followed the conversation without help. "Well . . . maybe," she said, "but that's old history now. Anyway, what I don't understand is, if the Jews *have* been so smart, why has everyone else been so dumb?"

Bell rose to the bait. "That's an interesting point. I'll answer it—as a German. A lot of us came back from the war and found that all the good positions—in business, in finance, in the universities, in the law—they had been taken by Jews while we were away fighting in the trenches. Their influence was far in excess of their numbers. That's what we are putting right now, in Germany."

Dahlberg exposed himself by nodding.

Dunsinnan put down his glass. "Have you ever heard, Ruth, of a document called the Protocols of the Elders of Zion? It's all revealed in there, the whole Jewish conspiracy."

"But that was a fake." She spoke with a new assertiveness. "It was faked by the czar's secret police in Russia, to discredit the revolutionaries."

"Is that so?" said Dunsinnan sarcastically. "On what evidence do you base that belief?"

"It was exposed in the *New York Times.* I recall the stir it made at the time."

"The *New York Times?*" Dunsinnan's sarcasm rose. "And who owns the *New York Times?*"

"You're not suggesting—"

"Oh, but, my *dear* Ruth, I *am* suggesting just that. . . ."

11

London, 1937

Ruth found herself unsettled by a detail: the look of the American postage stamps on her mail. Curiously evocative of home, they smelled of plain small towns. Instead of crowned heads they represented the unostentatious vigor of the New World. In Europe there was a contagion of fashion: seductive fashions in escapism and extreme fashions in government. America, three thousand miles away, seemed free of these extremes. Boston was the home of plain things and plain sense. She missed it. As compensation, she began to work with a vengeance, combing galleries, reading in the libraries, seeing art historians. Losing herself in medieval art at last provided the anaesthetic she had sought when she first left home. In London the spring was unlike any she had known; with no clear curtain between the seasons, it seeped into the city, the gray pall edged upward, and one morning she came out of the British Museum and found Bloomsbury suddenly in leaf. The light was high enough to break over the buildings, and even the people brightened.

Dunsinnan was in Germany, and his mother in Scotland. Ruth saw Seton at least once a week. She noticed that when he slicked his hair, he was always at his least serious; she didn't like his hair slicked—it aged him, and as they circulated the Savoy Hotel ballroom he merged with the other slicked heads too easily. Unslicked he was himself.

She divined that this slicked hair and the starched shirt were part of an act in which for some reason he wanted to become uniform, and slowly it annoyed her. One fugitive strand of the slicked hair fell across his brow and broke the effect.

"I'm done," he said, and they went back to the table.

"Edward, is there a lot of anti-Semitism in England?"

"Why do you ask?"

"I'm beginning to hear things, to pick it up. When I was

at the castle, at Christmas, Alastair seemed to be developing the symptoms."

"We do have our share of it, I fear. It's all very civilized, of course—golf clubs, the usual subtle social barriers, nothing too blatant, but it's there all right. Then there's Mosley, of course. He appeals to the lower class of bigot. Actually, I think I prefer the Mosley method—at least it's there, out in the open. It's not handled like that in higher places." He seemed to want to say more but checked himself.

"You look in need of a vacation," she said.

He tucked his shirt in at the waist and pressed the stray hair back into place. "Why do you say that?" He was aggressive.

"You look tired."

He called the waiter and ordered another bottle of champagne. "I'm not tired. At least, not physically. Tired, perhaps, of people. Some people."

It was a new note of complaint to her. "Bad day at the office?" she said, too flippant.

"It's all such a bloody muddle. Forgive the language. But I'll tell you what *really* worries me, Ruth. It's the kind of muddle that somebody has gone to a lot of trouble to arrange."

"Sounds like a definition of all government."

He took the new glass of champagne and held it to hers. "Never mind. Sorry to be such a bore. We can look forward to many distractions this year—it's a good time for you to be here. The coronation, all that stuff we do so well—parades, flypasts, race meetings—opium of the masses, takes the mind off other things. Cheers." His words were slurred.

She couldn't handle him in this mood. She lay awake thinking about what it was he really did, the subject he never discussed, and the other sealed compartments in his life. Sometimes, in glimpses, she had seen another man trying to get out, and it seemed to her—perhaps on the fringe of her sleep—that when she looked this other man in the eye, he dissolved.

And then Dunsinnan returned.

She was sitting one evening in her flat, with the windows raised, reading. The bell rang; she half expected Seton, who had lately been given to impulsive calls. But here now at the door—with a hovering Fraser behind, to make sure—was Dunsinnan bearing a dozen red roses.

"So!" he said, and it was a countenance more ebullient than Seton's.

Seeing her response, Fraser slipped silently away, and Ruth took the flowers as they went in, her annoyance at being drawn from study ebbing by the second in the refreshment of change.

"Stranger—I'd given up on you," she said, taking his arm.

"Ah, never do that," he said, examining the room. "So this is it—your little nest. Very nice . . . and quite handy."

"Handy for what?"

"Claridge's. Dinner. Tonight."

"Well. . . ." She maintained a dying pretense of commitment.

"That's settled, then."

The momentum of his arrival and presence easily overwhelmed her, and her submission to it was transparent. He walked to the window. "I like rooftops. Could look at them for hours. A fine selection you have from here." He sat on the sill, long gray flannel legs crossed, even darker with the light behind him, eyes on her. "You look absolutely marvellous. Work must agree with you. I can't *think* why I've neglected you." He smiled. "Sorry to gate-crash. Fact is, I just got in and thought of you—banked on finding you in."

"I'm glad," she said. "Would you like a drink?"

Dunsinnan was known at Claridge's. They were shown to a table on a small dais in a corner of the restaurant where they could see—and be seen. The piano hit springlike rhythms, the clothes were lighter, the food was irresistible, and she drank far more than she was used to. Dunsinnan presided with wit, and in the laughter she grew dreamily distant.

"You know there's going to be an absolutely unbelievable show for the coronation?" He was trying to attract her concentration. "Nothing like it before, ever. You're very lucky, being here now. You must—*we* must make the most of it."

"Ascot and all that rot," she said, mimicking the English accent drunkenly.

"Even better. Something rather special." He drew out the *rather* teasingly. "The naval review, at Spithead."

"Wh—what is that, Spithead? Sounds funny."

"You came on the boat last year, didn't you? It's the entire stretch of water between Southampton and the Isle of Wight, the whole thing—miles and miles of it, and it will all be packed with ships, the navies of the world, never been a sight like it."

"Mmmmm," she said, spotting the early strawberries on the dessert trolley.

"Would you come—I've been invited, to see it from a battleship, a pocket battleship?"

"A *what?*" She giggled. "In whose pocket?"

"The *Graf Spee—Admiral Graf Spee.* Latest in the German Fleet."

"German?" The strawberries appeared before her. "A *German* battleship, here?"

"That's right. There'll be ships from every major power."

"And you want me with you, on a *German* ship?"

He was patient. "There'll be a party. Special guests of the navy. Quite a night."

"Night?"

"The review goes on all day, then there are fireworks at night."

"I'll bet. Well . . ." She hesitated, then said, "I guess I can't refuse an invitation like that, can I?"

Her mind was racing, though. Who else would be there, on this Nazi battleship? It sounded harmless enough. And it would be a spectacle. Why had she drunk so much? It kept coming in waves. However, by the time they were finished, she was able to walk out quite steadily, without betraying how she really felt. She was careful to leave him in the lobby of her building as Fraser watched. She thought he half expected to be invited up, but wasn't sure. He took it gallantly enough.

Seton sank dispiritedly into a sofa, folding the newspaper as he read it, fingers blanched and tightening. "It's *deplorable,*" he said.

He and Endmere were the sole occupants of the Reform Club library. It was midmorning. The window was open, and the sound of traffic in Pall Mall made conversation difficult. Standing by the window, Endmere had almost to shout: "When somebody uses that term *National Socialist* instead of *Nazi* you know what they're up to."

Seton read aloud from the paper: " 'In England far too many people take an erroneous conception of what the National Socialist regime really stands for, otherwise they would lay less stress on dictatorship and more emphasis on the great social experiment which is being tried out in this country.' "

He broke off and repeated the phrase: *"Great social experiment!"* He threw the paper down. "That really is a contemptible speech."

"The new line."

"Yes—that's obvious. Neville Chamberlain as prime minister, and now Nevile Henderson as ambassador in Berlin, grovelling with a speech like this as his overture."

"There'll be applause from Cliveden," said Endmere, moving away from the window.

Seton looked up sharply. "You think those people will prevail?"

Endmere moved the discarded newspaper and sat on the sofa. "Henderson was their choice. Phipps was far too straight for them. Matter of fact, I've been checking up on Henderson. I think I can see how it started. Funeral of King Alexander, Yugoslavia, 1934. Henderson was our man in Belgrade. Göring went there on behalf of Germany, to the funeral— incidentally, right after the Night of the Long Knives. The start of a beautiful friendship. Henderson and the fat man discovered a common interest. Shooting. Animals, of course." Endmere failed to strike a chord of humor in Seton but continued: "Gradually they established a rapport, to the sound of falling elk. Hence, when it came to finding a successor to Phipps, up came the name of Henderson, though by then he was in Argentina. No doubt about his sympathies."

"I see," said Seton.

"I hope we've got it wrong—about Chamberlain, I mean. If we haven't, I hate to think of the consequences."

II

Visits

12

The English Channel, May 1937

The water for the whole stretch of Spithead was a dull gray-green. Lines of great ships reached as far as the horizon. Banks of mist kept the dawn light weak, and the ships and the ocean seemed variations of the same dim color. Sounds echoed from ship to ship: metallic sounds; muffled sounds from below the waterline; occasionally the thin sound of a small boat as tenders ferried between the ships and the shore; the piping of whistles and, gradually, the voices of men as the armada came to life. Shapes became more distinct: from the giant battle cruisers, broad in beam and seemingly weighed into the water by their guns, to the semisubmerged pencil outlines of the submarines. Incongruously, the larger ships were hung with strings of lights that in outline looked like fairground trimmings.

Still muffled in a coat, Ruth walked the deck of the *Admiral Graf Spee* with Dunsinnan. In a blazer and white scarf, Dunsinnan looked as though he had strayed to the great ship from a neighboring yacht. Crewmen scuttled by them without a glance, drilled in the waking ritual of a battleship. Under their feet was the almost imperceptible hum of vast power held to its idling speed: The *Graf Spee* was the first ship of its size to be powered by diesel instead of steam, and the faintly oily odor of diesel pervaded this end of the deck.

Dunsinnan pointed across the water.

"Rather sad . . . that all your people could send is that wreck of a ship."

The United States Navy was represented by the battleship *New York,* well past her prime, her antique superstructure contrasting with the lean outline of the *Graf Spee.*

"I guess the navy wanted to be discreet," Ruth said loyally.

Dunsinnan shrugged, without humor: "It's a display of power. It matters to show the best. Just look at the *Hood.*"

He pointed out the Royal Navy's principal battleship, at forty-two thousand tons the largest in the world. Neither of them could know as they looked at her that the *Hood* was already dangerously obsolescent, with flaws in her armor unremedied. But on this morning she was superficially intimidating, an extra muscle in the arm now being flexed at a psychologically important moment. Each admiral knew that his ships were being raked by the binoculars of other admirals, and that intelligence officers were swarming the lines— hoping to slip unobtrusively through the capital ships with the visiting parties as part of the diplomatic round. Some navies kept whole ships, or parts of ships, off limits, but the Germans were using the *Graf Spee* as an open model of the new generation of ships to serve the Third Reich.

In the light of day Ruth was impressed by the clinical efficiency of the ship. More compact than the older battleships, the *Graf Spee* was designed for speed, range, and deadly shooting, to be let loose in merchant-shipping lanes like a wolf amongst rabbits. The night before, it had been deceptively festive. Selected friends had been invited to a reception on board. Nazi banners and propaganda had been absent. The crew, especially the young officers of the generation given to idolatry, were smooth and talkative, like children proudly showing off a new toy. Captain Conrad Pratzig was indistinguishable in sociability and professionalism from any Royal Navy officer and spoke good English.

Ebullient from the champagne, Dunsinnan had said as they stood in a corner of the wardroom, "You see, these people are so much like us, it's unthinkable, isn't it, that we might end up blowing each other out of the water?"

Ruth looked round the room at the engaging company. "Well, if it was left to people like this . . ."

"*They* know where the *real* enemy is. Not here. In the east. It's the Russians who have to be stopped." Dunsinnan paused and looked around him again. "Together—we would be absolutely unbeatable."

Some of the young officers had had to make way for overnight guests. Ruth found herself in a metal cubicle, sleeping on a bunk hardly bigger than herself; how a large man got into it, she didn't know. Drowsy from the meal and from the air, she slept as though drugged until just before dawn the movement of men woke her.

Now Dunsinnan handed binoculars to her as they looked over the *Hood* and the British aircraft carriers.

"It's difficult to believe that people can be anxious about armaments when you see all this," she said.

Dunsinnan was thoughtful. "Yes, it *looks* as though Britannia still rules the waves . . . but you may be looking at the last of the great fleets. These ships are more vulnerable than they look—to planes, to submarines."

"So you think there's a false sense of security?" she asked, handing back the glasses.

"Perhaps."

They had breakfast in the officers' wardroom. Ruth felt herself the focus of the table. A young officer on her right asked about America in impeccable English. He had a fresh, virginal face, molded in the standard Teutonic cast. Across the table Dunsinnan was talking to a man Ruth had noticed at the reception: shortish, stocky, with the face of a bazaar trader, a complexion that could have been Levantine, an accent that could have been French, a manner that might have been American, and a mouth full of teeth that were certainly gold. His flashiness contrasted with Dunsinnan's conservatism. Ruth gained the impression that their conversation was a continuation of one that had begun the night before, after she had gone to bed.

After breakfast Dunsinnan introduced her to the man.

"Ruth, this is a fellow American, Charles Bedaux."

Bedaux flashed his gold and broke in: "Not *native* American. I'm very proud to have been naturalized. Miss Dexter, Alastair has told me about you."

The man seemed more reptilian in close-up, but she smiled, hoping that it didn't look as forced as it was. His cologne was too pungent.

"Charles has some business with me, we have some interesting news." Dunsinnan looked at Bedaux in a curiously impish way that didn't suit him. "But it will have to wait awhile."

Bedaux grinned. "A little while." He waved his arm toward the deck. "Magnificent, this boat."

"Ship," Dunsinnan said sharply.

There was a little more sun now, though the cloud banks persisted, and for a day near to midsummer, the air was cold. From the shore a steady stream of tenders came out, bringing parties of guests to each of the larger ships. Ruth scanned battleships from Sweden, Turkey, Japan, Holland, Rumania, and Russia—and a submarine from a country she had never heard of, Estonia. To identify it, they had to confer with a manual of national flags, helped by a German officer as bemused as they were.

As small boats cruised past the *Graf Spee* their passengers waved and looked up with glasses and with cameras. In full dress and in better light, the ships gained some color, the white of the upper decks reflecting light. Now, across the whole length of the Spithead water, the lines stretched for miles. The excitement on shore was audible on the ships.

A large party arrived at the *Graf Spee* from a liner anchored in the harbor. It was led by von Blomberg, tall and gray, with an air of sensuality. Dunsinnan pointed him out: "Hitler's first field marshal." With him came a group of British politicians, some ambassadors, and a young woman whom Ruth recognized, Unity Mitford. She was hanging on von Blomberg's arm and cooing in excessive pleasure about everything being "heavenly" and treating the battleship as though she expected it to be a yacht. She looked at Ruth with gimlet eyes but showed no recognition.

Dunsinnan introduced them formally. Von Blomberg surveyed Ruth too keenly, with a brazen connoisseur's look. Heavily perfumed with rose water, Unity Mitford had coarsened in the year since Ruth first saw her at the lunch in Belgravia. Her language was an uneasy blend of peppery superlatives and political references. Several times she spoke in snatches of German to Dunsinnan and von Blomberg—Ruth thought deliberately, to cut her out. There was much talk in Dunsinnan's vein, of world dominion for the Royal and Nazi fleets, of a new spirit of amity and understanding.

Canvas chairs were lined up on the foredeck to give them a grandstand sight of the review. As Ruth and Dunsinnan settled into the front row a photographer appeared, a blond young German with a limp.

Dunsinnan arranged himself carefully, putting an arm on

the back of Ruth's chair. *"Illustrierte Zeitung,* I think," he said.

The review began with a twenty-one-gun salute from the Royal Navy's capital ships. Echoes between the Isle of Wight and the mainland sent the salvoes bouncing over the water. As the last one died the antique shape of the *Victoria and Albert,* the royal yacht, appeared at the head of the first line to start the King's inspection. The battleships towered over the yacht, more suited to river cruising than the ocean, its long curved bow a relic of sailing days. Yet, as Ruth watched it pass down the line, there was the saving grace of royalty being modestly borne. The young King stood on the foredeck in admiral's uniform, taking the salute from each of the ships' crews, a slight, frail-looking man precipitated to the throne by the sexual obduracy of his brother. To her own surprise, Ruth's eyes turned moist at the sight.

As the morning went on the sun came and went fitfully, giving an occasional brilliant patch of light as it struck one or two ships against the grayness of the rest. Keeping tight formation, wave after wave of planes came over as the *Victoria and Albert* completed its tour.

Dunsinnan gave Ruth his glasses to watch the flypast. She saw the crewmen in open cockpits, the biplanes skimming at mast height.

"String bags," said Dunsinnan.

"They do look a little old," she said. Her father had scrapped similar planes a decade earlier.

The *Graf Spee*'s band began playing under a sun awning that was incongruous. A massive buffet lunch was served. They waited for a second flypast, but the clouds closed in and it was cancelled. Von Blomberg invited Dunsinnan and Ruth to return with his party to the greater comforts of the liner. They left the *Graf Spee* with the band still playing.

Party flowed into party. Unity Mitford entertained a circle of British politicians with stories of her life in Munich. Ruth found a bunk on the liner where she could snatch some sleep before evening; Dunsinnan, apparently tireless, was deep in conversation with von Blomberg.

Ruth awoke in a cold sweat. From the bunk she looked through a porthole and found the night sky ablaze with fireworks. She had been asleep for hours. She went up to a saloon, feeling weak and chilly, and found a waiter to bring her a cognac. Outside on the deck the revellers were outlined against the brilliantly colored display, the ships a phantom fleet in the intervals of light. In the same way, faces took on the glare of the fireworks, and in one burst she saw, by chance, Dunsinnan and Bedaux seated in a corner of the deck away from the main group. The waiter returned and looked at her, concerned.

"Are you all right, miss?"

She smiled wanly. "Yes, thank you—but I would love another brandy, please."

When Dunsinnan found her, she was feverish. He apologized for his neglect and became single-minded in his care of her. A doctor was called; he suspected influenza. Dunsinnan took her ashore to a hotel, where she had to remain for two days with a high temperature. Then, wrapped in rugs, she was taken in the Dunsinnan Bentley back to London, to the house in Eaton Square. It was another week before she could return to her flat, and even then, she wanted only to sink into bed. Dunsinnan arranged for a maid to feed her—and then left, with apologies, for France.

Seton, who had himself been out of London, came back and found her a sulky invalid. The spirited cockney maid was a well-intentioned believer in advertised remedies, usually those that she had just seen displayed on the side of a bus. Once the maid had left for the day, Ruth resorted to drafts of cognac in hot water. Her skin reacted, looking too florid. It was in the midst of an argument with the maid over how to treat this new condition that Seton arrived.

The maid looked at him suspiciously, even though he had obviously appeared with Fraser's approval, she and Fraser having conspired as Ruth's protectors. The maid perceived that Seton had some kind of authority, and changed her voice in exaggerated deference; but her eyes held the suspicion, unrelentingly puritan.

"Well, well," said Seton, with half a smile, "you do look sorry for yourself." He turned to the maid: "I think you can leave us, thank you." The maid pouted slightly, looked to Ruth for reassurance, and left, without accepting the idea of leaving a strange man in a lady's bedroom.

When the door was closed, Seton said, "I think she views flats in Mayfair as rather risqué to begin with. What's the problem, really?"

He sat on the edge of the bed, stiff, concerned. She realized that she was glad to see him.

"Nothing serious. Summer flu. The worst is over, or so

the doctor says. I just feel weak—and I can't stand the stuff they're giving me. Something called barley water."

"Not much fun, suffering alone." He noticed the flush in her color.

"No—not much."

He saw still the little girl in her.

Reading his thoughts, she pulled herself up on the pillow. "*You're* not going to pamper me. I won't have it."

He sank a little more deeply into the counterpane, relaxing. "I imagine you're a very difficult patient."

"It depends on the treatment."

"Yes, well. . . ." He noticed the thin gold cord around her neck.

"Anyway, where have you been?" she said, half in reproach. "You still look world-weary."

He realized that in resisting any sense of dependency on him, she was cleverly trying to reverse the roles. "Do I?" Each now understood the other perfectly. He got up from the bed and pulled over a chair. "Now, you can tell me about Spithead, and how you got to feel so sorry for yourself. It isn't like you."

Without slicked hair he was grayer. She liked that.

It had come to this: a wayward parson; an altar improvised from a wooden chest, covered with a tablecloth; a French organist struggling to find the right key for "O Perfect Love"; seven English guests, an American aunt, an American benefactor and his wife; an ersatz renaissance castle in France and its owner, their host, Charles Bedaux. Six months ago he had been King of England. Now his long abided love was consummated formally with Wallis Simpson on his arm as the parson, disowned by two English bishops for coming here, read the marriage service in plain northern cadences and waited for the responses, delivered quietly but clearly.

The small pale-green room had been relieved of its austerity and given fragrance by the flower arrangements of Mrs. Constance Spry. There were two photographers, a hasty Frenchman and the more elegant young Cecil Beaton, taking his time with the lights. The Duke of Windsor was normally fastidious about form and dress, but the wedding was surprisingly random in its costumes. Only one guest, Randolph Churchill, wore the formal frock coat that would have been mandatory had this been Westminster Abbey and not a fugitive ceremony. The calmest person in the room was the bride, who preserved cool regality while the groom, in his eyes, was still the ardent lover, now reduced to this in order to claim her.

After the wedding the guests relaxed a little, and a few others joined them, Dunsinnan among them. Toward dusk the Rolls-Royce left the Château de Candé, taking them down the long poplar-lined drive to a kind of obscurity.

Dunsinnan caught the poignancy of it as the Rolls disappeared.

"And where, now . . . ?" Bedaux asked rhetorically.

"The rest of their lives," Dunsinnan replied.

Somebody else said, "What do the British do with discarded kings?"

"I can't think of a precedent," said Dunsinnan.

"There is no precedent—for *her*," snapped someone else.

"That's true enough, I'm afraid."

Dunsinnan remained only as long as sociability required, then took the road back to Tours. He had left Lady Taverner at the hotel. They had dinner there on the terrace, and he described the wedding to her.

"It's a pity I couldn't have gone with you," she said, "after all, if Randolph could be there, and everybody knows *he* will be writing it up. . . ."

Dunsinnan's reply was indistinct.

"I said," she insisted with a pout, "it's a pity *I* couldn't have been there with you. Who would have objected?"

He looked at her over the wine. "*I* would have."

"*Well*, thank you *very* much," she rasped. "I know all about your passion for discretion, but what makes you imagine that they don't know already—about us?"

"My dear Margery," he said, more touchy than ever, "I thought you knew the rules. The great thing about discretion is knowing with whom to be discreet."

Throwing aside restraint, she snapped at him: "*Rules? What bloody rules?* That I stay in the cupboard while you moon around in public with that American bitch?"

He picked up his napkin.

"Took her to Spithead, I hear. How nice. You can parade *her* around in your distinguished company, but you can't show me. . . ."

As soon as the words were out she knew she had gone too far.

He got up. "I'll settle the bill. Don't bother to get up. You can take the train in the morning."

* * *

The Royal Air Force had better luck with the weather than the navy had had. Five parallel lines of planes appeared over Hendon airfield, each line composed of ten flights of five planes, two hundred and fifty in all, in the air at the same time. The engines swamped all other sounds. It was hot, and the sky was clear. Ruth and Seton, both shading their eyes with their hands, stood in an enclosure where the spectators included a group of Arabs in their tribal robes and one man whose dress seemed a parody of British formality: Prince Chichibu of Japan, in tailcoat and glossy silk top hat. They watched bombers converge on a fort and a series of explosions shatter the structure.

"Bit of a cheat, I fear," Seton whispered to her. "The bombs are blanks. There are explosive charges laid in the fort."

"Shame!" She liked sharing the secret.

It was the first time she had been introduced to a part of Seton's professional world. At lunch in a marquee she saw most of the R.A.F.'s senior men. Several Luftwaffe officers were also there, and a face she remembered from a past weekend: Baron William de Ropp, assiduously bringing together British and German officers.

The day in the sun, the sharing of Seton's interests, the comic aspect of the display—they all restored her spirits. When they went back to his car, a two-seater M.G., she asked him to put down the canopy.

"Are you sure?"

"I'm fully recovered. Don't *fuss* so much!"

On the road back to London it was too noisy to speak, but Seton knew that, occasionally, she was turning to look at him, and he felt uncommonly rakish. It was years since he had last had a passenger in an open M.G.

Only three of them—Ruth, Dunsinnan, and his mother— sat at the large dining table at Eaton Square. A crystal chandelier caught the reflection of the prolonged summer twilight. Because of its size, the room echoed no matter how soft the voices. Two maids and the butler clipped across the floor, and conversation stopped until they were gone. The butler was the last to withdraw, having decanted the claret and waited for Dunsinnan's approval. Lady Dunsinnan's head rocked gently, her eyes trancelike, in some private contentment; she receded to become a spectator. A tint from the twilight filtered through a window and caught one side of her face, adding to the flush already in her cheeks.

Dunsinnan spoke as though his mother were not there, with an intimacy inferring intrigue. The bloom of the claret had aroused his spirit, and across the table Ruth aroused it even more.

"Why so solemn?" he asked, raising his glass.

"Oh—nothing," she said absently, reciprocating the toast and tasting the wine. Each small movement—of glass on table, knife on plate, napkin at lip—had an exaggerated presence because of the room's resonance. Ruth felt that this was somehow a sepulchral supper. "I suppose I've been worrying too much about the newspapers," she continued.

"Ah. That's always a mistake. What, for example?"

"Spain. The bombing. The stories about the town, Guernica—they're still talking of it."

"Don't believe all that rubbish about it having been an atrocity. There was a very good piece in *The Times*. Apparently the real damage was done by mines they planted themselves, under the roads."

"What is it about Spain? I mean, nobody much cares—do they?" Her question was ambiguous, part troubled and part dismissive.

"*Some* people do." His mockery spoke only to the dismissive part of the question. "Bloomsbury has been emptied of communist poets."

Perversely she reverted to the first part of the question: "Seriously, please. I don't understand the terms. Nationalist and Republican—what do they really mean?"

Reluctantly he turned his mind to explanation: "It began as a revolution run from Moscow. The Reds took over, then the army rebelled, or sections of it. That's what's so confusing—the army being called rebels when they are really the loyalists. Now they're accepted as Nationalists."

"The Nationalists—they're the *Fascists?*"

"They're called Falangists." His smile conceded the mounting complexity. "But yes, they are the people we're helping."

"*We?*"

"It's not like the Reds. Franco doesn't take orders from Italy or Germany, he's not a puppet. But he needs outside help."

"What *kind* of help?" Her mind came more into focus, and she watched him carefully.

"Arms, planes."

"What have you got to do with that? I thought it was the Germans who were helping?"

He took another sip of the claret. "Oh, I've been able to help with some things, raw materials."

"I still don't see, Alastair. Why *should* other people get involved, feel so committed about it! I mean for example, why should a kid in New Jersey feel called upon to go out there and choose sides? I just don't see it."

"Sooner or later we're all going to have to choose, to take one side or the other. It's the way the world is going."

"*What* sides?"

"There are only two ways to go. Communism or fascism."

Her questioning tone gave way to a more emphatic one: "Oh, come *on!* Surely that's far too simplistic? You don't have to like either. If you're American—or British—that choice needn't arise. It's not your fight."

"Ah," he began airily, then changed his manner, leaned forward, insistent: "We can't afford the luxury of indifference any longer. More people have to understand that. It's clear which side suits *our* interests—and which doesn't. I'm in no doubt about it."

He took a long savoring mouthful of the claret, then he spoke again, softly: "Ruth, I think you should come to Germany. I think then you would understand."

Lady Dunsinnan's glass hit the table a little too firmly. "Oh, yes!" she said, looking at neither of them, "you *would* understand a lot then."

13

The heat had come suddenly as it often did in Berlin, the landlocked, airless heat from which the only escape was to desert the city, and Canaris could not leave even his office. His two secretaries left him late at night and found him still there in the morning, bathing himself at the metal washstand, dabbing his face with a towel. He waved the first girl away, but stubbornly loyal, she came back with coffee and hot cakes. In the morning light the chaos of the office seemed domestic: one crumpled sheet on the cot by the wall, the balcony windows open in a futile search for air, the desk littered with a succession of overnight messages. There was no portrait of Hitler, but there was one of Franco and another of the dachshund called Seppl, lamented forerunner of the present pair who were absent this morning.

The second girl came in with a set of photographs, enlargements with a glossy finish. She approached the desk gingerly, knowing the temper of the morning. He took the pictures without looking directly at her and let her get nearly to the door when he said quietly, "I'm not an invalid. You don't have to tiptoe. I like your new dress."

She turned and smiled over her shoulder.

He studied the pictures for some time, then rang the bell on his desk. "Ask Piekenbrock to come. Now."

Piekenbrock found him holding a fistful of telegrams.

"I wonder how the Wehrmacht General Staff will take this," Canaris said, handing the telegrams to Piekenbrock. "The assassination of the entire leadership of the Red Army. A bloodbath. Stalin has given the word *purge* a new meaning. And look at the charges. Collaborating with Germany to overthrow the leadership—quoting documentary evidence *from our files*."

Piekenbrock looked up from the telegrams, slowly getting Canaris's meaning. "You don't suggest . . . ?"

"You remember the fire in our filing department? And what was missing? Fake the evidence, and plant it—that's the classic Gestapo style."

"Heydrich?"

"He tried to get those files before." Canaris went back to his desk and sat down wearily. "Here—something better. Look at these photographs of von Klagen's."

Piekenbrock put down the telegrams and picked up the photographs.

"Look at the *Hood* particularly," Canaris directed. "They haven't touched the armor, on the top deck, you can see that. It's incredible, just as it was in 1918, before the new shells. One direct hit—pouff! Gone in seconds—the magazines are right underneath."

"Von Klagen did well."

"Yes." Canaris was thoughtful, tucking his shirt into his waistband. "That young man grows on me. Is he here?"

Piekenbrock nodded.

"It was fortunate that Patzig is now on the *Graf Spee*. He was very helpful to us. Look at that group photograph—there, at the bottom." Canaris waited for Piekenbrock to find it. "The whole group—what are those people doing there?"

When they found von Klagen, he was taking coffee with a girl from the Central Registry; he left her with his business incomplete. In spite of the heat Canaris was pulling a sweater over his shirt. He waved von Klagen to a seat and came round to the front of his desk, leaning back on it with palms pressed flat.

"I've read your report and seen the photographs. Excellent work. You're sure your cover is secure?"

"Yes, Herr Admiral."

"Good." He pulled out the group photograph. "Perhaps you could explain to us about this."

"I began with the Miss Mitford and von Blomberg. As you directed. They led me to the others. The man in the center of the picture. He is some kind of ringleader. That's Lord Dunsinnan."

"I know that name," said Piekenbrock.

"The memo from Bormann to Reithinger, six months ago," said Canaris. "The meeting with Heydrich in Switzerland. Yes, go on."

"The girl with Dunsinnan," said von Klagen, "the dark girl, she bothers me. I've seen her somewhere else, several times. With Group Captain Seton."

Canaris rubbed his nose and walked away from the desk to the open window. He looked out for a minute and then turned back toward them. "Can that be a coincidence? I doubt it. Then, what is going on? Mitford *and* Dunsinnan both seem very eager to be liked. And succeeding at it. We know, now, what Seton is doing. So . . . what is this other girl up to? The connection is too strong to be overlooked."

"All we know is what we don't know," said Piekenbrock, who liked irony.

"Precisely." Canaris looked at von Klagen. "From now on I don't want you to let this Lord Dunsinnan out of your sight. And the girl. I want to know about her—*everything* you can find out *without* becoming too obvious. Your cover is too valuable."

When von Klagen had gone, Canaris turned to Piekenbrock. "Why is it, the people who call themselves our friends are always the ones who bother me most?"

* * *

The conference on the mountain at Obersalzburg had been a trying one. Hitler's belligerence toward his generals was becoming more and more open. He showed total recall of their earlier promises and flung them back into their faces. On each of these occasions Canaris assembled in his head what could never be committed to a file, his private pathology, sensing already that one day his own survival might rest on where he stood in this uncertain court, what he had once said, how he responded to attack. Hitler—capricious, watchful, driving—remained to Canaris a bewildering set of contradictions, alternately demented and inspired, more often hovering between banality and strokes of cunning. While others flinched, Canaris was not intimidated.

On this afternoon Hitler gestured to Canaris to remain as the others left.

"Admiral, I want you to tell me more about Spain, about the religion." He pointed to a seat by the great window. "Please."

As they sat down, facing each other across a low round table, Hitler said, "How important is the Catholic church in this war?"

"Very important—as the real barrier to communism. Franco knows that. You have seen the photographs he has been releasing of the churches sacked by the Reds?"

Hitler's eyes settled on Canaris. "I have also seen photographs of churches bombed by Franco."

Canaris met the enigmatic gaze. "Accidents of war, my Führer. Bombs do not yet discriminate between churches and communists. Not even Göring can arrange that."

Hitler laughed. Any barb against Göring was the key to his humor. He sat silent for a while, looking out at the mountains, as though searching for some inspiration. Then he spoke. "You know, Admiral, I was born a Catholic. I have had to tell Göring and Goebbels to remain in the church. Himmler, meanwhile, is urging people to leave it, because of its criticism of the party. That is shortsighted." He paused again, turning back to Canaris. "We must be seen to have God on our side. *If not the Pope.*"

Suddenly energetic, he got up and stood at the window, looking at the Untersberg. Canaris joined him.

"Did you know, Admiral, that Europe was once very nearly lost to the Arabs? Imagine that! Bedouins from the desert, they rode from Arabia right into the heart of France before they were stopped! I often think of that. What was the energy behind them? *Their religion,* Admiral! What a faith that must be, that can send simple tribesmen that far. If only *we* could find that kind of energy!"

He looked at Canaris, eyes possessed by the thought: *"You see, it's been our misfortune to have the wrong religion!"*

From a distance Canaris appeared to be almost overpowered by his horse, a small man astride a strapping stallion. But he was a skilled horseman, and his appearance at dawn at the stables in the Tiergarten became a part of the waking landscape in this part of central Berlin. Riding was another antidote to sleeplessness.

He had cultivated a new riding companion, General Ludwig Beck, chief of the general staff. In appearance Beck was everything Canaris was not: indelibly Prussian, every bone of his body rigidly formal, upholding the precision of cavalry dressage. And yet the bond grew between them. Canaris felt that this austere and decent man was in some way testing him, discussing events to draw him out.

"You believe in the blitzkrieg?" asked Beck.

"Spain will decide that. A wonderful chance to experiment."

Beck caught the note of sarcasm with one flicker of the eyebrows. "The bombing is only a part of it. The age of cavalry is gone. Tanks, dive-bombers—you've heard the new gospel."

They cantered down the avenue, grateful for movement of air in the heat.

"Which way first—west or east?" Canaris asked.

Beck's spurs dug into the horse's flanks.

14

Dunsinnan was a different man in Germany. She noticed it in details: the way he organized her baggage at the station, his familiarity with dialect and custom. More assertive, more at ease, and more gregarious, even voluble. When he spoke in German, fluently, it seemed that the voice matched this personality, as though only here had he found himself. By recognizing this, Ruth was then able to see that the other Dunsinnan had—all the while—been reaching for this one. It was not that he was a chameleon, altering color to setting, but that where in Britain he was unable totally to merge into the setting, here he was so much a part of it that he seemed native. He knew all the codes.

With this understanding, Ruth felt a shiver of anticipation, a sense of having crossed a boundary. When he met her at the station at Munich, and on the drive to the Four Seasons Hotel, he was neither over-familiar nor distant but curiously correct, perhaps another sign of German manners, as though the absence of his mother demanded more impeccable behavior rather than less. He watched her as she took in the city.

"You could mix a little work with pleasure," he said, "after all, this city is your period."

She saw a medieval skyline, baroque spires, red-pitched roofs, rustic gabling, domes, towers—and, occasionally, signs of a new order. The streets were wet and fresh after a storm.

In the hotel lobby she could hear many English voices, but she felt an outsider: exotic, monolingual. Dunsinnan's discretion extended to her allotted room. He occupied a large suite overlooking the gardens; she was given smaller rooms several doors away on the same floor. Once he had directed the porters, he said in a carefully measured way:

"If you're not too tired, after the journey, I thought we might have supper up here, in my suite—that is, if you don't mind?"

"Fine. Just give me a couple of hours." She had not yet overcome the sense of strangeness and was glad that she would be with him.

She lay for a long while in the bath, thinking of the other abrupt dislocations in her life, and of how irrational it was already to be homesick. A memory of a Cape Cod summer persisted; she realized that in its insularity it was a haven for a person she no longer was. As she dressed, in petticoats under a billowing skirt and a high-necked blouse, Dunsinnan was on her mind. It amused her to appear so demure.

He was in a light-gray suit, white shirt, and dark-blue tie. A bottle of Moselle lay in an ice bucket.

First spreading her skirt, she sat down. He poured her a glass of the wine.

"Do you mind if I kick these off?" She pointed to her shoes. "The journey was hardest on my feet."

"Go ahead." He smiled. "It's a long ride, that one."

"Interesting, though."

"Yes. Not like that ride from Scotland."

"It's a long way from Scotland."

"Why do you say that?" he said, alert.

She took a calculated plunge: "Well, even after such a short time I can't help noticing how much at home you feel here. And I can't imagine anything more different—" she searched for the right phrase—"more *unlike* Scotland. And I wonder, just what *is* it that attracts you?"

He sipped his wine and looked at her. "That's a leading question. But I'll answer it, if I can." He uncrossed his legs and leaned forward, cupping the wine in his hands. "You see, my father always took the big view. His father had been content to play the laird; the wealth was in the estate, and that seemed enough for him. But my father—well, he saw the way things were going. He saw big changes and wanted a part of them."

She thought his earnestness had the strange effect of making him younger.

"Of course," he continued, "I didn't know my father that well. Nobody did. Except my mother, in a curious way. At any rate, Scotland was too small for him, and he developed many interests—as you saw in those pictures at the castle." There was a glint of humor in his eye at this. "The trouble was, he never really had time to complete the job."

He broke off and poured her some more wine.

"There was a time when I wondered whether to follow him—or whether to be content with what was there. Then, by the chance of looking for a good teacher—Hilbert—I came here, to Göttingen. At Oxford I was never a very political animal—the isms didn't much interest me. But here, in Germany, they were played out in front of my eyes. You couldn't *be* a spectator. The dissolution of the Weimar, the rise of the communists. It was then I saw how quickly, how very *easily*, it might all be lost. It had never hit me like that before—I'm sorry, is this all tiresome?"

She shook her head.

"Well, one night I heard a man speak. He was the most compelling speaker I had ever seen. You have to remember what this country was like then. In fact, he described it, and I remember his words: 'the people in debt; the currency worthless; the children going hungry; millions of young men waiting without any possible hope of a job.' It wasn't just *what* he said, or the way he said it. It was the effect on his audience. As it happened, that was the time of his emergence. The party got something like thirty-six percent of the vote. By then, of course, England was going the Weimar way, so it seemed to me. We'd had one general strike, we'd seen the possibility of a revolution. We had millions of unemployed—as you did, and still do. Well, compare that—only five years ago—and Germany now, the Germany you can see for yourself. I think *any* country can make that kind of change. If it has the will."

The whole thing had been said calmly, from within himself, with none of the fervor or rhetoric of the zealot. This made it all the more convincing as a personal testament, especially since he had identified his own interest with the success of the regime. There was even something physically attractive in the strength of his conviction, and she was sure it was the truth of how he saw things, why he was there—and why, perhaps, he had never seemed as self-assured in Britain. She didn't feel in the least offended, nor morally superior, and yet she found the avowal dispiriting for reasons she couldn't explain.

He went to the phone and ordered dinner, then looked at her with understated keenness. "I hope you're going to like it here."

She got up to bring circulation back to her feet and walked to the window, looking at the city beyond the terrace.

"I'll take my time to decide that," she said. "I don't trust snap judgments—on places, or people."

"Very wise," he said, moving to her side.

He knew her better than she had realized, she thought. And now that he had peeled away one layer of himself to her, he seemed to have decided that that was enough, to have been made wary—or perhaps he was still tentative about her. Their dinner arrived, and from then until near the end of the evening the talk was light, like a dance performed on eggs. Then she pressed him again.

"Do you think this is the *only* way to what you want—dictatorship?"

"It works." He wiped his lips with a large yellow napkin.

"Where have I heard *that* before?" she said, rolling her eyes upward sarcastically. "Let me see, I think it was about Russia—'I have seen the future and it works.' "

"This is different."

Against this adamantine front she pressed on: "I doubt that if you live in either place, Germany or Russia, it *feels* different. They're both totalitarian."

He was irritated: "It's the man that makes the real difference. You can't possibly confuse Hitler with Stalin."

"You really think a lot of him, don't you . . . ?" There was just enough of a suggestion of incredulity in her voice to continue the challenge.

He opened his cigarette case, took a cigarette, tapped it on the case, then lit it. He didn't answer until he drew the first taste.

"How would you like to see him?"

"Meet him?"

"Well—no. I can't promise *that*. But *see* him, at close quarters, as he really is."

"You make him sound like a species for study."

He smiled hesitantly: "I think you need to study it."

"I'm ready," she said, now appeasing him.

As they went to the door she took his arm and kissed him decorously on the cheek. "Thank you for supper," she said. He smiled and, in turn, took her with a hand on her upper arm and kissed her on the lips, gently squeezing the arm and holding the kiss just a second longer than was reciprocated. She realized that her body might get the better of her mind, and stepped calmly back, their eyes meeting. He checked his own instinct and wordlessly opened the door.

Back in her room she began to tremble. She undressed, opened the door to the terrace, and stood naked, staring into the night until she was under control again. The night sky was impersonal and a last refuge that had consoled her before. She breathed the scent of the gardens. In the colored lights strung through the trees she saw a Gothic fountain watering a large pool of lilies and heard laughter.

The next morning the telephone wakened her from a deep sleep. She groped for it, unseeing, and nearly dropped it.

"Welcome to Germany," said the count, already too ingratiating with just three words.

"Thank you," she said, deliberately prim.

"It is good you are here, Miss Dexter." He responded to the primness with this minor formality. "I do not like Munich. Too much sausage, too much beer. But never mind. You must enjoy yourself. We must enjoy *ourselves,* eh?"

"I think Alastair has some plans for that."

"Ah, yes." The count laughed. "Alastair *does* have plans.

Always, plans. It is good for him, that you are here." He had
understood her tone and became less importunate. "We are
meeting later, I think."

"We are?"

"There is a lunch party. So, until then. . . ."

In her mind she could see his teeth flashing. "Yes, until
then."

She went down for breakfast and was surprised to find in
the lobby the Paris *Herald Tribune*, one day out of date. In it
were evocative pictures: Harold Vanderbilt was about to de-
fend the America's Cup with his yacht the *Ranger*. She recalled the crescent of sand across from Newport when, in another year, the big boats zigzagged out to Nantucket.

"We'll lick you this time," said Dunsinnan, appearing at
her shoulder, seeing the picture of the *Ranger*. "Tommy Sop-
with's spent a fortune on his boat. It's the best we can turn
out."

"It will need to be." Nostalgia was still her foreground,
Dunsinnan and reality only slowly intruding. He sat down
breezily, the dark hair on his chest showing in the neck of the
Aertex shirt.

"I've heard from the count already," she said, taking the
coffee.

"I thought you might. He told you about lunch?"

She nodded and looked questioning.

"Just a few friends," he said, "nothing formal. I thought
you should meet our English colony."

But first they played tennis. It was already hot on the
court. Dunsinnan was a vain player, overregarding of his own
style, unaccustomed to a strong opponent, and visibly irked by
her strength as she took the heat better than he and steadily
outplayed him—drawing him to the net and then precisely
lobbing. A small group of people gathered, applauding her.

Afterwards, as they took their towels, he said, "My leg
isn't quite itself."

"Oh yeah?" she said, happily truculent.

From behind a copy of the *Frankfurter Zeitung* (the
only paper he now trusted) von Klagen watched the small
group as they tripped through the lobby to the reception desk.
Unity Mitford was in a flowered dress that showed puffy upper arms basted pink by the sun.

"And the Heavenly B is coming *too,"* she said; then fixing an eye on the desk clerk, she struck a pose of command:

"Lord Dunsinnan is expecting us. Would you please tell him we are here—Miss Mitford and friends."

Von Klagen waited until they had gone up in the elevator, folded his paper, and went to the desk. Asking for a pack of matches, he commented, "Not bad—those English girls, eh?"

The clerk embodied the discretion of years spent knowing the private side of public faces. The *Frankfurter Zeitung* under von Klagen's arm suggested a kindred spirit.

"Strictly for top people only," he said, "too dangerous for you to even think about."

Von Klagen played innocent. "Oh. Which top people?"

The clerk handed him the pack of matches and simply looked at him. After all, walls had ears.

Von Klagen disappeared toward the telephone kiosks and then, when he was sure the clerk was preoccupied, took the back staircase. The taint of stale food seemed ingrained in the carpet on the stairs; it must be the link between kitchen and rooms. On the first landing there was a small pantry, with hot-plate trolleys. Although it was nearly lunchtime, nobody was there. He slipped along the corridor, to where it took a curved turn to the right at the larger rooms overlooking the gardens. The staleness had gone; in its place was the smell of well-waxed woodwork and polished brass. Yellow shafts of light came from under the double doors to a suite, and he heard voices. One was already inimitable to him:

"Absolutely *beastly*, Alastair . . . *The Times* is usually so fair to Germany, but this man simply doesn't understand. It's upset the Führer *terribly*. He will have to be got rid of."

Von Klagen heard steps from behind and the banging of a trolley. He moved down the corridor and tried a door. It was unlocked. Inside the room the beds were stripped, waiting for new linen. He tried the windows to the terrace, and one of them opened. He stepped softly outside. On his left the voices were clearer. Through a trellis he saw a cluster of people on the neighboring terrace, standing around tables with several ice buckets full of wine.

Dunsinnan was wearing lederhosen.

Showering after tennis, Ruth had recovered her spirits, and finding that Dunsinnan was a bad loser had confirmed an expectation. Whether it had been the defeat in front of an audience, or a feeling of threatened virility, he was unable to hide his irritation, and the break before lunch was politic.

Walking back to his suite down the corridor, she heard the babble of voices. This time, as Dunsinnan introduced them, Unity Mitford remembered, looking at Ruth with an assumption that she found offensive: "Ah, yes—of course, Spithead. Cried off sick, if I recall."

"Bad touch of the flu," said Dunsinnan.

Ruth took the offered hand and found it clammy.

"She's quite fit now," he continued, giving Ruth a conciliatory look, his humor restored. "I can testify to that."

Misunderstanding the innuendo, Unity Mitford said, "Really? How nice."

The count intervened, making a courtly bow and kissing Ruth's hand.

"My darling Ruth—I feel better already."

Two young Englishmen and another English girl were on the terrace. The girl, very tall and skeletal, had a veined throat, and her voice piped as though squeezed from her.

"I hear von Blomberg has lost his heart—*again*," she said.

Unity Mitford turned: "When did you hear that?"

But it was Dunsinnan who answered: "You haven't heard? Your Heavenly B is in another heaven, I fear, Unity."

"Half his age, apparently," the thin girl said. "I hear he turns pink at the sight of her."

"Can't be true," countered Unity Mitford. "He *couldn't*, surely?"

"Oh, but he *could*," said one of the young men, enjoying her obvious discomfort. "He's quite rejuvenated."

"It's the best elixir there is," said Dunsinnan, steering Ruth away from the count with a light touch on the arm. Moving to the edge of the terrace, he said, "I'm sorry about that little tantrum of mine. You play very well."

Watching them through the trellis, his back pressed against the wall, von Klagen recalled Ruth's arrival the day before. There had been none of the familiar current he could usually detect when lovers attempted to seem not to be lovers, and there was something now, in the way she held her body next to his, that betrayed reservation. She was beautiful in a way seldom seen in a German girl, really dark and—slightly *Asiatic*, was it? No doubt Himmler would have asked for a blood test.

There was a sound behind von Klagen. A maid had come into the room and was making up the bed. There was no cover for him if she came to the terrace, and he heard her come over to the door, muttering. She took the handle and turned it, pulling the door closed and letting down the blind.

"I gather you've been to *Wasserleonburg*," said one of the men on the next terrace.

"Ah—*yes!*" said the thin girl. "Tell us about it, Alastair."

"Just a visit. Nothing more."

"But how *was* he, the King?" insisted Unity Mitford.

"Not a king—not anymore," said one of the men.

Dunsinnan sipped a glass of hock. "He's well. They're both very well. A little adrift, of course."

"Hmmmm," said Unity Mitford, "not so much adrift as his country. If that darling man had only remained—You know, the Führer told me, he would have welcomed him here, by now, as King—to Munich."

"Quite," Dunsinnan said ruminatively.

Von Klagen tried the door to the room, but the maid had locked it. He unfolded a small clasp knife and worked at the keyhole. Slowly he worked it back and forth, trying to avoid a noise. He could feel the spring weakening.

". . . And now we're in the hands of assorted wets. . . ."

The spring snapped.

"What was that?" said the count.

They stopped talking. Von Klagen froze. In the garden a merciful lawn mower sprang to life.

"What a racket," said one of the men, and they carried on.

Von Klagen let himself back into the room. The corridor was quiet. He slipped away, this time taking the main staircase and walking through the lobby, indistinguishable from the other guests. He realized that his back was damp with sweat. He didn't like Munich. It was aggressively provincial, too coarse in its recreation. But Munich was the Nazi capital, not Berlin—at least, emotionally and physically, it was where Hitler was drawn and therefore where his court had to follow. And the camp followers, as he had now seen. His disaffection with Munich was reinforced by the voice of the girl on the Abwehr switchboard, by her Berlin directness, and even more by his friend in the Central Registry. He asked her to check the significance of the name Wasserleonburg, and she didn't even pause.

"That's easy," she said, "it's where the count of Münster lives. He seems to have moved elsewhere, though, for the mo-

ment, to make way for guests. Honeymoon guests—I saw it in
the magazine."

"What guests?"

"The Duke and Lady Windsor."

Von Klagen didn't bother to correct the titles. Once he
had put the phone down, he wished he hadn't—it broke his
connection with his own world. In this mood he sought company.

"Where's the contessa?" said Ruth, edging clear of the
count as he lowered himself too closely onto the sofa.

"Rapallo. She's always there, this time of the year. She
does not like the heat here."

"That's a pity."

The party had spent its initial energy, and they were now
retreating from the sun into the suite, eating the buffet lunch
from plates balanced on their laps. Unity Mitford cornered
Dunsinnan, and Ruth was disinclined to rescue him. The trilling English voices grated—the voices of lives that knew no
labor. Unity Mitford still wore too much makeup.

The count followed Ruth's eyes and thoughts. "She is a
dangerous lady," he said quietly.

"Dangerous?"

"Too close to the throne. A whisper in the Führer's ear is
enough."

"What do you mean, enough?"

"She denounces people. A man I know, he was once a
favorite himself. But she told the Führer he had said something disloyal. He had to leave Germany—very quickly."

In his lederhosen Dunsinnan kept his knees discreetly together as he sat; on one of them rested a hand of Unity Mitford, like something with an independent life.

"Luckily," the count continued, "she likes Alastair." He
scooped out the claw of a lobster and dipped it into the may-
onnaise. "One of my weaknesses, my darling—lobster. What
are your weaknesses?"

"Popcorn. Hot buttered popcorn." Her eyes stayed on
Dunsinnan.

Von Klagen went to the Cafe Luitpold where Geczy the
bandleader appealed to matrons, mistresses, and ingenues alike.
Some of the clientele seemed to him to have walked straight
from the grotesque cartoons of *Simplicissimus*, pink rolled
necks stroked by hired fingers. Von Klagen dragged his bad

leg more than he needed to, to a table near the dance floor. A
dark-skinned girl with a fine Prussian nose watched from the
bar. She waited for the music to start again and went over to
him. She wore a yellow silk scarf around her neck and a very
thin woollen dress. He knew breeding and poverty when he
saw them united, and knew his luck.

"*Can* you dance?" she said, baring her sympathy.

"Of course."

A woman with a broad Bavarian face came to the micro-
phone and—inappropriately—attempted to sing like Dietrich:

> "*Love's always been my game,*
> *Play it how I may.*
> *I was made that way . . .*
> *I can't help it.*"

The girl put her face into von Klagen's shoulder, and he
could smell the freshness of her hair. Before they left, she
drank a great deal—green chartreuse.

His room in a dank side-street hotel looked into a courtyard, giving very little light. The heat of the day turned it into
an oven. Even after the window was opened, the room remained airless and caught the odors of the kitchen beneath—
and the flies.

The last thing she took off was the scarf. A light scar ran
from under one ear and halfway across the neck to a point
just short of the vein.

She looked at his twisted leg as he looked at her neck.
"We are both wounded," she said, and took his testicles in a
cupped hand. They didn't speak again. Suddenly she was
asleep, on top of him. He eased her over gently and then went
to the window. In spite of the heat he closed it and put out the
light.

Drugged by the wine and food, Ruth had gone back to
her room to sleep. In the interval between sleep and waking
she was tormented by confusions: confusions of place, of
faces, of past and present, and of her purpose. Once the room
had reassembled into clear focus, she felt claustrophobic and
opened the door to the terrace. The Gothic roofline jogged her
conscience about work. She had come primed with a list of
galleries and notebooks. She knew how easy it would be to be
mindless here; she remembered the vacuous faces of lunch.
She had just found the notebooks when the phone rang.

"You all right?" Dunsinnan asked.

"Perfectly"—she remembered her fuddled exit.

"That's good because I want to take you out. You've hardly seen the place."

She hesitated. "Well . . . there's some reading I ought to be doing."

"*Tonight?* I have something special in mind."

Her resolve wilted. "Well . . . you'd better give me an hour, to get myself together."

"Right. We'll see you in the lobby in an hour."

It was only after she put down the phone that the *we* registered.

When she reached the lobby, only the count was visible, standing by the door, restless. He wore rough tweeds and the same Alpine hat she had first seen on the grouse moor. He came forward.

"They are outside—Alastair and Unity," he said, seeing her perplexity.

"What *is* this all about?" she asked, unable to avoid the count's taking her arm.

"Alastair has not told you?"

She could see the collusion in his eyes. "No. He has *not*."

Dunsinnan was standing outside by a small black sedan, a convertible with its roof down. Two Nazi pennants were flying on it, one on each wing, and another, larger banner stretched across the trunk. Unity Mitford was at the wheel, wearing a black beret and leather gauntlets, the flowered dress exchanged for a black suit. Dunsinnan was still in the lederhosen.

"Good," he said.

From the car Unity Mitford gave her a short nod.

"It's Unity's new car," said Dunsinnan, opening the rear door for her. "Her father just gave it to her. Rather dashing, don't you think?"

There was just room for four inside, and with Dunsinnan taking the front passenger seat, Ruth found herself compressed by the count's ample thighs. Dunsinnan turned and looked at her just as the car started: "It's in the nature of a pilgrimage."

They passed through one of the city's ancient gates, the Isator, and then, continuing east, crossed the river Isar on the Ludwig Bridge. Unity Mitford drove impulsively. They came to a cluster of low, rambling buildings strung with colored lights already burning in the dusk. Only when the car engine died did Ruth hear the noise from inside. She recalled the din from the stadium at home before the Army and Navy football game, it seemed as great—and yet this building was only a fraction of the size.

"*This* is Bavaria," said the count ominously, climbing out and holding open the door for her.

Dunsinnan came round and put a hand on her waist. "It's the Bürger-bräukeller—a beer hall."

Going through the door was like experiencing a trick of perspective, a distortion from Alice in Wonderland, for it led to another world, strangely subterranean in feel, and the size of the hall confounded the modest exterior. Several thousand people seemed to be there, sitting at long wooden benches, being served large steins of beer by girls in Bavarian costume. Many of the tables were exclusively of men, some banging the steins on the wood as they sang.

Ruth had to shout into Dunsinnan's ear: "What *kind* of pilgrimage?"

He took her elbow, weaving through the press of people, making for a spot near a platform. He stopped in the gangway and pointed to the roof: "Look. Can you see anything?"

She followed his finger and then shook her head.

"The hole—just there, by the pillar. Do you see it now?"

She did see it, a perfectly circular hole in the wood with fractures radiating from it.

"Come on, let's take this bench," he said, and the four of them sat down.

"Now—enlighten me," Ruth said.

"It's a bullet hole. Hitler put it there, in 1923. Have you ever heard of the beer-hall putsch?"

"Vaguely."

"It was here, this is where it began. He fired the shot to get attention. Then he delivered one of the greatest speeches in German history."

"The putsch failed, as I recall."

Unity Mitford, pulling off her gauntlets, said: "It was the beginning. The real beginning. Every movement needs martyrs. The party got their martyrs, shot down in the square. The putsch might have failed, but after that, Hitler was the only man in Germany's destiny. The thousand-year Reich really began then."

There were many brown shirts at the tables, and some of the black S.S. uniforms. Old men mixed with young. Ruth was conscious of being stared at. The stench of beer and cigarettes was overpowering. It was not Ruth but the count who seemed the most uncomfortable.

"I wish I *liked* beer," he said as a brimming stein appeared in front of him.

"Poor Alfredo." Dunsinnan laughed. "He's a Mediterranean animal, not very good at adapting."

"It's a question of taste," said the count.

The vibrations of the peasant songs shook the steins. Unity Mitford spilt some of the beer in her eagerness to join the singing. She pulled out a handkerchief from her bag and wiped her suit. Ruth saw a head appear from the open bag, and then the body of a rat. It blinked myopically and, still bemused, crawled from the bag and sat on the bench, staring at the count.

"My God. What *is* that?" he said, suddenly seeing the rat.

Unity Mitford laughed. "Oh, that's Ratular. He's quite tame."

Ruth visibly recoiled. "You keep a rat—as a pet?"

"Why not? People have the wrong idea about rats. After all, a squirrel is just a rat with a larger tail. *You* like squirrels, don't you?"

"There seem to be a lot of misunderstood things around here," said Ruth, taking the beer.

Dunsinnan picked up the rat and stroked it, rubbing his forefinger under its chin. "Yes," he said, "quite harmless, do you see?" He dropped the rat back into the bag.

15

Ruth had noticed a nerve above Dunsinnan's left eye. It was a signal of agitation, even when everything else was under control. As he closed the door to his suite and turned to her the nerve moved once. "I think I'll send for some coffee," he said.

"On top of that beer—I'm afraid I couldn't." She collapsed thankfully on a sofa and kicked off her shoes. "Go ahead, though. I'll just have a glass of water." Somehow, she thought, his lederhosen looked ridiculous now. Perhaps it was the time of night.

"Did you find it interesting—the beer hall?" He sat opposite her.

"Educational."

"Just that? What about the spirit of the place? Didn't you find that exciting?"

She pulled her knees up under her chin and rubbed her toes. She decided to be blunt. "Alastair—I don't know why you have anything to do with that woman. She's nuts."

"A little odd, perhaps. But mad? I don't think so." The nerve moved again.

"What kind of person would keep a rat in her handbag?"

"You didn't like that, did you?"

"She says appalling things."

"A bit overzealous, perhaps."

"What *do* you see in her?"

Uncomfortable, he hesitated. "She's useful."

"How come?"

"You'll see. Tomorrow, perhaps."

The waiter came in with the coffee, and while he was there Ruth made her escape.

She found a note under her door in the morning: "Please be at the Osteria Bavaria by noon. The taxis know it. Will meet you there. Alastair."

When she announced her destination, the cabdriver gave her a knowing look and seemed from that second to become excessively silent. As the cab pulled up to the small inn on the Ramburgstrasse, dressed on the outside in heavy stone with leaded windows, she saw the small black sedan, its roof still folded down, the pennants flying. She was annoyed. As she got out she noticed a building nearby flying Nazi banners, and the inn itself had two uniformed guards posted at the door. Inside, it reminded her of any Irish chophouse in Boston, with its partitioned tables and austere fittings. Dunsinnan was waiting at one of the tables, with the count.

"Ah, punctual," said Dunsinnan, rising. "No, don't sit down, we were just waiting until you got here, to go in together."

He signalled to a stocky man, calling out "Domodossola." The man led them out of the restaurant into a small garden at the rear, laid out Italian-style with a fountain and dominated by a large table under a pergola. For a second the brightness of the sun, after the gloom of the interior, blinded her, and then as they followed the innkeeper Ruth saw that at the table under the pergola sat Hitler.

The sensation of recognition froze her for half an instant, the *frisson* of seeing in the flesh a face known before only in the flat dimensions of print or film. They were taken to a table under a tree. The count was almost incontinent with excitement—even before they sat down he bowed foolishly toward Hitler's table, though nobody took any notice.

From where Ruth sat Hitler was in left profile, fleshier in the face than she expected, a putative double chin pressing his shirt collar. His parchment skin was a lightly mottled pink under the cheek, the inimitable black hair slicked down precisely to the left ear. On Hitler's left was a young man in black S.S. uniform, on his right a youngish but stolid woman in a green tailored jacket. Hitler was in a soft gray double-breasted suit, white shirt, and dark tie. He was listening intently to a young broad-browed man sitting across from him at the round table. Between this man and another in brown uniform, by far the tallest and toughest of the men, was Unity Mitford.

"You see," said Dunsinnan, "how openly he lives—so much for all those ridiculous stories about his bodyguards, his being a recluse."

A girl brought them menus.

"Thank you, Rosa," said Dunsinnan, rather too obviously establishing his familiarity.

Dunsinnan nodded to the man speaking to Hitler. "That's his architect, Albert Speer. A useful man to know."

The count laughed. "Alastair always knows the man to know."

When Speer stopped speaking, Hitler leaned forward to reply. They were too far away to catch words, but Ruth recognized the coarse tones, even in modulation. She had to admit that the atmosphere was disarmingly unpretentious. Unity Mitford cast one short glance at them but betrayed no recognition.

Through the meal Ruth found it impossible to stop her eyes wandering to the table under the pergola. Occasionally either Speer or Mitford laughed, but Hitler never did. Dunsinnan, too, was looking across, though usually in the direction of Unity Mitford. Ruth, reading the faces at the table, saw interesting patterns. Whenever Unity Mitford spoke, Hitler would listen patiently while the others shifted in their seats uneasily. The lunch was unhurried, Hitler eating frugally, and little was drunk, but the party looked for all the world like colleagues from an office escaping dull work for the sake of gossip. It was this apparent ordinariness—contrasting with the outward panoply of the regime—that puzzled Ruth. She kept looking at Hitler, this man who was the embodiment of remorseless power, and yet could not feel in the least awed.

Just as they were finishing their own meal the tall uniformed man left Hitler's table and came over to Dunsinnan. They spoke in German, and then Dunsinnan got up, saying: "You'll have to excuse me." He spoke calmly, but Ruth noticed that his hand was shaking.

As they watched Dunsinnan walk over, bow, and shake hands with Hitler, the count said, needlessly, "Lady Mitford has arranged it."

Dunsinnan took an empty seat between the woman in the green jacket and Unity Mitford, who seemed to be talking to Hitler about him, because Hitler nodded attentively while he scrutinized Dunsinnan. Then Hitler asked a question, and Dunsinnan replied, sometimes tapping a finger on the cloth. When he was finished, Speer asked a question. As he answered Dunsinnan continued to address Hitler.

When Hitler spoke again, he was more animated, waving his right hand, palm down, then at the end closing the hand as though punching the air. Dunsinnan nodded eagerly.

"Who's the gorilla—the one who came over?" Ruth asked.

"That's Brückner, his adjutant," said the count, "a strange man. Very religious."

"Can you be religious *and* a good Nazi?"

The count looked at her cunningly: "As long as you don't confuse your gods." He observed Ruth with new interest: "Are you religious?"

"I'm not sure—anymore."

Dunsinnan had stood up, shaking Hitler's hand again and making a very military bow. The woman in the green jacket dipped her head and smilled. Speer rose, they shook hands. Brückner escorted Dunsinnan back to the table.

Dunsinnan was flushed. He took a long draft of beer.

"Alfredo, you'll be interested to know that Mussolini is coming here next month." Then he turned to Ruth. "You see, he's only human."

* * *

Like a sleepwalker not knowing the real from the unreal, and muddling both, Ruth wandered through Munich for another week, disoriented, hearing a babble of voices, seeing face dissolving into face, growing more and more uneasy, too often deflected from her work. Every other name seemed double-barrelled, in any language: Sykes-Maclean, Reck-Malleczewen, Faucigny-Lucinge, Conta-Faemino (what explained this—stubborn genealogy?). The voices were to match: piping and effete, diffident and epicene, arrogant and regal. Some of it seemed a continuous party, not knowing night from day, spinning with the visceral narcotic of Nazism, against a backdrop divided between old Bavarian Gothic and neo-Roman buildings decked in Wagnerian heraldry. In the wings: a gutted aristocracy, aloof but hoping that these new vulgarians would replenish the vaults. But there were alleys and crevices down which people dared not look nor go—and signs saying *"Juden sind hier nicht erwünscht."* Jews not welcome here. In such places, only the nearsighted were left; the farsighted already knew enough and had gone.

At the hotel she saw young bucks in cars with looping chrome exhausts, some of them wearing lederhosen and Alpine hats, in the company of girls in peasant dresses. There were other young men, who knew the aphrodisiac appeal of boots, belts, and uniform caps, whose bodies were tuned for procreating the master race, whose inseminations obliged the eager virgins of kindred races. Thigh met thigh as they played the "Horst Wessel Song" and thought of the martyrs falling as the Führer marched on, miraculously saved by a shield of other bodies, knowing his destiny before others did.

The pervasive *Zeitgeist* sprang incredibly from the man she had watched eating semolina noodles while his cronies wolfed down sausages, a man of superficial anonymity. Now that she had seen him she still could not understand.

Then came the pageant. The city's medievalism—the cathedral's bulbous bell towers, the severe angled churches, the riper stone of the Renaissance, the flights of mad Ludwig—all this seemed preparation for a new dementia given final expression by a parade of medieval knights with swastikas embossed on their breastplates in the place of the holy cross. To mock the bathos or to fear the aspiration? Still she did not know. But the beginning of understanding was not far away. Only one unwary step from the street into the Haus der Deutschen Kunst built by decree to purge the art world of all but Germanic purity. Here in the colonnaded halls hung the work of Picasso, Matisse, Cézanne. But something was amiss. The paintings were stripped of frames and hung crazily, some deliberately upside down, others with labels attached: "German peasants looked at in the Yiddish manner." And these works were interspersed with those of lunatics so that the public—if it persisted—could be challenged to tell the difference. "Looked at in the Yiddish manner." Fingers pointed, here was the scapegoat.

An omen: Hitler had laid the foundation stone for his temple of art, and the silver hammer had snapped. Now the flaw bore its fruit: Ruth walked from the gallery of Degenerate Art to the assembled masterpieces of the Third Reich, into the world of cleansed images, and she found—a void. All that was left was insipid realism, the master race at work and play, culminating in sculpture thirty feet high: bodies without veins or hairs or life, pallid unraised penises, and breasts that could have been molded by Krupps. Some were incomplete. The artisans of this clinic in their white coats still crawled along a thigh or sat astride a shoulder to chisel away the last imperfections, like lice on a corpse.

She saw Dunsinnan wiping his mouth with a yellow napkin and saying "It works"; she heard the relished anecdote of Streicher's Jews eating from his carpet; she saw the young Speer laughing at a table in the sun; she began slowly to shiver not because of anything she saw here in this temple of madness but because of what she now saw of herself; and then the shiver turned to a chill as she began to speculate on what might lie beyond the pageant, behind the ordained art and the bannered horsemen. As she went out they gave her the brochure, art through the eyes of Dr. Goebbels, a lasting evocation of the malignancy.

These introspections degraded her, as the museum had its art. The affront of her aesthetic nerve ends was, she realized, an indictment of some moral infirmity on her part, of the way other nerve ends had failed. She recalled that during the Olympics the *Juden sind hier nicht erwünscht* signs had been removed, temporarily. She too had practiced selective exclusions. They began to dissolve. Light fell where there had been shade. She saw her own face, eyes betraying conscience, her mindless dance over the graves.

The green Moselle wine tasted as though pressed from the grape that afternoon, flowery and innocuous. She sat on the terrace and gazed sightless at the gardens. The first bottle gone, she ordered another. The wine waiter was stunted, with a face of vellum and nicotined fingers straining at the cork. Too obsequious. He took the dead bottle from the ice bucket, and it dripped across the table. She waved him away. She saw Dunsinnan enter his terrace with the count. The count saw her first and came leering to the trellis. Something stopped him in mid-effusion.

"I'm having a private party," she called, waving the glass.

Dunsinnan joined the count at the trellis, straining to see her clearly across the distance. "So I see," he drawled. "That's a little selfish." He, in turn, began to comprehend.

The count looked at Dunsinnan and then called to her, "Please, why don't you join us . . . it would be more fun."

"Oh, yes—*much* more fun," she said to herself. She pulled the bottle from the bucket and disappeared, to reappear in seconds at the door of Dunsinnan's suite just as he opened it. Without a word she walked in, bottle in one hand and glass—tilting too much—in the other, and kicked off her shoes. On the terrace she put the bottle in the center of the table and sat down, raising her glass to them. "Okay, then— time for fun."

The two men watched her warily.

"You certainly have a start on us, Ruth," said Dunsinnan.

"Yes, don't I?" She grinned up at him. "So don't just stand there—get moving."

The same wine waiter appeard, this time bearing champagne. He looked from Dunsinnan to the count, and from the count to Ruth. The cork flew over the terrace and into he garden.

"I'll bet you two have done some fine deals . . . it's a good time for deals. . . . Alastair . . . business good?"

He raised his glass uneasily: "And what are *you* celebrating?"

"Oh, me? Nothing, very much. You can just put it down—to general high spirits, you know—getting into the real spirit of things, *at last*."

Neither of them was sure of the irony. The count chose to disregard it and did his impersonation of gallantry: "A toast to beauty."

"Ahaaaaah . . . now *that's* quite a toast, Alfredo." She put down her glass and pulled at the neckline of her dress, curiously demure, looking to check that the slip was covered and then staring at the count. "How is the Sistine Chapel these days?"

"Pardon?"

"Is the fresco—is it on the approved list? Or do the angels have black shirts *now*?"

Dunsinnan sat down. The count faltered and then laughed. "Such an *American* sense of humor."

She turned to Dunsinnan. "You know, Michelangelo was a homosexual. Surely, they—I mean, *your friends*—they can't approve of *that*?"

Dunsinnan glanced at the count and then leaned back in the chair, sipping the champagne calmly. "So you've been to the exhibition?"

"Do you think—do you think that truth and beauty—do they go together?" she asked with a dangerous reasonableness.

"Such cosmic questions!" Dunsinnan said. "I doubt we could successfully discuss *that* at this moment."

To Ruth his face was moving in and out of focus, assuming unfamiliar contours, only the voice remaining clear and patronizing. The champagne caused her to belch. She put her hand over her mouth after the release, mistiming the movement. "Pardon *me*." She giggled.

She woke up to find the room mobile, diagonal bars of light from a window shade increasing the uncertainty of horizon. Dimly, from a corner, she heard Dunsinnan's voice as she turned her head sideways.

"Are you conscious?"

"Probably." She seemed pressed to the bed as though on the wall of a revolving drum, held down by centrifugal force.

The indistinct form appeared at her side. He put a hand on her brow. "That's good. You've had a good sweat—you're a lot cooler."

"Is that right?" She lifted her head from the pillow and then sank back again. "Jesus—was I *that* bad? I guess so." She recalled the count's face, the terrace and gardens, but nothing else. She put out a hand and met his. "I'm sorry." She moved a leg and realized that she was still dressed. A blanket covered her.

"That's all right," he said, squeezing the hand. "Would you like anything?"

"Just water. Plain old iced water."

When he came back with the water, she had managed to sit up. She drank it slowly. He sat on the bed. The water congealed on impact with her stomach. "I think I'm going to have to find the bathroom. . . ."

Fifteen minutes later she returned to the bedroom. The last of the twilight had gone. He had opened the shades, and the room was illuminated by reflections from the garden. He was now clearly reassembled from the blurred fragments. So, too, were other memories of the day. She put an arm over each of his shoulders and buried her head under his chin as his arms folded over her back. The touch of his hands felt contaminating, but she yielded to it, as to a commanding incubus. She pressed her nose into his neck and licked the skin between the chest bones. Then she looked up and said, "There's no dog around, is there?"

His hand began to unbutton the back of her dress, but she drew away. She pulled off the shoulder straps and undid the remaining buttons, letting the dress and slip fall to the ground. Still in underwear, she went to him and unbuttoned his shirt and trousers, clasping his erection as she found it. He released her brassiere and began biting at her nipples. All she wore now was the thin cord of gold with a bone pendant, and her stockings.

"Wait," she said, and went to sit on the bed to pull off the stockings. He got into the bed and lay on his side. She was quite clear in the head now. An image recurred of the mammoth Aryan Adonis with whitecoated figures polishing its slack pudenda. She rolled into the bed and slid downward, licking first around his genitals and then closing her mouth on him, and then biting. He screamed and ejaculated in one movement, and she lay back.

"You bitch—I'm bleeding!" He sounded slightly hysterical. She closed on him again, drawing herself to his face, pressing her chest into his. She forced her right knee between his legs and then put her hand there, feeling the blood and stroking his testicles.

"It's all right," she said, as though consoling a child, "only superficial. Keep still, leave it to me."

She felt him shiver beneath her. He looked into her face, his mouth tight, his eyes still liquid from the pain but now relenting. She massaged him carefully and slowly until her hand was full, and then she guided him into her and pressed with her knees so that she was able to take his full, deep strokes, wanting the self-abasement to be absolute. She saw the pain rising in his eyes again and his teeth clench, and she kept moving until her own lubrication eased him. "Bitch!" he said again, but this time smiling. She felt the tears across her cheeks and began sobbing. She closed her legs on him and pressed him deep into her, locking there, inner muscles taut. He gasped and screamed again. She looked at him and saw other faces. Inside she was dry. She dipped her head to his left shoulder and bit deeply, holding long enough to taste the blood.

When they broke apart, they both lay silently on their backs, not touching.

"I don't understand you," he said after a while.

"It's what you wanted, isn't it?"

He turned to look at her, the sheet pulled only to her waist, the gold sliver on her breast. "What are you trying to prove?"

"*Prove . . . ?*" She continued to look at the ceiling. "It didn't need proving, did it?" She began to cry again, quietly. She felt very alone, and wanton.

16

"On this I agree with the Gestapo, so help me!" This young woman is a menace." Canaris was sitting so far back in his chair that von Klagen, at the other side of the desk, could see only his head. One dachshund—von Klagen could never identify either by name—was lying at the front of the desk panting from the heat, and the other was foraging somewhere by Canaris's feet. It was a Sunday morning, and through the window came the dolorous ringing of a church bell.

Von Klagen raised himself slightly in his seat as he answered: "Brückner complains that the Lady Mitford seems to know where the Führer is going before he does. She parks her car illegally outside the Osteria, nobody dares to do anything."

"And" said Canaris, "she wears the *goldenes Abzeichen*, with the Führer's own signature on the back of it—*engraved*."

Leaning against a wall in the background, Piekenbrock, for once out of uniform, wore a severe gray suit; he had come direct from early morning mass. "Can the British secret service be as clever as this?" he said, looking at Canaris.

"It doesn't matter if they are or if they are not," Canaris replied. "She exists. As long as the Führer wants her around, we have the problem."

"He never allows her near the lady on the Obersalzburg," said Piekenbrock. "She seems no threat to that arrangement. What *is* the attraction?"

Canaris sank lower into his chair, looking at the ceiling. "The Mitford sisters—he called them, what was it? *'Perfect specimens of Aryan womanhood.'* He talks with the eye of a herdsman at market." The dog at the front of the desk overcame its lethargy and slithered between the pedestals to Canaris's feet, to its companion. Canaris continued: "There are too many connections here." He pulled himself to the desk again, taking von Klagen's report. "This Bedaux. He was with Dunsinnan in Munich, yes? He has been here in Berlin. The Duke of Windsor was married at his home."

"Dunsinnan was there, too," von Klagen added.

"Exactly. And Schellenberg—you say *he* makes regular contact with Dunsinnan?"

"Yes. They go to great trouble to avoid being seen. The last meeting in Munich was in the Englischer Garten, at three in the morning."

"What about the American girl?"

"I'm still not sure."

"Not sure of what?"

"She doesn't fit. Not with the Lady Mitford, not with any of them—only with Dunsinnan."

"How with him?"

"They argue."

Piekenbrock said, "What is that supposed to mean?"

Canaris, looking carefully at von Klagen, answered: "It means that von Klagen may be losing his judgment, is that not so, Oberstleutnant?"

Canaris had not used von Klagen's rank since their first meeting. It was a form of reprimand, but the shrewd inference reminded von Klagen of something. Getting up to go, he paused and said, "Dunsinnan and his friend seem to know about von Blomberg."

Canaris and Piekenbrock exchanged glances, and then, in an almost bored tone, Canaris said, "What about von Blomberg?"

"His girl friend. The whore."

Piekenbrock said, "Those are just rumors—why should you be concerned?"

"If the Lady Mitford knows, then it could get to Hitler."

With evident distaste, Canaris said, "Von Blomberg is a fool. If the rumors about this girl turn out to be true, it's making it too easy for Heydrich, he'll make a scandal out of it—then. . . ." Canaris drew his hand across his throat.

There was a scuffling on the floor around Canaris's feet. *"Kaspar!"* he cried, reaching down. The dog was eating a page of von Klagen's report that had fallen from the desk. It looked up soulfully and wagged an appeasing tail. A quarter of the page was already digested. The remainder was smudged with saliva.

For two days Dunsinnan had been insufferably correct in his manner, a parody of a Prussian nobleman. The count noticed it. He looked from Dunsinnan to Ruth and then, when the opportunity came, asked, "What's the matter? Alastair—he is very strange."

"I think he has a problem," said Ruth, unhelpfully.

The count looked at her suspiciously. "His mother is coming, did you know that? I only found out this morning."

"Yes, he told me too. It's the only reason I'm still here."

Suddenly wise, the count smiled. "Maybe we could have lunch together, you and I? It is high time."

"Why not?"

Apart from a hand on her knee, the lunch was harmless. The count's distaste for Munich was not so much moral as cultural. His snobbery was unconsciously funny and relaxed her.

Lady Dunsinnan arrived in the evening. There was something intuitive in the way she looked at Ruth. Dunsinnan's excessive formality persisted through dinner. It made his mother edgy and the count testy.

"I'm proposing that we go to Nuremberg," Dunsinnan announced, "Mother, Alfredo—and you, too, Ruth—if you wish."

"You mean, the party rally?" said his mother.

"The *Parteitag*," corrected Dunsinnan in his most clipped German.

Lady Dunsinnan looked at Ruth. "I hope you'll come, my dear?"

Recognizing a cry for help, Ruth nodded. "Of course." She looked at Dunsinnan. "I may never get another chance."

Dunsinnan hired a large open touring car. It had a long, low hood, a windshield that folded down and forward, one

passenger seat next to the driver, a jump seat facing forward
behind the front passenger, and room for two more passengers
behind. The highly buffed metalwork reflected the light, even
the spokes of the spare wheel strapped on the side of the hood
above a long running board. It was a powerful barge of a car
with a throaty, expensive sound.

Ruth sat alongside Dunsinnan in the front; the count
rode the jump seat and Lady Dunsinnan sat alone in the rear.
Their appearance exaggerated their élan. When they neared
Nuremberg, the converging traffic slowed them to a crawl.
Limousines, trucks, and smaller cars carried people from all
over Germany. In the distance they saw the old castle of the
Hohenzollerns against a skyline of mountains. Banners and
uniforms were everywhere.

Ruth shared a room with Lady Dunsinnan. The journey
had left an almost visible film of dust and oil on their skin.
Ruth unpacked. From the bath Lady Dunsinnan called out to
her:

"Tell me, do you think Alastair realizes—fully realizes—
what he's involving himself in?"

Ruth knew evasion would serve no purpose. "Yes . . . I
think he does. He speaks like a man who knows absolutely
what he's doing—and why."

"Yes. I'm afraid that's true," said Lady Dunsinnan pensively. "I must admit, my dear, that it concerns me, concerns
me quite a bit. I don't really know what I can do about it,
what I *ought* to do." She hesitated. "At one time, I had hoped,
perhaps. . . ."

"I realize that." Ruth spoke steadily. "I think I knew
that, in Scotland."

"I'm sorry, it was presumptuous of me."

"No—it wasn't. But I don't think you can do anything to
change his ideas now."

Lady Dunsinnan fell silent.

In the morning they joined Dunsinnan in his room for
breakfast. There was a pungent trace of a man's cologne, a
scent that Ruth half remembered, and an ashtray held two
fresh cigar stubs. Dunsinnan explained that in an hour an official car would collect them and take them out to the Zeppelin Field, where the world's largest stadium was under con-
struction. He rattled off statistics like a paid guide: "The
tribune is thirteen hundred feet wide and eighty feet high.
You'll be in the privileged seats." Dunsinnan's boasts stung
the count into retaliation:

"Rome wasn't ordered by the cubit. The true art lies in proportion, not size." He sprinkled cigar ash over the remains of his breakfast. "If you say to Speer, 'Give me a building of a hundred meters,' he answers, '*Mein Füher*, how about two hundred?' The Führer slaps him on the back and says, 'You are my man!' "

When they got to the Zeppelin Field, the sun was burning off the last traces of mist. Entering from the rear of the tribune, they came out suddenly into light and the sound of thousands of hushed voices. Ruth's first dazzled look into the vast arena was dominated by thousands of points of light, sun on metal. Once her eyes adjusted, she saw that the reflections came from spades, polished like mirrors and held like guns on the shoulders of a sea of khaki-clad youths, ten parallel lines of them, each block at least a dozen men broad and reaching in tapering perspective to the distant end of the stadium. Dunsinnan's obeisance to this sight was in every movement and gesture.

In the exact center, beneath the tribune, stood a granite stele hung with two enormous wreaths decked in Nazi ribbons. Lined up before it was another group of young men, stripped to their waists and leaning on their spades as though in prayer.

Dunsinnan's party was led to seats beginning at number 720 in the center tribune. Ten yards or so below them, and a little to the right, was Hitler's enclosure, with a granite lectern. Ruth heard English voices around them and saw old men in winged collars, younger women, and other faces remembered from Munich. Dunsinnan exchanged nods of recognition. A few minutes later Charles Bedaux and his swanlike wife slipped into seats next to the count.

The voices died, leaving only the sound of feet and scattered nervous coughs. Below them Hitler appeared with his entourage. The man Ruth had last seen slumped in a gray suit in the Munich garden had become the bearer of a nimbus, brown shirt overlaced with leather belts, a hat so large that it came low on his brow. He had the studied movements of a man who knows himself to be the focus of scores of thousands of eyes. With a shiver Ruth realized that by a single action—the man filling his place—the whole mass had, in that instant, been coalesced into something more than its parts, an organism surrendering will and mind to him. Dunsinnan's words came back to her: ". . . any country can make that kind of change, *if it has the will.*" She glanced at Dunsinnan now. His submission was almost sexual.

After Hitler was seated, the silence held for another minute, then was broken by slowly paced beats on a bass drum joined gradually by other instruments until the band was delivering a dirge. The phalanx of bare-chested youths began to sway with the music, their heads still bowed to the tribune. Then they began to sing a funereal hymn culminating in dedication:

> *"O Führer, in this solemn hour*
> *Unto the utmost of our power*
> *We vow that all our life shall be*
> *Labor for Germany and thee."*

The words were translated on sheets given to the foreign visitors before they took their seats. Ruth slowly screwed up her sheet in her hand.

The heads fell again to their spades, and silence descended while, below Hitler, a uniformed figure stepped forward and prepared to speak. Ruth realized that the tension in the stadium was in danger of dissipating; the speech was too flat. But the band, taking an urgent cue, broke in, curtailing the speaker.

Hitler moved forward to his lectern. His arms hung stiffly at his sides. In his left hand he held two cards but made no use of them. The stadium was so large that each of his sentences took seconds to issue from the network of speakers and rebounded across the terraces. Ruth saw that Hitler was using this time lapse deliberately, sending each phrase through the system like a volley gaining power in the reverberation. After five minutes he raised his right forearm, still keeping the elbow as a pivot by his side, and the right hand with its palm down swept the phrases into flight. After ten minutes the arm was straightened, raised clear of the body with fist clenched, punching the air. Then, coming to climax, both arms sprang out to punctuate the final phrases:

> "The German nation has
> *(has, has, has . . .)*
> after all
> *(all, all, all . . .)*
> acquired its Germanic Reich.
> *(Reich, Reich, REICH . . .)*"

The words ignited the audience; a wave of applause seemed to explode over the stadium, reaching to the great mountains beyond the city—the cry of a manic destiny.

As Ruth watched, her eyes were drawn hypnotically to the back of Hitler's neck, a thin ribbon of skin visible between collar and hat, slowly turning pink and then crimson as he pumped his last words into the air. The disembodied applause now gone, he spun on his heels in a strange half step. His chin jutted upward, his eyes bulged, his face was transfigured by a spasm, and stepping back, he brushed Goebbels's shoulder. It was only a fraction of a second, barely a movement at all, but in it Ruth recognized the impulse of a man incapable of personal touch who in his ecstasy had been swept to a crippled, fleeting intimacy.

Afterwards Bedaux led the way down. Ruth heard the English voices murmuring: "Frightfully impressive"; "The man is here to stay"; "Lovely boys"; "What an example to us" (this from a throat carrying three strings of pearls); "I wonder, Harry, if we could find a house here, it's so nice. . . ." Ruth wondered if she was the only one with doubts, and then caught Lady Dunsinnan's eye and knew that she was not.

In the nearby restaurant a table was reserved for them. "I have something to announce," said Dunsinnan as they sat down. There was only mineral water to drink, but he poured it as though it were champagne. Raising his glass to Bedaux, he continued, "Charles here has been responsible for an important event—though, mind you, it's not official yet."

"It will be announced soon," said Bedaux.

"The Duke and Duchess of Windsor are coming to Germany, next month."

"They'll see Hitler?" Ruth was astonished.

"Why, *of course!*" There was a note of triumph in his voice. "The Führer is most anxious to meet His Royal Highness. Let me explain. Charles and the Duke have common interest, modern labor techniques. Through Dr. Ley, the director of the German Labor Front, Charles is opening a branch of his business here. He suggested the visit to Ley, and so it came to pass. What could be better?"

"A lot of people won't like it," said Lady Dunsinnan.

"A lot of people have much to learn," said Dunsinnan. He turned to Ruth: "Well, what did you think of it today?"

"I've never seen anything like it," she said truthfully and ambiguously.

Outside, a bank of photographers waited for the foreign visitors to leave. As they came down the steps Ruth thought for a second that behind one of the Leicas she saw a vaguely familiar face, but as she looked a second time another photographer moved into the place. While they stood waiting for their limousine a curious miniature car, bulbous like an inverted bathtub and painted an austere gray, drove off making a sound like whirring chains.

"What on earth is *that?*" said Ruth.

The count grinned. "They call it the People's Car—Volkswagen. One for every family, that is the promise."

"It'll never catch on," she said.

17

Southern England, October 1937

Seton parked his car at the end of the runway. He could hear the distinctive note of another distant engine at idling speed. There was a slight rise in the center of the runway, obscuring the plane from his view, and the sound was his only guide to its position. By the time the bark of the Rolls-Royce Merlin engine at full throttle reached him, the plane was already over the hump of the runway and coming straight for him. He saw the minutest of gaps open between its wheels and the tarmac, then the wheels tucked up into the wings. But the plane kept on coming at the same height, gathering speed all the while. Seconds before it reached the car, its nose rose and it bolted into the heavens, leaving Seton incredulous at its performance. The wings of the plane were unlike any others in the air: perfectly curved through their whole span, like a scimitar at the tip. Within half a minute it was above the cotton-wool flecks of cloud, a shrinking black dot against the blue, its sound fading.

Seton climbed out of the car and walked over to the grass; he kicked at it. The mingled smells of grass and aviation fuel touched off too many sensations. No tarmac then:

just rutted fields, tents, the wind sock, and a Flanders wind to fill it. Other smells: cordite, canvas, oil, blood.

From behind him, and only a little above, came first a rush of air and then the engine, flat out. The Spitfire did what they called the "daisy cutting" run across the field, diagonal to the runway, then climbed over on its back, flew upside down back across the field without apparently losing speed, rolled out the right way up, banked almost at right angles in a turn that Seton could not at first believe possible, throttled back, and came to earth as lightly and passively as a gull. Seton climbed back into his car and drove to the apron by the hangar. A man of about his own age climbed down from the Spitfire, wearing an all-white flying suit with the entrails of an oxygen system dangling at his chest. "What d'ya think?" he said, betraying his New Zealand origins.

Seton walked around the plane, touching it as though pressing the flanks of a thoroughbred. "Couldn't do a turn like that in a Camel—not without bits falling off," he said.

"It's not much like a Camel"—the pilot laughed—"no bloody fear." He bent under the wing to look at the landing gear. "You have to watch it, though, in those turns. Easy to black out—especially at my age."

Seton stopped and looked at him. "At least you can still qualify. Nobody flies one of these wearing a pair of glasses."

The pilot put an arm over Seton's shoulder in mock commiseration. "It's not the end of the world. It comes to all of us, if we live long enough." They walked over to the hangar.

"No vices, really?" asked Seton.

"I wouldn't say that. For all its looks, it's a delicate beast. They stripped everything down to the limit for speed. It's not as rugged as the Hurricane. There's something more serious, too." He became confidential. "The armament. I don't think those peashooters are going to be enough, from what I hear of the Luftwaffe. We need cannon. Can you do anything, Edward?"

"I'd heard about that," said Seton, stopping. "Keith, I'll be frank. The big worry now is sheer numbers, not just planes but pilots."

"You're telling me. You should see the people I'm getting. Still wet behind the ears."

"Still," Seton went on, "it is worrying about the guns. I've seen the reports from Spain. Ironically it's the Russians who've taught the Luftwaffe that lesson—their I-16's are ripping the Messerschmitts to bits."

"D'yer think we can stuff a cannon into *that* wing?"

Seton looked back at the Spitfire as the ground crew clambered over it, pampering every inch. "We'll have to."

"So you think it's coming, then?"

The single Spitfire seemed somehow too fragile. Alongside it on the grass stood a row of biplanes, their silver wings bearing a black-and-white checkered pattern. None had fired a shot in anger and—they both knew—none was now capable of doing so. Finally Seton answered:

"Let's go on that assumption, shall we?"

When Seton returned to London, he sought out his patron; they took another walk in the park.

"We're just not moving fast enough," said Seton.

"I fear you can put a lot of the blame for that at Lindbergh's door. Of course, you might imagine that listening to him, they would be panicked into action, but it seems to have the reverse effect. You know he's just been to Germany again?"

"Yes. I saw that."

"More and more horrors, about the invincible scale of the Luftwaffe. The result is that they're becoming totally paralyzed."

"Look," said Seton, finding the leisured cadences too complacent, "we can't let him get away with this. I *know* they're taking him for a ride—his figures are just not possible. I want a chance to shoot them down."

They walked in silence for a minute, then Seton's companion stopped. "Give me what you have, as concisely as possible, on paper. I'll see it reaches the right people. Then— you'll probably have to face the music."

A week later Seton was called to a windowless cavern in Whitehall. A dour clerk noted his name on a pad and waved him in, with a look of pity. Only one item furnished the walls, a 1910 Bartholomew map of the world, its pigment cracking to expose the linen beneath, the decomposition symbolic, since the map showed a world still girdled by pink, the British Empire at its peak. Seton put his briefcase on the table and, still standing, took out his papers and waited.

Two men entered. The one in uniform he recognized; the other, a civilian, was far younger. The elder man—small, compact, military, with a toothbrush moustache—was a marshal of the Royal Air Force. "Group Captain," he began, extending a hand, "I do hope you don't mind, I brought along Kincaid, from the ministry, just a watching brief." Kincaid nodded coolly. Seton was surprised to see that even Hugh Dowding, the new head of the R.A.F.'s Fighter Command, was not allowed to talk without a shadow bureaucrat.

They sat down, and Dowding continued: "I have, of course, read your paper. There is no need to go through it all." He glanced at Kincaid. "It has caused some perplexity in the ministry."

Speaking slowly, Kincaid said, "You seem to be implying that Colonel Lindbergh is gullible."

Seton unwound the fingers of his right hand. "We know from the amended budgets imposed on the German armed forces this year that the Luftwaffe is getting around fifty thousand tons of metal *less* than it asked for, *every month*. They cannot turn out anything approaching Lindbergh's figures. It's inelastic, finite. If you don't have the metal, you can't make the machines."

"What's *your* figure?" Dowding asked.

"It's a guess, but an informed guess. Their current plan calls for about seven thousand planes in the year. I'd be surprised if they did better than, say, five and a half. That is around half of Lindbergh's figure."

"Why did you produce this memorandum, now?" said Kincaid quietly.

"My value is that I don't have a sectional view—I look at the whole picture. I wanted to put a case that I thought was going by default."

"About the cannon," said Dowding, "I'll do what I can. Your assessment of Spain was very useful. Trouble is, we don't make any suitable cannon ourselves. The Czechs or the Belgians, it seems, are the people."

"It's urgent," said Seton.

Dowding's right hand glided over the table and settled on a pencil. "Quite so. Tell me, Seton, the Luftwaffe's top men are due here soon—Milch, Udet, Stumpf. The minister is rather keen on these exchanges. We haven't yet decided how much we should show them. What would be your advice?"

"In machines? Anything but the Spitfire. They must be kept in the dark on that, for as long as possible."

"I rather thought you might say that," said Dowding, with a tentative smile. "I will have to persuade the minister. He's rather keen to show it off."

* * *

Seton was still haunted by a vision of the Luftwaffe's commanders climbing over a Spitfire when the call came from Ruth. Already drinking whisky, he asked her to come to his flat. She was there within an hour.

She flicked her head to free a lock of hair. He took her coat, sensing agitation. "Sit down. Please. I'll get some coffee."

"Oh, no . . . your coffee is rotten. Make it tea."

She arranged herself on the sofa, putting her bag beside her, straightening her skirt, the nervousness unusual. He didn't speak until the tea was poured. He remembered how she had reacted to his avuncular nature when she had been ill, and he took care this time to conceal the instinct, though as he looked at her he felt it difficult to repress. He sat opposite her, a low table between them.

"Well . . . how *was* Germany?"

She settled her hands across her lap, fingers clasped, too tense. "I didn't realize, Edward, what it's all about, not until now. I don't know why I didn't, I should have. . . . God, *it was awful.*"

"Tell me."

Her hands unclasped and one of them went to the gold cord at her neck, tugging at it. "The crazy thing is, he seemed so *ordinary,* Hitler himself."

"You saw him?"

"Twice. The first time, just sitting there, in a restaurant, having lunch. The second time, the Nuremberg speech. He wasn't ordinary any longer. The real demagogue."

"I heard. On the wireless."

"The sound is only the half of it. But I understand now. His hold over them is really terrifying. But that wasn't the worst part. It was an art exhibition in Munich, what *they* call degenerate art. All the really good things—impressionists, cubists, Picasso. Something just snapped inside of me. I saw how it all added up—the signs about Jews, too many flags, silly saluting. It's *evil.*"

"Yes," Seton spoke quietly. "I wish more people knew that—understood it."

"That's it, isn't it? I'd like to pretend that things crept up on me until it became obvious. But I know it wasn't like that. I was shutting things out, all the time. It's very easy to do that, Edward. Not wanting to know. Still, that's not he same as knowing and not minding."

"Who, for example?" He knew already before she answered.

"Alastair, and his kind. There are a lot of English people there, in Munich. That awful Mitford woman. She arranged for Alastair to see Hitler."

"When was that?" Seton was still casual.

"When he took me to the restaurant where Hitler goes. Alastair was asked to the table, for about ten minutes. Alastair's been doing *a lot* of talking. Which reminds me—it seems to have been arranged for the Duke and Duchess of Windsor to go there, to meet Hitler."

"Are they, by God? When?"

"It's going to be announced soon."

"How much do you know about that—how was it arranged?"

About to answer, she stopped, suddenly alert, as though seeing outside herself for the first time in the conversation. "Are you fishing for something?"

Seton stood up and walked a few paces. When he turned and spoke, it was with a quiet gravity that she didn't know. "You'd better listen to this carefully. I wish I could tell you everything, but I can't. It won't be hard for you to guess why. I do have a professional interest in Dunsinnan—"

"You mean—all this time . . . ?"

"I'm afraid so."

"You've been using me—for information about him?"

"You must understand why—*now*."

"The hell I do!" Her hands clasped again, and she dipped her head, her eyes turning moist.

"You must have an idea of what he's up to—" Seton stopped, realizing that she was crying. In spite of himself he kept his voice firm: "He's a part of some kind of conspiracy. I don't know exactly how big. . . ."

She looked up at him. "You're pretty unscrupulous yourself, aren't you? *You used me*."

"I think you forget. You've made a confession yourself. You said you didn't want to know. Well—now that you *do* know, you might be able to do something about it, if you *really* care.

She wiped her eyes, leaving a streak on the cheek. "I know his beliefs, he's talked about it. But what can *you* do about that? It's not *illegal*, what they're doing or saying. It may not seem respectable, but it's not *criminal*, not yet, surely?"

"Somebody killed that man McCabe—or had him killed."

She froze into a momentary silence, then burst out, "You *knew* that, when I asked you about it?"

"Not at first, we weren't sure, but we are now."

"We? We *who?*"

Seton didn't answer.

She moved to the edge of the sofa, eyes now dry and accusatory: "You let me go to Germany, knowing that?"

"I'm afraid so."

"Well—*thank you!* There's not really much to choose between you, is there? At least *he* doesn't try to seem what he is not."

"It was better that you didn't know. You were safer that way."

"Oh. You cared about that, did you? Safer than *what?* Than if I had gone there as your willing spy, your Mata Hari?"

"I don't have the right to ask you to do that. But if you feel as strongly as you say you do, now—"

"Oh, *no.* . . ." The dawning understanding curtailed the protest.

"So you're not really committed, even now?"

"That's *not fair.*"

"How much does it take to get you involved, to find your conscience?"

She got up and walked to the window, talking half over her shoulder: "You really manipulate people, you know that? What *are* you, anyway? *Really?* You can't tell me that, of course. I can guess, though." She sighed.

"In the end we're all going to have to choose sides."

"That's funny—*really* funny. You know who said that to me last? Alastair." She turned from the window. "You people are all very anxious for the rest of the world to line up, aren't you? Well, I'll tell you, you and he can fight your war as you see fit. But don't involve me."

"So that moral outrage that you brought here this evening, that you couldn't wait to get off your chest—where does that end?"

Slowly she walked back to the sofa. Sitting down again, she said quietly, "You're a real shit, you know that?"

"Who were these people, with him?" Seton remained standing.

"Bedaux, the guy who owns the château where the Windsors married. He was on the *Graf Spee*, too. Albinoni, of course. Unity Mitford. They talked of getting rid of the *Times* man in Berlin—and your consul in Munich."

"Yes—well, they wouldn't find that too difficult."

"Give me a drink—a large one—would you?"

The fluctuations in her, from girl to woman, were like a kind of schizophrenia. The woman now prevailed, disturbing him more.

"What kind of terms are you on with him, now?" he asked, handing her the whisky.

"Not good." She fingered the gold cord and looked at her lap.

"But you get on with his mother?"

"If this is leading where I think it's leading. . . ."

"If you agree to help me again, I'll feel obliged to tell you what this is all really about."

She took several sips of the whisky and looked at him with a new boldness. "Okay. But first you tell me *your* story."

18

Canaris wore two oiled wool naval sweaters and a dark-blue serge seaman's jacket but was still cold and kept the horse at a gallop. It was the first really bitter morning of the winter. He called the wind the Prussian Chiller; it swept into Berlin from the east, laden with Baltic ice. As he reached a crossing of the lanes in the Tiergarten he saw a familiar rider converging on him from the south. General Beck had timed the interception with his usual precision, knowing Canaris's own regular habits. Canaris stopped, and Beck cantered up on his fine gray horse.

"General," nodded Canaris.

"Admiral." Beck seemed preoccupied. They broke into a trot in parallel, each looking ahead as they spoke.

"You've heard of the chancellery conference?" Beck asked.

"No more than that it took place."

"I was excluded also. We seem to be outsiders now."

"Only the party faithful admitted."

Beck held the reins short, arms crossed over his tunic and hands resting on his lap, turning red in the wind. His buckles glistened like mirrors. Still looking fixedly ahead, he said quietly, "It has gone far enough. Hitler will lead Germany into the grave. He must be stopped."

For months Canaris had known that this rigidly formal man had been forcing himself to a point of indiscretion, looking for some sign of Canaris's own views, having to overcome a torment of training and loyalties, awaiting some final provocation. But Canaris remained wary, his own inclination to avoid open commitment prevailing. "Is it *that* serious?" he said.

Beck turned to him: "We must talk. But not here. There is something you have to read. Will you come to my office?"

At his desk, instead of astride a horse, Beck looked strangely reduced, out of place, uncertain even of the impartiality of the walls. "Please. Look at this." He handed Canaris a plain file. It contained a memorandum written by Colonel Fritz Hossbach, Hitler's Wehrmacht adjutant, summarizing the conference called by Hitler a week earlier from which both Beck and Canaris had been excluded. As Canaris read the precise, matter-of-fact account his brows rose.

"You see?" said Beck. "For the first time it is all revealed—what he really wants, what he wants us to take for him. This idea of *Lebensraum*. Austria and Czechoslovakia, they will be the first targets."

Canaris looked up from the file. "No surprise, to anyone who has read *Mein Kampf*."

"It will bring war with Britain and France. We could not survive that."

Canaris stroked his nose. "The Führer appears to believe that the British won't care what happens to Czechoslovakia, and the French won't honor their treaties."

"The army is not ready for such a war. It does not want it." Beck got up and paced the room. "You remember, Admiral, when Hindenburg died, in 1934? We generals swore an oath of loyalty to Hitler, pledging the life of every soldier to his service."

Canaris nodded. "I, too."

"There was one general, Stieff, who did not take the oath. He said it was giving our fidelity to madness. At the time, well—I thought that was farfetched."

Canaris remained silent.

Beck returned to his desk. "We must break the spell this man has cast on our people."

Canaris did not conceal his reservations. "There is no basis for a popular revolt. The people know too well what Hitler has done for them. They are not going to believe that he is leading them to destruction."

"Then we must prove it—disclose what his plans really are."

"*Suicide!* That would be suicide, General." But Canaris was more shaken than he seemed. Finally he said, "You know, there could be another way, a safer way. If we could warn the British and the French. If they could be made to see what his real aims are, then they could call his bluff. It could be stopped without a shot being fired."

Beck was hesitant but interested. "You think so? The French and the British, they don't seem to know how weak we still are. After all, they let us take the Rhineland with a cardboard army."

Seton shot up from his chair like a rocket. *"What? They asked what?"* He took the telephone with him and nearly pulled it from its anchor. Pickles's excited voice was crackling through the receiver. Seton listened and then said, "Just slow down, Pickles, and repeat that again, will you?" The voice subsided, and as he listened Seton turned distractedly to the window, watching a flight of starlings swoop over the Foreign Office courtyard. "Right," he said at last, "how many people were there? Just the Germans and Swinton and the air marshals? No journalists, I hope? Thank God!" He sat down again. "Look, Pickles. For God's sake, make sure that nobody flashes a Spitfire at them, will you? Dowding assured me on that. They can climb all over the Furies, of course. Let's hope they think that's as far as we've got." He put down the phone and sat scowling at his pad. Then he lifted a second phone. He had to wait several minutes for a connection, then he was insistent: "Most urgent, as soon as possible. In ten minutes—by the bridge?"

As soon as he got to the lake in the park Seton could see the man, already on the bridge, and—an extraordinary deviation from character—he was throwing bread to the ducks from a brown paper bag. Still dipping into the bag as Seton reached him, the man said, "My dear Edward, I've never heard you so anxious. Pray, what is the matter?"

Seton looked at the impassive face and realized that this

man had survived by never revealing a single emotion. The feeding of ducks was an extension of this composure, shaming Seton into equanimity.

"I'm sorry, if it sounded a little hysterical. I felt you ought to know, at once. You'll have seen that we have the Luftwaffe's top men here, at the minister's invitation."

"Hmmm. I don't know that Swinton is any more prudent than Londonderry."

"No. Well, it couldn't be headed off. We have tried to limit the risk. There was a reception for them today, they've been up at the college at Cranwell. Milch was talking to an air marshal and, quite casually, as though remarking on the weather, he asked how we were getting on with R.D.F., our radio direction finding system."

"*Did* he, by God? And what did they say?"

"I think they choked on it, as well they might."

"So much for secret weapon number one."

Seton leaned over the parapet of the bridge. "It's even more important than that. If they know about R.D.F., which has been kept under the tightest of wraps, what else do they know about?"

There was silence for a minute, and the last of the bread was dispensed to the ducks.

"Do they have it, too, do you think—R.D.F.?"

"We don't know. They could. These things seem to occur by simultaneous osmosis; nobody has an edge for very long, the bloody scientific papers give away a lot, they all read each other's stuff. But R.D.F. is our last line of survival, it covers for the other weaknesses, which are legion. Dowding is staking his whole defense system on it. *If Milch realizes that. . . .*"

"I don't *believe* it!" said Ruth, her Boston inflection rising. "I just don't *believe* it. Here. Take a look for yourself." She passed the copy of the *New York Times* to Seton, who read:

THE DUKE'S DECISION TO SEE FOR HIMSELF THE THIRD REICH'S INDUSTRIES AND SOCIAL INSTITUTIONS AND HIS GESTURES AND REMARKS DURING THE LAST TWO WEEKS HAVE DEMONSTRATED ADEQUATELY THAT THE ABDICATION DID ROB GERMANY OF A FIRM FRIEND, IF NOT INDEED A DEVOTED ADMIRER, ON THE BRITISH THRONE. . . .

Seton looked up. "None of our papers has gone *that* far."

"Humph," said Ruth, taking back the paper. *"That's* why I get the *Times* sent here at such great expense. If you really want to know what's going on, don't rely on the London papers." She read through the account again and then, still volatile, said, "In Berlin they actually called out *'Heil Edward'!"*

Seton nodded sadly. "His right arm followed suit."

She seemed to have changed, almost imperceptibly but significantly. No longer did he feel that he was talking across a generation: Some experience had brought her to parallel comprehension. From the moment that she came back from Germany there had been this shift, a maturing in her—and an adjustment in him. Neglected notebooks lay with a stack of reference books. Other books began to appear, on recent European history. He wondered if, almost without knowing it, she had acquired a cause. Seton still hesitated to ask for more— the rancor of the deception remained in the background, not yet dispelled, flaring occasionally; and he changed the subject.

Her flat was again permeated by the pungent smell of onion and garlic. Seton's nostrils twitched. "You have been cooking that stuff for hours."

"Be patient! You know it can't be hurried." Gradually she had worn down his reserve. He had even removed his jacket. And this good-natured questioning of her cooking had an almost domestic intimacy to it, of which he seemed unaware but which she subtly tried to cultivate.

After the meal, fearing dyspepsia but not yet falling to it, Seton subsided into the embrace of the sofa while Ruth put on a record, "Love Is Good for Anything That Ails You," recorded at the Gleneagles Hotel in Scotland.

"Funny thing, that," he said, tapping his right foot and feeling inept, "I can never make out whether these singers are male or female anymore—perhaps it's an occupational hazard, in that business."

She folded herself alongside him. "It's the fashion— phony American accents add to the confusion." She put her head back on his shoulder, staring at the ceiling and feeling wilder than she seemed. She kicked off her shoes and put her legs over the end of the sofa, wriggling her toes. *"Ho hum,"* she said, and knew that he was getting uneasy. The needle stuck on the last chorus, altering the pitch. "Damn," she said.

"I'll get it." He got up, and escaped.

She turned, pulled her knees to her chin, and wrapped

her arms over her legs, looking at him from a face dipped down, so that her pupils rolled up and gave her a kittenish look, beginning deliberately to tease. "Play the other side," she said. "It's your song."

He looked at the title: "West End Blues." "Am I that dull? I'm sorry. Shall we try a dance?"

She got up and looked at his shoes. "You'll do me an injury. Take them off." He obliged, with strange misgivings. She stood on tiptoes and did an exaggeratedly formal move-ment, as if beginning a gavotte. He took her in his arms as the music began. After a few steps in his Savoy style she broke away with one arm and began to shake her body with the rhythm. "It's *jazz*, dammit! *Move!*"

Seton did his best, but nothing in his body could match her instinctive movements. She seemed frenetic, gradually en-circling him, dodging his arms, and then confronting him with a laugh. "Oh *well!*" she said as the music stopped, "you need a *lot* of training." Walking about in his stocking feet, he felt gauche. She felt sorry for him. "I'll make coffee," she of-fered, accepting the anticlimax. She ruffled his hair as she passed.

Over the coffee she became solemn: "Edward, what do you know about the Americans in Spain? Do you hear any-thing about them?"

Relieved, and surprised to be back to a manageable sub-ject, he said, "There's the Abraham Lincoln Brigade. About three thousand of them, on the Republican side."

"What about pilots?"

"Only a handful. Why do you ask?"

"Oh—nothing important, just something I saw. I was in-terested. Is it dangerous?"

"Flying, out there? It's not a way to reach old age. Two out of three never come back. But at least the Republicans have the edge—for the time being."

She feigned indifference. "Really?" She poured another coffee and tried to hold her hand steady.

When he had gone, she pulled out the letter again, and the photo: A young man in a leather flying suit stood by a plane with a Mickey Mouse emblem painted on the fin. Across it was scrawled a message, in ink: "Escuadrilla de Moscas, Brunette, Spain, July 1937—Russian leader, Russian plane, Yankee motor, Yankee pilot—what a team!" She sat down and stared at the picture and then read through the letter again. It had come via California and had taken two months to reach her. Her eyes were moist. She picked up a coffee cup and threw it at the wall.

"Damn, damn, *damn* airplanes!"

Though different in personality, Seton and Endmere understood each other and gently traded confidences. Seton knew of, but did not envy, the rakish side of Endmere (the dissolute *brio* of Regency England somehow survived in people like Endmere). But what *were* Endmere's real beliefs? In some unarticulated way Seton knew that Endmere shared with him a certain kind of Englishness: Seton whose family line came from rural clerics steeped in the high Anglican mores of Dr. Arnold's Rugby School, and Endmere whose family had produced gifted mountebanks in the mold of Byron, dandies, cardsharpers, and a bishop or two—a common and unadulterated fiber ran through both men.

They were in the Reform Club. Reclining in leather and well lunched, they enjoyed the peculiar security of such places where unwritten laws assured their members that conversations would not be overheard. Endmere pressed on Seton a huge ruby goblet of port that was called a Double Burgess in honor of its principal client.

"It's only a matter of time," said Endmere, half his face in lemon light from the window and the other half in shadow. "Chamberlain is not so foolish as to have a head-on row with Eden, nothing as *open* as that, it's not his nature. Eden is a man of principle. So Chamberlain has to undermine the principle just enough, and Eden will have no choice but to resign, thereby looking wet, which is how, I fear, those bullocks in the cabinet see him anyway."

"Yes," said Seton, "I can see that a man of principle might be an embarrassment." He watched a gout-laden duke waddle painfully to a chair and then collapse into it like a felled bison. "But on what issue will that be tested, do you know?"

"Mussolini, most likely. Eden's very stubborn on that. Won't talk to the Wops at all. Chamberlain isn't so fastidious. As a matter of fact, it's already started." He pierced a cigar and sniffed it, running it under his nose. "There's a back-door route. Austen Chamberlain's widow lives in Rome. A messenger picks up Italian notes from her, delivers to somebody in Tory party headquarters here, who gives it directly to Chamberlain, behind Eden's back—it never goes through the Foreign Office. Or, as an alternative, through the Italian embassy

here and then to Chamberlain via Sir Horace Wilson in
Downing Street." Endmere drew so keenly on the cigar that
its tip, in ignition, flared scarlet. "That man—Wilson—can
stand watching. All the strings converge in his hands. I doubt
anyone's enjoyed as much hidden influence since Cardinal
Wolsey."

Despite a shearling coat, thick boots, a scarf, and a hat
Seton was frozen to the bone. A junior airman slipped into the
hut, allowing a blast of wind to emphasize the bleakness, but
he brought two mugs of steaming noxious tea, which Seton
gratefully shared, gulping it down before the taste registered.
"Do they still put bromide in this stuff?" he said, wiping his
lips and pushing away the mug.

In the darkness a weak square of light came from a small
screen in the center of a large console. Around the console
stood other bulky equipment, electric cables trailing from it.
Seton stood behind a man seated at the console, who was peering into the screen through a hood. The screen glowed incan-
descently with uneven strength and was flecked by bright
spots. Across the center of the screen ran a thick horizontal
bar of stronger, green light. Intermittently this green bar con-
torted and then streaked into short vertical bars like a fever
chart. The man pulled his head clear of the canopy and beckoned to Seton: "Here, look at that—quick, while it lasts."

Seton leaned over the man's shoulder and squinted into
the canopy. The green bar faded, rematerialized, ruptured,
smudged, and then held in place with the vertical shoots bob-
bing up and down.

"Doesn't mean much, I'm afraid," said Seton. "Where
are they supposed to register?"

"Each break in the horizontal—that's an interception."

"Can you tell how far off they are?"

The man consulted a pad on the console and adjusted a
dial. "Let's see, the angle is . . . well, roughly, as near as I
could say, about thirty miles."

Seton pushed his hands deeper into the coat and stamped
his feet. "So. That would give us about ten minutes? Hardly
enough time to get airborne and catch them—even with a
Spitfire."

The hut was on a hill overlooking the Thames estuary
near the port of Chatham. The wind came directly off the
North Sea, and the hill was the first obstacle it met in its
course from Norway. When, once more, the door opened, it

was nearly ripped off its hinges. A man in uniform, almost doubled up, pressed himself in, holding down his cap. With an effort he got the door closed and slid home a wooden bar. "Jesus *Christ!*" he said, "we chose a good night for it."

Seton's face was outlined in the glow of the cathode-ray tube. "It seems to be working—once or twice," he said.

"That's good, because nothing else is. There's supposed to be a total blackout in Rochester and Chatham, but nobody told them to switch off the pier lights at Southend, so it looks like an amusement park. In fact, that's about what it is, even an Italian navigator could find his way up the river. And that's not all—" He broke off and peered over Seton's shoulder at the screen. "See that? It's not what you think it is. The poor buggers are chasing each other's tails. The Hurricanes from Biggin Hill are believed to be the Blenheims from Northolt, and the Blenheims from Northolt are having a nice clear run without opposition, so if they really *were* the Heinkel One-elevens they're pretending to be, well, cheerio, Chatham. What a bloody mess."

Seton stamped his feet again, but the cold had frozen out any feeling in them. "We have a long way to go, it seems," he said.

"That's right, we do," said the flying officer. "How long do we have?"

Seton inclined his head to the screen again as it seemed to disintegrate into a snowstorm of green flecks. "What's happened?"

The operator looked up. "*Kaputt!* Something's blown again. It's always happening. And we can't get to the mast, not in this weather."

Seton was grateful. At last he could pick his way down the path from the hut to where the staff car was parked. He was enjoying the rare facility of official transport, as the guest of the Air Staff who had organized the air-defense exercise. The rudimentary radio direction finding system was having one of its crucial trials: Many of the Air Staff were unconvinced of its effectiveness and, Seton knew, would remain so after tonight. The frustrations of the flying officer were echoed in most of the people he had seen. He knew that if Britain was to have any chance of adequate defense, this still ramshackle equipment would have to be transformed.

"*How long do we have?*" The unanswered and unanswerable question stuck in his mind.

19

Baden-Baden was a curious place to meet, but then, Dunsinnan had become a rolling stone. As arranged, Lady Taverner took a room in a hotel near the Kurhaus casino and waited. She had a view across the foothills to the Rhine, a softer face of Germany with as yet little trace of the Nazi presence. The gaming tables of the Kurhaus had been revived in 1933 and now drew the drifting, displaced roués of Europe whose old haunts had been washed away by the war and the Weimar and who had now settled into Baden-Baden for their last resort. Alongside these fragile and aloof people flowed another stream of life, gawping trippers filing through the rooms craning their necks at ceilings with lascivious frescoes—a new bourgeoisie glimpsing fragments of a lost regime.

The Hotel Frankfurter Hof—"wholly renovated, a home-from-home, Manager's Wife English"—seemed to be a practical joke of Dunsinnan's. It was too genteel, with a polished mustiness that warned of another English connection in the kitchens. Rhubarb tart was on the dessert menu, to aid geriatric bowels into motion.

The morning after she arrived, a black-booted chauffeur came with a note, to be handed to her personally. The lapse in accommodation was being put right. "Please come back in an hour," she said, wondering why Drummond was not there. She breakfasted and repacked, annoyed by the inconvenience.

The black Mercedes limousine took her along a mounting and spiralling road until she was able to look back and see Baden-Baden well below and, beyond it, a silver line, which was the Rhine. The car turned between two red marble pillars, each crowned by a gunmetal Minotaur, and pulled up a gravelled drive to a villa, a stucco structure with a timber frame.

Dunsinnan was waiting on the steps, pink and wind-blown, wearing plus fours and a black leather jerkin. He himself opened the door of the limousine.

"Sorry about the overnight delay," he said. "This place

had no spare rooms until this morning. I hope you liked the hotel."

She got out and straightened her skirt. "I couldn't have survived another night of it." She turned to look back at the view and inhaled pine and mountains, purging the last trace of the English cooking.

"You'll like this place," he said.

She turned, brushing his chest with her breasts: "I like the black leather." She plucked at the jerkin. "It suits you."

The German chauffeur pulled her valise from the trunk of the Mercedes and followed them into the villa. A small, owlish woman with stout trunks for legs curtseyed as they came through the door.

"This is Elsa, she runs the place," said Dunsinnan, perfunctorily sweeping her on past the woman.

Lady Taverner's nostrils twitched. "What on earth is that scent, Alastair—not your cologne?"

He sniffed the air. "Of course not. No, I'm afraid that's the mark of a departed guest. Rather *lingering*, isn't it?"

"I'm glad Bedaux isn't," she said.

"And I'm glad you've arrived." He took her arm and led her upstairs.

So, too—in a different sense—was von Klagen. The vigil in Baden-Baden had grown monotonous; the town's ossification made him listless and dull in the eye. His usual skill in corrupting domestic staff had met stubborn resistance in Elsa, whose Alsatian nature combined French perversity with Rhineland obtuseness. Finally he had increased the bribe but even then was dissatisfied with the collaboration and resorted to veiled hints about the Gestapo. There was also the problem of the chauffeur. When not driving the Mercedes, this man ranged the grounds of the villa and kept no predictable routine, making von Klagen's several attempts to enter both risky and futile. The chauffeur—and of this, von Klagen had no doubt—was a gift from Heydrich.

Bedaux, Albinoni, and others had come, and so, too, for an afternoon, had Schellenberg. Margery Taverner was a welcome addition to the familiar entourage. Von Klagen had easily found the details of her identity at the Hotel Frankfurter Hof and had no trouble in guessing whom she had come to see. There had been hints before in England and Switzerland. And given, for once, reliable advance warning by Elsa, he was in place when they entered the Green Room of the Kurhaus on the second evening, she in a full-length silver dress that left her back bare to the base of the spine, and a conceited-looking Dunsinnan in a quilted smoking jacket.

They were the most crisply minted couple in the casino, almost offensive in their glamor. The croupiers were obsequious, transfixed by her scented bosom as it hung over the baccarat table. She flicked glances around her and caught several faces paralyzed by baleful impotence. She murmured suggestions as Dunsinnan recklessly lubricated the casino's treasury. For those who could just meet the minimum stake of twenty Reichsmarks, his flow of notes was the smell of another world, of Monte Carlo ahd Biarritz where only royal senility was admitted. Von Klagen could not take his eyes off her back: The shoulders melted into an arching, creamy glacier divided by the merest declension of bone and agonizingly terminated where new surfaces formed, as though her bosom found symmetry with her haunch, and in the light of the chandeliers he saw a wisp of honeyed down.

He realized that there was a kind of sadism in Dunsinnan's conceit, in possessing this exquisite creature—this *event*—and his financial virility, too. Like gods descended for a bacchanal, they taunted and then left, aloof and ethereal. Hopelessly bewitched, von Klagen sank into inadequate dreams. Had he known the reality, he might have been surprised.

Wearing only the black leather jerkin, Dunsinnan was spread-eagled on the bed, hands and feet tied to each corner post. The silver dress had given way to knee-length suede boots and nothing else.

"It may not quite be the Salon Kitty," she said, standing over him, "but we can improvise."

He smiled nervously. "Take it very *slowly*, please."

Elsa, at the keyhole, was beginning to feel a cramp in her legs. A coarse hand came over her mouth, and another pulled her back from the door. The chauffeur moved without a sound, his look enough to freeze her cry and leave her safely mute. He bent down and watched for five minutes. The pine floor on the landing flexed with the boards on the other side of the door, and they heard successive but muffled cries and then sobs in the rhythm of the movement. Finally the chauffeur rose and turned to Elsa with a tilt of the head; his raised eyebrows told of a man who had seen much but knew that there was ever more to learn. Safely in the kitchen, he said, "Never breathe a word about this—to *anyone*." She knew better than to consider it but understood it would not stop with him.

At breakfast Lady Taverner seemed able to trespass on Dunsinnan's most guarded ground with impunity; he, for the moment, remained in a strange mood of compliance. For once the relationship of the night extended to the day. She noticed that while he was in this state his jaw had an abnormal defensive movement, working sideways, leaving flecks of egg on his lower lip.

"You know, without your mother within reach you're better."

"Really?"

"Must she *hover* so?"

"That's why I like it here. She doesn't."

"But why play the fugitive? Why not have her stay in Scotland, leave you alone?"

"Maybe."

"I suppose she's still trying to land you with the American girl."

The jaws sawed on a piece of toast, and then he looked up. "No, not anymore."

"Pretty little bitch."

"You think so? I suppose so, in a dark kind of way." A thought struck him: "Anyway—when did *you* see her?"

"Ah. That would be telling."

"She has the American disease. Idealism."

"Meaning, I imagine, that she disapproves of the Nazis."

"They're so *unworldly*, the Americans."

"Well, that's one word for it." She sipped the coffee. "I hear that Halifax is over here—what's that about?"

Dunsinnan put down his napkin. A mannerism of tilting back his head and looking over his nose as he talked returned. "There's quite a bit going on. Officially Halifax is here for the hunting exhibition. In point of fact he's seeing Göring *and* Hitler. I think he'll understand Göring better. Edward's such a snob—that's something Göring understands, even likes in the English; but Hitler—he doesn't like airs."

"Hunting? That's quite a freemasonry, isn't it? Here and in England."

He looked at her sharply. "Yes. Very useful."

"You spent rather wildly last night."

"They need all they can get in hard currency, pounds especially. It's why they're so keen on tourism."

"So *that's* why you. . . ."

He smiled. "I don't look on it as a wasted investment."

The rain came horizontally across Leicester Square, and
Seton held the umbrella like a shield, providing Ruth with
some shelter and himself with none. A taxi mercifully appeared; the driver was a cockney comedian of a kind Seton
could happily live without.

"Been for a swim, guvnor?" he said, pushing down the
Hired sign.

"Bayswater Road," Seton snapped. The driver recoiled.
"Don't take on, guv, only jokin'. Filthy night."

The umbrella jammed in the door, and a rivulet of rain
spilled from it into Seton's neck. Wrestling with the umbrella
while the cab waited, getting wetter by the second, he only
just held himself in check. From inside the cab Ruth laughed
out loud: "Oh, Edward! You're like a drowned rat!"

He heaved himself and the umbrella, only half retracted,
into the seat and felt the water running down his back. "Damnation!" he said.

She squeezed his right arm. "Tut tut tut!"

He sighed.

"Why don't we go to my place—it's nearer," she said.
"You need wringing out." Without giving him a chance to
reply, she tapped the partition. "Driver, Davies Street, *not*
Bayswater Road. Near Claridge's." The driver nodded but
cursed to himself, as he had to turn back through the square.

She looked again at Seton, imposing the choice without a
word.

Fraser looked on him pityingly as they entered the lobby.
"My word, sir, you have caught it."

Seton sneezed. " 'Fraid so." He left a wake of water like
a dog coming out of a stream. The more miserable he seemed,
the more pleasure it gave Ruth; she was unaccustomed to such
ready submission from him.

Inside the flat she took his jacket. "Crazy, not going out
with a coat," she said, shaking it. The neck of his shirt was
sodden, and the silk backing of his vest rippled. "Here"—she
steered him into the bathroom. "Dry yourself down. I'll fix
something." She closed the door on him.

He came out wearing her terry bathrobe, grinning like a
small boy. "Sorry to be such a nuisance. . . ."

"Take this." She handed him a steaming mug.

"What on earth . . . ?" He swallowed the liquid, then coughed.

"It's all right—it kills all known diseases."

"But what *is* it?" He took a second mouthful and held it down.

"My own potion. You remember how you ministered to me when I was sick? This is my revenge. One part bourbon, one part Jamaica rum, one part tomato juice—and other things you'd best not know about."

"Ye gods! I'll never walk again."

"Don't make such a fuss!" She looked him up and down. "You look just dandy in that robe."

"I *feel* like Oscar Wilde."

"I hope not," she laughed. "Come, sit down."

"That's odd," he said, looking at the low table, "I didn't realize you read things like that."

"Oh, that—*The Field?* That shows how little you know about me." She broke into an aped English accent: "I'm a terrific hunter, foxes, doncherknow. Tally ho, old bean!" She relented. "Okay, seriously, then. I do ride, you know. I was looking through this copy and came upon something I thought you should see." She picked up the magazine. "Here, look."

He saw the photographs. "Ah, yes. The hunting exhibition in Berlin. Göring, with his severed heads, only this time they're animals."

"All very sporting, isn't it?" she said, sitting down. "Feeling better?"

"Not like Oscar Wilde anymore."

"That's good. Wasn't the movie fine—worth the soaking?"

"I'm not normally a fan of that kind of thing, but it was awfully well done. That chap who played Baby Face—what was his name?"

"Bogart. Humphrey Bogart."

"Odd-looking bird, rather, well—"

"Sinister?"

"Not quite. Tough, but vulnerable."

She looked at the yellow bathrobe. "Just like you."

He drained the last of the drink. "I think I've lost the use of my legs."

"My God," she said, "what's that *smell* . . . ?" She put a hand to her mouth and let out a sophomoric shriek. "It must be your shirt. I put it over the radiator." She disappeared into the bathroom and returned holding a steaming garment. "Er—I hate to have to show you this." She turned back the collar and saw a scorch mark—and the label. "Turnbull and Asser, oh dear! Maybe I had better buy you a new one."

"At their prices? I couldn't let you." He smiled ruefully. "It doesn't matter, really."

The joke embraced a strange, intimate, domestic understanding, introducing a new ease between them.

"I was supposed to be taking you to supper."

"In a yellow bathrobe?" Damp stockinged feet and trouser cuffs, still sodden, showed under the robe, and his woollen undershirt with its old-fashioned high neck protruded from the top. Thus stripped of his social armor, he looked younger, better. She curled her toes in pleasure at the sight and blessed the luck of the rainstorm. "No," she said, "I'm not going to be seen in public with *anyone* who looks like that. We'll stay here. Nothing special, just an omelette, okay?"

He felt cornered and didn't mind. "You seem to have the advantage."

Camped at the kitchen table, gratefully scraping the last of the omelette from the plate, Seton saw the contentment in her eyes and saw that the old mistrust had finally gone.

"I had a letter from Father," she said, taking the plate. "He asked after you."

He got up and followed her to the washbasin, taking a towel, ready to wipe. "He's still prospering?"

"Yes. And he told me something interesting—who the new ambassador here is going to be. A very odd choice for Roosevelt to make. Joe Kennedy."

"Is that good or bad?"

"He'll stand for money, wherever it points."

Seton frowned. "It could be absolutely crucial, who comes here now. We may need all the help we can get."

She handed him a plate. "I know. But there are strange things going on at home. Did you see that picture in the paper, of Nazis marching through New York? They call themselves the German-American Bund. They claim Lincoln as the first fascist. They think of themselves as *patriots*."

He was not good at wiping plates. She looked at him sideways, a satisfied grin on her face.

"The infection could spread," he said. "It seems to offer a lot of people what they're looking for."

"I think," she said carefully, "that to *really* understand what they're about, you have to be a Jew. Then you don't have any doubts, none at all. . . ."

* * *

"How would you like to take the waters?" Dunsinnan asked.

"You think I need that?" she said doubtfully.

"Good for the body—if not the soul."

Having walked round the spa, they were now drinking chocolate at the Kurhaus.

"It's self-defeating," she said. "You lie in the sulphur bath, embalmed in rose petals, and they serve you *brioches* on a tray."

"You've done it before, then?"

"Not here. In Schwalbach, years ago."

"There's a lot I don't know about your past."

"My *past?*" She laughed. "You make it sound scandalous."

He pursed his lips.

"No," she said, "you don't know everything."

"My father, you mean?"

"You're not unlike him—in ways." She looked about the room, at the chandeliers with stained bulbs. Rooms like this held dead music as they held dust. "Your father was a survivor. While all the others were falling he came up. Is that what you're up to?"

"I think it's time we went back—back to London."

"We?"

"You'll come?"

"I'm going to Rapallo. The contessa asked me."

"I didn't know. . . ."

"We've mended our fences."

"We had better make the most of it tonight, in that case."

The spa did not agree with von Klagen's leg; far from proving therapeutic, the baths seemed to exacerbate the pain. He couldn't bother to follow them back up to the villa again, and he was tiring of the game. Piekenbrock had teased him too much with stories of the cabaret. He was preparing a valid case for nosing back into the files on Dunsinnan in the Central Registry, and another prospect it held. Only one thing detained him here, and that was unattainable: the vision of Margery Taverner.

Thus resolved and already packed, he found that Dunsinnan was leaving—on his own. While the chauffeur took Dunsinnan to Strasbourg, Elsa came into the town to arrange another journey, to Rapallo.

Von Klagen called Piekenbrock and, after a mild argument, was allowed to travel south instead of north. He devised for himself a new personality and profession, testing his manner in the mirror by thinking of Ribbentrop. He would put more emphasis on his leg; perhaps she would find it within her to take pity.

He waited until the train got to Basle where they changed to the Genoa Express, and then timed perfectly his arrival in the dining car. She was just taking a table facing him as he walked down the aisle, limping, wearing his most tragic face.

"May I?" he said, pausing tentatively by the opposite seat.

"Of course." She smiled.

Von Klagen's progress into Italy came near to causing a rupture between Canaris and Piekenbrock.

"I don't want agents in Italy," said Canaris, eyes raw from insomnia. "There's a new situation to consider there. Officially, they are allies. It could lead to trouble."

"This is a new line. I think he had to follow it through."

Canaris was mocking: "I can imagine why." He paced the floor and spoke with his back to Piekenbrock: "How many women *are* there in Dunsinnan's life? I think I've lost count."

Piekenbrock persisted: "I think this one is different. It may be what we have needed all along."

Canaris was suddenly amenable: "Very well, for the moment. Perhaps the American girl was a coincidence, after all. But Seton—that man makes me uneasy. I don't know why."

20

As usual Fraser gave Ruth her bundle of mail as she went out, and on this morning, feeling lighthearted and frivolous, she stuffed the envelopes into her coat and forgot them. She had read a glowing review of a new young actor playing Macbeth, Laurence Olivier, and went to the New Theatre to get two tickets, a surprise for Seton before he left London to spend Christmas with his mother in Wiltshire. From the theatre she walked through the park and then along Piccadilly to see the Christmas window displays. On an impulse she went into Fortnum and Mason and bought scandalous luxuries. Then she sat at the soda fountain for an early lunch and ordered Welsh rarebit, scorched cheese on toast. Then, slipping off her coat, she remembered the mail.

Waiting for the food, she looked at the three envelopes. One was recognizably from her mother, another from a friend, and a third from California, in unfamiliar script but with a familiar postmark. She hesitated and then opened this envelope first.

The smell of the toasted cheese was its own messenger. The waitress smiled and asked if she wanted sauce—the strange spicy sauce that the English seemed to spray over their bland food. Ruth didn't hear the request; the waitress pouted and moved away, having banged the sauce bottle on the counter.

After the first few lines of the letter her eyes seemed to lose focus. She felt fiercely hot, then began to shake. She put the letter on the counter and held to the chair with her left hand, whitening at the knuckles. Quietly, almost inaudibly, she sobbed. The waitress returned and changed her manner: "You all right, miss?"

Ruth looked up: "Yes, thank you."

The waitress looked dubious, saw the open letter, looked at Ruth, again, brushed a hand on her apron nervously, and moved away. Ruth slipped a ten-shilling note from her bag, which covered the bill by at least a factor of six, and slipped off the chair, pulling her coat behind her. She clutched the open letter with the unopened envelopes in her left hand and prayed that she could reach the door and a taxi.

Pickles took the call first, and when Seton came on the line, his voice was jocular and expectant.

"Edward?" She sounded frail.

"What is it?" He was instantly alert.

"I'm afraid I have to go home, to the States. Something has happened."

Seton tensed. "Family?"

"No, no—they're all fine. No, it's something personal—I'm sorry, but I can't explain, not now. I have to go to California."

"That will be a difficult trip, this time of the year."

"I know, the crossing. But I have to go. I can get on a boat tomorrow. I. . . ."

"Is there anything I can do?" He could tell how distressed she was.

"No—no, thank you. I'm sorry—about it being so sudden. Don't worry, I'll be okay. I just wanted you to know. . . ."

"I can come round, this evening—if you need a hand." He sensed a risk of intrusion.

"Well . . . no, thank you, but—I have to take care of some things. I'll write you, of course." She was silent for a few seconds. Then she said, "Take care."

The next morning there was a note from her, enclosing two theatre tickets: "I hope you can use these, Edward. They were meant for us. Have a good Christmas. Please don't worry about me. Love, Ruth."

It was only after several days that Seton was honest with himself about the sense of loss. It caused him to question many assumptions until then secure, and to see the past more sharply. There were prosaic symbols, like the scorched shirt, which surprisingly overshadowed the more portentous moments, even the exposure of his deception. It was the scorched shirt that was—he now saw—adventitious and catalytic. Another side of his nature intervened, telling him that it would pass. Then he realized she might have gone for good.

21

England, March 1938

On the second hole of the Stoke Poges golf course in Buckinghamshire a thickset red-haired man lined up his iron for a shot. He felt his balance on the balls of his feet, flexed his arms, and took the iron on a trial curve. They had said that the golf in England would be good, and this was his first taste of it. The stroke was made, and the ball followed a perfect arc over 128 yards—and landed plumb in the cup. Joseph Kennedy had posted notice of his arrival in a way that the

English newspapers could find generous space for, even at a time of crisis. Not only was the new American ambassador a break from the mold of Brahmins who were usually preferred for the post, not only did he have nine children and a winning wife—he could bag a hole in one.

Lady Dunsinnan folded the paper with a long sigh, then put it down. Her son lay back on the chesterfield, reading his own paper and enjoying the account of Ambassador Kennedy's game. He glanced away and caught her look.

"What's the matter?"

"Austria is the matter. It's just the beginning, isn't it?"

He swung his legs off the chesterfield and turned to face her, knowing the warning signs. "Not one bomb was dropped," he said. "It was perfectly peaceful. I don't know what the fuss is about."

"Oh. You don't?" The lilting edge of her accent shaped the challenge.

"No, I don't. What's happened, really? Germany and Austria, two peoples with the same nationality, have been reunited, never should have been split. I should have thought *you* could see the historical parallel. It's like the Act of Union, Scotland and England—different but together. Perfectly healthy, natural union."

She pitched her chin upward. "Your history is weaker than I thought. I don't think the Act of Union is a good precedent. *That* was rape by the English."

He laughed, not attempting mediation. "That's the difference in the Dunsinnans, Mother—the male and the female. Don't forget, it was the male line that moved up there to civilize the barbarians, where even the Romans had failed."

Her temper was already incandescent. "Oh, is *that* it?" With each word her accent broadened. "Well, as a Gordon I know better, a lot better." She stood over him. "Yes, you're a good example, I must say. Not content with *civilizing* the Scots, you now want to join that *very* civilizing influence in Germany—that's a real chip off the old block." She spun around and walked off, her small heels clicking in anger.

He picked up the paper again. One of the pleasures of provoking his mother was to bring out the Annie Gordon rather than the Lady Dunsinnan, to see that other part of his own nature, a kindling force rather than the calculating one that normally prevailed. This perception brought him to the business of the day. There was the question of Drummond.

Was it, he wondered, a case of the devil making too good a job of his apprentice? Ever since Drummond had replaced McCabe as manager of the estate, he had dismissed and recruited staff, until now he had control over the minutest details. His mother complained—and he himself was bothered: Drummond had become indispensable.

This morning, dipping his dark head at Dunsinnan with the usual mechanical deference (so correct that it bordered on insolence), Drummond said, "For a few days I've had a funny feeling, of being followed—nothing I can pin down, mind you." His dank breath came too close.

Dunsinnan raised a brow: "Oh?" He moved clear of the baleful face. "Perhaps, after all, one little accident might not have put them off."

Drummond was behind him in one pace, hovering: "I think, with everyone being so edgy, sir, we should take more care, *especially* today." His hair was plastered with Brylcreem, the sweet scent countering his breath.

Dunsinnan paced to the other side of the room, looking out into Eaton Square, as though in one glance he might apprehend the supposed pursuer. "You may be right."

So they went west instead of east from the square, down the King's Road, squealed through some of the smaller streets of Chelsea, slipped across the Albert Bridge to the south bank of the river, then turned east as far as Tower Bridge, recrossing the river there. Dunsinnan thought the whole maneuver tediously dramatic but indulged Drummond. By the Tower they turned right into the seedy world of Wapping, along streets still cobbled, the Bentley so conspicuous that rude faces stared at them. Warehouses like cliff faces rose at each side of the street, cutting out direct light. Then suddenly the line of warehouses broke into a small square lined on two sides by Regency terraces, a small lawn between them, an oasis of green in the gray. Even Dunsinnan's philistine nature responded to the relief.

They drove down one side of the terrace and parked by the river wall, where there was a small slipway. Dunsinnan stepped out and sniffed the air, aware of an alien pungency. The little square, overlooked by spice warehouses, was impregnated with oriental bouquets—turmeric, cumin, mace. Dunsinnan disliked spices; there was, he felt, something corrupting in them. He turned to the river. Opaque and viscous, it left a watermark of corrosive scum on the slipway.

An open dinghy was tied to the mooring; a man was at

the oars. He gestured to them to sit in front of him. The dinghy wallowed as they climbed in, and they crouched quickly to steady it. The oarsman cast off, and with only the lightest touch on the oars he steered out into the current so that they drifted downstream. Six hundred yards or so to the east floated a small yacht with a single funnel rising from a glass-framed saloon. The dinghy pulled alongside, and they boarded.

It was surprisingly warm in the saloon—the oily warmth of a heated greenhouse. There was a long leather banquette and a low table covered in an elaborate lace cloth. No one else was visible. Drummond remained at the door while Dunsinnan sat at the table. The lower half of the saloon's windows were misty with spray. The boat had its own low chorus of straining timber and lapping water, punctuated a moment later by steps and the squeak of brass.

Two men appeared in outline, one familiar to Dunsinnan and one not. Walther Schellenberg stepped forward with a handshake. "This is Fritsch. Karl Fritsch." He introduced the svelte man.

"Ah, yes," said Dunsinnan as the man shook his hand, "I know the name."

"Please," said Schellenberg, indicating the seats. He looked at the table, then frowned and walked to a bell at the door. "Coffee?" Dunsinnan nodded. Drummond faded away, and a white-coated attendant appeared, taking an impatient command from Schellenberg. Schellenberg rubbed his hands. "The river is not warm."

Fritsch spoke in English: "I am to be your new contact here. With things going so well"—he looked at Schellenberg and then back to Dunsinnan—"we need more regular communication, outside the embassy, of course."

"Of course," said Dunsinnan, lighting a cigarette.

The boat began to sway as a tug passed. Schellenberg grimaced and held on to the table. "Water is not my element." The boat settled down once the wash passed. "Now—" He stopped, irritated, while the attendant brought the coffee and disappeared. "Now, Lord Dunsinnan, you expect, with Eden gone, things to move our way faster?"

"There are still powerful influences against us," Dunsinnan replied.

Fritsch smiled knowingly. "One, in particular. We think of the same person, do we not? Churchill? Too wild to be given office—but too much in evidence to be ignored."

"That's very shrewd of you, Herr Fritsch," said Dunsinnan. "Yes, he is a major obstacle. But the British would need to be pushed a lot further before they turned to such a man."

"And you think Austria may have pushed them a little in that direction?" Fritsch asked.

"It will pass," said Dunsinnan, looking at Schellenberg.

"The point of this meeting," said Schellenberg, seeing Dunsinnan's impatience, "is that you should know of something called Plan Z."

"A little melodramatic," said Dunsinnan.

"Not our title," said Schellenberg, "nor our idea. It is, so to speak, a gift from the gods. Since Fritsch is our man here, he can explain."

Fritsch moved earnestly to the table. "We have discovered that Sir Horace Wilson has drawn up this plan. Its objective is for the prime minister to visit the Führer."

"At last!" said Dunsinnan excitedly.

"Well—not exactly *at last*. There is no date for it, yet. Chamberlain has to be persuaded. But the germ has been planted. Unlike his predecessor, he is not averse to travel."

"So you see," said Schellenberg, "all of your original objectives may well be met."

Dunsinnan leaned back, drawing on the cigarette. "Quite so. It shows how to get things done here, the way things have always been done." He looked at Schellenberg: "If you know the right people."

"How *was* the Duke when you last saw him?" said Schellenberg.

On the north bank of the river, opposite the yacht, von Klagen eased himself from the platform and watched his step on worn wooden slats. Back on the planked floor, he recovered his bag and put away the binoculars. A pocket of wind, trapped in the loading bay, stirred into a vortex that spun across the floor and spent itself into another layer of the exotic dust. He nodded to the foreman, still beaming at von Klagen with gratitude for the unexpected windfall. "Cheerio, mate," called the man.

In the street von Klagen dusted himself down and then realized that his coat had an indelible taint of spices. He walked along the cobbles, shivering in the sunless canyon. First the spices, and now a brewery. In Wapping people must be marked for life with one smell or the other. Accidental stigmata like this annoyed him and reminded him of the elaborate clues of Sherlock Holmes in the Limehouse stories. It suggested carelessness on his part—and the results of his observation were meagre. Not even a lip-reader would have made anything of it.

England played its tricks on him. There was a gaffe with a pipe he bought: Unwittingly he selected one with a thin mouthpiece designed for use with dentures. The shopkeeper pointed out the mistake, but von Klagen stood on his pride and kept it. He smoked a brand of tobacco called Dr. White's Presbyterian Mixture, which the advertisements said had been the secret of Stanley Baldwin's composure; the idea of sharing tastes with the most otiose of British prime ministers gave him covert amusement, till his landlady in Kensington revealed that her poor departed husband liked the same brand, and looked incautiously at von Klagen.

The one bathroom in the boardinghouse had a volatile machine, called a geyser, for providing hot water; it greedily consumed coins in a meter before gurgling anything. He lay in the tepid bath as the thing shuddered and fumed; the spices, he discovered, had penetrated to the skin. Carbolic and sponge were not abrasive enough; the scent persisted. Retreating back up the stairs in his gown, he saw a turbanned head staring up at him and pointedly slammed his door. Better things were in prospect.

When, later, he limped into the Cafe Royal, the mirrored walls made him feel self-conscious. Margery Taverner was already at the table, and already with champagne. She nodded to the ice bucket: "I do hope you don't mind, Erich, I was absolutely *parched*."

His "Erich" persona was not so easily unsettled: "Of course, why wait? I'm sorry . . . but the traffic." He slid into the banquette and deliberately let his right thigh meet her left one, getting a satisfying pressure on contact. "Now," he said, taking the ponderous menu, "we must have a celebration!"

"Oh? Why, particularly?"

"Because—I have not seen you for three days."

She put a hand on his thigh. "You must learn to suffer."

Having ordered, he looked around the restaurant. "This is my idea of decadence," he said with an air of satisfaction.

"I thought you would like it. You know, once it was *really* decadent, in Oscar Wilde's time. They had little dining compartments upstairs, they were called *particulières*, and once they brought the food, the rest of the evening was your own, if you understand."

The colloquialism baffled him.

"They closed the curtains."

"Ah. I understand. Why did they stop that?"

Her hand pressed further on his thigh and confirmed its attractions. "Because people go home to do that kind of thing now."

By the time they returned to her flat, she was drunk and playful in a strange, obsessive way that bordered on neurosis. She pushed her face into his, baring her teeth. "My mystery man. What *are* you—really?"

"You know what I am, I'm a wine salesman. What did you think I was?"

She hissed. "I think you're a mystery man. Why is it that *everybody* I know has secrets?" She kept her face pressed into his, picking at his jacket. "In this country everybody is playing games." She turned her back on him suddenly and walked away into the bedroom with precise steps. "I like you, Erich, but you're a bad liar."

He frowned. In a minute she called him. He found her sitting brazenly spreadlegged on the edge of the bed, nipples upturned. "My God," she said, "you're taking your time tonight."

He undressed slowly and then walked to her. He sliced his right hand, knuckle first, across her face.

"You bastard!" she cried stupidly, and kicked out, catching him in the groin.

He bent forward, gripped her shoulders, and spun her over facedown on the bed. She kicked upward but had no strength. Pressing down on her shoulders, he pushed his right knee between her legs and forced it up. "You shit," she said, biting the pillow. He held her there and calmly looked down, remembering the first time he had savored that back at Baden-Baden, denied the sight of what was below. The compound curves of pelvis and buttocks were stretched into an ivory tautness. He moved his knee back and pressed into her with slow deliberation. She had stopped fighting and held the pillow in her teeth.

Afterwards she lay on his chest. "You smell funny. Have you been trying some new cologne? Is it *musk?*"

"You ask too many questions," he said.

* * *

From the flying boat Ruth's first glimpse of land was through a gap of cloud—a wedge of green tipped by chalk cliffs, a disembodied and unattached place, as gaseous as the clouds.

The size of the plane gave the illusion from the ground that it was moving slowly. At first Seton could hear only the engines, and then he saw the Boeing Clipper break beneath the clouds. It banked over Portsmouth, turned out toward the Isle of Wight, losing height all the time, and then into the wind along the line of marker buoys. As it came down under the horizon of the Isle of Wight, Seton lost it for a minute against the gray of the island behind.

Ruth saw a flotilla of small boats strung out across Spithead water beneath her. Transoceanic flights were still enough of a novelty to attract this kind of attention, and the boats drew toward the buoys as the plane's four engines throttled back.

From the shore Seton saw the plane's sharp hull cut into the waves, sending white spume underwing. As the hull settled more deeply into the water the floats on its wingtips touched, too, and sent two more wakes of spray behind them. Now it looked an ungainly hybrid, neither boat nor plane, curiously ponderous. It turned in toward a jetty of pontoons. A front hatch opened, and a crewman appeared, ready to throw a line.

It was bleak at the jetty. Spray on the windows had obscured Ruth's view. She felt the first draft of salt air from the open hatch, and the passengers were at last allowed out of their seats in the saloon. She tried again to see through the window, but it remained opaque. The plane rocked a little.

As the passenger door opened Seton saw the cabin steward recoil from the wind and reappear in a coat. Ruth was the third passenger to step out. The wind caught her coat and it billowed; the steward handed her a small white case while she pushed the coat down in a shy, modest gesture. She seemed even darker against the silver hull and the other passengers. She bent her head forward into the wind, and it wasn't until she came to the final feet of the jetty that she looked up and saw him.

Waving seemed totally inadequate to him, and she, holding her coat with one hand and the bag in the other, made just a grin of recognition before she disappeared into a reception hut. A bus took passengers from the hut to the customs shed, keeping them out of view. Seton walked back and joined the other people waiting at the barrier. It was twenty more minutes before she came through. She stopped a step short of him, characteristically critical. "Hmmm," she said, putting down the bag, "you look in need of attention." Seton stepped forward, feeling too paternal. Then she embraced him.

Familiar sensations came back to him: her hair, her scent, things memory was fallible in preserving. The sharpness of her nose bone again: as though finished by a lapidary.

She pulled back from him, keeping her hands on his shoulder. "Yes. You're *definitely* suffering from neglect. Too pale. And a bit flabby."

"You look marvellous. And now you're a pioneer—coming over in that thing."

She laughed. "Father didn't want me to do it—*him*, the hypocrite! He said it still wasn't proven. *Imagine* that." She slipped her right arm into his, and they walked over to the baggage trolleys. *"However*, as you can see, I prevailed."

"Naturally."

She gave him a sidelong look.

"It's early in the year to be that punctual," he said, "you were late leaving Lisbon."

"Oh? You took *that* much interest?"

"I've been up there with you every minute."

She squeezed his arm. "I wish you had been. I have to admit it, Pan American does it well. Whatever Father says. So, why *are* you looking so *withered?*"

"Perhaps I need a plate of chili, to bring the color back to my cheeks."

In the car to London she slept, slipping to his shoulder. He had to wake her at the last turning into Davies Street.

"I'm sorry. I guess I'm pooped."

"The time change, I believe, can do funny things."

"It is *weird*—waking up here, only a day after leaving Long Island. I guess we'll have to get used to that kind of thing."

At Seton's suggestion Fraser had filled the apartment with flowers. Fraser himself was almost tearful at seeing her again, a crack in his facade that amused Seton and greatly moved her. Seton watched as she familiarized herself again with the details—opening a window to smell the air, coming out of the kitchen once she discovered that he had replenished the supply of Colombian coffee beans. In a confusion of emotions he fell silent.

"You thought of everything," she said, standing again by the window. "How are things here—really?"

"Not good."

"No? Well, I can tell you, Austria has changed things in the States. People are waking up." She turned and looked at him: "I'm glad I'm back."

"I wondered if you would—come back."

"Why on earth would you doubt that?" She walked toward him. "I have unfinished business here."

22

Horcher's Restaurant was too voluptuous for Canaris's taste, but there was security in its sheer size. To make the meeting look even more natural, he uncharacteristically wore uniform, as did his companion, Rear Admiral Pratzig. Any observer might have thought it a naval reunion, two officers on a Berlin fling: Pratzig, promoted from the captaincy of the *Graf Spee*, had been Canaris's predecessor at the Abwehr, and the man who had nominated Canaris for the job. But their conversation was not pleasantly nostalgic.

As the senior officer, Pratzig felt he could press Canaris in a way that others could not: "We are wondering where exactly you stand."

But Canaris was no longer willing to defer. He leaned forward and spoke quietly: "I cannot jeopardize the Abwehr. If I go, Heydrich takes over. I cannot allow that."

Pratzig was clearly displeased. He waited for a waiter to replenish their wine and withdraw, then said, "You cannot go on serving gangsters. Submit your resignation: I can get you a good command, in spite of Admiral Raeder."

"I serve Germany, as long as that is possible."

It was too disingenuous for Pratzig. "These people *are* Germany. They have stolen it." He gulped the wine and steadied himself. "You have never joined the party. Heydrich complains about that to Hitler."

Canaris didn't respond.

"You know," said Pratzig, "when Generals von

Schleicher and von Bredow were murdered—the Night of the Long Knives . . . ?"

Canaris nodded.

"They were killed because of what they knew about Heydrich and Himmler. But Heydrich never found that dossier. He always thought I had it."

"And did you?"

"That dossier is better for not being found. In a way, it must still work, still keep them at bay. You know what's going on? The generals?"

"Beck dreams of restoring the monarchy," said Canaris dismissively.

"They need help."

"I'll tell you something, my dear Admiral." Canaris offered a cigarette across the table. "The generals were happy enough, in 1933. We all were. The monarchy seemed irrelevant, washed away. Thank God, for order." Canaris lit his own cigarette and looked steadily at Pratzig. "I seem to remember you saying something of the kind. Well, we have done our jobs, you and I—and the generals. Who did we imagine it was being done for? Some disposable politicians? Or something finer, some honorable abstraction?"

Pratzig drew on the cigarette and didn't speak for a minute. The waiters in their black knee breeches and red waistcoats reminded him too much of Göring's personal staff. "So you're a patriot?" he said.

"If you dropped a few bombs on this park at the right time," Seton observed, "you might wipe out half the British government—politicians, mandarins, hangers-on."

"Would that be so bad?" Ruth threw bread at the ducks. Already swollen with attention, they ignored it.

"You've become very harsh," said Seton.

"If you really wanted to lose American public support, you couldn't have done better than to choose a man like Neville Chamberlain." She gave up on the ducks and slipped an arm into Seton's. They walked on, parallel to the pond, and found a free bench seat. In the flower beds the primulas and magnolias were out. The paths were thick with people, and on the newly mown grass office girls lay staring at the sky. Mayfair nannies wheeled bulky carriages. Children took impulsive runs over the grass.

"It *is* strange," said Ruth, leaning back on the seat and crossing her arms behind her head, "to think that all these anonymous men walking around here—just like you—are responsible for the country. In one way, it's nice, kind of democratic. They don't seem to manifest power. But in another way, it bothers me."

"Too much like amateurs, is that it?"

She considered the point. "Yes. I guess that is it—I like politicians to *look* like politicians, aggressive, ambitious, greedy, you know—as it is in Washington, they leave a kind of wake behind them."

"Tell me, Ruth, would Roosevelt dump us?"

She looked at him, the tawny hair with a touch of gray lightly disarranged by the wind. "He has to be very careful. You know, there's just been an attempt to amend the Constitution, so that we could not go to war without a national referendum. He only just stopped that."

"This new ambassador, Kennedy. He's been saying things off the cuff—'America won't pull England's chestnuts out of the fire.' "

"Would you like to see him, hear him, in the flesh?"

"Kennedy?"

"He's talking to the Pilgrims Club. I can get us two seats."

Seton remembered the Pilgrims Club, the speeches heavy with Anglo-American sentiment: "I'm game." He saw the winter visibly receding and felt a new lightness of spirit. "By the way," he said, "I nearly forgot. Olivier was marvellous as Macbeth. Thank you for those tickets."

"He is rather smashing, isn't he." She liked Seton with a touch of gray but hoped it wouldn't spread.

Starched into the appearance of a penguin, Seton felt as though he had aged ten years just by the change of clothes. He knew that uniformity was only a mask for personality, not a substitute for it, and yet amongst this conforming surface of white shirts and ties, black barathea, patent leather, and miniature medals, even the peculiarities of physical features seemed secondary to costume. The presence of Americans did introduce one or two anomalies: a white tie askew, a cuff link too bright, one jacket with *quilted* lapels.

Seton had discovered that his waist measurement was two inches more generous than when he last wore a white tie, a mortifying sign of the bureaucratic life, and he had had to go out and hire the dinner dress. He kept this revelation from Ruth who now, in orange chiffon, glided at his side and caused several of his acquaintances to look at him in a way that formal introductions did little to dispel. She was the most exotic flower of the evening.

Endmere had the assurance of a man whose suit was his own. Loose-knit and boozy, he put an arm on Seton's shoulder after the reintroduction and regarded Ruth with open admiration: "He's a deserving case, this Edward. Take good care of him. There aren't many like him made anymore." Endmere enjoyed Seton's embarrassment but was shrewd enough to see that this praise was not falling on deaf ears. She, too, enjoyed Seton's rising flush. She picked up Endmere's tone of detached affection:

"I know. He is rather special, isn't he?"

Fearing that Seton would retreat, Endmere hastened to seriousness: "And what do you hear about our guest of honor tonight, from your hometown?"

Ruth, with one eye on Seton's visible discomfort, said, "Oh—the ambassador? Well, he's plain potato."

Endmere laughed. "That's a Murphy, surely, not a Kennedy—in the Irish lingo."

"This is no simple Irish mind. Though he might want you to think so."

Seton, recovering, said, "An odd choice, though, for Roosevelt."

"Yes," said Endmere, "and not one he's finding easy to keep gagged. Kennedy gave us a briefing the other day. He seemed to be tempting fate. He said 'I hope all you boys will be down to see me off when I'm recalled.' Sham courage, perhaps. But I understand that his speech tonight has been cleared in advance."

"Which makes it either significant, or—"

"Or very bland, which is not like Kennedy," said Ruth, completing Seton's observation.

Endmere looked at the top table. "He's certainly drawn a high-powered audience. The Bank of England, captains of industry, Whitehall—they're all here. I don't think I've ever seen so much power at one table." Among the white breasts he picked out one scribbling a note on the back of a menu. "Cadogan," he said, nodding toward the small man with the large head, "he doesn't get much peace these days. Hitler keeps them on the hop."

"*That's* just the trouble," said Ruth cuttingly. "From the States it looks just like that. You people are second-guessing all the time, not reading the play at all."

"Reading the play?"

Seton interpreted: "American football. You must forgive her these lapses."

She rose to the bait. "Don't evade the point. You know what I mean."

"Yes," conceded Endmere, "I do know what you mean, and of course you're right. Hitler acts, we react. And as long as Chamberlain is there it will be like this. Chamberlain looks at the world through the eyes of a Birmingham ironmonger. No ironmonger has ever met anyone like Adolf Hitler before."

There was a movement of chairs and the brittle snap of bending starch: People were settling at their tables. A toast-master in red tunic and knee breeches positioned himself behind the center of the main table. Several men self-consciously moved down the table to their seats. In the midst of them was the American ambassador, with freckled face and circular-rimmed glasses, red hair thinning at the brow. He nodded to several of the men on the opposite side of the table and sat down.

Endmere moved off to his table, and Seton guided Ruth to their own. Their companions were a voluble American matron and her taciturn husband—"in railroads"—and a Whitehall mandarin, vaguely familiar to Seton, with his owlish aristocratic wife. The matron, discovering Ruth was from Boston, recounted through the meal the tribualtions of furnishing a new mansion at Newport, Rhode Island. Seton and the mandarin managed two or three monosyllabic asides.

As soon as Kennedy opened his mouth Ruth heard the street voices of home, the echoes from the parlors of her childhood: broad-hipped men come to the social graces late; patriarchs making small talk until the women withdrew, then filling the room with sour cigar smoke, and emerging, much later, with the deals done. Once, she remembered, a man much like Kennedy had been wheeled out on a stretcher; one side of his face and body was rigid, the look of a broker petrified by the stroke. Now Kennedy took this taxidermic assembly as he would have a barful of cronies—by the ears. Glasses of brandy and port stopped moving; cigars flickered out in the ashtrays.

He would explain, he said, how Americans felt about Europe—if at all. Their government was not going to bind itself to any entanglement without great caution: "In some quarters, it has been interpreted to mean that our country would not fight under *any* circumstances, short of actual invasion." He paused, then continued: "That is a dangerous sort of misunderstanding to be current just now."

The suspense broken, there was a murmur of applause; Seton looked at Ruth, visibly relieved. But Kennedy continued: "Others seem to imagine that the United States could never remain neutral in the event of a general war." Again he paused for effect. "That, too, is a dangerous misapprehension. My country has decided that it must stand on its own feet. . . ."

It was the turn of the Newport matron to applaud. As she broke into motion her husband woke up and stared blankly at the top table. Kennedy moved on to a kind of maxim, which Ruth had heard before: "Nations, like men, do not consider undertaking business transactions unless they are convinced a common interest exists. War is *not* inevitable."

Afterwards, in the men's cloakroom, Endmere, finding Seton, commented, "That was clear enough, I should think."

"Clear enough to be heard in Berlin."

"I can see where *his* heart is, all right. Somewhere around the center of Wall Street."

There was much comment of the same kind around them.

Outside Claridge's, the chiffon showing under her coat, Ruth said, "Take me home." It was, after all, only half a minute away. She pulled closer to him. A Mercedes with a diplomatic pennant rolled by, the first in the procession of waiting limousines. Neither spoke as they turned the corner and walked down Davies Street. The American embassy was only a block away, and they saw Kennedy's car go up to Grosvenor Square, its passengers engaged in animated conversation.

As soon as they were in her flat, Seton pulled his tie loose and removed the collar with its stiff breast piece. "Like armor, isn't it?" he said. She pulled off her white gloves and saw the red line around Seton's neck where the collar had chaffed.

"More coffee, okay?" She went into the kitchen. While she was gone, he found the records and put on Mozart.

Bringing in the tray, she said, "That's an ironic choice of music—the *Prague*."

The slow first movement was finely balanced between exultation and morbidity. Seton sat down next to her on the sofa, and she poured the coffee. They listened to the music. When she got up to change the record, Seton said, "You know, listening to Mozart, you can hear all the tides of the German character."

"The distant thunder of the soul."

He looked at her. "*Yes . . . yes.* That's it, isn't it?" He lay back on the sofa, tilting the cup, feeling the tension of the dinner drain away. His shirt had begun to rise from the waistband, the unfamiliar trousers too loose after all.

He waited for the record to end and then, quietly, he said, "Your mother wrote to me, while you were away. She told me about the young man in Spain. I am very, very sorry."

She fussed over the record for longer than was necessary, not speaking, and then came back to him, perfectly composed. "He was a fine person. But it was over before it started. More like losing a brother, I suppose. I really always took second place. Edward, what *is* it with airplanes? I always seem to be competing with them, you know—Father, my brothers . . . !"

"You might just as well ask, what is it about railways, about ships—even about money. Look at Kennedy."

"I just did." She frowned. "I was forgetting—you have it, too, don't you? The thing about flying."

"I did. But I'm past it."

"Thank God for that."

"Was he—did they bring him home?"

"There was nothing to bring." She turned away.

"His family—were you close?"

"Not until now."

He got up and paced behind the sofa, where she couldn't see him. "I fear that a lot of other parents are going to go through that, the way things are looking."

"It's coming, isn't it?"

He was at the window, looking at the roofs. "Yes. It's no longer if, but when. And the when is very important."

"Why don't more people *see* that?"

"They don't want to. I suppose it's understandable. One war is enough for one generation."

She swung her legs off the floor and put her stockinged feet on the sofa.

He went to the sideboard. "Would you like a drink? If I may, I think I'm going to help myself to one." She nodded. "Whisky all right?" He put soda in both glasses and handed one to her. Then he began pacing the floor again.

"You know, Ruth, I've already seen one world lost forever." He sipped the drink, reflecting. "It's odd, but I have only a hazy memory of it. How the world was before the war.

It seems long ago—not in years but in state of mind. The values I had, growing up in the rectory, then school at Rugby, the aura of Dr. Arnold—God, *what* a man! For people of my age, our youth didn't just end with the war—it *evaporated*."

She tucked her legs under her and sat up, listening intently.

"It seems a gilded youth. But I suppose it wasn't, at least not for many. The war was at least a great leveller. It was a time of brief lives. We were losing in 1917. Then came Uncle Sam—your father—just like the cavalry in the pictures." He smiled wryly. "The Huns very nearly won. Consider the implications of *that*. And now, this world, that's over too—the brave new world, the jazz age, call it what you will. It's finished. I feel it slipping away from under our feet, the harder we dance. Like on a moving staircase, going up the down part."

"What your friend, Endmere—what he was saying earlier, about Chamberlain, the ironmonger mentality, was that fair?"

"We've been caught with the wrong lot in charge. They're Victorians, all the virtues, and all the vices. They belong to that other world, the one I can barely recall. They remember too much and learn too little. Endmere was right, they've never met anyone like Hitler before."

"There never was anyone like Hitler before."

He took another draft of the whisky. "No—nor Goebbels, Himmler, Göring. *They* are the new men, if you like. The vanguard of something, I hate to think what. But I'll tell you, the enslaving of public opinion—that's the first step in the process, the first step in the enslavement of the people. They know that. That's why they're getting away with it."

She finished her whisky and walked over to him. She stroked his hair as they stood looking out the window. Then she turned away and went into her bedroom, putting on the light. As she sat on the end of the bed he came to the door. She flexed her toes, and he saw the slight ruck of silk at her ankle, lighter in shade where it had freed itself from her skin. She reached under her skirt, not raising it more than a few inches, and detached the stockings from the garters. She did all this without taking her eyes from him.

His control depended on words. Words were his mask, which seldom slipped. But words were drying in his mouth, unuttered, yielding to another self. What decided the matter was her own knowledge of him before he knew it himself. She saw into him, and in the end he knew she had seen into him, before his only words croaked out:

"It cannot be."

Still sitting on the bed, she raised her legs until the knees were under her chin, and pulled the chiffon up her legs. Then she pulled off one stocking, bringing it over the knee and gathering it in her hand as it came away from the foot. Without the stocking the leg was an even shade of dark honey, a faint halo of hair on the calf. As she pulled off the other stocking he moved away to the bedroom window. The street was empty. He closed the curtains.

He unbuttoned the back of the dress for her, and she stood up and let the chiffon collapse onto the floor, stepping out of it. She wore no bra. She went over to the light and switched it off, then took off the garters and pants. He still stood by the bed. Slowly she pulled the tail of the shirt out from his waistband. "Come on," she said quietly.

He remembered long afterwards how all the scents of her body—perfume, talcum, hair—were fused as they touched skin to skin for the first time. And then, as she took him and guided him and then clung to him, all the secretions of love mingled with the other scents. The shell of his celibacy fell away like the discarded shirt breast, all the pain of self-denial gone, and they lay together quite still.

23

"I'm used to livin' at the center of storms, Mr. Kennedy."

The ambassador grinned hugely. "Me too, Lady Astor. I guess we weren't meant for the quiet life."

"Nancy. Please call me Nancy." She took his arm and wheeled him through the scattered groups on the terrace. Pertinacious but disarming, she was about to make another meeting of interests. She spotted Lindbergh's head above the rest of a group at the edge of the terrace and made for him like a dart.

"Colonel Lindbergh, this is Ambassador Kennedy. I want

you to tell him what you've been tellin' us." She tugged Lindbergh away from the group. "The ambassador has been explainin' his fears about being counted a member of the wicked Cliveden Set." She laughed thinly. "I told him, it's all a lot of nonsense put about by that communist rag of young Cockburn's."

Lindbergh fixed on Kennedy: "Yes, sir, Mr. Ambassador, I'm very glad to make your acquaintance. Very glad." He turned to his hostess. "Nancy has told me about you—that you think straight, unlike a number of people on this island. Now, see here. . . ." Lady Astor, consummation achieved, smiled and left them.

In another corner of the terrace Lady Dunsinnan sat with Ruth. She was drinking more than she used to, Ruth noticed.

"Do you really *like* this house?" said Ruth, watching the ambassador being backed into a corner.

"Oh, it's fine enough. But it's not really a *home*, do you know what I mean? How can it be? It seems to be run more like a country club, always full of these people. Poor Waldorf, he's a good man, but left in the shadows. It's almost as though he's never here."

"Yes," said Ruth, "I wondered what it must be like, married to the most famous woman in England."

"It was good of you to come here with me, Ruth. I know it's not much fun for you, all these old men." There was a hint of curiosity in her voice.

"Oh, it fascinates me, ever since the first weekend, when I came with Alastair. It's a bit like watching history *before* it's made, all these powerful people. . . ."

"Yes. That's what draws Alastair, too. But not as a spectator."

"Why did he go off so suddenly?"

Lady Dunsinnan took another long gulp of the champagne and coughed. "Why does he ever keep doing it? You know how it is. . . ."

"Germany again?"

She nodded. "You're looking very well, my dear, *very* well."

Politely, Ruth steered away her curiosity. Her pervasive well-being probably did show, but discretion prevailed. As they went in to dinner she wished devoutly that Seton could have been with her—even more so when she found herself seated next to the gnomic figure of Thomas Jones. Something in his fluency was too easy, a mind without pauses or hesitation. Ruth pressed him to explain the new Hitler, conqueror of Austria.

"Oh, I admit it," he said, chewing sagely while he spoke. "I have been in favor of trying to reach some amicable understanding with Hitler, for the very reason that I believed him to be a fanatic to be humored. We could not take any offensive with our forces so unprepared."

"Surely to humor him is to encourage him more?"

Jones cast a patronizing glance at her. "No, I thought it might keep him in his place. As it is, well—I don't think 'scoundrel' describes him, it applies more to the people around him."

"I thought that in that regime everyone dances to his tune."

"He's not like the rest of them. He's a mystic, a recluse."

"He didn't look much like a recluse, riding through Vienna."

Jones began to look uncomfortable—and impatient. "Ah, but that was a *homecoming*."

This was too much for Ruth. She swivelled in her chair, forgetting where she was in her passion: "I see. And what about the eighty thousand people arrested by the S.S.? Where is their home? And what about the Jews being made to scrub the streets. Have you seen the pictures of *that?*"

Around them people had stopped eating and looked embarrassed. Jones's defense was to become didactic: "We must distinguish between Hitler's aims and his methods . . . we have to convince the world that for peace we are prepared to go to absurd lengths. Our people will not fight unless they are satisfied that fair treatment of the potential enemy has been tried."

"Peace at any price?"

He ignored the jibe and moved his ground, becoming falsely congenial: "Tell me—Miss Dexter, isn't it? Tell me, do you think we could expect any help from America, if the worse came to the worst?"

Ruth looked to the top of the table where Kennedy sat next to Lady Astor. "The ambassador seems to hope not," she said.

For the rest of the meal Jones skillfully avoided talking to her. Later, lying alone in a vast bed, she remembered what Seton had once said about Jones: "He's never opened up on the subject of appeasement, not in public. He's the only one of

them like that, he works at it in private." Jones's calculating
finesse, evading the macabre realities of Vienna, kept her
awake.

At breakfast Lady Dunsinnan already had malt on her
breath—the flask from Pitlochry could not be far away. She
looked at Ruth shrewdly. "What's troubling you, my dear?"

"Nothing serious. Just something somebody said last
night."

"The Welshman. Alastair thinks a lot of him."

"I know." Ruth saw the paper. "I see the shops in Vienna
now have to display notices declaring themselves to be Aryan."

"Oh, it's a lot of nonsense, all this harping on race. What
are Aryans, anyway? Do I qualify, as a Celt?"

Ruth knew that the frivolous answer was a form of defense, by proxy. She chose to leave it.

"Ruth, I'm going up to the castle next week, it's a lovely
time of the year up there now. Would you like to come? I'd
love you to."

"Well—thank you, but— My plans are rather in flux, I
haven't quite—"

"You needn't decide now. Let me know in a day or so."
The appeal was more earnest than she made it sound.

"Will Alastair be coming?"

"I don't know. We *never* know, these days."

Several times Seton had to bite his tongue when about to
call her "darling" in public, and each time she knew his difficulty. She didn't like the affair's being clandestine but accepted that for the moment it had to be. She thought she detected a look in Fraser's eye, the savvy Fraser, as they walked
in together, but the established precedent of their friendship
should hold good for a while longer.

She told him about the invitation to Dunsinnan Castle,
watching him warily.

"It could be useful," he said, and then hesitated. They
were having breakfast. She, in a thin silk gown, seemed too
fragile. And too much in his care.

She saw the cause of his hesitation. "I'm not afraid to do
it, you know."

"That's exactly what worries me. You should be. It could
be dangerous—this time."

She put down her knife. "Look, Edward, don't you understand? If it has to be done, I'll do it, because nobody else

could. I know it's different now, being a witting agent instead of an unwitting one."

He colored. "I thought. . . ."

"Okay. That's all over, *believe* me. It's forgotten. I don't bear a grudge."

"It's just that"—he got up and came around the table to her—"I can't ask you to do it, not any longer."

"You can't stop me." She stood up and put a hand firmly on each of his shoulders. "You've probably never had anyone say that to you before, have you?" She was plainly defiant.

"No. But then, I've never given assignments at breakfast before."

"I'll hope not!" Her right hand moved from the shoulder to the back of his neck, behind the ear. "You're going to have to get used to doing a lot of things you haven't done before." She kissed him hard, her tongue ranging his mouth, both their lips sticky from the marmalade. Then she drew back and looked at him more solemnly: "I will do it, because I know, now, how important it could be. Remember, he doesn't know anything about us, he won't be on guard. He just looks on me as a hopeless case, no more. I irritate him, nothing worse. And as long as he thinks like that—well, I can keep my eyes and ears open."

"Austria really upset you."

"It's far more than that. It was the kind of things Jones was saying, the indifference to what's happening."

"Yes. That's the worst of it." Suddenly, on an impulse, he said, "I could fly you to Scotland."

She looked at him sharply: "Your flying days are over, you said so."

"Officially, maybe. . . ." He grinned sheepishly. "But a private plane is different. No rules there about pilots wearing glasses."

"You see, you are incurable, just like the others." She tapped him on the chest like a schoolmarm. "Okay, just this once."

They took off from an airfield just north of London in a single-engined Percival Vega Gull. The moment she sat alongside Seton, Ruth, who was already familiar with small planes, recognized all the movements of the instinctive pilot—as soon as his feet touched the pedals and his hand the control stick it was as if man and machine were fused. It was the same with her father.

Once he had reached his cruising height at four thousand feet, he turned to her: "Beautiful, isn't it?"

There was just an occasional wisp of cloud beneath them, and she misunderstood. "Yes, a lovely day."

"No. I mean *the plane*," he shouted, laughing. "One of these won the race to Johannesburg two years ago—did it in just over two days. Just think of that, six thousand miles!"

She saw an England that she had never seen before. From the air and away from roads and railroads it seemed very thinly populated, great swathes of rich land, forests, and a surprising number of large houses behind the walls of great estates. She picked out a castle, dull yellow in the sun, standing on a rise at the edge of a wood. Behind the castle a geometrical garden extended over at least a quarter of a mile. She pointed down: "Look at that—those gardens."

He banked the plane slightly and looked over her shoulder. "It's one of the things you realize from up here—England's capacity to swallow enormous wealth. From the ground you'd never know it was there."

He banked the plane back on course. Just over two hours later they landed at Newcastle for fuel. While they stood by the plane he looked at his watch and checked his maps. "We have time to spare. What would you say to passing over Edinburgh and snooping around Dunsinnan Castle from the air? I'd like to see it."

"Fine," she said.

There was thicker cloud over Scotland at the dangerous level of two thousand feet. Only intermittently could she see ground, bare moorland, and hills. With the map on his knee Seton checked the compass points and then eased the plane down through the clouds. For a minute they seemed to be in dense fog, then suddenly it was light, and they were over water. "The Firth of Forth," he said. "Now we'll do some hedge-hopping." She nodded uncertainly.

As they followed the line of a road across the Fife Peninsula flocks of sheep stampeded, horses took off at a gallop, and a car stopped dead in the road, its occupants staring up. She saw another estuary ahead, the Tay at Perth, and then the cloud was less dense and he gained height until dead ahead of them she recognized the great spine of the Grampian Mountains. He checked the landscape with the map, then banked steeply to the right, so that she could see over his head and through the canopy to a belt of forest in the foothills, and a loch. "That should be it," he said, pointing to the loch. "Dunsinnan Castle, on the edge of the tree line."

He throttled back and let the plane take its own speed down until they came over the loch at barely two hundred feet. Directly ahead she recognized the road up the hill and the castle's outline against the trees.

"Mustn't make them too curious," he said, and banked away to the right so that she could see the grounds, and over the brow of the hill to the moors beyond. "Quite a place," he said, looking back. He opened up the engine again and climbed in a wide turn; as they gained height she could see a progressively enlarging view of the Dunsinnan estate. There was one small boat on the loch, and she knew who was in it. From the air the loch looked even more forbidding. There was no transparency in the water at all, and toward its center it was the color of ink.

Seton checked his watch. "Right. Now we should be just right for Edinburgh."

She had flown enough with her father to know that Seton's navigation over that terrain, and in that weather, had been impeccable, and she knew that the low-flying episode was more than curiosity. It was something irrepressible in him wanting the merest excuse, a reliving of an earlier life. This one indulgence was now forgotten as he began the disciplines of radio contact with the airfield at Edinburgh, for all the world as though completing the normal flight path, and they had no means of knowing otherwise.

The masquerade of propriety had to be maintained when they landed. The only gesture of intimacy he could safely make as she prepared to climb out was to squeeze her knee and look to her silently. After the heated cabin the wind coming over the Forth was a rude welcome to Scotland, and she took her coat gratefully as a porter removed the bags from a small hatch behind the cabin. By the wooden hut that served as control tower and terminal stood the familiar brown Bentley, with Drummond at its door—unusually, since his new rank had required the hiring of another chauffeur. She glanced back across the airfield; the plane's canopy was already latched down, the propeller turning, and the pilot was only a dim outline. Drummond, too, watched the Vega Gull taxi to the end of the field; and then, as Drummond opened the door with a slight bow, the plane flew out low across the metal-gray estuary, turning gently to the right and disappearing over the city.

* * *

Canaris and Piekenbrock stood by the open window of Canaris's office, their voices deliberately overlapped by the traffic in the Tirpitzufer. Piekenbrock bent down to pat a dachshund and said, "What does Oster *do* with all those telephones on his desk?"

"I never ask," said Canaris.

"You don't think he might be going too far? We could all be implicated."

Canaris left the question unanswered. He went back to his desk. "The report drawn up by Professor Bonhoeffner—now *that* is a dangerous document. What were the terms he used—psychopath, paranoiac? Ironical, to apply Freud to Hitler, is it not? I didn't need a medical report to tell me that."

"It could be important—to have it certified."

"I'll tell you what worries me most, Piekenbrock, not Oster and his telephones, not even making out psychiatric reports on Hitler. *Why doesn't the Gestapo know?* Do you really believe that all this is going on and Himmler remains in ignorance?"

"Perhaps, Admiral, we overrated Heydrich."

Canaris fell silent for half a minute, then said, "It cannot work when it's left to men like Beck to organize. Would *you* go into something like this with him, Hans? Beck is a man of principle but not a man of action." Canaris, uncharacteristically anxious to confide, had slumped at the desk. "I wish I found it as easy as Oster to make up my mind. But I don't believe it's that simple. Beck could just be leading others to slaughter. We have to find another way—"

"The London contacts?"

"Not promising, so far." Canaris seemed suddenly to realize the impression his own despondency was making, and pulled himself up squarely in the chair. "I'm sure of one thing. If Hitler goes too far, there is a danger that America would become involved. Then we could never win. Remember 1917, Piekenbrock. I can't forget it."

As the steaming dish came to the table Lady Dunsinnan looked across to Ruth, watching her face.

"So *that's* it," Ruth said weakly.

"That's it."

"What, exactly, *is* it? Sheep's intestines or something, isn't that so?"

"No, though you're getting warm. Sheep's stomach lining,

stuffed with all manner of things. Don't think about it, it doesn't help. Just try it . . . you'll be surprised."

"*That's* for sure," said Ruth as the first portion was placed in front of her. The idea of eating haggis had been a joke between them until then, something mysterious, ever-threatening.

"Really, we should have had a piper here to bring it in, that's the proper way." Lady Dunsinnan laughed as she watched Ruth peck tentatively at the plate. "You can always wash it down with whisky afterwards."

But she digested the haggis without anaesthetics. In fact, she found it more interesting than the usual bland diet of the castle. As they finished dinner Lady Dunsinnan said, "Alastair is coming, after all. He's bringing a photographer, a German, from one of their magazines. I don't quite know why."

They were standing on the steps of the castle, and they could hear the car already climbing up through the trees. The new chauffeur had gone to collect Dunsinnan from Edinburgh. Drummond stood next to Ruth. Quietly he said, "There was quite a flutter up here the other day, miss. Grant was in his boat, on the loch. An *aer-o-plane*"—he licked every consonant of the word—"came over the water so low he thought he might be decapitated."

"Is that so?" she said calmly.

"Yes," he said, gazing upward as though the plane might materialize again, "there are not many *aer-o-planes* hereabouts."

"I've noticed."

Von Klagen stepped out of the Bentley behind Dunsinnan, dragging his bad leg. Ruth had two successive reflexes: The first identified him with Spithead; the second one, barely subliminal, was of a face amongst a line of photographers at Nuremberg.

"*Well,*" said Dunsinnan, showing his teeth. "I *am* glad to see you back in the clan." He was slightly awkward, kissing her lightly on a cheek. "It's been a long time." He turned to von Klagen, whose Leica was strung around his neck. "You may remember this chap—he certainly remembers you, he tells me. From the *Illustrierte Zeitung*. Remember?"

"Yes," she answered, then von Klagen bowed and took her hand. At first she thought he was going to kiss it, but he shook it lightly, looking at her with a hint of a smile.

As they turned into the house Dunsinnan said, "Walther

has been telling me that in Germany they think very highly of the Scots. They regard us as the last healthy racial influence in the British Isles, the most upright and Germanic—wasn't that the phrase, Walther?" Von Klagen nodded. "His magazine wants to introduce Scotland to its readers—by showing the castle, the land around, that sort of thing."

She noticed the nerve above his eye was more active.

When she came down to dinner, Dunsinnan sat her next to von Klagen, across the table from himself. Casually he said, "I'm told you flew up this time. That must have been interesting."

"Yes. It was."

"In a small plane?"

"That's right."

"Rather than the regular service?"

"Someone happened to be coming up, offered me a ride."

He picked up his napkin. "I see."

Dunsinnan and von Klagen remained at the table long after Ruth and Lady Dunsinnan retired. Ruth lay awake, still troubled by the questions about the plane. Then she began to turn over an idea in her mind. That morning, before Dunsinnan returned, Lady Dunsinnan had shown her his library, a large corner room on the ground floor. The selection of books was predictable, from early tracts on the Aryan view of history to *Mein Kampf*. Many of the titles were in German. Lady Dunsinnan had surveyed the shelves dolefully but passed no comment. Ruth had noticed a Chippendale desk in one corner. Her knowledge of the castle's layout was now extensive, and lying in bed she realized that there was a way into the library that avoided the main staircases—through a servants' corridor and a staircase leading off the kitchen.

For several hours she remained awake until certain that everyone else was asleep. Then she slipped a coat over her gown and put on a pair of soft shoes. The bedrooms in the guest wing were empty, apart from her own. Von Klagen had been put in another part of the castle. There was no light in the corridor, but an uncurtained window at the turreted corner gave enough light for her to pick her way to the staircase, and once her eyes adjusted, she easily reached the ground floor.

She was worried about the dogs. Two of them were kept somewhere. But the kitchen was away from the central part of the building; when she reached it, she was startled to see a pair of eyes, staring at her. She stifled a cry. Then she realized it was an unskinned rabbit, left on the table. A short flagstone passage by the pantry ended at a door that she believed must open into the library. At first she thought the door was locked. She turned the handle but nothing happened. She felt around the handle but could find no latch. She tried again, turning harder. There was a click and the door swung open. She realized how heavily she was breathing and disciplined herself to calmness.

The windows of the library had been left with the curtains open, and for the first time she could see clearly outside. A faint, watery moon gave enough light to see into the woods. Though it was cold enough in the library to make her shiver, she wondered whether this was in fact nerves. She went straight to the desk. She tried the central drawer, but it was locked. The top left-hand drawer was open but contained only stationery, and the drawers below it were locked. On the right-hand side there was one deep drawer, unlocked. It contained some manila files. Carefully she pulled them out and held them open to the window, but they were only the accounts of the estate.

Just as she was about to close the drawer she noticed that, if she bent down, she could see the underside of the locked central drawer. She put a finger under it and pressed upward. There was a little movement. She tried again, slipping her hand as far as it could go to the left, and felt the catch. She pressed once again, and there was a click. The drawer slid open without a sound.

Inside, there was only a copy of a magazine, *The Field*. She checked again, because the light was poor, but found nothing else. Then she noticed the edge of what appeared to be a loose page in the magazine. She opened it and saw several closely typed sheets of paper. To read them, she had to move to the window. It was a memorandum from Dunsinnan to someone called Fritsch, carrying a date two months old. As she read it she understood a great deal, not without a sense of dread.

It took her ten minutes to read the document once. She realized how cold she had become. But she read it through a second time, trying to memorize salient details. Then she slipped the papers back into the magazine and returned it to the drawer. As she turned to go she saw von Klagen, in outline, standing by the door. A cry died in her throat.

"I'm sorry—if I startled you," he said, keeping his voice down and walking toward her.

"Yes. You did," she said faintly.

"I heard somebody moving about." He looked at the desk. "My room is above."

Surprised by his manner, she thought quickly and desperately, disbelieving herself even as she spoke: "I—I couldn't sleep. I came down for a book." She was, she realized, nowhere near a bookcase.

Von Klagen's features were sharpened by the moonlight. He moved from the desk to the nearest bookshelf and ran a finger along it. "Here." He pulled out a book. "This might send you to sleep."

It was a copy of *Mein Kampf.*

"It's not very light reading, is it?" she said, her nerve slowly returning.

Still by the books, von Klagen surveyed the whole collection. "It is odd, is it not, that the British prime minister should be called Chamberlain? You see these books, here? Written in the nineteenth century, by another Chamberlain. The Führer is a great admirer of them. They interpret the whole of world history from the Aryan point of view. You are interested in that?"

"Not my subject, really."

"No. I suppose not." He looked at her speculatively: "What is your subject?"

"Medieval art."

"So? Interesting."

She sensed that he was coming to a decision.

"When tomorrow I take the pictures—I would like you to pose for me. I have heard about your horse. You will ride that for me, perhaps?"

24

Neville Chamberlain's collar had a life independent of his neck. The winged collar remained rigidly facing forward while his neck moved with his head, as though the body were a shell, and the head nervously explored the world beyond it. In spite of the summer heat he wore a thick three-piece suit. He was bareheaded and carried an umbrella, handle down, under his left arm. His wife walked alongside him in the park, wearing a fur coat and a small-brimmed felt hat with one feather.

The people who encountered them on the path among the beds of primulas reacted in two ways: The more formal of them doffed their hats as they passed; the majority were flustered, not quite sure if it *was* who they thought it was, not knowing whether to store or to look elsewhere.

Overlooking the park from his dark corner of the Foreign Office, the permanent under secretary, Sir Alexander Cadogan, watched Chamberlain leave the park, cross Horse Guards parade ground, and enter 10 Downing Street by his garden gate. Cadogan was still musing on this phenomenon when the buzzer on his desk came to life. Still standing, he pressed down the switch. "Yes?" An aristocratic voice crackled from the small speaker. "Coming up," said Cadogan, and he gathered a cardboard file bulging with telegrams.

In the room immediately above Cadogan's, Lord Halifax, the foreign secretary, had also been watching Chamberlain's progress. He was standing by the window when Cadogan came in. They made an ill-sorted pair: Halifax the languid giant, Cadogan small and peppery. Halifax motioned Cadogan to a leather chair by the window.

"Something is definitely going on," said Cadogan, swallowed in the leather.

Halifax remained standing. "What does Henderson say?"

"He says they can't organize an invasion of Czechoslovakia *and* the Nuremberg rally at the same time. Nuremberg is still on."

Halifax complained, "Henderson said we should keep Germany guessing, but it seems to me all the guessing is done by us."

Cadogan was silent. They heard the first notes of the Guards band striking up from Horse Guards.

"D'you see Neville, just now?" said Halifax.

Cadogan nodded.

"Pretty fine that, wasn't it? I think *that's* what we stand for, don't you, Alex? Can you see Herr Hitler doing that?"

Seton ran through Ruth's notes several times, pressing her on apparent gaps, getting her to search her memory—quietly impressed by her thoroughness. Finally he took off his glasses and rubbed his eyes. Then he put the glasses back on but pulled them to the tip of his nose. He looked across the table: "You see what it all means, don't you? So far it's gone precisely as they wanted. The devil of it is, it's impossible to tell how far they were able to push it this way, and how far—well, how far it was predestined."

She saw in him a new uneasiness as he peered over the frame of the glasses, his concern visible.

"*Nothing* is predestined," she said. "It takes a smart mind to make it look that way."

"Yes," he said, drawing out the word, slowly accepting her perception. "That's the art of what they seem to have done. Getting Henderson installed as the ambassador in Berlin. Building up the pressures on Eden—"

"*Was* he a good foreign secretary, Eden—I mean, isn't he too—well, *pretty?*"

Seton took off his glasses and dangled them thoughtfully. "I don't think you can hold his looks against him. No. You can tell his quality by the pleasure his resignation gave to Hitler. And others."

"But couldn't Alastair be claiming more for himself than he actually achieved?"

"He could." Her casual use of "Alastair" mildly irritated him. He put his glasses back on and read through his notes again. "There are clues here. Take this guidance to the Germans on how to handle Chamberlain. It could have come only from someone really close." He brooded for a second. "All too shrewd; I fear."

"Then *how* could they have done it?"

"The trouble is, you'll never be able to pin a name on it,

that's not the way it works. A word here, a word there—*there* being, more often than not, Cliveden. That's how it's done. I suppose there's a polite term for it, taking soundings, something harmless like that. But, in the end, see what it's already achieved: Phipps chucked out of Berlin, Eden betrayed into resignation. Then the steady drip of defeatism."

"I guess my fellow Americans have made some contribution there. . . ."

"Lindbergh—certainly. Now I hear that Kennedy has been busy dispiriting the King, with visions of invincible Germany."

"But they haven't pulled off the last stroke—yet?"

Seton readjusted his glasses and looked at her notes again. "No. But I have a feeling it won't be long in coming. The words are already on the wind. Mohammed unto the mountain—what a vision that would be: Chamberlain making the final ascent, to the feet of the Führer. I wonder, could he *really do* that? And have it not look like self-abasement?"

"They know the man now."

"Yes. They do." Seton pushed his chair back from the table. "You did well. I don't know how this is going to be received, what can be done about it."

"*Well now*," she said, pertinently curious. "That's what you've never really explained. How do *you* know, when you see whoever it is you have to see, that *they* don't think this way too?"

It was uncomfortably close to his own nagging doubts, but in answering her, he reassured himself: "There's only one thing that makes me certain that that can't be the case. I wouldn't be where I am, doing what I do." He saw the question taking shape within her and cut it off: "And *that* I cannot elaborate on."

She moved round the table. Standing behind him, she ruffled his hair with one hand and rested the other on his shoulder. "You can leave it to my imagination," she said.

He was getting used to her attacks on his hair, which had become a tolerated delinquency. He bent one arm back and his hand met hers on the shoulder. He could feel her breasts on the back of his head and somehow, though there was no eye contact, they were extraordinarily close. "You know," he said, "I still don't understand that incident in the library. You *knew* that von Klagen didn't believe you, and yet. . . ."

"After the first shock he wasn't frightening at all, that's

the odd thing. It was like we had just met casually, in broad daylight, instead of at two o'clock in the morning. And he was dressed—fully dressed."

"He never mentioned it again?"

"He looked at me once or twice, in a funny way. But no, he never breathed a word. Something else, though. He was there to photograph the house, okay? Not just the outside, the gardens, that kind of stuff, but the interiors. Well, all he had was a Leica, no plate camera. You wouldn't take that kind of stuff with a *Leica,* would you?"

"It was clever of you to find this place," said Endmere, sitting on the terrace sipping a glass of wine.

"I didn't *find* it, actually. It was offered out of the blue," said Margery Taverner. She was standing at the terrace door. "Bunny and Toby suddenly shot off to Italy and wanted it taken care of. Suited me."

"Dunsinnan still in Scotland, then?" He knew the inference would annoy her.

She turned away. Her buttocks were stained with grass. "It's getting a little cool. I think I'll put something on."

He followed her inside and found two candles in the kitchen, vivid orange, and put them on the table. She came back in a regal gown drawn in at the waist with a loose knot, and bare-footed. Her hair, still wet from the pool, was drawn up from the back of her neck into a Regency crown. Seeing the candles, she began to improvise a charade of maidenly deference, curtseying and lowering her eyes, her breasts nearly coming out of the gown. "Master," she said, "dinner awaits."

The game was out of her character and made him feel clumsy. He indulged it until the food was on the table, and he had poured the champagne. Then, bluntly, he restored reality.

"I'm going away. To Germany."

"Oh?" Reluctantly she adapted.

"Things are hotting up."

"You think they'll invade, then—Czechoslovakia?"

"Not invade. Just take bites."

In the candlelight her neck was like jade. She chewed the lamb slowly, sorry that the fantasy was dispelled.

He poured her more of the champagne. "Of course, we're almost begging him to do it gently, so as not to require action on our part. Chamberlain is rehearsing in front of the mirror—all the arguments that it's none of our business. He needn't worry. As far as I can establish, not *one* of the chiefs of staff—the War Office, the Admiralty, the Air Ministry—none of them is against appeasement. No guts at all. Not like their German colleagues."

"What do you mean?"

"It's *very* hush-hush, but there's talk of a putsch—against Hitler. The generals appear to have had enough. They've sent somebody over here, trying to rally support, hoping that if we give the nod they can pull it off."

"Really?" She sipped the wine and thought of her German wine salesman. "That's a bit farfetched, isn't it?"

The flat at 11 Morpeth Mansions was modestly Victorian: The visitor was shown into a long but narrow room, still in semidarkness. It was a room decorated more by books than by paint: They lined shelves, lay on mantels; and more were stacked on tables, with page markers protruding. The flat had an indelibly masculine and clubbish atmosphere. A decanter of whisky, half consumed, stood on a desk next to a foolscap notepad covered in a racing, spiky hand, marked with revisions. The room might have been the haven of an academic historian—but for the traces of vigorous good living, including the presence of a butler.

The visitor, a man in late middle age with cropped gray hair, wore a dark suit. While he waited he stood nervously near the window, looking out on the incongruously mock-Byzantine Roman Catholic Cathedral in Westminster.

"Ah, good morning to you, sir." The voice from the door was fruity and resonant. The visitor turned from the window and saw a bulky figure wearing a thick woollen dressing gown and carpet slippers. "Von Kleist?" He advanced, moving a cigar from right to left hand as he offered a handshake. "Pray take a seat."

The visitor bowed first, with a military reflex. "It was good of you to see me, Mr. Churchill."

Churchill stayed on his feet, scrutinizing the visitor. "I have, of course, been informed of your other meetings." He put the cigar in his mouth and drew on it; then he walked to the desk and half turned: "Cigar?" The man shook his head. Churchill picked up a sheet of paper and then faced the man again. "Now, sir. You have my undivided attention."

Sitting stiffly upright, von Kleist spoke urgently in crisp accented English: "I believe that war between us would be a great catastrophe, Mr. Churchill. Not only I, but my friends the generals know it. To invade Czechoslovakia, as Hitler intends, would mean war."

Churchill lowered himself into the opposite chair. "And the date is set?"

"Your prime minister knows the date."

Churchill frowned. "I was not aware. . . ."

"Mr. Churchill, I have come out of Germany with a rope around my neck, to warn your government. *You are my last resort.*"

Churchill's face was hidden by a haze of cigar smoke. For a moment he was silent, then he said, "I am aware of your allegiances, sir. I have no *official* position, you must understand that. However, I am not without some influence. You realize that England will march with France, and certainly the United States is now strongly anti-Nazi." He spoke with a slight lisp, rasping out the last word: *Naaaaarzee.* He continued: "Such a war, once started, would be fought out like the last, to the bitter end. Tell me, how many in Berlin want such a war?"

"There is only one real extremist. Adolf Hitler."

"And the prospect of removing him, that is realistic?"

"It has been planned for many months. If we can rely on support from your government, we would have a new regime installed within forty-eight hours."

Churchill's cigar was spent. He put the stub in an ashtray. "What kind of support did you have in mind?"

"Simply a speech, at the right moment, making clear what you have already said: that Britain and France stand together. That would be enough."

Churchill rose and went to the desk, sorting through papers. He found a small booklet and gave it to von Kleist. "You must read this, it is a full statement of *official* British policy. Before you came, I consulted Lord Halifax. He asked me to make it plain that this policy stands." While von Kleist read the paper Churchill stood by the window. Seeing the German look up, visibly disturbed, Churchill said, "A speech, you say? When?"

"Before the Nuremberg Rally—you know how important that is, as a demonstration of public feeling. The right speech before that would undermine him." Von Kleist stood up. "You see, *we have so little time.*"

"Speaking for myself," Churchill said slowly, "I believe that a peaceful and friendly solution can pave the way for the true reunion of our countries—on the basis of the greatness and freedom of both." Seeing von Kleist's expression, Churchill said, "If you wish, I will give you a letter confirming these views."

The royal box at the Nuremberg opera house was framed in heavy velvet curtains, bowed at the bottom. Under the center of the box hung a swastika banner, not the usual burst of scarlet but a domesticated version woven in tapestry. Standing at the front of the box, right arm extended, Hitler took the applause of the audience before the curtain rose on a gala performance of *Die Meistersinger*.

From a smaller box to the side of the gallery Canaris found the applause disturbing. He sat down and waited for the opera to begin, letting five minutes or so pass before he moved back into the shadows and slipped out of the box. He walked along a carpeted corridor, then found the men's lavatory.

Piekenbrock was already waiting, by the washbasins. "It's all right," he said, nodding toward the cubicles, "nobody else is in here."

Canaris was even more uncomfortable in evening dress than in uniform. He stood looking at himself in the mirror, pulling one eye back, looking at the ravages of insomnia. He unbuttoned his jacket and pulled at the starched shirt, then brought out a small packet from his trousers pocket.

"Here," he said, "would you like one? Something new, very good for the liver."

Piekenbrock shook his head, and Canaris slipped a tablet into his mouth and chewed it, still looking in the mirror. He caught a sense of his cumulative weariness—a weariness that could be resolved only by doing something against his whole nature. As he came to this truth he saw from behind him Piekenbrock's eyes, which reflected the same understanding. The clinical lavatory, crudely scented, intensified the sense of isolation and introspection. "Well?" he said, turning away from the mirror.

"It's agreed," said Piekenbrock. "It can be done. The date is fixed now. September fifteenth."

"Well, at least Halder is running things instead of Beck. I have more faith in it now. There is one detail I do not like. It is a mistake to leave the Potsdam garrison to take the chancellery. Their reliability is in question, they have been penetrated by Nazi elements. A small number of officers, absolutely trusted, must be sent to Hitler on some pretext. They should spirit him away quietly—no shooting—before anyone realizes what has happened."

Canaris moved across the tiles to a urinal and continued, talking over his shoulder: "I expected more from Churchill. Doesn't even *he* realize what's at stake? I think Hitler already has them paralyzed."

"We could make one more attempt," said Piekenbrock.

Canaris turned away from the urinal, buttoning his trousers. "Kordt—at the embassy in London. He has good connections with the government there. I think he should do it. Perhaps, even now, they will give us what we need."

Piekenbrock knew that Canaris was still trying to convince himself.

The lavatory door swung open, and boots hit the tiles. A man in the full dress uniform of the S.S. walked in, silk gloves against the black of his pants, already unbuttoning his flies. He saw the two men at the basins and stopped. "Herr Admiral," he said, "it is a long opera for weak bladders, is it not?"

Von Klagen had forgotten the way Margery Taverner drove. She moved into the center lane of a three-lane highway to overtake a cruising M.G. The M.G. was driven by a knight of the road who, seeing a woman driver as provocation, suddenly accelerated and left them no escape as they came into the bend just as an ancient bus came around it from the other direction. For a few seconds there was virtually no space between all three vehicles. The M.G. driver lost his nerve first, and his front wheels wobbled. In the slipstream of the bus Margery Taverner found her car sucked sideways. Von Klagen watched the margin narrow between his door and the M.G. She regained control and deliberately edged to the left. The rear nearside fender tipped the outside wing of the M.G. In the mirror, as she accelerated away, she watched the sports car waver and then spin into a ditch. Von Klagen looked back. All he could see was dust and then a small orange glow.

"The bastard," she said, keeping her foot down.

They left the main road west of Reading and drove up a wooded hill and then along the rough track to the cottage. She switched off the engine and smiled at him: "This is it. My little nest."

"Perfect," he said.

She put a hand on his groin. "Nobody will bother us here, Erich."

As he carried the hamper inside she watched the bad leg dragging.

"It's all right," he said, deflecting the offered hand.

"Why don't you take something, if it's bothering you so much?"

"I'm not a cripple. It will pass."

She brought him a large whisky, and they sat by the small pool.

"Strange man," she said, "you keep turning up."

"Like a bad penny?" He gulped the whisky gratefully. It was better than medicine, he thought—and quicker. It seeped through his nervous system. He pushed out his legs, hoping the whisky would settle in them, and looked at her: the swan neck and the eyes like bullets. Where the throat met the edge of the breasts there was the slightest shift of color, a darkening. Otherwise, an even lightness.

"So," he said.

It was cool enough, after the meal, to light a fire. He squatted by it, pushing another log into the flames and watching as the bark curled from it like parchment, and the sparks were sucked up into the draft. She stretched out naked behind him on the rug. She was slightly drunk.

"How's the leg, *now?*" she said, stroking the calf.

"Can't you tell?"

"You're quite a gymnast, even— You've never told me how it happened."

"Riding."

She looked at him insolently. *"I've* never seen a riding injury like that."

His hand slipped inside her thighs and gripped. He moved the thumb in the way she liked. Her eyes dilated. He kept the hand working and felt the membrane swelling. There was a sweet smell to mingle with the burning wood. Her eyes closed. "Mmmmmmmmmm *oh. Chrrrist!"*

Later, as he brought the coffee, she said, "The wine business seems to have a lot of slack times."

"The peak is over. People don't drink German wine in winter."

"There's a hell of a lot of drinking going on at the moment. The idea of war must be good for business."

"War?"

"Oh, come on, Erich. Czechoslovakia. He'll do it, *you* know that." She cupped the coffee in her hands, holding it between her breasts, the light of the fire behind her in her hair. "I hear he might be stopped, though. By his generals."

He moved away from the fire so that he could see her face more clearly. "Why do you say that?"

"I heard. Apparently some of your people have been trotting over here, asking for support. Planning some kind of putsch."

The coffee burned on his throat. He took an iron and moved the logs in the fire. "Who told you that, Margery?"

"That's odd. You've never called me that before."

He smiled.

Before she awakened the next morning, he walked a mile down the track beyond the cottage to where it crossed a small river, a tributary of the Thames. He had not slept. It was already sultry and the stone of the bridge was warm when he sat on it. He watched a frog haul itself through the reeds and then, seeing him, stop. It sat staring at him, its throat palpitating. As soon as he moved it vaulted into the water.

When he got back, she was frying eggs and bacon.

"Early bird," she said. "Where have you been?"

"I wondered where the track went. I followed it down to a river."

"It's nice, isn't it? A piece of old England. Beyond the river it runs down into Wiltshire. Good picnic country."

"A good idea—a picnic."

"You *are* going native, aren't you?" She was pleased as well as surprised, looking at him less warily. "I can make some sandwiches, we'll take the car down the track—that leg of yours wouldn't go the distance." He didn't object.

She backed the car out to the track and there it stalled. She tried the starter again but nothing happened. She pumped her foot in frustration.

"Let me," he said, then climbed out and raised the hood. He came back looking puzzled. "I don't know this car. Could you help me?"

"All right. But I warn you, I'm not much good with cars." She got out and peered under the hood. The side of his hand sliced into the precise spot on the back of her neck, and she crumpled without a sound. Her weight renewed the pain in his leg, but he managed to drag her back into the driving seat. He returned to the engine and readjusted the carburetor and put down the hood.

Her head slumped forward, her brow rested on the wheel. He edged her over gently and started the car, keeping her feet just clear of the pedals. He eased off the brake, and

the car pitched forward down the track; he kept the speed low
because it was difficult to control the car while lying across
her body. He stopped about thirty yards short of the bridge
and opened the driver's door. He moved her back fully into
the seat and balanced himself on the running board alongside.
He leaned across and released the brake, catching the scent of
her. The car began to roll without any touch on the pedal. He
waited for it to reach about twenty miles per hour, keeping his
left hand on the wheel. Just before the bridge he gave the
wheel a flick and jumped, hitting the grass with his good leg
as if in a parachute fall and rolling over to keep the weight on
that side.

Just as he got back to his knees the car reached the
bridge, at a slight angle. The right wing hit a parapet, and the
car tried to spin. He heard the leaf springs tear into the top of
the low wall and saw sparks. The nearside front tire was ruptured by the impact with a sharp stone and exploded. The
deflated tire acted as a sudden brake, and the car tilted at
about forty degrees to the left. It keeled over the edge of the
bridge and fell on its side into the water, not yet out of forward motion, so that it nosed to the far bank of the river as it
sank. Only a quarter of the rear offside and an edge of the
spare wheel remained above the water. As the car settled it
slewed around slightly in the current. He was surprised how
deep the river was. A great bubble of air came to the surface
with a limp plopping sound.

Von Klagen stood by the track for another minute, making sure nothing moved. Then he turned and walked back up
to the cottage. The killing was a step in self-knowledge: Given
the sudden imperative, it caused him not one second of mis-
giving.

The two men crossed Horse Guards to the garden wall of
10 Downing Street. They stopped at the small black gate set
into the wall. One of them tapped on the wood. The door
opened, he whispered a name, the two went up the garden
path, past a small conservatory, and into the house.

They were met in an anteroom and ushered through a
door. "Mr. Conwell Evans—and friend," the secretary announced.

Sir Horace Wilson waved them to seats by his desk without getting up and offered cigarettes, which were declined.
The secretary melted from the room. During the last few
years in Downing Street he had grown used to clandestine

meetings, but there seemed a tension to this one that was unusual, reflected even in the demeanor of Wilson, Neville
Chamberlain's alter ego.

"Well . . ." said Wilson, with a studied weariness, "I
gather there is another message from Berlin?"

"Herr Kordt has come to me at some risk," said Conwell
Evans, "as you will appreciate. In my long experience as an
intermediary between our two countries I have to admit that
this is the gravest hour. He brings a message from his brother
in the Foreign Ministry."

Kordt moved his spectacles nervously, looking from Conwell Evans to Wilson. "The invasion date is certain now. October first. The military plan is code-named Green. Before it
begins there will be provocations, to create a pretext."

Wilson raised his eyes slowly. "Provocations?" He spoke
like a man finding grit in an oyster.

"An incident will be contrived, requiring the Sudeten
Germans to appeal to Germany for help."

"Rather transparent, I should have thought," said Wilson.

"It must be stopped," Kordt said with sudden insistence.
"The German patriots see no other way to stop it but through
close cooperation with Britain and France. If you can make
public your knowledge of the invasion, and your support for
them—"

"Yes, yes," said Wilson, moving to impatience, "we have
heard all this before. You must understand the prime minister's reluctance to become involved in what is, strictly speaking, an internal German issue."

Conwell Evans protested: "The invasion of Czechoslovakia is hardly an internal issue."

Wilson, stung by the sharpness of the comment, fell silent, turning in his chair to look out the window. After a minute he turned back to face them and said, "You really must
understand that we have already gone a long way to settle this
amicably, by diplomatic means, which is the only proper conduct. I really cannot take it upon myself to give you an answer. We might see if we can have a word with the foreign
secretary."

There was a brief telephone interchange, and then Wilson led the two men back the way they had come, but this
time they turned left out of the garden gate instead of right,
into a small rear entrance of the Foreign Office.

Halifax listened silently as the two men repeated the

message. Then he said, "A coup is a dangerous quantity. One doesn't know the risks, which could be disastrous."

"How are we to know that this is not bluff?" said Wilson.

Kordt's lips tightened. "Hitler is seriously talking of the political domination of Hungary, Rumania, and Yugoslavia—*after* Czechoslovakia."

"But that is madness," said Halifax.

"Just so," said Wilson.

"The view is that Hitler *is* mad," said Conwell Evans. "That will be the basis for removing him."

Halifax looked at Wilson and then back to Kordt. "I am most grateful for your taking the risk of coming here. Of course, no record will be made of this meeting, for your own protection. In any discussions I will refer to you only as Herr X. Is that satisfactory?"

"That will become academic if nothing is done," Kordt replied. It was now dark outside, and Halifax's domed head was waxen under a chandelier. Kordt and Conwell Evans got up. Halifax came from behind his desk and shook their hands. As Wilson was about to leave with them Halifax said, "Horace, would you stay?"

When the two men had gone, he said, "I'm afraid they've got Neville wavering. Yesterday he said to me they should be left to do their own dirty business. Today he said—let me think, it was *typical* Neville—ah yes, he said, '*I do not feel sure that we ought not to do something.*' What d'you think, Horace?"

Wilson stood watching the two men recross Horse Guards. "There's always something suspicious about anti-Nazis coming to this country in fear of their lives . . . especially if they get away with it."

"Yes, but what d'you advise?"

"Nothing should be done to jeopardize Plan Z—not now."

The Scotland Yard inspector was a brisk, cunning man with broad Yoskshire vowels and a manifest contempt for London beer. He found Endmere more congenial company than others he had so far encountered in his brush with "society." Endmere, he thought, was more candid, more genuinely distressed, and he just might be telling the truth. He drained the offensive brew and put the glass back on the pub counter with clear disdain. "Theakston's, now *that's* a beer,

Theakston's Old Peculiar. They make a good barrel, do Theakston's—six pints of that and you could see off anyone."

"Really?" said Endmere. "I must try it, if I ever get to Yorkshire."

"Yes, sir, you do that." The inspector consulted his notes again. "Now, sir, we have only this one sighting, and that's what bothers me. I don't like being bothered. There was an incident on the road near Reading, I came on the report quite by chance. Nobody got a clear view, but the car fits the description as near as may be. Young man in an M.G. forced off the road, cut up a bit, lucky to get away with his life. He said there was a man in the car, with the woman. The woman's description *could* have been Lady Taverner's—it's a long shot, I admit, everything happened so fast, bad witnesses. But there it is."

"No other trace?"

"Not yet." The inspector ordered another pint of the beer and bought Endmere another whisky. "I'm desperate, to be honest, sir."

"So," said Endmere, raising his glass to the inspector's, "it mightn't have been an accident, you think?"

"Nothing wrong with the car. Simple piece of driving. Of course, I gather she was a bit of a wild driver. Nevertheless, sir, as I said, it bothers me."

"And you don't like to be bothered."

The inspector quaffed half of the beer and put the glass back on the counter. "Gnat's piss," he said in earshot of the publican, but in a way that intimidated reply.

25

Theodor Kordt's limousine took the main west road out of London, following other black official cars, to a cluster of huts and aircraft hangars on the perimeter of a suburban field. Noting the diplomatic pennant, a guard waved them through, and they parked with the other cars near the largest of the hangars.

A new Lockheed 14 of the Imperial Airways Fleet, regis-

tration G–AFGN, stood on the apron, silver against the dull
gray morning. Its passenger door was open, and Kordt saw
men put some small light metal steps under it. Above a small
group of British officials he saw the giraffe head of Lord
Halifax, crowned with bowler. The men turned up their coat
collars against the damp wind.

Two more limousines, ponderous and stately, drew onto
the apron, and a passenger left each of them. As soon as
Kordt saw Sir Horace Wilson and Neville Chamberlain he
knew, finally, how futile had been his clandestine meetings.
Chamberlain walked across the apron to a small line of press
photographers and called for some of his officials to form a
group by the steps of the plane. Instinctively, Wilson took a
pace into the background while Chamberlain, game for the
pose, waved his hand several times to make sure all the photographers were happy. Then, taking his first step into an air-
plane, he disappeared through the door, followed by Wilson.
Two small steps, thought Kordt, and the world collapses.

At 5:30 P.M., nearly nine hours after leaving London,
Neville Chamberlain climbed into a dark-blue supercharged
Mercedes and left the town of Berchtesgaden, the car climbing up through the two checkpoints to the Berghof. The cloud
was too low to give a view of the Untersberg. A guard of
honor lined up, and as the car stopped at the foot of the steps
Hitler stepped forward.

Chamberlain's advisers followed him up to the terrace
and into the reception room. As they passed through the door
a German staff officer recognized one of the British aides.
The German took the Englishman's arm and moved him to
one side.

"My dear Bartlett," he said, "it is too late."

"What is too late?"

"You knew the plan."

It was September 15.

Ruth walked for the first time across the great stone
floor of Westminster Abbey. She had gone there on an impulse after brooding on the news of Chamberlain's flight.
Skeptical as she was about the trappings of patriotism and of
the pomp of the high Anglican church, something secular in
the building now overrode its sacramental images: She realized it was an accretion of a particular life force in the stone
itself; the plainer the stone, the more potent seemed the

spirit—of weathering, of enduring. The Abbey was silent witness to that native drama that had been played out here since London was little more than a village, where dynasties were punctuated by regicides heroic and squalid and where people came, as they did now, to renew their sense of belonging.

The Unknown Warrior's Tomb lay in the west wing of the nave. A crucifix flanked by two candles had been put there that morning as the focus for a period of unbroken intercession, day and night. The smell of candle wax blended with incense. The flames bent with the draft from the movement of people about the tomb. The stone magnified the hushed voices into a low, undulating murmur. People of all ages came and rested their spirit here, hoping a whole spectrum of hopes, from surrender to resolution. There Ruth began to see into the heart of an anguishing division: One man's honor would be another man's abdication.

She came out into Parliament Square knowing that prayer was as futile as debate but feeling that she now understood a little more of her own commitment—and how easily and decently hope could be misplaced.

A fussy point Seton noticed in himself: the squaring off of the papers on his desk, as he talked. There was a meridian on one wall of the office at the end of the bookcase. When the evening sun reached this point, summer was running out. On such details a man became familiar with confinement. Seton despaired of himself. He took another sheet of paper from the telegrams Pickles had just dropped into his tray.

Every day brought more of these messages from Spain, clinical assessments of what he knew must be far from impersonal experiences for his agent—though Seton knew how impersonal it could be for the deliverers of the carnage, squatting over the bombsights ten thousand feet over the cities. It was the final part of this message that jerked Seton from his melancholia. He read it twice and then called Pickles.

"Did you see today's message from Oloroso?"

"I didn't read it."

Seton still had the telegram in his hand. He got up from the desk and began pacing the room, taking his glasses off, almost declaiming:

"I should have thought of this *before*," he said as Pickles stood back. "We could have—" He broke off and turned on Pickles: "This single piece of information, Pickles, changes everything—the whole premise on which this wretched man is talking to Hitler!" Aware suddenly of breaching a professional discretion, Seton waved his glasses at Pickles: "Please disregard that comment."

Pickles grinned. "That's all right, sir. He sickens me, too."

Seton stopped walking and slowly conceded a grin. A professional alliance. had grown a personal confidence: "Really? That's good to know." He gave the telegram to Pickles. "Read it—the last paragraph."

Pickles read:

STAFFLEN K88 OF THE CONDOR HAS BEGUN OPERATIONS WITH ITS NEW HEINKEL 111B BOMBERS IN THE BATTLE OF THE EBRO. THESE SUPPLEMENT GROUP A88 WHICH HAS FLOWN THE DORNIER 17F SINCE OCTOBER LAST. BOTH TYPES VERY EFFECTIVE ALMOST IMPOSSIBLE TO INTERCEPT OWING TO SPEED. CONVERSATION WITH PILOTS OF BOTH GROUPS REVEALS INTERESTING COMPLAINT. LOAD AND RANGE OF AIRCRAFT SACRIFICED FOR PERFORMANCE. HEINKELS CARRY HALF TON OF BOMBS FOR JUST OVER FOUR HUNDRED, REPEAT FOUR HUNDRED MILES. SIGNIFICANCE OF THIS FOR YOU IS NO CONSOLATION FOR ME. OLOROSO.

Seton looked at Pickles as he finished reading. "Don't you see, *they can't reach southern England and get back!* The same goes for the fighters. *Göring has built the wrong air force!*"

"You mean—" Pickles himself became flushed. "—unless they operated from France, they are no use against us?"

Seton went back to his desk. "I should have seen this before. Just a few weeks, and I might have been able to convince *somebody* that as long as France holds firm, this idea of London being defenseless is entirely unfounded. You see, Pickles, *this* is the answer to Lindbergh's mischief. He has them cowering because they see the Luftwaffe over London tomorrow, but that just could not be!"

"It's a bit hard, isn't it, sir? I mean, to know this today, of all days."

"That's the devil of it, the real devil of it, Pickles. I can hardly call Chamberlain out of the meeting." He picked up the phone. His frustration on hearing the answer was clear.

"Not in London? Oh. *I see.* Very well, as soon as he's back. Would you tell him that it is extremely urgent? No, nothing that can be said over a line to Germany. Thank you."

"*He's* there, too?"

"That must be pretty hard for him to bear," said Seton.

"You asked for the psychiatric report on the wrong man, Oster."

The two colonels, Piekenbrock and Oster, were suffering Canaris at his most lacerating.

Canaris's head nodded several times with the motion of his temper. "Yes. It is Chamberlain whose head should have been studied. You should have sent your Professor Bonhoeffner to examine *him*. For myself, I am beginning to think Hitler a genius. It is said that genius is close to madness, you obviously couldn't tell the difference. He's *playing* with Chamberlain. The English are unbelievable, to send such a man to deal with Hitler."

Even the two dachshunds cowered.

"There's no hope now, you realize that?" he continued. "You can no longer present Hitler as a man about to destroy his country. The people won't have that."

Oster sighed. "Chamberlain has saved him."

Until now, Seton had only seen his patron in the armor of Whitehall, and here, suddenly, he was in worn tweeds, bareheaded—and without the umbrella. It heightened the sense of intrusion.

"I'm sorry," said Seton, "but I had to see you."

"Sit down, Edward."

The table was of white wrought iron with a marble top stained with bird droppings. The wooden seats were similarly blemished. Seeing his host settle his tweeds uncaring onto the pine, Seton did the same, knowing that his gray flannels would bear the mark. Slack attention marked the whole garden: untrimmed bushes, rampant shrubbery, stone vases on pillars trailing ivy. Seton thought of the precision and fussiness of the man's professional work and realized that this was where he let himself go.

"My wife will bring some tea." There had never been any indication of a wife before. "Now, why so much of a hurry?"

"Our man in Spain, watching the Condor Legion, something of the utmost importance. I've explained before, they're trying out their latest bombers—the stuff that will be in the front line, in Europe. For the sake of speed they've sacrificed range. As they now are, the Luftwaffe bombers could not reach southern England and return to Germany. Nothing like enough range."

"You mean—from German bases?"

"That's right." Seton saw that the significance had gone home.

"I see."

They heard steps behind them. A broad-hipped woman in a floral dress came up with a tray. Seton began to rise.

"No—please," she said, "I mustn't interrupt. Very nice to meet you, Group Captain." She had a white, very open face. She turned to her husband: "There, your favorite fruit cake. Must go, the jam is on the boil." She gave a parting glance to Seton: "Apple and rhubarb, you must take a jar with you."

Seton's host poured the tea.

"You're sure of this?"

"Four bomber wings have just been moved into Luft-flotte Two—their crack unit in Europe, on the western front. They have the same aircraft. They're committed, now—for years ahead."

"So, unless they take Belgium, Holland, and France. . . ."

"They're useless against us."

Seton was offered, and took, a slice of cake. His host sat back in the chair, dropping crumbs as he ate, ruminating. Finally he said, "A month ago, I might have done something with it."

"But—surely, there's still time?"

"Things have gone too far. The P.M. is committed."

"To what?"

"To negotiation. Peace with honor, he calls it. The phrase was Disraeli's, I believe."

"He's not going again?"

"There's a joke going the rounds: If at first you don't succeed, fly, fly, and fly again."

Seton fell silent. From the house came the sickly smell of boiling jam.

Chewing on a second slice of cake, his host said, "There's something else you should know. Germans have been coming over here trying to enlist our support for a coup against Hitler. Men have risked their lives. We had the whole timetable on Czechoslovakia."

"A coup? You think that is possible?"

"Was."

Seton put the jar of apple and rhubarb jam on the table. "There," he said, *"that's* all I got for my trouble. Rather apt."

Ruth was dismayed by the desperation of his appearance as soon as she opened the door; now she heard it in his voice. "You look awful," she said.

"That's right."

She went to the whisky and put in very little soda.

He took the drink and sat down. "I'm sorry, it's really bad."

"You'd better get it out of your system."

"The hell of it is, there's nothing I can do."

She poured herself a whisky and stood over him. "I don't understand you—do you know that? You just let things brew inside of you. And you come in here like a drowned dog looking for comfort. I can't *stand* that."

He finished the whisky and said, "No. You *don't* understand, do you?"

"How can I? I *want* to. But you're so damned *taciturn*—so *English.*"

"Oh. You're tired of England now, is *that* it?"

She wondered how their tempers had risen so quickly, but she was undeterred: *"Yes*—if you want to know. This country is a joke. What does it take to get you people mad enough to fight, for chrissakes? Don't you realize you're not dealing with gentlemen? They're *monsters!*" She began to pace the floor.

Seton turned facetious: "Oh, that's *rich,* coming from you! Who was it who was telling me, not so long ago, that this was not *their* fight!" As soon as he said it he realized how wounding it was. "You don't understand, Ruth—how this country works. You can't get anywhere by raising hell. For God's sake—look at Churchill! Tolerated, barely, because of his high birth. But ignored. And what does *he* do? He keeps quiet, *even now.*"

She turned on him: "And you're a part of that? You believe—*knowing what you do*—in lying down and letting them roll over you? You make me sick."

He stood up and went to the window. "Churchill knows. You have to wait. It's the only way."

"My God!" She put down the drink and went to him. "You're too *buttoned up*—do you know that?" She put both

hands on the lapels of his waistcoat and pulled hard. The buttons tore away in succession, from top to bottom. *"Too fucking buttoned up!"*

He looked at her calmly. *"I* can handle this, but I'm not sure you can."

She turned away and walked out, taking her coat and slamming the door.

He went to the phonograph and took out the Mozart set, beginning with the *Jupiter*. The whisky decanter was slowly drained. The needle skated in its final groove impotently for an hour as he slept. The bell became insistent. On its third prolonged burst he heard it and rose drowsily, at first disoriented. He went slowly to the door.

She looked at him. "In the first place, it's *my* flat. In the second place, I considered the alternatives. Will you *hold me*, please?"

In the morning he told her everything.

"My God—they let *that* chance go?" she said, incredulous.

"I'm going to do something. I *have* to."

"What?"

"Get to the right people."

"I'll have to sew those buttons back on, first."

Ambassador Joseph Kennedy paced the room listening to a monologue:

". . . The rate of progress in German aviation is without parallel. . . . German factories can produce twenty thousand airplanes a year. . . . Civilization has never faced a greater crisis . . . Czechoslovakia has no modern aircraft. . . . Germany can destroy London, Paris, and Prague if she wants to. . . . It is essential to permit Germany's eastward expansion. . . . Germany is inseparable from the welfare of European civilization. . . ."

As he spoke Lindbergh's head rolled like a metronome in the rhythm of the litany. Watching Kennedy's face to judge the impact, Lindbergh took care to harp on the chain-reaction risk to America if war came over the invasion of Czechoslovakia. Judging that his message was delivered, he stopped, patting his right knee with a final emphasis and then licking his lip.

Kennedy continued pacing. "I'm sure you're right. Nothing in Hitler's present ambitions ought to bother us. I just don't know why the British and French don't calm down. Jesus, you only have to look at Spain to see what would happen to London." He stopped and pushed a finger at Lindbergh: "Look here, I want you to put all that down in writing—here and now. I'll call a secretary. I want your view in the hands of Neville Chamberlain—*before he leaves for Bad Godesberg to-morrow.*"

26

Reinhard Heydrich took a yellow chrysanthemum from the vase and held it to his nose, squeezing the stalk between index finger and thumb until it fractured and the head hung limp. He left the broken flower on a table and turned to Dunsinnan.

"This was the Führer's idea," he said, indicating the vases of red and yellow flowers filling the suite. "Flowers in every room. Perhaps, now, a little optimistic?"

Dunsinnan sat in a hard moquette-covered chair, slightly slumped. "I had hoped for more, I must admit."

Heydrich turned to the window and watched a tourist steamer coming down the Rhine. Across the river, on the far bank, was the long solarium of the Dreesen Hotel at Bad Godesberg. The bow wave of the steamer slapped into the river wall by the hotel.

"If Chamberlain had been reasonable, they would have been sailing together down the Rhine by now. I don't understand this change. It was to have been the finale—a true gesture of peace." Heydrich's smile was arctic. "Now all we have is the flowers." He turned away from the view as the steamer's horn rasped out and echoed up the hill toward them.

"It's not lost—yet," said Dunsinnan. "Chamberlain may still see reason. He could come back again. He seems to have taken to flying."

"Those warmongers—Churchill and his Czech friends—they are behind it." Heydrich's voice hovered between accusation and question. He glared down at Dunsinnan.

Dunsinnan shifted his right foot, drawing it back an inch or so from Heydrich's, for fear of contact. "The personal rela-

tionship seems to have worsened. At Berchtesgaden I thought
they rather hit it off."

Heydrich, pleased with the intimidation of the withdrawn
foot, remained where he was. "I always thought the English
were supposed to be the best dressed men in the world. Why
did your people wear such clothes? The Führer *hates* tired
suits. He said if they came here looking like that again, he
would go to London wearing a sweater."

Dunsinnan's trousers had a knife-edge crease, and his Vi-
yella shirt was freshly pressed. "Tired clothes, tired men."

Heydrich suddenly relaxed, as though completing an interrogation and now seeking to lull his subject into grateful
humor. "Don't worry. There is still time. But not much."

Von Klagen was so worried about keeping out of Dunsinnan's sight that he nearly missed them as they walked across
the lobby. The hotel's flunkeys quivered visibly in the presence of Heydrich, whose plain suit did nothing to mask his
psychopathic presence. Von Klagen, keeping his distance,
watched them take the official car and head down to the
river. Since there was no evidence of Dunsinnan's baggage, he
assumed they had unfinished business. A mutual toast to the
looming war? he wondered. War hysteria was in every eye. In
the hotel the bad news from the conference had spread fast.
Von Klagen had relayed it to Canaris: Hitler had given
Chamberlain an ultimatum, demanding the dismemberment of
Czechoslovakia. Canaris had fallen silent so effectively that
von Klagen had thought the line had gone dead.

By the time von Klagen's taxi reached the ferry point at
the Petersberg side of the river, Heydrich and Dunsinnan
were aboard a small gray motor yacht, slipping from the ferry
quay into the current, almost overshadowed by a barge. Not
for the first time, von Klagen was beaten by the effectiveness
of water as a rendezvous. The barge, seeing the yacht cross its
bow, gave a blast of its horn. The master of the yacht was
heedless in a way that was ominously familiar to von Klagen—a way that spoke of a man who acted within the protection of the ultimate power in the state.

That power was invested in the man Dunsinnan now met
for the first time: Heinrich Himmler. Here, in only slightly
less measure than Hitler himself, was embodied the countenance of Nazi Germany, the true expression of its temper, the
odd admixture of civility and evil. Yet—to Dunsinnan—
Himmler seemed to possess a kind of grace which Heydrich

lacked, giving an impression of academic fastidiousness, almost feline. In Himmler's presence Heydrich fell deferentially silent, and Dunsinnan saw more clearly the apprenticeship. The light reflected off Himmler's glasses in such a way that his eyes were completely masked.

The three of them sat at a small table, Heydrich next to Himmler, facing Dunsinnan. In the manner of a man seeking counsel, Himmler said:

"I wanted to meet you, Lord Dunsinnan, because you have done so much for us in the past that I hoped you would be able to help us understand the present difficulty. In fact, when I planned this meeting, I expected it to be a celebration."

"I am as worried as you by this setback," said Dunsinnan. The Rhine shoreline passed across Himmler's glasses. "Personally, I will go to any lengths to achieve a lasting relationship between our two countries."

"Yes. I am sure you would," said Himmler. "Tell me, Lord Dunsinnan, I have watched these men, at Berchtesgaden and now here, at Bad Godesberg, and I still do not understand: Who is really in charge?" He took a silver pot of coffee and filled the three cups—Dunsinnan's first, his own second, and lastly Heydrich's.

"No," Dunsinnan began, "I don't suppose that is very clear." He sipped his coffee and then leaned across the table, hoping to penetrate the barrier of Himmler's glasses. "The advisers are the key. Who has the prime minister's ear. Fortunately, at the moment, that is principally one man—Sir Horace Wilson."

"I have watched him," said Himmler. "I still do not understand: What is his political view?"

Dunsinnan permitted himself a smile. "Professionally he doesn't have one. As a civil servant he is above that."

Heydrich said, "Where does he stand?"

"He's a very valued adviser," said Dunsinnan carefully, "taking into account Chamberlain's nature, *the* ideal man."

Himmler finished his coffee and at last moved his head to a position where Dunsinnan could see his eyes. "Lord Dunsinnan, we spend a large amount of money, time, and manpower trying to find out things like this. We have agents in more than sixty countries at this moment. *Sixty countries.* And yet of all of them, England, so close to us, so easy to penetrate, is the greatest mystery."

"I think," said Dunsinnan slowly, "if it was any other way, it would be harder for us."

Heydrich sat stony-faced. But the riddle percolated Himmler's humor, and he leaned back in his chair. "Just so, Lord Dunsinnan."

Seton went into the room with no sense of awe, although he had never before set foot inside 10 Downing Street. His determination made him immune to the simple intimidations of setting. He found a table covered in green baize with seven chairs on each side and a pair at each end. Only five places were filled, all at one end of the table—three on the far side and two at the far end. Seton was invited to take the seat nearest to this end on the empty side, placing him opposite the man who emerged as his principal interrogator: Sir Horace Wilson.

Seton suspected that the asymmetry of the seating was intended to put him at a disadvantage: The two men on his right, who remained in profile, doodled on pads; the two men to Wilson's right leaned back and studied the ceiling.

Wilson's heavy-lidded eyes settled on Seton: "We are obliged to you, Group Captain, for your memorandum. We felt it only fair to give you a chance to elaborate." He took up a pencil. "First, I think we were rather surprised by your view of Colonel Lindbergh."

Seton put his right hand on his manila file but left it closed, then—as he had rehearsed—spoke with quiet deliberation: "Lindbergh's figures are beyond anything I consider realistic—way beyond it, from what we know of their industrial capacity."

The man immediately to his right, fleshy and smelling of stale cigar, stirred from his pad and interrupted, looking not at Seton but at Wilson. "The group captain seems to discount Colonel Lindbergh's firsthand experience in Germany—something I believe denied to the group captain himself."

Wilson put both elbows on the table, threading the pencil through his hands and raising his eyebrows as an invitation to Seton to respond.

"I don't for one moment question Colonel Lindbergh's reputation as a pilot. But as a military analyst he is apt to come to superficial conclusions."

The man on Wilson's right, young and sandy-haired with a compressed, simian face, lowered his eyes from a distant cornice and began speaking:

"If we were to accept that there might be an *element* of exaggeration in Lindbergh's figures—after all, nobody can be sure of this kind of thing—would it still not be true to say that in *quality* of equipment Germany does, at this moment, enjoy ascendancy?"

The questioning seemed carefully orchestrated, coming from unpredictable directions. But this was an opening Seton had anticipated:

"It is perfectly true that their latest types are superior in performance to those in our own front-line squadrons—though not to the new types we are bringing forward. That is not the point, however. As I pointed out in my memorandum, they are not the right aircraft for an attack on us."

After a few seconds of silence, and some scratching of pencils on pads, Wilson spoke: "But they are a threat to France?"

"Without the conquest of France, Belgium, and Holland they are no threat to us."

The simian face showed interest again: "Is that a prediction of Hitler's plans?"

Confidently, Seton made his first mistake: "It seems likely."

Wilson nodded to the so far silent figure on his left—a man Seton knew to be from the War Office. Turning to Seton for the first time and speaking mildly, he said, "Would you accept that strategy is indivisible from diplomacy?"

Seton saw the danger. "Yes—I would accept that."

As though taking a cue, Wilson spoke: "You see, Group Captain, this is just the problem we have with your memorandum. Your whole drift seems to be to translate this theory of yours into diplomatic action. Coming at this particular time, with the prime minister making every effort to reach an understanding with Herr Hitler, it is hardly helpful."

"Even though you know that Hitler's own generals want to see him brought down?" That was Seton's second mistake.

The simian face looked at him. "How did you know of that?"

"It's my job to know."

Wilson's face was a mixture of suspicion and hostility. "I must emphasize that those approaches were very suspect. The prime minister will not lend encouragement to people involved in an internal party squabble."

Disregarding the now clear risk, Seton interrupted: "But, surely—they cannot be discounted so readily? The German

General Staff clearly has no appetite for war. The Luftwaffe can have no faith in a western offensive. I would think that if we gave them even a discreet indication. . . ."

A bronchial sigh came from Seton's right, then, still not looking directly at him, the man spoke: "*Really*—you are stepping outside your brief. Do you *seriously* suppose that we could have anything to do with—anything *at all* to do with a conspiracy to remove a head of state—a head of state of a country which is in no meaningful sense a belligerent, with whom we are involved in the most serious efforts to achieve a lasting peace, and on whom we believe we can exercise a moderating influence?" He dipped his head obliquely to Seton. "You have become carried away with your case—with *one* technical observation, it seems to me."

Seton comprehended the unstated but implicit purpose of the meeting. He had the sense of a closing trap.

Wilson said, "I know you have the confidence of Air Marshal Dowding, and we must put weight on that. But, great as your technical knowledge undoubtedly is, this is a time of great delicacy in our relations with Germany. We could not—*under any circumstances*—give encouragement to these factions within Germany."

"It's a matter of propriety, man," said the man on Seton's right.

Seton clenched his hands and leaned over the table, talking directly to Wilson: "Don't you *see*—this is probably the *last chance* to avoid war? Hitler is engaged in a campaign of bluff. A stand by us now could produce a bloodless coup and a completely new situation in Germany. *War could be averted.*"

Four faces gazed at the ceiling. Wilson was curt: "There is no serious risk of war, neither side wants it. Intrigues of the kind you appear to favor might well, on the other hand, so gravely compromise us that war *would* follow." He pulled the top sheet from his notepad and screwed it tightly into a ball. "This committee will take note of what you said. Thank you."

Seton picked up his folder. His throat and mouth were dry, and he realized that his anger had been overtaken by another emotion—a sense of betrayal; at last he had seen the true nature of what he opposed, and what he would have to go on opposing. He got up and walked out, leaving the five men seated in silence under the portrait of Sir Robert Walpole, the founder of cabinet government.

* * *

Ruth was concerned that Seton began turning up at her flat the worse for wear. This time the vapor of brandy was overwhelming.

"You'd better have some coffee—quite a *lot* of coffee."

"It's all right," he said, throwing his trilby to a hook with great accuracy, "my aim is still good." A crease of guilt came to his mouth. "You're right, I have been indulging." He took her in his arms, hooking a hand to her waist. "This time, though, there is hope on my breath."

"Not only hope," she said, drawing away, still apprehensive.

"Seriously, there is a turn for the better. The navy has been mobilized. Perhaps somebody *has* got the message."

"What difference can *that* make—now?" She went into the kitchen to make the coffee, and he stood leaning on the door, watching her.

"It was Churchill's idea. The navy still counts for something. Of course, they daren't give Winston the credit. The minister, Duff Cooper, gave the order."

"I still don't believe that they'll call Hitler's bluff."

She brought out the coffee, and he drank it greedily. Looking at him, she said, "That's not it, is it? Why you've been drinking."

He put down the cup and poured more coffee. "You know, I feel naked in front of you, these days. You do see through me, don't you?"

"Not *through* you. To you."

"I've been warned. That meeting was a bit of a personal disaster."

"That warning took a lot of brandy, I guess." She went to his side. "It may look like a personal disaster to *them*, but not to me."

"The trouble is, my dear Ruth, people don't go to war to improve a man's principles or morals."

"But surely you understand *why* they didn't want to know? Why they couldn't accept the idea of the German coup?"

"They talked about *propriety*."

"It's a kind of club. You broke the rules. When they hear of plots, they think, 'There but for the grace of God. . . .' "

He took her hand. "This broadcast of Chamberlain's, this could be it. The balloon going up. Shouldn't we be packing you off home? Plenty of others are going."

"No chance."

He looked at his watch. "Ten minutes, and we'll know."

She lay on the sofa and put her head on his lap. A dispassionately crisp B.B.C. voice announced that the broadcast was "direct from Number Ten Downing Street by the prime minister, the Right Honorable Neville Chamberlain." There was a gap, a crackle of static, and then the fluting, hesitant voice:

"How horrible, fantastic, incredible it is that we should be digging trenches and trying on gas masks here, because of a quarrel in a faraway country between people of whom we know nothing—"

"God,' she said, looking up at Seton.

"—still more impossible that a quarrel which has already been settled in principle should be the subject of war—"

"Principle!" exploded Seton.

". . . However much we may sympathize with a small nation confronted by a big powerful neighbor. . . ." The platitudes worked to a resolution: "War is a fearful thing, and we must be very clear, before we embark on it, that it is really the great issues that are at stake, and that the call to risk everything in their defense, when all the consequences are weighed, is irresistible. . . ."

Seton felt a wave of nausea. Ruth repeated the words: " 'a faraway country between people of whom we know nothing.' " She snorted: "And care even less." Her anger was nearly translated into an attack on the radio. There was another click, and Chamberlain evaporated into the void. She got up and looked at Seton. Even the brandy flush had drained from his face.

Seton guided Ruth through the lobbies of the House of Commons. "You'll never see the like of this again," he said.

"It's a bit like I imagined the opening day at Ascot," she whispered. There were men in tailcoats, some women in severe suits and black veils, others in bizarre hats and summer dresses, and an array of ambassadors in full diplomatic dress. Some members of Parliament were in uniform. The air of privilege, the sheen of wealth, the look of power, all were mingled into one mass with a common apprehension as yet only in the eye. Finally, reaching a bench seat in the gallery, she was shocked to discover how small the famous chamber really was. She had always thought of it as a hall and now saw it as a cockpit with steeply angled benches and many gray

heads crammed together. In the center of the narrow strip of
floor was a table with the great gold mace in its cradle.

She recalled the *frisson* she had felt in the Osteria Bavaria when she saw Hitler for the first time, and here now
was Chamberlain coming into the chamber—his hair grayer
than she expected and the face rouged rather than sallow—
and none of the same electricity. At the end of one of the
benches she saw Churchill, a domed head and a broad belly,
clutching a wad of telegrams held together by a rubber band.
The effect when Chamberlain rose was that of a laywer as-
sembling his case: holding pince-nez in one hand, notes in the
other; moving with overrehearsed vanity and, conscious of his
profile, elevating his face into the beams from the skylight.
The voice that filtered from the radio the night before was
now more assured, more stagey. He feigned spontaneity,
breaking away from the notes for effect, gazing up at the
galleries, hand on lapel clutching the notes.

Seton whispered to Ruth, "Over there, look." She recognized the Duchess of Kent, who sat in a small gallery; behind
her, she saw a small woman in black, almost lost in the shadows. "Queen Mary," said Seton, "don't think she's ever been
here before." Other faces in other galleries peered down;
among the ambassadors Ruth spotted Kennedy's red hair.

Chamberlain knew the power of chronology to play on
tension: He worked through, stage by stage, the history of his
dealings with Germany, reserving the two meetings with Hitler for his climax. "My first flight," he said, to emphasize
the heroism of his journey to Munich. Then Ruth noticed a
stirring in one of the galleries. Someone got up to leave and
moments later reappeared on the floor at the back of the
chamber, passing a note. The note reached a man sitting behind Chamberlain. He tugged at the tail of Chamberlain's coat
but was ignored. He tugged again and passed the note. Chamberlain faltered in midsentence and peered at the paper.
"Shall I read it now?" he said. The man nodded. Chamberlain
adjusted his pince-nez; his tongue flicked lizardlike across his
lips. He said, "Herr Hitler has just agreed to postpone his
mobilization for twenty-four hours and to meet me in conference with Signor Mussolini and Monsieur Daladier at Munich,
tomorrow."

There was a moment of stillness and then the chamber
erupted. Some sang "For He's a Jolly Good Fellow." Seton
turned to look at Ruth, who stared down on the scene in
disbelief. Below, a few figures remained impassive on the

benches: Eden and Churchill among them, Churchill still fingering new messages.

Afterwards, in the lobby, there were many exultant faces. A hand took Seton's arm from behind: "What did you think—perfectly timed, wasn't it?" It was Endmere. Ruth heard the voice and turned. Seton said awkwardly, "You remember Ruth . . . ?" Endmere smiled. "Could I forget?" Bodies pressed into them; voices were shrill and insistent. A corpulent man stumbled by them: ". . . I think Neville is the reincarnation of Saint George. . . ." Ruth watched him disappear and said, "About to be devoured by the dragon, I think." Endmere said, "Now, *now*—you mustn't destroy the atmosphere, it's a moment of history." He was pushed into her by the crush. "You must find all this rather primitive." She said, "I've never seen *anything* like it." Seton said, "I hope not." The jostling continued. Seton took her arm, and they moved through a tide of sycophantic comment, swept out into Palace Yard. Big Ben was just striking 4:30 P.M.

The passage of Chamberlain's news was physical, reaching daylight as they did, going visibly from the Yard into the street outside, across Parliament Square, from one cluster of people to the next—an uncritical wave of relief so great that Seton wondered if people would kiss the grass. Instead they congregated around Parliament calling for Chamberlain. He came out and, stepping into his car, waved his umbrella.

Endmere stood with them, watching. "That man has the kind of vanity that is very close to stupidity." Then he left them, disappearing into the mass, in search of a taxi.

"I think I need a walk," Seton said.

They crossed Westminster Bridge to the south side of the Thames and took the path eastwards by the river. They could see, on the opposite bank, trams clattering by with people leaning from the open platforms waving and cheering and singing. Ahead of them, around the curve of the river, the dome of Saint Paul's Cathedral was white and matte gray in the evening sun.

Seton stopped. *"We can't have this,"* he said.

Ruth drew closer to him.

A sheet of low cloud hung over London as the Lockheed came in from the east and turned in a wide arc to line up with the still shrouded runway at Heston. Only half a mile from touchdown it came out of the cloud and passed over the suburbs, beads of rain on the windows blocking the passengers' view. By the time the plane rolled to a stop on the apron the drizzle had eased. Chamberlain took the two steps back to earth and walked to the waiting microphones. The newsreel cameras began to turn. From inside his coat he pulled out a piece of stiff legal-sized paper and unfolded it. He stepped to the microphones.

"I have here an agreement, signed between Herr Hitler and myself today. . . ." He looked up at the cameras between sentences, coming slowly to the climax: "We regard the agreement signed last night, and the Anglo-German Naval Agreement, as symbolic of the desire of our two peoples never to go to war with one another again."

His mouth curved in an inverted smile, eyes raised again to the heavens, and he held the paper aloft as the flashbulbs went off. It began to rain again.

Ruth took in the post while Seton was shaving. There was a letter from her father. She sat in the kitchen and read it:

SOMETHING HAS CHANGED IN THIS FAR-OFF LAND. WE LISTENED TO MURROW AT FOUR IN THE MORNING FROM LONDON AND WE HEARD CHAMBERLAIN. IT ALL SEEMS CLOSER TO US NOW—AND YOU, TOO. WE HEARD THE CROWD IN DOWNING STREET AND THOUGHT YOU MIGHT BE THERE. YOU CAN'T ESCAPE THESE THINGS NOW. THE WORLD, BECAUSE OF THE RADIO, COMES INTO YOUR OWN HOME BEFORE BREAKFAST AND THEN ALL DAY WITH THE SPECIAL BULLETINS. WHEN WE LISTEN TO HITLER'S RAVINGS I REALIZE WHAT RADIO HAS DONE FOR DR. GOEBBELS—OR WHAT DR. GOEBBELS HAS DONE TO RADIO. THERE ARE PLENTY MORE FOLK HERE WHO HAVE GOTTEN THE MESSAGE, AND OTHERS WHO WOULD LIKE IT ALL TO GO AWAY. THE GERMAN BUNDS ARE QUIET. THE CZECHS HAVE STARTED TO ARRIVE AND MORE JEWS FROM AUSTRIA. HOW MUCH DO YOU KNOW OF WHAT IS GOING ON THERE? IS IT GOING TO HAPPEN AGAIN IN CZECHOSLOVAKIA? I WANT TO THINK DISPASSIONATELY ABOUT IT BUT SOMEHOW CAN'T ANYMORE. THE EDITORIALS IN THE TIMES HAVE BEEN CALM AND FINE BUT I SEE THAT THE MORE PIECES YOU OFFER TO A DICTATOR THE MORE HE IS GOING TO WANT. LADY ASTOR IS NOT MUCH

REGARDED HERE THESE DAYS. FOR MYSELF I FIND
CHAMBERLAIN A PATHETIC FIGURE BUT IT IS AN IM-
POSSIBLE THING TO KNOW RIGHT FROM WRONG JUST
LIKE THAT. YOUR BROTHERS ARE NOT BEING MUCH
USE TO ME RIGHT NOW. WE HAVE THE LINE TO HA-
VANA GOING SWELL AND WE'RE GOING TO EXTEND
TO GALVESTON BECAUSE I THINK THAT'S A BACK-
DOOR TO THE MIDWEST. BUT THE BOYS WISH THEY
WERE FLYING THE NEW B-17 AND THEY ALREADY
HAVE THAT LOOK IN THEIR EYES IF YOU KNOW WHAT
I MEAN. YOU SHOULD TELL THE GROUP CAPTAIN
THAT HE'S GOING TO NEED ALL THE HELP HE CAN
GET AND I HOPE WE GET AROUND TO GIVING IT—BUT
MR. KENNEDY WON'T HELP MUCH. SORRY ABOUT
THESE MUDDLED THOUGHTS BUT SITTING HERE BY
THE RADIO WE CAN'T GET YOU OUT OF OUR
THOUGHTS AND WE WORRY. WE SEND OUR LOVE. IF
IT GETS ANY WORSE I WILL COME GET YOU. . . .

Seton came into the kitchen and found her absorbed in
the letter. She looked up and smiled. "There," she said, holding out the letter, "you read it."

He polished his glasses on a napkin and read while she
made the coffee.

"I hadn't realized," he said, putting the letter on the table, "how important the wireless is."

"You mean radio." The language problem was a recurrent joke.

He took off the glasses and sucked the frame. "It's different here. We only have the B.B.C. They never give you anything you can't read in the papers. There's censorship, too—
they've been got at by that man Wilson."

"Funny, isn't it?" she said, looking over the rolling script
again. "They have more of a sense of outrage at that distance
than most people here. I've never known him to be so wound
up. I wonder—if he really will come over." She stood up and
walked behind his chair.

"Would you like that?"

"It would kind of bring things to a head, wouldn't it?"

He fingered his glasses nervously. "Yes—it would." She
tousled his hair—there was more gray than before—and bent
over to kiss the top of his head.

There was still much unsaid between them. Each had
made adjustments, up to a point, but she knew his nature

rested on layers of reserve, progressively more opaque, and that at the core he had still to come to terms with their affair. She had to let him find himself.

She knew that Seton thought it risqué, but she pressed him and he relented gracefully; so they gave their first invitation to dinner at Davies Street—to Endmere. For an hour before Endmere arrived, Seton was trying to be someone else: the uninvolved family friend. It annoyed Ruth to see this piece of social cowardice, but she held her tongue. As Seton answered the door and came back a pace behind Endmere she knew already that Endmere knew. That was revenge enough, and the mutual recognition remained an unspoken complicity through the evening.

Ruth liked Endmere; she liked his balance of confidence and dissipation, and saw a quick brain behind his affability. She also saw that Seton and Endmere were in ways complementary, each respecting the other's individuality. Watching them together made her curious about the things that Americans were always curious about: the hand of the English public school on character, the incarceration of boys together, its renowned virtues and infamous vices. Endmere wasn't pompous, but she noticed that when he said *off* and *cross* he actually said "orf" and "crorse," whereas Seton did not. Choosing her moment, she said, "Did you go to Eton, Peter?"

"How did you guess?" he said, already conceding the joke against himself.

"I'm learning."

Seton laughed. "Ruth is doing *Pygmalion* in reverse— *we're* the specimens."

Endmere said, "Then you can tell the essential difference between us—Edward went to Rugby."

"I used not to mind that," said Seton, "until I realized that Chamberlain did, too."

"I wouldn't lose sleep over it," said Endmere, "you can't blame Rugby for that. The essential thing about *him* is that his father was a bully—and his brother mocked him. A dangerous combination."

"I remember what you said outside Parliament," said Ruth, "about vanity close to stupidity."

"So I did." He sat back reflectively. "You know, I think Hitler understands that, too. He's convinced Chamberlain that he, Chamberlain, is a world statesman instead of an ironmonger."

"Yes," said Seton, "it's *all* bluff. If only Chamberlain, or somebody, could see through it."

Endmere's professional curiosity stirred. "*All* bluff, Edward? Surely there's substance to his threats? You must know that—if anybody does."

Ruth looked at Seton quickly.

Seton murmured, "Not as much as you think."

"*Tell* him." Ruth's tone was suddenly sharp. "*Tell* him!"

Endmere looked from Seton to Ruth, surprised by the outburst. "Tell me what?"

They had all stopped eating. Seton took another drink of his wine and then looked across the table to Endmere. "It's been hushed up. Like a lot of things. But the Luftwaffe is not what it seems. Their bombers can't reach London and get back—not from Germany. They don't have the range."

Ruth's left hand moved to Seton's thigh and rested on it, under the table. Endmere's chair scraped back over the floor. He spread his feet, his whole frame tightening. "But that's *fantastic!* You mean—we knew that, *before* Munich?"

"Well before the last meeting."

"Did you know about the attempted putsch?" said Endmere quietly.

"Nobody took any notice."

"I know that. But—"

Ruth finished the thought: "The two together, that really says it all, doesn't it?"

"Can you prove this—about the bombers?"

Seton hesitated, then said, "What are you suggesting?"

"I'm suggesting that it should come out. Nobody need ever know where I got it from. I could write a piece—" Endmere hesitated, then found the right words: "—a bit cloudy, just enough fact at the nub of it, you know the kind of thing."

Ruth looked at Seton, the enormity of the idea sinking in.

"That would finish me—if it ever got out, where it came from. The Official Secrets Act, the lot—they would throw the book at me."

"But you'll do it?" Endmere asked.

Seton looked at Ruth, and then to Endmere, and sighed. "Professional neutrality has got us nowhere—yes, I'll do it. Somebody *has* to."

Later, as Endmere left, he said, "Edward—I can give you a lift home, if you like."

Seton hovered at the door. "Thanks, but I think I'll walk. It'll do me good."

"Yes." Endmere looked over his shoulder to Ruth. "I'm sure it will."

Endmere's short walk from Fleet Street to the Thames embankment was, he reflected, to cross a gulf from one kind of journalism to another: The aloofness of *The Times* from the rest of the British newspapers was partly geographical and partly vocational. *Times* journalists were gentlemen, not tradesmen. To be an amateur, to be closer to diplomacy and scholarship, was more godly than to be a professional, if that meant Fleet Street's idea of professionalism. Endmere had early come to terms with this doctrine. He had slipped comfortably into *The Times* because of family connections, drifting through salons and chanceries, writing elegantly; he enjoyed the fellowship of the knowing even though it often denied him the right to tell what he knew.

Seton's document, slowly burning a hole in his acceptance of this custom, was a watershed for Endmere. He had drafted and redrafted the story until he judged it sufficiently opaque, and early one morning—when the office was virtually deserted—he left the final version in the political editor's basket. Nothing happened for three days, and then he was called to the office before he had finished breakfast.

There was a plaster coat of arms under the eaves of *The Times* building, its centerpiece a clock arrested at 4:30. Nobody knew whether it was A.M. or P.M., or why *The Times* stopped the world at this hour, unless it was to take tea.

Endmere seldom saw Geoffrey Dawson, his editor, in the office: They crossed more usually at places like Cliveden, and there was no real familiarity between them. In the grate behind Dawson's desk burned a fire tended by the butler who served the editor. Endmere was directed to a hard chair to one side of the desk.

Dawson held Endmere's story aloft, ominously virgin, without editor's marks. "Did you seriously expect me to publish this?" He put the sheets back on the desk as though they might be contaminated.

"It seemed important." Endmere was stiffening.

"Important?" Dawson let the word hang in the air for a few seconds. "Where did you get this information?"

"I'm afraid—"

With a speed that surprised Endmere, Dawson intercepted the phrase: "—that you can't disclose the source, is that it?"

"No. I cannot."

"Really?" Dawson's eyes ranged Endmere's crumpled suit, settling somewhere on his midriff. "You will appreciate that the editor of *The Times* takes personal responsibility for everything in the newspaper? The idea that correspondents enjoy confidences denied to the editor would put the system in jeopardy." His gaze moved back across the desk to the offending text. "As it is, my dear Endmere, I regard this particular piece of work as too slapdash—and too *viewy*. Its conclusions seem too hasty for the substance of the material. Of course, I need hardly add that to follow the logic of this piece would be to seriously embarrass the government at an extremely sensitive time."

Endmere thought the language more that of a government spokesman than an editor. He was openly incensed: "I would have thought that, at the very least, the subject could stand a little debate."

Over the years Dawson's plain face had thickened and developed character lines thought to register sagacity and caution in equal measure. Both aspects were now summoned to deal with the intransigence. "The new columns are not the place for debate. The paper is built on steadiness." He pulled at the skirt of his waistcoat. "I am curious about the motives for this particular piece of yours. As a matter of fact, I have made inquiries of my own. There is some dismay that such information should be in circulation at all. If you are still unable to enlighten me. . . ."

Endmere remained silent.

"Very well. I must warn you, though—this could have been a serious breach. In time, perhaps, you will come to appreciate why it is out of the question to publish."

In time, thought Endmere, it will be too late.

27

Just before 1:00 A.M. pandemonium erupted through the Vier Jahreszeiten Hotel in Munich. Canaris had taken a dose of Phanodorm, and Piekenbrock had to shake him awake. The room was already acrid with fumes, and through the window the buildings in the street reflected an orange glow. Still drowsy, Canaris grunted, "What is it?"

"The synagogue next door. It's on fire."

Canaris looked out and saw hoses snaking across the street. "The hoses are on the hotel—not the synagogue."

"They're letting it burn."

Canaris pulled on his clothes. In the corridor Wehrmacht adjutants were knocking on doors and retrieving baggage. Once outside, Canaris saw that the synagogue was already a shell, its roof gone and the column of flame so high that it was reflected on the clouds.

"Now I know what Himmler meant," Canaris said grimly. He remembered the phrase from dinner: "The Jews have to be driven from Germany with unexampled ruthlessness." They stood in the street for ten minutes and then, ignoring the evacuation, Canaris took Piekenbrock back to his room, to a bottle of schnapps. They were the only people on the floor.

"You see, Piekenbrock"—Canaris was now settling on his bed, drink in hand—"why I don't like coming to Munich? They always use the anniversary of the putsch for something. God knows what madness this is."

Piekenbrock straddled a chair back to front, arms resting on its back as he held his drink. "Every time I see that Brownshirt parade I realize the party might have remained a provincial rabble, just the old gang in the beer hall—but for Goebbels."

"This circus has several ringmasters," said Canaris, knowing that the sleeping pill had already worn off. "If what I think is happening *is* happening, they might have gone too far this time. Something like this could turn the world against us."

Ruth came into the room white and shaking, holding the paper and reading it aloud: " 'In almost every town and city in the country the wrecking, looting, and burning continued all day. Huge but mostly silent crowds looked on and the police confined themselves to regulating traffic and making wholesale arrests of Jews—for their own protection.' "

"Back to the Middle Ages," said Seton, staring vacantly into the street. "The Jews are running into the forests to hide."

She continued to read: " 'Ten thousand Jews rounded up in Munich were told to leave . . . embassies besieged by

Jews wanting to emigrate . . . Jews committing suicide
. . . two hundred synagogues destroyed, and hundreds of
shops. . . .'" The paper bunched in her hand. "And this is
only what we can *see* is happening. What must be going on
behind it?" She went to Seton. Her head sank into his shoulder. "Sometimes—sometimes I think they're setting out to
eliminate the whole Jewish race."

Seton held her head. "There are millions of Jews in Europe—they couldn't get away with such a thing, even if they
wanted to. Not after this. Something on that scale would be
unthinkable. Oh, I'm sure there's a campaign of quite deliberate terror, what we're beginning to see now, and some awful
things going on in the camps—but the idea must be to drive
them out. They can't liquidate every Jew in Europe."

"There are men there who are mad enough to try."

"Well . . . maybe. But in spite of everything, Germany
is, after all, one of the world's most civilized countries. People
can take only so much, even from Hitler. I would think they
must be pretty near the limit. They won't take much more."

"I hope you're right. I'm not sure you are." She unfolded
the paper again. "After all, for every one of them who can get
out there must be hundreds who can't. Parents are sending
their children out, without being able to leave themselves. Anyone with relatives to go to, they can try to get out. But the
others, they just can't. *Where would they all go?* Who would
take them? You know how it is here. You hear people saying
quite openly they don't want them here."

"Yes," said Seton slowly, "there are broken shop windows here, too."

She broke away from him, going to the breakfast table.
"One thing, though—Kennedy's going to have a hard time
convincing people that we can live with a regime that does
this."

But something else was on his mind. Drawing up a chair
and taking the coffee, he still hesitated. In the loose gown at
breakfast, recoiling from the shock of the newspaper, she
looked too fragile.

"You still see Lady Dunsinnan, don't you?" he said.

"Occasionally. Why?"

"Is he here—Dunsinnan?"

"You want me to go back again?" She had seen the ambivalence in his face.

"There's something else I think might be there—related
to what you found before."

"I'll do it on one condition."

"What's that?"

"That you stay someplace near. I don't want to go there again and have you so far away."

His hand met hers across the table.

When Ruth called Scotland, she had the feeling of having thrown a lifeline into an empty stretch of ocean and finding someone surfacing beside it.

"*Of course*, my dear. Of course you can come. I must warn you, though—I'm in bed. The weather has been awful. I caught cold. You would be the best cure."

Just as Ruth wondered how to put the question an answer came:

"Alastair is away, again, but that won't stop you, will it?"

Ruth and Seton travelled on separate trains to Edinburgh. The lugubrious Drummond did not meet her—this time it was the new chauffeur, old, small, and courtly. The season was between the colors of autumn and the snow, a monotonous time of capricious winds and frequent rain. The castle was oppressive; it was gradually acquiring a barren feeling. When Ruth arrived, Lady Dunsinnan was already asleep. Ruth had a light supper sent to her room, and wondered if the journey would, after all, turn out to be as futile as it was uncomfortable.

The next morning a strange car, black and flaked with mud, stood in the drive. She went to Lady Dunsinnan's room, thinking it might belong to a doctor.

The patient was, however, alone—and unusually free of the trace of whisky.

"You saw the car?" she said, and then explained: "It's a policeman, from England. Rather a coarse man, but then he's from Yorkshire. He's seen me already, and he's talking to the staff."

"Why?" said Ruth, puzzled.

"Too long a story to tell, my dear. But as far as Alastair is concerned, there's been a kind of bereavement." She gave Ruth an old copy of *The Times*, folded open at the obituary page. There was a brief notice of Lady Taverner's death—"from an old county family," it said, heavy with discretion. Lady Dunsinnan tapped the paper as Ruth held it. "This woman—she's the cause of the policeman's travels."

Ruth read the notice, guessing the rest.

"As far as I'm concerned, my dear, it's a deliverance."

"That's harsh."

"It was mutual, I assure you. She couldn't wait to see me gone." She laughed. "And I thought she would—see me go. How reassuring."

"Why, though . . . ?"

"A whore, a highbred whore."

"No. I mean the policeman. What's his interest? From this account it seems perfectly straightforward."

"Nothing about that lady was straightforward. I don't know—he didn't tell *me* much. He saw Alastair in London. But he wouldn't be on it unless something was wrong. He seems to think the accident was arranged. Accidents can be arranged, you know."

Ruth thought of McCabe and remembered why she was here. She said, "Why would anyone do that?"

Lady Dunsinnan pulled herself up on the pillows. "My dear—in the drawer there—could you get me the flask?"

The inspector left before lunch. Ruth, reunited with the Arab, went high onto the moors. She realized how familiar she was with the tracks, and how natural the horse was with her. She thought of Seton in the hotel in Edinburgh, kicking his heels. There were strict orders to make no contact with him— and she didn't know whether she would keep them. When she got back, Lady Dunsinnan was downstairs.

"Alastair will be here in the morning. I think it was hearing that you were here."

Ruth sensed that Lady Dunsinnan viewed her son's return as an infringement of her freedom to talk to Ruth. All through dinner there was a tone of hurried intimacy, and afterwards she took Ruth back to her room, anxious to be out of the servants' earshot.

"That woman we were talking about this morning," she said, "there's something you should see." She had drunk a great deal and went unsurely to a bureau. She pulled out a large photo album covered in red leather and embossed with the gauntlet clutching an arrow. "Here." She passed it to Ruth.

For fifteen minutes or so Ruth sat silently turning the pages. The earliest photographs—many of them flared at the corners—were in sepia, with a lack of contrast, so that every group appeared to be out of direct light. The subjects stood or sat in the way people did for long exposures. At the beginning the pictures showed Dunsinnan's father and the young Lady Dunsinnan, with various transient guests, and then, about a quarter of the way through, one young woman began recurring—appearing at first on the fringe, then toward the center of the second or third rows. At about the same time Alastair appeared—at first in the oddly feminine dress typical of a time when nurseries made no distinction of gender, and then as the self-conscious heir. By the end of the album Margery Taverner was at the shoulder of Alastair's father, with Alastair in flannels at her other side.

Ruth pointed out a man in tweeds with a heavy Edwardian moustache who seemed to appear with Margery Taverner for a while and then went missing. "Who was he?"

"Her unfortunate husband. It took *him* a while to realize what was going on. He was like that."

"How did *you* put up with it?"

"My dear—people did. It's all very Greek, isn't it?"

Dunsinnan's sustained geniality put Ruth off balance, though not off guard. Only the raven presence of Drummond in the background provided a discord; otherwise it seemed almost as though no interval had passed between her first visit and this. The feeling was reinforced by the absence of other guests, and Dunsinnan's single-minded readiness to enjoy himself. They rode twice a day for three days; they compensated for the weather by eating enormous meals; they were peculiarly isolated from reality. Playing her part, Ruth had sometimes to remind herself of Seton and why he had sent her there—a lingering reluctance, perhaps, to accept her role as his agent.

When the change came, it was all the more traumatic, for this euphoric prelude and for its suddenness. They were finishing dinner, just the three of them—Dunsinnan on his mother's right and Ruth on her left. Ruth had been avoiding talking about Germany and was surprised that it had not been pressed upon her. It was Lady Dunsinnan, who had drunk whisky steadily through the meal, who said to Dunsinnan, "I see Duff Cooper has resigned."

"Silly man," said Dunsinnan, "bag of wind, really."

"Oh. Is that so?" said his mother. "I've another view."

"I expect you have," he said impatiently. "It was just Churchill's dog, barking."

The change of temper took Ruth by surprise. She spoke mildly: "Aren't you surprised there weren't more—resignations?"

"Why should there be? Events have vindicated Chamberlain, he has the country behind him."

"A faraway country of whom we know nothing—the popular view of Czechoslovakia, you mean?"

"I told you before, over Austria. The same was even more true with Czechoslovakia, a hybrid concocted at Versailles. Reunification, high time."

Ruth was still deceptively conversational: "In this process of reunification, isn't there a little clearing out to do? I mean, aren't some people in the wrong place? The Jews, for example. They're not hiding in the Grünewald for fun, surely?"

"Oh—not *that* again." Dunsinnan sighed and sliced an apple, not looking up.

"Freud didn't leave his clinic in Vienna for a change of wallpaper, surely? Albert Einstein, now there's someone else—Wasn't his brain equal to the requirements, is that why he left? They're not even playing Mendelssohn anymore—and Wagner has to be played without Jewish violinists."

The knife became more pedantic in its attentions to the apple, gouging the core. Dunsinnan said nothing until the first slice was in his mouth, and then he looked at Ruth as he had before, months before. The nerve above the eye moved. "The Jews are trying to push us into war."

She flung down her spoon. "*Do you know*—do you *really* know—what's going on?" The question arced from her throat across the table. "I'll tell you, just in the remote event that you don't. Thousands of people—maybe *hundreds* of thousands, men, women, *children*, too—they just get on a train and disappear. One moment they're walking through a town, to the station, very orderly. The next, gone. Have *you* taken a ride to Dachau?"

"Nonsense!"

Ruth turned from him to his mother. "Odd, isn't it? Nobody knows—*wants* to know. I guess Adolf doesn't know, either. But it's not the kind of thing you write to *The Times* about, is it? It's all happening to somebody else, somewhere else."

"Where's your evidence?"

"The smell is enough." She steadied herself. "Take a look at Julius Streicher next time you're hanging around with them. Have a word with Goebbels, ask him to lunch."

Now near to tears, she got up and walked out.

Lady Dunsinnan took a gulp of whisky and looked at Dunsinnan: "Is any of that true?"

Dunsinnan, his face curiously mottled, looked at the space where Ruth had been and wiped his mouth. "I think that girl has a touch of the tarbrush."

Within five minutes Ruth, now sitting on her bed, knew that she had gone through a catharsis. The falseness of the last few days, the strain of deception, was expelled. In its place came a sureness, a determination free of misgivings. She could do it now—without any fear. She waited until there had been no sound for an hour, and retraced her previous nocturnal route to the library. The pigskin case was lying on top of the desk. It was done in half a minute.

Her only pain of severance was with Lady Dunsinnan. Making her leave the next morning, Ruth felt strangely that it was Dunsinnan's mother, alone and uncertain, who was the true continuity of whatever was important in this bleak place; the hereditary line had been derailed somewhere and the real roots lay with her. Lady Dunsinnan squeezed her hand. "You'll still come to see me, in London?"

"Of course."

Kissing her, Ruth smelt violets and whisky in equal measure.

The valet loading her two suitcases into the Bentley was watched over by Drummond. It was he, not the chauffeur, who took her to Edinburgh, and his manner was perfunctory. For the whole of the journey she kept the partition between them closed. She noticed that once or twice he seemed unsure of the road and nervous. But this was ridiculous, she knew, since the road was so familiar. On the pretext of an overnight stay to await the morning train she went to the station hotel. The Scottish wariness of single women in hotels, rooted deeply in Calvinist hypocrisy, mildly embarrassed her. Every member of the hotel staff, however humble, seemed an agent of this suspicion. Thus it was that passing Seton in the restaurant, she imagined that the heavens might open and send a searing retribution. But he barely glanced from his copy of the *Evening Despatch*, no bolder than any itinerant seeing an unescorted nymph. She admired that.

It was not until 1:00 A.M. that he came to her room, and then it was he who felt the transgressor. Tapping the door, he imagined a thousand eyes on him and rehearsed the feeblest of alibis to himself. She was careless enough to embrace him before he was able to close the door with a back heeling movement. Her linen nightshirt rubbed incongruously against his coat—the alibi called for an early morning walk and a mistaken room. Reluctantly he unhooked her hands from the back of his neck.

Having explained all, she concluded: "I've burned my boats. And I'm not sorry. Deception consumes the deceiver. I think I forgot who I really was—until the row."

"You did well."

"I hated it."

"I know." He held her face.

In a while she went to the largest of her suitcases. "It weighed so much more than when I arrived, I thought they might notice." She opened it and pulled out the pigskin case. "I haven't dared open it myself."

It was an Asprey travelling case. He turned it over, looking at the lock, gold-plated. A nail file broke it open. The contents were prosaic: shaving mirror, shaving brush and soap, brilliantine, hairbrush, packet of laxative tablets, cologne, spirit flask, and black leather address book. Seton went straight to the address book.

It was sparsely filled, and all the names were German, with German addresses. He frowned. "This means nothing—it can't be it." He opened the flask and sniffed. "Schanpps! His German accoutrements." He pressed the lining, then took the nail file and tore away the red watered silk to the wooden frame. He prized out the mirror and removed its back. He opened the shaving soap and cut it in half. "No. *Nothing!*"

Her disappointment was evident.

"Never mind. A good try."

The fatigue of released tension mingled with the depression of anticlimax. They were soon asleep.

Seton awoke and realized that her left arm was across his chest and that she lay behind him bunched in the fetal position. Beyond the end of the bed, without moving his head, he saw the back of a man, head down, going through one of the cases. Seton cursed his carelessness. He would have to make one coordinated movement, which he rehearsed in a few seconds silently: to roll to the floor, never minding the noise, and to push himself very low and fast so that the man would be presented with the smallest target, like a dog coming at him. Seton had never done anything like it, but he had played Rugby for Cambridge and was vain enough to put his faith in technique as a substitute for diminished powers.

The first sound he heard was Ruth's cry; the second, the

man's cry as he fell with Seton on the back of his thighs. Seton's knees pressed down, but he lost his balance and the man pushed sideways. As they fell together Seton brought his right hand down, hard, on the man's neck. Ruth grasped for the light cord over the bed and then sat up with her hand over her mouth. All she could see was Seton's head above the end of the bed.

"Cord. Quick, give me the light cord."

The cord came out of the socket complete with its wooden toggle. She came from the bed and gave it to him, at the same time getting her first look at the stunned figure on the floor. "My God, it's the photographer—the German photographer."

"Not really," said Seton. "Oberstleutnant Walther von Klagen, late of the Luftwaffe, now of the Abwehr." He secured von Klagen's hands at the base of his spine and rolled him over. In the half-light von Klagen's face looked deathly, the blood gone from it.

"Is he—is he all right?" she said, then realizing how foolish it was to sound solicitous.

"Give him five minutes." Seton got up, aware that his knees were badly bruised.

On the floor beside von Klagen the travelling case—or as much of it as Seton had left—lay open.

By the time Seton had dressed, von Klagen had come round. He looked up first at Ruth, showing recognition. Then he said to Seton, very slowly, "How did you know—my one weak point?"

Seton was nonplussed.

"My leg."

Ruth said, "Of course. He limps."

Seton smiled grimly. "Pure luck."

Von Klagen hunched over his knees and sat up painfully. "So," he said, "you have what I want, but you don't seem to know that you have."

Seton frowned but stayed silent.

"It is too much like one of your Sherlock Holmes stories, really." Von Klagen managed a laugh, then regarded them both: "Since I can give you what you want, although you don't know that, I think we should come to terms. You will find it difficult to believe, no doubt, but our interests happen to be mutual. I will share the information if you release me."

"Explain," said Seton.

Von Klagen moved his captive hands. "That's hardly practical."

Trying bravado, Ruth said, "Why should we?"

"This could be very embarrassing, especially in Edinburgh. This is not Brighton. Not only a diplomatic incident, but a mistake in a hotel room, the group captain with his lady."

"You *have* done your homework," said Ruth. Seton flushed.

Von Klagen nodded to the gutted case and then spoke to Ruth: "Dr. Watson—will you play him, my friend? Surely the most attractive Dr. Watson in history. Please take the flask and tell me what's in it."

"We know that," said Seton tartly. "Schnapps."

But Ruth was quicker. "*Of course!* Why on earth would Alastair carry Schnapps when he's obsessed with malt whisky?"

Von Klagen smiled. "*Well done*, Dr. Watson. Now, tell me, please, what is the brand of laxative?"

She took the packet and read the label: "Plural."

"Exactly. Do you happen to know if Lord Dunsinnan has that particular problem? No—you do not know, forgive me. Let me explain. One of the ingredients of Plural is phenolphthalein. If you dissolve one tablet in schnapps, fifty-fifty, you get a very effective invisible ink. Yes, we still use invisible ink. As soon as I saw the tablets. . . ."

Seton grunted.

"May I have a cigarette, please?" said von Klagen, "and an ashtray, of course." Seton nodded to Ruth, and she lit the cigarette and put it in his mouth.

"Now, do we have a deal?"

"So far you have only explained how it gets written, not how we get to see it." Seton remained cool.

"Be patient," said von Klagen. "Now, Dr. Watson, would you get some water—just a little—in a glass." She went to the bathroom, then put the glass by his side.

Von Klagen drew on the cigarette and held his head over the glass. The first deposit of ash fell into the water. "I am afraid we shall have to wait for some more." When another finger of ash had fallen into the glass, he said, "Now, Dr. Watson, kindly stir the ash to mix it with the water." He watched her, nodding. "Please take out the address book, and very slowly, with one finger, rub this solution over the first page."

There were only three names at the top of the page, with the German addresses. Ruth smeared the solution over the remainder of the page. At first nothing happened. Then, like a photograph in developer, more script began to appear in pink, identical with the hand above.

"Oh," said Ruth, "that's *really* neat."

"My God!" said Seton. He looked at the names. They were now English—some familiar, some not, enough of the familiar ones astonishing.

Von Klagen sighed in the manner of a teacher who has only painfully brought illumination. "Now, to assure you of my part of the bargain, I will wait while you develop the rest. Then, if you don't mind, I would like to copy the names down for myself—you can keep the book. Is that not fair?"

Ruth offered him the flask of schnapps, ready to hold it to his mouth.

He shook his head. "I too prefer whisky."

It took Seton three hours to go through the revelations of the address book, and by then it was dawn. He opened the curtains and raised the window, trying to dispel the smell of cigarettes. Ruth lay on the bed blotting dry the last page with a towel. Von Klagen was asleep on the floor, his hands still bound.

Seton looked down on the hotel's kitchen roof and heard the first stirrings of breakfast. He realized how hungry he was.

Ruth left the address book open at the drying page. "Did you think there were so many of them?" she said, pulling the counterpane over her because of the draft from the window.

"The kind of people they are?"

He put down the window. "I had no idea."

The noise of the window woke von Klagen. Seton saw in him the reflexes of a man used to instant alertness. There was no disorientation: Von Klagen rolled over and looked up at Seton wide awake.

"So—do we share the secrets?"

Ruth looked curiously at Seton, not knowing his mind yet.

"You really have nothing to bargain with," said Seton. "It's not going to cut any ice, that stuff about a compromising discovery in the bedroom."

Ruth smiled, but Seton kept his gaze on von Klagen.

"No," said von Klagen with resignation.

"You're really quite a catch," said Seton with a suggestion of mockery.

"You don't *arrest* spies in England, not in peacetime," said von Klagen. "So—what will it be, some kind of accident?"

"This is not Nazi Germany," snapped Seton. He was slightly disconcerted by von Klagen's directness, the calling of the bluff. "We can, however, detain you. There is a lot I would like to know, if you felt able to help."

Von Klagen laughed with hard insolence. "I am sure there is." He managed to sit up, leaning forward to his knees so that he could take in Ruth. She turned away defensively to Seton. Von Klagen moved a leg and grimaced. "Very well," he said slowly, "I will tell you why I want those names. You just used the phrase *Nazi* Germany. It is too simple. It is not Germany that is Nazi. The party is not the country. Many of us have never belonged." He caught Seton's look of contempt and paused. "You cannot understand that? No. I can see you don't. At the beginning, when the party came to power, I didn't realize. . . . There seemed so much to hope for. And so much to forget. I joined the Luftwaffe—"

Seton interrupted: "A very *peaceable* intention."

Von Klagen lost control: "*You* can build bombers, the French can build bombers, and Germany makes do with gliders. *That* is peaceable?"

Ruth saw the anger in his eyes. Seton was impassive and still silent.

Von Klagen modulated his voice: "You know that in the past some of us tried to warn you what would happen. We spoke to deaf men. I know why—now."

Seton relented slightly. He sat on the bed by Ruth and looked from von Klagen to the address book. "Come to the point. Why do you want it?"

"If the German people ever came to believe that Hitler can make an alliance with England—what is it you call it, an *Axis?*— if they ever thought he could deliver *that*, and without war, then he would be invincible. A Nazi Caesar. There could never then be any question of removing him."

Ruth saw his logic. "So *you* have to stop Alastair?"

"It's ingenious, even plausible," said Seton. "Tell me, you work for Canaris?"

Von Klagen hesitated, then nodded.

"Where does he stand?"

Von Klagen laughed wearily. "His position, it is very dangerous."

"Meaning?"

"He does not confide in me."

"Then *who* does?"

Seton's asperity was beginning to shift Ruth's sympathy to von Klagen, who sensed the change.

"Group Captain, please. I have told you why I want those names."

"Yes." Seton got up again, picking up the address book and leafing through it. "Canaris *would* appreciate it, I'm sure. As evidence of how undermined we already are." He looked at von Klagen steadily. "You appreciate that there is nothing I could possibly do to verify your alibi. I want you to know that I do *not* take it on trust. Your credentials are not encouraging. You have been very active with your camera."

"I'm a professional—like you."

Seton did not improve with flattery. "At the moment you do not seem it."

"Without me you'd have a blank address book, Group Captain."

Touché, thought Ruth, keeping silent with difficulty.

But Seton's thoughts had already moved from animus to expediency: "You will be allowed to walk out of here with a copy of the names. I'll take that risk. But your career as an agent here will become rather more difficult, if not impossible. I'll make sure of that."

"My hands," said von Klagen, "there is no feeling in them."

It was Ruth who went to him and untied the cord.

Drummond sat in a nondescript car across the street from the main entrance of the hotel. He had been there since dawn, waiting for the exodus to the London train. When he saw von Klagen appear, he was unprepared. Not knowing whether to follow him or continue the watch for Ruth, he got out of the car and went to a corner, in view of the station. Von Klagen carried a small suitcase and seemed to be waiting to catch the train. But the time for the train's departure approached without any sign of Ruth. Drummond went back to the car.

It was another two hours before Ruth appeared with Seton. They took a taxi, not to the station but out of the city. Drummond followed. He realized where they were going after several turns: to the airport. As they left the main road for the terminal he continued on along the perimeter of the airport and parked in view of the runway. Two small private planes came and went, without any sign of Ruth and Seton. Then he saw a twin-engined plane come in over the estuary and, as it landed, the R.A.F. roundels. Seton led Ruth to the cabin, helped by an airman who had flown in with the plane.

Drummond watched as the plane was refuelled—obviously for a return flight to London. He took the car back into Edinburgh and exchanged it for the Bentley, then recrossed the Forth and headed north, worried more by the discovery of von Klagen than by the appearance of the R.A.F.

28

When Ruth came into the living room of Seton's flat, the man was framed in the window, the light behind him. All she could see of his face was a fleshy outline—unsettled by the movement of his jowls when he spoke, like a rubber mask shifting its contours. His voice was that of a man not used to including a woman in a confidence, careful and too didactic. She wondered whether he chose to stand there to conceal his awkwardness. Even his use of Seton's first name was forced, an intimacy out of its familiar boundary: "Er . . . I would like—Edward has told me of the risks you ran, I felt I had personally to thank you. . . ."

Seton stood to one side, himself edgy with the sudden enmeshing of professional and private lives. Ruth, conscious of both men's uneasiness, determined to do nothing to make it any easier, was amused and yet annoyed.

There was the gentlest change of tone: "Of course, I don't have to stress how *sensitive* this has become. . . ." The jowls fell into temporary repose, the man slightly disturbed by Ruth's steady stare. "*Very* sensitive." He shot a glance at Seton, and she saw their shared anxiety. "Obviously you will be concerned as to what may now follow. . . ."

Suddenly and decisively he moved from the window, equivocation gone. She saw the face clearly, strong nose and—fixed on her—eyes of a peculiar opacity like smudged film, faintly yellow. "The list of names is not in itself conclusive. We cannot be sure that the Germans have misplaced their hopes . . . to expect so many collaborators at this level—" He hesitated, seeing Ruth's reaction. "Of course, for myself, I take it very seriously. Have no doubt of that."

"So what happens?" she said, looking at them both.

"If we were to act on it now, it would split the country from top to bottom. When the time comes—*as it will*—we will deal with them. There will be legal means of doing so." He became sardonic: "War makes such things much simpler."

He looked at his shoes for a second, and she saw thinning hair and a scalp flaked with eczema. He looked up again. "It's like a cancer. It will be cut out, however high it goes. At least, now we know the difference between appeasement and treachery."

"I don't see much difference. The appeasers haven't done such a bad job for Hitler," said Ruth.

"Quite so." The jowls sat creased over a ring of starched poplin. "We are in your debt, very much. It will, of course, be unwise for you to go near that young man again—he will doubtless associate his loss with your departure. In fact, you will need to be careful." He looked at Seton and back to her. "We will mark him closely now, and he will know that we are doing so. His problems are just beginning."

"A drink?" said Seton, suddenly at ease.

When they sat down, the man sipped his sherry with feline delicacy, then spoke to Ruth: "I confess to still being bothered by the role of von Klagen."

Casting formality to the winds, Seton sat on an arm of the sofa, over Ruth. "I think," he said, "that things in Berlin are quite Byzantine. Some kind of internal war is going on. Canaris runs the Abwehr like a privateer. Apparently he won't let any Nazis into the place."

Ruth said, "Do you believe von Klagen's story—about their need to stop Alastair?"

Their guest put down his sherry. "It's a double-edged sword. If we were to act against these people now, it would expose to the whole world the degree of our own rot. At the same time it would greatly embarrass the Nazi intriguers."

"And since you're *not* going to do anything . . . what will they make of that?"

Her asperity gave him pause. He sipped the sherry again, running his tongue along his lower lip. "I should think they would hold us in low esteem—wouldn't you?" He knew that at last he had struck an empathy with her.

After the visitor had left, Ruth said, "Do you *like* him?"

"That doesn't come into it. What matters is that I trust him."

"Nobody else?"

"Not at that level."

"What an admission!" She wanted to push Seton further. "Is he—well, is he *it?*"

"He has to be very careful."

"I'll bet." She recalled Seton's words as the pink script materialized on the pages of the address book: "Good God! Two generals, an admiral, *three* judges, even a bishop. A whole bunch of noble lords—my word, *him!* Naturally, *this* one. Five M.P.'s . . . can't take this one too seriously. Funny lot, mixture of Cavaliers and Roundheads. They've lain *very* low. . . ."

"As the man said, war will make it all much simpler," she said, going to Seton's arms.

"Yes—in more ways than one." He held her. "We'll have to take care of you, as he said." He felt her hand on his neck. "There might be greater security—I mean, perhaps it would be simpler—living in one place instead of two."

For a second or two she seemed not to understand, and then she moved away from him slightly, letting both hands fall to the small of his back. "What are you trying to say—that we should live in sin?"

"No. That's *not* what I meant." He looked at her steadily. "What I'm suggesting is that we get married."

Her arms slipped away from him, and she stepped further back. "Do you think you could try that one again?" She didn't quite know why, but she wanted to prolong his agony; in some way it deepened her feeling for him.

"Would you marry me, Ruth?"

"I thought you'd *never* ask." She fell into his arms, at first laughing and then crying uncontrollably. She looked at him: "You strange, *strange* man. I *love* you. I've loved you for—oh, I don't know *how* long." Then she wiped her eyes and gripped him harder. "You're not just doing this out of your very peculiar sense of duty?"

He put his hand to her neck and ran his finger along the thin gold cord. "I'm sorry you should even think that." The hand moved from the gold to her chin, lifting her head slightly. He saw the wet streaks across her cheek. "There's no question of that. I didn't really *know*. . . . After all, in some ways it won't be easy for you."

She felt the cropped hair at the back of his neck. "It's not a problem, Edward. Has it ever *been* a problem, so far? It doesn't *matter*. You're *not* an old man." She knew he was still too tense. "After all, your boss, if we can call him that, I think he was quite envious."

The next day the cable arrived from her father. She had to wait until the evening to see Seton, and she was still uncertain of his reaction. She gave it to him without saying anything and watched him closely.

"We'll have to tell him, of course," he said. "How's he going to take it?"

"Better than Mother."

"Yes. I expect you're right. You had better let me do it."

"On your own?"

"That's right."

"Absolutely not. Do you think this is a Henry James novel?"

He sighed and looked at the cable again. "So, from here he's going to the Paris Air Show." But his mind was on her mother, left behind in America—how *would* she take it? She had been particularly close to his wife, and he knew the effort of tolerance it would require to see her succeeded by her own daughter, even though a widower was a shade more respectable than a divorced man.

"It'll be okay," said Ruth, taking the cable and steering him to the sofa. "I guess we both need a drink, though."

Seeing his mood, she put on a record—Beethoven this time, not Mozart, an early quartet. Then, as he settled into the whisky and the music, she went into the bedroom. She came back into the room naked, walked up behind him, and slipped her hands down his neck, unbuttoning the shirt. They had always made love in bed, but now she came to him on the sofa. She had still not convinced herself finally that his proposal was not the product of rectitude, a wish to end the ambiguity. She guided him to all the sensual resources that she had, hoping that his own last layers of reserve would now fall away. But as she joined and moved with him to a deep intensity she realized that she would have to leave him some core of privacy, which might always be there. She understood that now and did not resent it.

* * *

The all-night tram car came slowly over the bridge at Blackfriars, its weak yellow lights blinking on and off as the power circuit was broken by the switch of tracks. There was no other traffic in sight, and the grinding of the tram echoed down the alleys running from Fleet Street to the Thames. The conductor jumped off the rear platform before the tram stopped, and went forward to await the driver. There were no passengers, and the two men left the tram at its stop and walked over to the small kiosk that served as all-night cafe, its trade mainly consisting of tram crews and the men who drove newspaper delivery trucks. Six or seven men were standing in the light of the kiosk drinking tea and eating sausage rolls.

Dunsinnan crossed the embankment and climbed the spiral stairs to the top deck of the tram. It was cold and he tightened the woollen scarf around his neck. He sat on a wooden bench at the rear, anaemic under the discoloring bulbs. Two minutes later Karl Fritsch arrived. Dunsinnan had watched him walk over the bridge, recognizing the head of cropped hair.

Fritsch looked down to the kiosk as he settled next to Dunsinnan. "You didn't have some tea?"

"I don't think it would be recognizable as tea." Dunsinnan loosened the scarf to seem less at bay.

"Probably not." Fritsch rubbed the misting window, to keep his eyes on the street, avoiding Dunsinnan's scrutiny. He watched a car judder over the cobblestones and tramlines. Then he said, "How did they find out?"

"Somebody found the book, the book with the names."

"*Somebody?*"

"A guest at the castle. A girl."

"The American?"

Dunsinnan was dismayed by Fritsch's knowledge. Before he could answer, Fritsch continued:

"We have had our suspicions since she was in Munich. I would have raised it before, but the relationship seemed to be in decline." He turned to look at Dunsinnan for the first time: "I hope you're not thinking of retaliation. That would only compound the trouble."

"I realized that. With some reluctance."

Fritsch did not seem reassured. "There are enough repercussions in Berlin, as it is."

The windows around them had become opaque. Dunsinnan felt claustrophobic. "They don't have *all* the names," he said.

"They have enough." Fritsch took out a gold cigarette case and offered a cigarette to Dunsinnan. Neither of them spoke until each had inhaled. The luxurious cigarettes helped to suppress the odor of cheap tobacco that permeated the tram. Fritsch waved his cigarette in the direction of Westminster, a diffuse entity ahead of them at the end of the embankment. "They'll certainly keep on your tail now."

"That's already happened. I had to be very careful tonight."

Fritsch rubbed the condensation away from the window again, this time with a sleeve. The same men were huddled around the kiosk. "I hope so. In any case, this will be our last encounter."

"I'm untouchable, I suppose." Dunsinnan was aggressively sarcastic.

"I'm going to Berlin."

"Permanently?"

Fritsch nodded. He watched the driver and conductor break away from the other men and walk toward the tram.

For the first time Dunsinnan realized the change in Fritsch. In place of the suavity was a kind of resignation, almost fatalism. "Look here," he said as the conductor reached the platform below them, "it will turn our way again—once the pistol is at their heads."

The conductor rang the bell. Fritsch flicked out his cigarette. "By then it will be too late." The tram jerked into movement, and its whole frame vibrated. The abrasion of wheel on track was transmitted directly, without intervening relief, to the hard bench seats. The noise swallowed Dunsinnan's reply. Fritsch looked at him, but Dunsinnan thought better of it. He tightened the scarf again, got up, and went down the staircase, jumping from the platform to the street.

"Hey, mate . . ." shouted the conductor in the wake of the lost fare.

He came up the stairs. Fritsch said, "Two to Westminster Bridge, please."

The conductor looked back through the window and saw the disappearing figure, then back to Fritsch: "Right you are, guvnor." He was used to all sorts on the Route 38.

Patrick Dexter had the build of a slightly overweight fighter, and even at fifty his body kept a suppleness that showed in his impatient walk. They met him at Waterloo, from the train that delivered the Pan Am Clipper passengers from Southampton. At the barrier Seton stood back while father and daughter embraced. It was strange, the sensation of his own intimacy with this girl shared with this other kind of intimacy in reunion. He noticed the peculiarity of two bodies apparently dissimilar yet with features in common—something in the father's way of holding his head, something in her purpose of movement, and more in their manners.

Dexter disengaged himself, eyes still glowing, and looked at Seton over Ruth's shoulder.

"Well, well—*isn't* she something, my little girl?" He grasped Seton's hand. "And you, you old fox. You're not looking so bad."

As Ruth watched the two men her anxiety dissolved: Whatever was to come, these two had long reserves of amity to summon. It came out even in the polarity of their personalities: Dexter the pugnacious extrovert, Seton the seemingly more diffident and fragile of the two, but she knew that they had equal strengths.

They had planned to tell him at dinner that night. But while they both quietly waited for the right opening Dexter persisted through the meal with urgent questions:

"Edward, I'm not just here for the air show. I represent some people who might be ready to give you some help. You know we're already supplying planes to the French. We know your own weaknesses—maybe we can answer that." He leaned across the table, pulling some of the cloth with him. "But first, I want answers. It comes down to this. We don't want to supply stuff if it's going to end up in the hands of the Germans."

Such bluntness was Dexter's style, and Seton knew better than to resent it. "You mean, are we going to collapse? The Kennedy line."

The close-cropped gray head lunged toward him again. "Don't underrate Kennedy. He has powerful support. It's not only him. Munich has made a poor impression. You've got to convince us that you have it in your guts to fight. With Chamberlain, a lot of people just can't see it."

Before Seton could answer, Ruth spoke: "Father—you ought to know better. People here are as sick of Munich as you are."

Seton changed his answer to that of the conciliator. "No, Ruth. He's right. You can't expect them to believe anything else. Munich is what they saw." He looked directly at Dexter: "We're going to have to be pushed to it. Not many people are ready yet to stand on the line. But when it comes—as it will—we're not quitters. You know that."

Dexter looked unconvinced. "*You* may not be. But Munich wasn't Chamberlain acting on his own. He delivered what people wanted." He paused, then turned to Ruth: "I guess you've become partisan. If it was up to you—you'd give the British everything they asked for, right?"

"Right. After all, it's *our* civilization too."

"*That* partisan, eh?" He looked curiously from her to Seton. "You know, six months ago you couldn't have sold me on any *kind* of involvement. I didn't want to know about it. What with Roosevelt to worry about. . . ." He grimaced. "But then came this stuff with the Jews. You know, I just don't get it. Hitler lost America with that one night. What *is* it with them?"

"Ask your daughter, Pat. She saw it."

Ruth looked at her father: "I *didn't* see it, not at first. Then I did. It's the imperative of his kind of power—offering something to hate. The Jews were perfect."

"Yeah . . . I guess so." Dexter put both elbows on the table and propped up his head. "So it's an inevitable war, now?"

"A necessary war," said Seton.

"That's a hell of an idea to have to sell to the American people."

Ruth was vehement: "It has to be a *moral* judgment, Father."

Dexter looked at her with a confusion of affection and skepticism. "That's even harder to sell. Maybe it already is, for you. But that isn't why people go to war, not in 1938. There are two reasons I can think of why they won't want to fight. Reason one: Hitler just isn't morally offensive enough. Reason two—the big one: Hitler will knock the shit out of you, if you'll pardon the phrase."

Seton heard the authentic voice of Dexter country, of a thousand conversations in the Racquet Club bar.

While Seton and Ruth were still preoccupied with this cynical but too accurate assessment, Dexter's tone changed: "Edward, I want to know, what have you done to my little girl here? She's become a political animal."

Though they had rehearsed for such an opening, they were still tense. Seton put his right hand on the table, unconsciously crumbling a bread roll as he answered: "Pat—there's something I have to say. It's the most difficult thing I've ever had to say, to you. I'd like your consent to marry Ruth."

The reflex hit Dexter slowly: His mouth fell slightly open; his eyes narrowed and creased; his hand went to his head and he rubbed the cropped hair.

As she watched the two men, Ruth's hands tightened on the cloth.

Dexter's voice came low and slow: "Well . . . I'll be *damned!* Isn't that the *damnedest* thing!" He looked from one to the other. "You two?"

"I want it, Father."

Dexter sat back in his chair and scrutinized her. "Yes. I guess you do." He began to laugh, but the pitch of the laugh was ambiguous. Then he repeated: "The *damnedest thing!*" He looked again at Seton: "Well, Edward—you're, you're— It's the best goddamned news I have had in quite some time." He swiveled in his chair and waved to a waiter so forcefully that people at nearby tables turned. "Champagne, waiter. Bring a bottle of the best champagne in the house."

Ruth got up and went to him, holding him by the shoulders and kissing him. "Oh—Father. You've made me so happy. I never thought. . . ."

"He's the guy you should be kissing—not me," laughed Dexter. He squeezed her hand and then looked at her more earnestly: "I know you know what you're doing, and I'm very happy." He looked over to Seton, who had turned pink: "There's nobody I'd rather have join the family, you old fox." Still holding Ruth's hand, he said, "I'm gonna have to go through hell to sell this to your mother."

"I know," said Ruth.

"No offense, Edward. But she's gonna regard you as Bluebeard—or worse."

"Well," said Ruth, going back to her seat, "I guess I'll just have to spell it out to her."

"How about, for a start, spelling it out to me?" said Dexter.

The walls of the corridor were ridged roughly where planks had held the concrete in place until it dried, and the whole place had the damp chill of a cavern. Green service pipes ran along the walls, and from somewhere beyond them came the throb of the generator pumping air through filters from above. A young R.A.F. pilot officer led Seton and Patrick Dexter to a double set of steel doors forming an air lock between the corridor and a lighter, less improvised area where the walls were painted white. "If you would wait here, please, sir," said the officer, leaving them and disappearing into another corridor.

An older officer appeared and recognized Seton. As they shook hands Seton introduced Dexter, and then the three of them went through a red door. They entered the high gallery of a surprisingly large auditorium. Beneath them was another smaller gallery fronted by a continuous desk on which stood a bank of telephones, a chair by each telephone. Most of the auditorium below was filled by a map of the southeastern corner of England, with London near its center and on the right-hand side the English Channel and the French coast from the Brittany Peninsula north to the Belgian border. The map was like a huge gaming table segmented into numbered squares. Long sticks like croupiers' rakes lay on the map next to stacks of numbered moveable counters. On the far wall there was a bank of narrow columns, each headed by the number of a squadron and the name of an airfield. The columns were divided horizontally into illuminated legends indicating the degrees of readiness of the squadrons' aircraft. A smaller group of columns to the right gave weather conditions for each airfield.

Seton had very little explaining to do: The purpose of the place was clear to Dexter. One innovation drew his attention: "And you say that with this radio direction beam device you can plot the height *and* speed?"

The officer replied: "That's right—and while they're still far enough away to give us the time to get airborne, and our planes can be directed accurately to an interception point."

Dexter gave a low whistle. "I'll be damned."

Seton was more cautious: "There are a few problems to be solved before I'd say it was foolproof."

"Well," said Dexter, "if you wanted to convince me that you still had some tricks in this game—you did right."

"Men and machines," said Seton, "that's the real problem."

In the car going back to London Dexter was silent for a while and then turned to Seton: "You know, Edward, one thing bothers me . . . about that map. It seems to assume that the Germans are already at Calais."

When they went to the Paris Air Show, one long-guarded secret was allowed briefly into the sky. A prototype Spitfire flew from London to Paris in fifty minutes, was refuelled discreetly in a distant corner, and then flew back again. It made several fast passes over the crowd. Dexter turned to Seton. "What the hell was *that?* It's too pretty for a warplane."

"If you can offer us anything as good, which I doubt, I would take the lot," said Seton, watching not the Spitfire but the binoculars of some Luftwaffe officers spinning in agitation. Seton knew that Dexter would go home as committed as his daughter.

29

Canaris had spent the night on the cot in his office but was testy from insomnia. He went through the empty outer office and into a corridor. The absence of activity unreasonably angered him; in such moods he wanted the rest of the Abwehr to share his sleeplessness. He prowled further, looking for a victim. One light showed at the end of the corridor. His circulation was at a low ebb, and he shivered and thought of coffee. Pursuing the light, he pushed open a door.

Major Helmuth Groscurth, chief of the Abwehr's Sabotage Section, was lying across his desk fast asleep, his head resting on an uncompleted memorandum. The sight of someone even more fatigued than himself dissipated Canaris's annoyance. He leaned over the desk and shook Groscurth by the shoulder. Groscurth stirred hazily.

"Good morning, Major."

Groscurth's senses returned in a rush. He sat up and smoothed his hair. "Admiral—what time is it? I'm sorry. . . ."

"If we can find an orderly alive in this place, we'll get some coffee, you and I, and have a talk."

While Canaris took a chair Groscurth found a telephone operator to summon the coffee.

"It was easy—Czechoslovakia?" said Canaris.

"The Czechs could have mobilized seven hundred and fifty thousand men and more than thirteen hundred airplanes. Our signals didn't work. The tanks broke down. We ran out of food. It's unbelievable—it just fell into our hands. If this part was so easy, the rest can't be long in coming."

"Another proof of the Führer's genius—psychological victory."

"That's right. On the second day, Admiral, we stopped at a village inn for lunch. Hitler, the generals, some junior officers. The dining room door was left open. Our drivers and people from the village came to the door to listen. He raved away, for their benefit. The British were enemy number one: *'It's always the British who criticize me,'* he said; "they're decadent, led by degenerate aristocrats or by idiots like Chamberlain. They dare to cross my path, I will not have it, I will destroy them. . . .' "

An orderly came with the coffee.

Canaris stared into the cup, gratefully inhaling. He was solemn: "By taking Hitler's word, Chamberlain has made war inevitable—and yet he talks of saving the peace of Europe."

Groscurth sipped his coffee and confirmed the observation: "At the end of lunch he was still ranting about Chamberlain: *'That brute prevented me from making an entry into Prague!'* "

"Our people don't *want* war," said Canaris between gulps of the coffee, "but when it can be waged as cheaply as this— they won't object. And the generals, they are beginning to believe in it. Even Halder. A month ago he thought we could get rid of the Führer. Now he's dreamed up this plan, *Sichelschnitt,* for invading France! Major, Hitler understands generals. Ask them to draw up a plan, and they forget the politics."

Groscurth grinned ruefully. "It's a beautiful plan—you have to admit it."

"You, too, Major?"

Von Klagen in Berlin was a man rejuvenated: Once the plane landed, he knew it—despite everything, Berlin was still *Berlin;* even Göring's economies had not impoverished its spirit, the streets had that distinctive libido of a cosmopolitan city, the women the surer stare and the sanguine walk. At a traffic crossing in the flick of a second a girl glanced at him in the black official car and completed the sense of homecoming. You could simply assume more, say less, and satisfy any taste in Berlin. The girl's glance enshrined it all; it was a conspiracy they shared, with thousands of others. Nobody had looked at him like that in London.

The car followed the canal for the short journey along

the Tirpitzufer. It was still dark enough for some of the lights to be burning in the windows of the Abwehr. He looked up and saw that in the big office overlooking the canal someone was already at work. He decided to give it time and went to find breakfast in the canteen. One of Canaris's secretaries was there, filling a tray for her boss. She had advanced maternal instincts and said, "I should wait for half an hour, at least. He's like a bear with a sore head." The aphrodisiac effect of the city began to wear off.

When finally he arrived in the outer office, Piekenbrock was waiting. "You'd better be convincing," he said, flicking nervously through a file.

The second of the secretaries came out of the door. "You can go in."

Denying the predictions, Canaris seemed congenial. He was slumped in his chair, the high neck of a thick sweater almost swallowing his head. "A good flight, von Klagen?"

"Thank you, Admiral."

"Sit down, both of you." Canaris looked at von Klagen: "They have the list, but they do nothing. Can you explain that?"

"I don't know, Admiral. I don't understand. By now, I thought. . . ." He was still suspicious of Canaris's mood. "The situation in London is unclear."

There was a short, hissing laugh. "We can agree on that." Canaris flipped through several pages on his desk. "I can see why the Führer is taking such risks with the English. He can't really expect them to fight, not if these people really represent British opinion." He looked up, at von Klagen again: "Seton must find it difficult to distinguish between his friends and his enemies."

Von Klagen grinned.

"Oberstleutnant, there are extraordinary things happening here in Berlin, too. And yet the Abwehr preserves its reputation. We do our job, but our job is usually clear. I wonder, are you confused? Did you think you were working for Heydrich—or even Himmler, perhaps?"

"Admiral?" Von Klagen was uneasily on guard.

"The woman, Lady Taverner. Not as tidy as you believed. The English police are taking an interest."

"She had to be killed."

Canaris pulled himself wearily to the desk and leaned over it. "*Had* to? It wasn't any part of your orders."

"She knew about the putsch. She was talking openly of it."

Both Canaris and Piekenbrock were startled. It was Piekenbrock who said, "How could she know?"

"From a journalist, I think."

Piekenbrock spoke Canaris's thoughts: "The *newspapers* knew?"

"Nothing appeared, but Kordt's visit was known to some of them. And the meeting with Churchill. It seemed to me that if she was talking about it, she might tell Dunsinnan. And then—"

"Straight to Heydrich," said Piekenbrock.

Canaris looked at von Klagen with a new comprehension—for once unable to conceal his surprise. "How long had you known what was happening?"

"The Luftwaffe is not yet full of trained dogs, Herr Admiral."

"You and Oster," said Canaris, "you share the same views?"

"There are many of us, *still.*"

Canaris nodded resignedly. "Unfortunately your method was not entirely convincing. Perhaps you left some traces."

"I don't think so." Von Klagen was self-assured again.

"You can't go back—to England. Seton will make sure that you are useless to us there. You broke all the rules." He smiled at von Klagen remorselessly. "I think you need a change of climate. You don't know our Moscow station, do you?"

Drummond showed the visitor into the drawing room at Eaton Square. "Mr. Barrington."

"Lionel," said Dunsinnan, already sensing trouble. "Sit down, won't you."

Barrington had elaborately waved flaxen hair and a pinched face that seemed adolescent, although he was in his early thirties. He sat in a tentative way, as though it might prove necessary suddenly to leave.

"Sherry?" said Dunsinnan.

"No. Thank you." Barrington looked at the lingering Drummond.

"Thank you, Drummond," said Dunsinnan. Drummond left.

Barrington waited for the door to close. "Look, Alastair, sorry to barge in like this, unannounced. Fact is, I've had a pretty unpleasant experience. Friend of mine at the club, somebody I've known for years, asked me to drop by his flat for a drink. Thought nothing of it. When I got there, there was another chap with him. Little chap, strange eyes. Never seen him before. At any rate . . . we were introduced, I had a drink, and my friend made some excuse and disappeared into the bathroom. Whereupon—" Barrington gulped. "Whereupon this other chap starts speaking, very quietly. He says—as far as I can recall the exact words, 'It has come to our notice that you have been keeping in touch with certain figures in Germany. It's my duty to warn you that these contacts are very unwise.' *Unwise*—that was the word. Then he paused, fixing me with those hard little eyes. I didn't say anything, so he said, 'We know about your friends also. This sort of thing can get you into trouble. I think you should know that.' There was something quite threatening about it. I was quite shaken, I can tell you. When my friend came back, it was obvious he knew what was going on. He's been rather evasive since then. So, I've noticed, are other people in the club. I tell you, Alastair . . . I think it would be as well if I were to drop out of this scheme of yours, for a while, at any rate."

"Until you see which way the wind is blowing?" said Dunsinnan acidly. He saw that the headlong recital was a form of irrigation for Barrington, leaving him in a state of nervous exhaustion. The man was dispensable, anyway. There had been doubts before, a suggestion of drugs. Now the weakness was explicit, marked by a yellowing skin—appropriately, thought Dunsinnan. It wasn't Barrington that alarmed him but the clear indication that the names were being followed. Perhaps they had deliberately chosen the weakest link. After all, nobody else had yet come squealing. It would make sense: scare one and hope to panic the rest. Dunsinnan turned away. "Have you told anyone else—any of the others?" He lit a cigarette, looking out into the street.

"No. You're the first, of course."

A lie, thought Dunsinnan. "And the last, I trust," he said, turning back toward Barrington.

"What will *you* do?" said Barrington.

Dunsinnan flicked cigarette ash onto Barrington's knee. "It must be awkward for you, Lionel, at the club."

Drummond came into the room.

"Would you run Mr. Barrington to his club, Drummond? White's, isn't it?"

Dunsinnan was schooled enough in the signals of the British social semaphore to realize what was being done to him. It seemed ironical to think of the term *beyond the pale*, with its Jewish associations, but that was his destiny and he knew it. Now it would be left to the hard core. This knowledge did not, to his own surprise, depress him. It had concentrated his allegiances, simplified his future.

The image that was to stay with Seton after the meeting was a surrealistic detail: There were three deep leather armchairs in the room, he sat in one, his master in the second, and the third, though empty, retained the impress of a body and all the while slowly recomposed itself, the leather rising silently. The image of this chair never left him.

"Impetuous, ill-judged, highly compromising. I simply can't think why you did it." Seton's accuser in agitation was totally still except for his mouth and eyes. The hands rested on each arm of the chair, their stiffness curiously terminal.

"There seemed no alternative," said Seton, beginning to be unnerved by the unfamiliar stillness. "I considered it very carefully, it was a last resort."

There was a silence in which Seton was conscious of their respective rhythms of breathing: his own unsteady and his master's more nasal, a sound extraordinarily capable of conveying weariness, exasperation, and sorrow. Then, finally, a melancholic echo: "Last resort. . . ." One hand, his right, moved to displace the symmetry and fell on his thigh, where it relapsed again into lifelessness.

"I've been holding them off for some time. At first I don't think they were sure. I imagine there were the usual consultations. You realize, of course, how close Wilson and Dawson are?"

Seton didn't answer.

"That ought to have been obvious. However, for whatever reason, they let it simmer for a while. No doubt other things preoccupied them. When they came back with it, they had chapter, book, and verse—the minutes of your meeting with Wilson's committee, your own memorandum—and the damning thing, a précis of the unpublished article. They couldn't show me the actual article—that would have been a shade too revealing." He stopped and sighed. "The connection was uncontestable."

"I'm sorry if it makes things difficult for you."

The replying glance was cool and dismissive. "They

wanted to use the Official Secrets Act. Their view is that you are unsuited by temperament for this kind of work—'too committed,' I think somebody said. I talked them out of a secrets trial. It might have raised too much interest. Then they wanted you out—entirely."

"You mean—retired?"

"Oh, nothing as unsubtle. Some distant station. You were not to become a conspicuous casualty. You know the sort of thing. We do have airfields in the desert, I believe." It was the nearest he came to humor in the whole conversation, and it was bleak enough.

"I see."

"You have a useful ally in Dowding. It was he who fixed it."

"Fixed what?"

"The point is—the point is, you must drop out of view, lie very low. You're being sent to Cranwell."

"*Cranwell?*"

"To lecture. Don't imagine, for a minute, we're letting you fly again. I insisted on that. You are to lecture on strategy. I thought that rather apt."

Seton's sense of disgust overcame his abjection. "That's *exile!*"

"It was very nearly disgrace. Don't forget that."

Seton sank back into the chair, thinking. Then he said, "What about the list of names? Isn't *that* behind it—why they've moved now rather than before?"

The hand on the thigh moved slightly forward. "They don't know of that."

The empty chair completed its reassembly with one last crease.

On the eastern faces of the low hills, in clefts never reached by the low winter sun, streaks of snow remained. The patches of white were faults in an otherwise cohesive landscape: Dark-red soil turned into spiralling ridges by the plough, grassland dulled by the gray light, bare woods breaking the skyline. Even at its bleakest it seemed to Seton the quintessence of the English heartland, a place free of extremes, its texture shaped not just by hand but by social adjustments in a country coming to the edge of revolution and then always drawing back, ground gained, ground lost. For Seton this harmony embodied both the virtues and vices of

English compromise, accepting inequalities for the sake of peaceability.

An old Roman road, the Foss Way, ran northeast, surviving in intermittent stretches whose flawless straightness and drainage mocked the shoddy meandering medieval lanes, a physical trace of the incompatible temperaments of Roman commanders and feckless peasants. As the Foss Way came over the brow of a low rise a Norman church was set back from it on a knoll, its castellated tower expressing yet another alien temperament. At the rear of the church was a cluster of gravestones, some upright and freshly cut, most moss-stained and pitching into long grass. A low wall of yellow stone enclosed graveyard and church.

A light wind caught Ruth's lace veil and lifted it from her eyes. Her dark-brown skin against the gossamer layers of wedding dress made the one exotic mark in the gray setting as the photographer crouched under his black hood. Seton wore a morning suit with gray top hat. To his right, in a wheelchair, sat his mother wrapped in fur, only dimly aware of her surroundings. To Ruth's left was Patrick Dexter, bareheaded, in a dark serge suit, feeling the cold. A small group of Seton's kin, ranging from an elderly curate to a fidgeting infant, stood behind them. On the fringe Pickles stood awkwardly balancing on one foot next to Endmere, the most urbane of them all. The last notes of the organ came from the church, and the photographer pressed the button. A mischievous instinct made Ruth realize that original sin was now sanctified—and a countering instinct, that Seton was still too paternal.

It was the reversion to uniform that rubbed in Seton's sense of exile. It was years since he had lived in the precisely stratified society of an officers' mess, and within the professional insularity of the service. The R.A.F. College at Cranwell emphasized his age: Like a man realizing that suddenly all the policemen seem too young, so Seton, confronted by adolescents in uniform, was made to feel of a distant time. Ruth recognized that she, too, seemed an agent of this gulf. She did what she could to reclaim him, but it was a hard start to married life.

Her solution was to enlist Endmere as a lifeline. She insisted on weekends in London; they disposed of Seton's old flat and used Davies Street as the refuge. Endmere kept Seton supplied with political gossip, willingly exchanged for Ruth's cooking. As, month by month, the war came closer he watched her struggle with Seton's morale. The strain matured her.

One evening, settling with his brandy, Seton said to Endmere, "Tell me, Peter, did anything more ever come to light about the Taverner death? The papers seem to have lost interest."

Endmere stubbed out his cigar. "Scotland Yard seem to have given up on it, too. They did find something, but it led nowhere. Somebody saw her from a distance, at the cottage, with a man. He had a limp."

Seton's hand, resting on Ruth's, tightened.

"Not much use as a clue, that, is it?" said Endmere.

Ruth looked at him carefully. "What are you so pleased about, suddenly?"

He had just come into the cottage from his car, stooping under the door, too light in his step. He pulled the scarf from his neck and threw his cap onto the peg with precision. "Nothing. Nothing really."

"Come on. You're like a dog with two tails."

"It shows that much?" He sought out the whisky decanter from a small table overflowing with freshly picked flowers.

"It does."

"Whisky?"

"Yes.'

"I flew a Spitfire today."

"You did what? I thought. . . ."

"Yes, well—here, I'm afraid I've rather drowned it with the soda. Well, you see, when I said I was visiting that airfield today it was true, and that was all, the usual things planned. Then Keith Park—you know, the New Zealander—he let me sit in the thing, supposedly showing me the controls—and well, suddenly he said, 'How would you like to try it?' I didn't even have to ask."

Reluctantly she grinned. "The rest is obvious." She sipped the whisky, looking at his still flushed face. "Well, how was it?"

"Not bad—for a man with glasses."

"The plane, not you. I know what you can do, with or without glasses."

"If we had another five hundred, I'd rest content. And, of course, the pilots to go with them."

The Spitfire, she thought, had virtues other than being a

fighter plane: One flight in it seemed to have returned to her a lost man.

"It's taken a long while," said Endmere.

"Will you be glad to have it settled?" said Ruth.

"Glad? Hardly the word. Relieved. It decides things." He looked at Seton: "And you, Edward?"

"There's a difference between declaring war and actually fighting it."

"Ahhhh," said Endmere, "how very true. You've had to learn that the hard way."

Ruth looked at Seton. "Yes, he has."

The three of them stood at a window of the flat, looking over roofs toward Whitehall. Barrage balloons ringed the London skyline. The streets were curiously empty of people.

"Tell you something, something that might sound far-fetched—swear it's true," said Endmere. "Until last week all the chiefs of staff were on holiday. So were Chamberlain and Halifax—Chamberlain shooting in Yorkshire, Halifax fishing in Scotland. He sent a salmon down, packed in ice, to the Foreign Office. How do you like that?"

"God help us,'" said Seton.

"Another straw in the wind," said Endmere, "a little scene outside the Savoy the other night. Churchill and his pals, you know, the warmongers, they were holding court inside. Duff Cooper had been with them. As he was leaving he bumped into the Duke of Westminster—you know, one of the really hard-liners, very pro-Hitler. Westminster went for Duff; said the war, if it came, was the work of the Jews, that Hitler knew, in spite of everything, that we were his best friends. Duff was rather good. He said, 'I hope that by tomorrow he will know that we are his most implacable enemies.' "

Ruth said, "Are people like the Duke going to count for anything now?" A memory of names on a list came back to her, and she looked at Seton as Endmere answered:

"They'll try."

"Somehow," said Seton, "I don't see Chamberlain embracing that phrase—what was it, implacable enemies?"

"More like Churchill," said Ruth.

"Wishful thinking," said Endmere, turning from the window. "He's settled for First Lord of the Admiralty. In any case, he's getting on."

"Sad, that," said Seton.

It was September 2, 1939. At 11:00 A.M. the following morning Britain was formally at war with Germany.

At Cranwell Seton was encircled by avid questioners. Younger officers, and flying instructors, were pressing to be released to the front-line squadrons. Older officers argued priorities.

One of them said, "Bomber Command is still dropping bloody leaflets, nothing heavier."

Another said, "They did ask for permission to bomb the Black Forest. You know what they were told? 'We can't do that, it's private property. You'll be asking us to bomb the Ruhr next.'"

There was a collective groan. Seton shared the despair over unresolved policy. Already the war was being called the Phony War, though not by the Poles.

An orderly called Seton away to the phone.

The voice on the other end was placid: "Ah—Edward. How are you? Glad to have caught you. Connections are not easy to get. Edward, I wonder—could you come up, say, to-morrow?"

"To London?"

"Ten o'clock sharp. The Admiralty."

"The Admiralty?"

"Not in uniform, please. You'll be expected." The line went dead.

The Admiralty was not like the Air Ministry. Its age gave it a tangible sureness and sense of purpose. He was led deep into the sprawling building, down steps into corridors lit by lamps inside blue shades. Gradually the gold braid on coat cuffs became thicker, and finally he was put into a waiting room, converted to double as an emergency bedroom. Three cots almost filled the floor. Two thick woollen dressing gowns hung from coat pegs. Stacked against a wall were ministerial dispatch boxes, some black and some red. On one wall was a large map of Scapa Flow, the deep-water Scottish harbor. Seton felt out of his element.

A young woman naval officer came out of an inner door, her face scrubbed carbolic clear. She spoke briskly: "Group Captain Seton? Please go in."

The door opened into a room of astonishing size, down its center a long oak table. The room was in an even shade of dark wood except for the chairs, padded with brilliant red leather. The table was empty except for a half-filled whisky decanter. The smell of cigar hung in the room. At the far end of the table Seton saw a familiar form, perhaps a little grayer, hunched in a chair, one hand apparently lifeless on the oak.

"Change of atmosphere, Edward. Please sit down." He waved Seton to the chair beside him. "Yes," he continued, "a definite change of atmosphere, at least in *this* building. Your wife—is she well?"

"Thank you, yes."

"Good. I expect she'll be glad to leave Cranwell."

Seton settled into the chair. There were two glasses by the whisky decanter, each with a drop left in them, judging by the smell left there from the night before.

"There's a post in Paris I've recommended you for. It won't be the same system as before, not exactly. Boundaries are very much more fluid these days, all sorts of things being tried out."

"Paris?"

"I think you'll understand. Ostensibly you'll be liaising with the French Air Force on intelligence. There is quite a legitimate job to do. But the duties will be, er, a little *mixed*. You know somebody in the Deuxième Bureau, do you not? Martel, isn't it?"

"Yes."

"That's a great help. Better to work through the natives, wherever you can. And no more uniform. I'll see to it that you have whatever help you think you need." He saw Seton's uneasiness. "Wives *are* allowed."

Not until Dunsinnan had crossed Berkeley Square and reached Davies Street did he realize what was distracting him from his purpose. Then, looking ahead toward Claridge's, he remembered the impulsive call at Ruth's flat and the dinner when he invited her to the Spithead Review. He had never quite been able to reconcile himself to her apparent enmity and—even more incomprehensible to him—her marriage to a middle-aged bureaucrat. His mother had never mentioned Ruth to him again, but he knew there was an indictment of him in the selective silence. Now his mother sat morosely in Scotland while he defended his ideological ground elsewhere. An urgent concern had brought him back to Davies Street, to the house of the Duke of Westminster. A block short of where he had called on Ruth he turned into the small courtyard and rang the bell.

Inside he was suddenly aware of being the youngest member of the gathering. There was a fellow Scottish peer to whom he nodded without getting acknowledgment, a sign of an imperishable Highland feud, a sprinkling of other faces known from the House of Lords, several clerics, some members of Parliament, and one or two uniformed figures ostentatiously wearing decorations from the First World War. Dunsinnan saw in the room what he had feared: an unstable alliance of the serious and the eccentric. Dispirited by the rambling conversation, he sat silent while the meeting attempted to produce the draft text of a memorandum to be sent to the cabinet, calling for the immediate opening of negotiations for peace with Hitler. When the meeting broke up, Dunsinnan lingered behind, standing by a mantel in the room, drawing on a cigarette.

The butler closed the door on the last departing member of the meeting and, in another minute, came back into the room.

"His Grace would like you to join him in the study, Your Lordship."

Dunsinnan crossed the hall into a much smaller, shaded room.

"Why so quiet, Alastair?"

"A warning is only as strong as the names attached to it."

"It mayn't be as weak as you think. A drink?"

"Thank you, yes."

"You take it straight, do you not?" The Duke went over to a cut-glass decanter. "No, Alastair. I shall make it my personal concern to ensure that the prime minister realizes he has been tricked into war by the Jews. *They* are the only people who want it. The Jewish newspapers have a lot to answer for." He filled two glasses generously and then turned to Dunsinnan showing signs of sudden agitation. "Poland. Good God, man—how *did* we come to go to war on *their* behalf? Because some intriguing woman comes to London and panics us into making that ridiculous guarantee. *Poland!*" He thrust the glass of whisky into Dunsinnan's hand and sat down.

Dunsinnan remained standing. He said, "Churchill's malignant influence is beginning to show."

"Perhaps . . . but he is still not really trusted. Too much the wild man. Given time, I'm convinced Neville will not have the stomach for this war. After all, Germany is impregnable, is she not?"

"I have no doubt of it."

"Sit down, Alastair." The Duke waited for Dunsinnan to settle. "They're bringing the Duke of Windsor back," he said quietly. "And the Duchess. Of course, it makes the King very nervous. Very few people know."

"What will they do with them?"

"Ah—Alastair. That won't be simple. They'll obviously try to keep him away from the palace."

"Your house at Chester, perhaps?"

The Duke shook his head. "I'm afraid not. Not this time. It's too obvious."

Dunsinnan stretched his legs, picking up interest. "I know a way—to keep in touch."

III

Pursuits

30

Paris, May 9, 1940

Summer had come early. In the cafes on the Champs-
Elysées most of the tables were packed night after night. Seton and Ruth walked under the continuous canopy of chestnut
trees down the great boulevard. In the twilight the white stone
of the mansions, hotels, and stores turned pale pink. The
pavements held the heat of the day, and the warm, stagnant
air was permeated with the smells of fresh coffee, ambitious
kitchens, and coagulating drains. In a succession of balmy
weeks this walk had become a ritual for them whenever Seton
was free to make it. They left the Hotel Metropole at the
Etoile and walked down the Champs-Elysées to the Rond-
Point, and there turned left to the small restaurant where they
regularly ate.

The *patron* was a roguish Breton who from a squalid
kitchen conjured simple artistry. Some supplies had become
irregular, but he had his own resources; when the normal sup-
pliers ran dry, he disappeared into the country and came back
with fresh vegetables, cheeses, and game. Seton had planned
this dinner as an ironical celebration, marking the two
hundred and fiftieth day of the war. The *patron* assembled
the ingredients on the table before them: raw fillet steak
ground into pink beads; two raw eggs; a bowl of plump sour
capers from the Midi; a dish of finely chopped onion; and a
small bottle of Worcestershire sauce, the sole concession to
Anglicized taste. He broke the raw eggs into the meat and

stirred the two, meat and eggs, into a thick paste. The capers and onions followed, then the sauce, until all the flavors were blended. He divided it into portions and put each on a bed of lettuce: *"Voilá! monsieur-dame. Le steak tartare!"*

There was one minor technical violation of wartime stringencies. Officially it was a "spiritless" day, imposing the hardship of replacing cognac or whisky with champagne or other wines. The *patron* knew that their favorite drink was a blend of black-currant liqueur, classified as a spirit, and a dry white wine, Chablis when it could be found. "Nobody can tell it from *rosé,*" the *patron* confided, laughing as he shared the toast: ". . . *two-fifty,* maybe we will still be able to toast *five hundred* days, *monsieur-dame!*"

"Nobody lives like this in London anymore," said Seton, forking the raw meat. "You get one lump of sugar and a sliver of butter, one kind of cheese, no more iced cakes."

"Iced cakes? *You* never ate iced cakes, anyway."

He grinned. "That's true, but it's causing pain in high places."

"Oh, *him.* Yes, he would definitely be an iced-cake type—with sherry."

"I wonder what they're eating in Berlin?"

"According to the *Herald Tribune,* nobody's going hungry."

The sweet dark syrup in the drink countered the sharpness of the grape. Seton was conscious, almost absurdly so, of illicit self-indulgence. Or was it self-deception? Ruth had bloomed like the chestnuts, the creases of anxiety of the previous autumn now gone from her eyes. Each time they came to the restaurant Seton had a sense of being part of a great delusion, of dining at the edge of an abyss. But each morning the sun came up and Paris remained intact, slowly refilling with those who had fled to the country six months before; Maurice Chevalier sang "Paris reste Paris," and everyone believed him.

Reading his thoughts, she said, "How much longer?"

He shrugged. "As long as this weather holds—it could be anytime."

"I got the *Atlantic* magazine today. Lindbergh is offering his wisdom again: Germany is as essential to civilization as England or France, the Germans only claim the right of an able and virile nation to expand—you know the kind of stuff."

"If you had the misfortune to be Polish, you'd know what he means by virile."

"I wonder—do you think Roosevelt will just stand by and watch?"

"We're on our own."

She stretched across the table and held his hand. The *patron* brought a second bottle.

Before dawn the next morning he left her sleeping and went out to his car, the R.A.F. driver, as usual, raw-eyed from debauchery. They reached Château-Thierry as the sun came up, blinding the driver even with his visor down, but there was remarkably little traffic and virtually no sign of any French military activity. To the right the vineyards of Epernay already carried the fruit for another vintage of champagne; he knew Frenchmen who worried that the Maginot Line was sited too far north to save the vineyards. At Reims they turned into the yard of a château flying the blue ensign of the R.A.F. Although Seton was not in uniform, the guards knowingly saluted just the same. He cast one more uneasy glance to the east, at the azure skyline, and went inside.

Six months earlier racks of champagne had filled the cellar; now, in their place, was a long low table covered with a map of northeast France. Young R.A.F. officers and one French airman were watching as W.A.A.F.'s moved several red counters from the Channel coast to the east. The French officer glanced up and acknowledged Seton. "As you promised, they're coming," he said, with unrestrained excitement. Six R.A.F. squadrons were being transferred that morning from their English bases to airfields around Reims.

A young flight lieutenant gave Seton a telegraphed message. "Look at this, sir. It seems ominous." Seton read that the Dutch had blown the bridges on their border with Germany three hours earlier, and intelligence reports indicated heavy troop movements toward Holland and Belgium.

There was worse to come: At the edge of an airfield on the far side of Reims eighteen Blenheim bombers had been lined up immaculately according to regulations. Three Dorniers came out of the sky, destroyed six Blenheims in one run, and left the rest unfit for service. At another field an R.A.F. transport crashed, killing several fighter pilots. But by then Seton saw a more concerted pattern emerging in the reports: The Germans had begun a massive invasion of the Low Countries, supported by lethal bombing. The Phony War was over.

* * *

The radio that Ruth had put in their room at the Hotel Metropole had trouble picking up London: The building masked the signal, and the B.B.C. news channel fluctuated wildly in strength. On this evening she turned it to full volume, but this heightened the static, not the voice from London. She heard the announcer faintly: "This is the Home Service. Here is the Right Honorable Neville Chamberlain, M.P., who will make a statement."

The voice she despised came on the air, surprisingly composed. She strained to hear it. Chamberlain said he realized that the country wanted an end to party divisions in war, that there should therefore be a coalition government, and that the one obstacle to forming the coalition had proved to be himself. He had therefore resigned. The new prime minister was Winston Churchill. While Ruth still clutched the volume control Chamberlain delivered a final—and belated—condemnation of German aggression. And then he was gone.

A news bulletin resumed with a list of the cities bombed by the Luftwaffe and a sketchy account of the invasion of Holland and Belgium. She shivered with comprehension, wrestling with conflicting impulses: joy at the departure of Chamberlain and the succession of Churchill; foreboding about the enormity of the war; anxiety about Seton—and, overlaying it all, a surprising surge of homesickness, a desire to share the crisis with her family and to know how her own people would respond. The radio became imbecilic, giving out racing results. She turned it off and went to the window, switching off the light before opening the heavy curtains. Although Paris was blacked out, unrestrained lights glared from the suburbs: She could see the glow of Saint-Germain on the horizon, making a convenient homing beacon for the Luftwaffe. They had yet to come.

She was asleep, still dressed, when Seton came in. He touched her brow, and her eyes focussed slowly; she was still in another place. Then she touched him and said, "Chamberlain—"

"I know."

She sat up and saw a new gauntness in his face. "What's happening?"

"It's bloody awful." He pulled off his tie and turned to look at her. "We won't be able to take these losses for long."

"What are you going to do?"

"Not what I *should* be doing. I feel superfluous. Intelligence games aren't much use any longer—the hordes have descended, predictably." He saw her anxiety. "Do you want to get back to London, while you can?"

She stood up, straightening her skirt sleepily, and walked across the room to him. "Definitely not."

He kissed her on the brow. "Well, at least we have a leader now."

"Is it too late?"

He didn't answer.

Seton was appalled that such a high-level figure could fly from London in an unarmed Avro Anson without escort. Waiting at the terminal at Le Bourget, he knew how defenseless the airfield was, too, and how infested by the Luftwaffe the French skies had become—and yet here was the Anson droning serenely to a landing as though making a scheduled peacetime flight. The second surprise was the transformation in his visitor. Instead of the ponderous, slow-moving man in the park, here was a man apparently rejuvenated, as though from a cup of elixir. His jacket was unbuttoned, his tie slightly crooked, his step springy. Before Seton could say a word of reprimand for the carelessness of the flight, he was swept along in a new grip.

"Now then," said his master, waving a slim attaché case in the other hand, "tell me how things are."

But even Seton's dolorous account of the opening days of the battle did not depress his companion, although he listened in silence. When Seton had finished, he said, "I know . . . I know. We can't go on taking these losses. We'll be left naked. Winston knows that."

"The French will want more."

"You think they should have them—more planes? Our planes?"

Seton hesitated, and before he could answer, he was anticipated.

"I can tell you, Edward, Dowding has done the sums. He was called to the cabinet. He didn't say one word. He just walked round the table until he came to Winston. I thought he was going to hit him, astonishing scene. All he did was hand him a graph. In ten days, at the current rate of losses, Fighter Command would be wiped out—nothing left." He leaned over Seton, putting one hand on Seton's knee, his eye drawn to something in the street. "I see the escargot are still on the menu. Not much sign of austerity here."

Seton tried to keep to the point: "What will Winston tell them?"

"You'll dine with me tonight, I hope?" said his master with implacable evasion, sinking back into the seat.

Seton had reserved for his master a large corner suite overlooking the Arc de Triomphe. Once the porter left them, Seton was directed to a seat while the other man remained looking out to the street. Without turning, he said pensively, "We've very little to fall back on. The narrowest of margins." He turned from the window. The buoyancy had suddenly deserted him. He sat on a fragile Empire chair, seeming to overburden it. "It may not be enough—I suppose, of all people, you'll hardly be surprised. Having done what you did. There's no consolation in being proved right, not now."

Seton, expressionless, said, "Churchill must know that feeling, too."

"Yes . . . *yes,* he does. But it doesn't seem to get him down. You know what I think is Winston's greatest gift? He can tell the country how it needs to think of itself. Nobody else can do that."

"That's something else we could have done with a long while ago."

The edge in Seton's voice discomfited his companion, who crossed his legs and brushed a knee lightly with his right palm. "Quite so." Then a twitch of amusement came to his mouth, though not to his eyes. "You know, I wish you could have been there—the morning after Winston arrived. It was quite a thing. *Quite* a thing! Arrivals and departures. Horace Wilson, for example. He turned up as usual, at ten. Opened his office door and looked straight into Randolph Churchill's belligerent face. A clean sweep—Randolph as Winston's broom. Wilson didn't say a word. Just turned and left. Haven't seen him since."

"Oblivion is too kind a fate for some," said Seton.

"Yes. Well, he's fortunate, he comes under the heading of the misguided, to be charitable." The legs uncrossed, and the body leaned forward confidentially. "Look—when you provided me with that list, I promised that their time would come. Well, it has—at last. We're invoking something called Regulation Eighteen-B. Quite sweeping in its powers, no legal restraints. We can arrest anyone regarded as in the slightest way a risk, and that can be quite widely interpreted—quite widely. We're pulling in Mosley and the worst of his lot. And the other real nasties. That leaves three more groups. The yellow livers, they've already fled across the Atlantic, no doubt believing that they will hold our civilization in trust for us. Then there are a few nasties with friends in high places. We'll have to try warning *them* first, it might be tricky to go further—yet." He looked slightly apologetic. "And that leaves the hard core, the *really* dangerous people, the quislings." He stood up and returned to the window. "I'm afraid somebody must have tipped them off. They've hopped it. Don't know *why* they were left for so long, but there you are."

Seton looked up sharply. "Dunsinnan? Does that include Dunsinnan?"

His master continued to gaze at the Place d'Etoile. "I'm afraid so. We've lost track of him. I think he was forewarned—there are people who look to him, even now."

"Is that why you're here?"

The discord of the intemperate traffic beyond the window engrossed the watcher for a little longer. "Appalling. Quite appalling, the way these people drive. An expression of national character, I'm afraid." He walked back across the room. "I'll order something to drink. What would you like?"

Not until they were settled with a bottle of cognac five minutes later did the purpose of the meeting emerge, and by then Seton's master was improbably without his jacket, and even his tie was loosened. Seton realized now what had changed. A long cultivated mask had been dropped, though incompletely—the habit of years could not be shed in hours. That candor could suddenly be without risk was unnerving. Seton wondered at the cost, over the years, of this man's survival, of the compromises made and the dissembling. And he saw, too, how dangerous his own indiscretion must have been. There was one thing they both knew and showed in equal measure: the insidious attrition of despair.

"Now. As to why I am here. There is something I want your help with, something needing a great delicacy, *very* great delicacy." He had moved to a more accommodating chair and now rested in turquoise velvet. "The request comes from the highest quarter, as I'm sure you will come to appreciate. You may know, when the war came, there was some anxiety about the position of the Duke of Windsor. He was brought back to London from the Continent. However, that caused more problems than it solved. Family tensions. Two kings do not sit easily together, even if brothers."

"So you sent him back here."

"It was thought appropriate. He had always shown an interest in the military life."

"A dilettante, it turns out."

"Look, Edward. It's become quite a worry. I'm afraid he can't go back to England again, without causing the most awful rumpus. The King just won't have him there. Nor, *especially*, will the Queen. And his position here in Paris is, as things are—well, it's increasingly embarrassing, not to say precarious. We'll try to find a place for him in the Dominions. Some sinecure, to save his face. But in the meantime, in the meantime—there are dangers. As long as he's accessible, there are people who might influence him, get at him, the old set."

"Bedaux?"

"For one. Certainly. We know now, he took money from Bedaux, so-called expenses. Quite a lot. There have been awkward questions, about the dollars he was spending so freely. Bedaux was certainly running him for a while. He's been prey to anyone with money and ideas. There was a Swedish millionaire, touting what he called world peace. I'm afraid the Duke falls for that one too readily."

"It sounds like cupidity."

"Yes . . . well, the lady has expensive tastes. It is costly, to compensate. . . ."

Seton put down his glass, wary. "I still don't quite see—what can *I* do?"

"I want you to keep an eye on them. At arm's length, so to speak. Not to be at all evident, that would only exacerbate things. We don't want to make him feel caged. But you must keep a special lookout for anyone likely to try to subvert him."

"*Subvert?*"

"At this time, with so much uncertain, it could be an embarrassment were he to repeat the kind of things he's said in the past. I've no reason to suppose he's altered his vision since then. Could have got worse. There are still people who look to him, who would like him to appear now as the bearer of an olive branch—his old friend the Duke of Westminster, for one. Winston's had to slap him down *very* firmly, I can tell you."

Seton was silent for a minute. Then he said, "You didn't explain—about Dunsinnan. Is he part of this problem?"

"I don't know. That worres me."

"I see. It's not very tidy, is it?"

31

The dawn sky was ribboned with thin columns of black smoke, the traditional mark of hasty evacuation through the ages—the burning of the files. Seton realized the smoke was coming from the French ministries. He wondered what potentially incriminating details were now floating as incinerated flakes safe from the reach of historians. History! Again Paris was ready to give up her body to it. The city was too voluptuous for war; even now the music had not stopped and "J'attendrai' had lodged in his mind as the requiem. The dawn chorus from the park trilled confidently, the birds more composed than the citizens. He turned from the window. Ruth slept with one arm across the pillow where he had been, golden against the white. The beauty was hard to bear.

In his car, going east to the daunting Château de Vincennes, he noticed more cars reaching Paris with Belgian number plates and others with the French designations of AF for Aisne and NA for the Pas de Calais, messengers of distant disasters. At Vincennes the French commander, the inscrutable General Gamelin, too slowly grasped the pattern of his defeat from behind a barrier of confusions.

Later, when Ruth awoke, she was angry that Seton had not disturbed her. She went naked to the window and looked down. She, too, saw the migrant cars. Half an hour later she crossed the street to buy a *Herald Tribune* and went to the corner *brasserie* for breakfast. The paper spoke of the "reconquest" of a fort at Sedan. She knew the French map now: *Sedan!* Thus did the disaster leak through the censors. The Germans were across the river Meuse. Her waiter's gravity confirmed that the clue had reached the French papers too.

While her head was still deep in the paper a dark, stocky man came to the table. She looked up and smiled spontaneously: *"Louis!"*

"Madame."

She had never adjusted to French formality, the incessant shaking of hands between people meeting for the third time in

277

the same day. Louis Martel remained courtly after months of acquaintance.

"Please—sit down, Louis."

Martel did so with evident relief and ordered a cognac.

"I am looking for Edward," he said, tapping the tabletop nervously.

"He's at Vincennes."

"Ah." Martel registered despair. "It is the shame of France, the Château. You saw—Sedan?"

"Yes."

"I don't think they can be stopped now." The whole *brasserie* had succumbed to the same realization. No music played. Martel took the drink and downed it in one gulp. His face conveyed how comprehensive the catastrophe was.

"Can I help?"

"It is something I found last night, in a report. I remembered your story of the Scotsman, Dunsinnan."

"What is it?"

"He has been seen here, in Paris." He called the waiter for a second cognac. "Of course, British problems are a low priority at the Deuxième Bureau. We have our own fifth column to worry about . . . but I thought Edward should know." He produced a slip of paper. "Give Edward this. It is the address where I think Dunsinnan is staying. It is a neighborhood where the White Russian émigrés live."

She had to stand up to respect the formalities of departure, made mellower by Martel's kissing her hand; perhaps melancholy would unbend him. She went back to the hotel and asked if there were any messages. The desk clerk was distracted. "No, madame, no messages." Then came a nonsequitur born of his panic: "The line to Saint-Quentin is dead." She noticed a pyramid of baggage in the lobby, women in plain black dresses fretting and looking for their cars. In the hour she had been out, panic had begun to displace the unreal calm.

"This is worrying," said Seton, holding Martel's note.

"Why would he come here, *now?*" she said.

"That's what concerns me."

She saw the toll of the disaster in his eyes and cupped his head in her hands, kissing him hard. When they broke apart, she said, "How bad is it?"

"Winston flew here today. All hell is breaking loose. The

French are asking for ten more squadrons. *Ten!* They'll bleed us dry—*before* we face the Luftwaffe ourselves."

"You mean—alone."

"The people here know already, you can see what's happening in the streets. Paris will be left in the hands of those who don't really mind staying."

She sat down. "It was extraordinary today. Just in an hour. It all changed."

"The French army is split from top to bottom. Left and Right. Phobias about the fifth column."

"Louis mentioned that."

"Yes. The Bureau has its hands full."

"Will Churchill give them the planes?"

"I hope not. But they've made it clear that if he doesn't, they'll regard it as betrayal."

"Nasty."

He poured two cognacs and gave her one. "I think I know why Dunsinnan's here."

The mood of the city had touched Seton, too. He sat in the *brasserie* with his jacket over a chair, and his shirt open at the collar. Louis Martel was also dishevelled, his beard three days old. They shared a bottle of white wine.

"How did you get on to him?" said Seton.

"You remember something called the Croix de Feu?"

"The old Fascist organization?"

"Not old anymore. They were banned, they changed their name, but the faces were the same. We have watched them, always. The other day a new name appeared on the report. Your man."

Seton opened another button of his shirt, trying to get cool. "Tell me, have you heard of someone called Bedaux, Charles Bedaux?"

"Of course. He was one of them—the Croix de Feu. He is American, now."

"Is he here?"

"But yes. He moves in high places these days—higher than I can reach. You know, the blue-blooded circuit. Why are you interested in him?"

"What kind of blue-blooded circuit?"

"Wandering royalty, you know the kind. Your Duke of Windsor—he is often with Bedaux at the Boulevard Suchet."

Seton poured more wine into each of their glasses. "You know what the Duke has been doing?"

"He is at Vincennes. Liaison, with the military mission."

"I've been asked to keep an eye on him. It seems nobody knows what to do about him—or with him. The worrying thing is, I think Dunsinnan and Bedaux have an interest in him, too. If they've already got at him, through Bedaux, it could be a big problem for me."

"Then why don't you just pick up Dunsinnan?"

Seton gulped the wine. "I've already suggested that. They're worried about him, but they don't want to be bothered with him, with things as they are. I get the impression they would like to dump him here—on your plate."

Martel protested: *"Alors!* We have other things to worry about, too." He became conspiratorial, a look that Seton knew from the past: "Why don't you take care of him? We could arrange an accident, perhaps. It would be very easy."

"You know—we don't do that kind of thing."

"No." Martel was despairing. "That is one of your mistakes. So, *what* will you do?"

Seton slumped back in his chair, pulling at his collar. "My orders are to keep the Duke and Duchess out of trouble—or, rather, to keep trouble out of their way. I can't actually get too near. It's thought that the Duke might throw a tantrum if he feels he's under guard."

"It's a fool's errand, Edward."

"I was given no choice. *Fait accompli.*"

"My friend, you have my sympathy. I can offer nothing else." He drained the bottle into their glasses, and an accordion began playing drunkenly somewhere behind them.

32

Ruth found that the hotel lobby was now a muddle of arrivals and departures. Paris was a comparative sanctuary for the richer refugees from the north, while to the jittery Parisians it was becoming too obvious a target, still lying unmarked in the sun. The desk staff had lost control. Someone cried, "The Boches are at Laon," and a stooped old man croaked, *"Ils ne passeront pas!"* which earned him derisory or pitying looks: Valiant rhetoric was out of fashion. It was no good any longer even trying to ask for messages. She went up and waited in the room for Seton.

It was another two hours before he returned, and he came urgently into the room. "We have to pack—just as little as you need—for a resort."

"A *resort?*"

"We're going to Biarritz. They left together, this morning. All I know so far is that that's where they're going, not *why.*"

His R.A.F. driver and Humber had been appropriated by a more needy cause. The black Citroën parked outside the hotel was on loan from the Deuxième Bureau, given by Martel, he suspected, as an expedient for removing him from their hair, and it came replete with passes and the other documentation now required to navigate the bureaucratic barriers to flight. Amid all the hysteria Ruth had a curious feeling of leaving for a holiday, a part of the annual August exodus from Paris, and the unblemished sky did nothing to puncture the illusion. But for Seton it was a Göring sky: just what the Stukas thrived on, the roads constipated with refugees and the remnants of an army.

At first, going southwest on the N10, they could make little headway. Paris buses had been requisitioned and were packed with poorer families. Others had horse-drawn carts, children trailing behind. The one-way column took both lanes of the road. The occasional truck or car coming in the opposite direction had to crawl perversely through, glared at.

Ruth said, "It seems crazy—all this happening, and *we're* chasing the Duke of Windsor to Biarritz."

"Louis found it bizarre."

"Why *don't* they spirit him back to England?"

"His brother won't have it. Winston's trying to find a safe haven for him, somewhere well away, one of the Dominions perhaps."

"You mean, *Churchill* has to bother with this, too?"

"He has no choice. Just imagine, if Hitler got his hands on an ex-King, what kind of trouble that could make."

She sank back into the seat, shaking her head in disbelief. "It just seems so crazy, with everything else that's happening, to have to bother with it." But she didn't dwell on the point, seeing that Seton felt the incongruity of the assignment as sharply as she. The shade trees gave respite from the heat; their reflections moved across the windshield of the Citroën

like a rhythmic kaleidoscope and slowly hypnotized her into
sleep. When she woke, they were approaching Chartres. On
the right a field of rapeseed lay like a deep pile carpet, the
yellow tinted crimson in the setting sun. The great cathedral,
ahead of them, was opalescent.

"It'll be bad as far as Le Mans," said Seton. "There's a
back route, keeping clear of the N10."

The minor road was empty, and they made good time to
the rolling hills of the Loire Valley. The night sky was as
peerless as the day, the landscape metal blue, and they saw
the river first as flashes of silver to their left. The Deuxiéme
Bureau were not ascetics: In the glove compartment of the
Citroën she found a current copy of the *Guide Michelin*. She
turned to a map in the front marked *Les Bonnes Tables*. Just
south of the river, in a village that would otherwise not have
appeared on a map, was a single rosette denoting a restaurant
attached to a small château. Surrendering to hedonism, she
guided him to it.

They dined on a terrace with a view of the valley. The
privations of war seemed distant, left in France's northern
hemisphere. Here the air was humid, and a chorus of crickets
came from the gardens. The specialty of the chef, *sole farci*,
was served with a bottle of Sauvignon *blanc*, flint-dry but
grapy in the way of the Loire.

"*This* is war?" she said.

Around them a few tables were still occupied, and an
epicurean haze scented the terrace. An obese patriarch heading a table of five poured heavy cream over a pyramid of wild
strawberries and sent for more champagne.

"You know," said Ruth, "in the car, half dreaming, it
came back to me, about Dunsinnan and the Duke. In Munich
when they arranged the Berlin visit . . . this could all have
started then."

"I know. It would fit. They could be playing on his vanity, which is colossal, suggesting that he is the last hope of
making peace with Germany, before we get smashed. If they
got him to agree to make a peace overture—"

"They don't have much time."

"No."

It was Ruth who had the idea in the morning as they
dressed and looked out at the valley. "Isn't the Bedaux
château near here?"

"Château de Candé. *Yes,* of course, the other side of

Chaumont, not far." His mind synchronized with hers. *"That's a thought. . . ."*

She found the hamlet of Candé-sur-Beuvron listed in the *Michelin,* on the map for *"hôtels agréables, tranquilles, bien situés."* The description was not exaggerated. A small road snaked into the Touraine backwoods, and there they found the Bedaux estate, the castellated château striking a discord in the soft harmony of the valley. Strands of mist hung in the shaded parts of the valley.

"What do we do now?" said Ruth.

Seton realized how formless his ideas were. "Well, it's a long shot, but if they *are* doing what I think they're doing, they may come through here, too. I think perhaps we had better get some cover."

He drove the Citroën a short way beyond the gate to the château, where a track ran into a wood. He pulled off the road and under the trees. "If anything is coming, we'll hear it without any trouble."

An hour passed and the only sign of population was a peasant in a blue smock on a bicycle who saw the car and leered at them, as they intended, assuming a hasty and illicit assignation. Then they heard a car coming from the direction they had taken. They went on foot to the edge of the wood for a view of the château entrance. A dark-green Renault appeared, with another car behind it, a black Ford convertible. The Renault turned into the gate, but its occupants were indistinct. It was easier with the open Ford: There was no mistaking either Drummond or, sitting beside him, Dunsinnan. Trunks were piled on the backseat.

"Looks as though they've been driving all night," said Seton. "The chances are, they'll rest here, if they are going on." He looked at his watch. "I don't think we should hang around. We know we have a start on them, we can make Biarritz by tonight."

The sound of barking dogs came from the château.

South of Tours the traffic on the N10 thinned out, with only sporadic clusters of refugees. They passed one convoy of army trucks going north and saw men listless with the expectation of defeat. From Poitiers they crossed a monotonous plain and eventually, ahead of them, saw a pinnacle: the fortress town of Angoulême. Six main routes converged here, and there was more evidence of flight. They drove up a winding pavé road to the summit, under the castle wall, and parked. Lines of poplars and plane trees fanned out like the

spokes of a wheel into the somnolent country below them.
They ate *sandwichs jambon* in a cafe. Seton found English
beer—and German pilsner.

"You British, old chap?" A young man in flannels and a
tennis shirt had spotted the bottle of Bass. Seton was discour-
agingly curt: "Yes." The man looked from Seton to Ruth:
"Not going south, by any chance? I could use a lift." Seton
lied: "No. Limoges." The man looked dubious. "Limoges? The
only thing there is porcelain." Seton persisted: "I buy it, porcelain." Still suspicious, the man said, "What—*now?*"

"Where are *you* going?" said Ruth.

The American accent temporarily diverted him as he
came to some conclusion about their true activity. "Bordeaux.
Getting a boat home—I hope." On the tart note he left.

"You were very rude," she said.

Seton watched the man walk across the square. "I'm not
taking any chances. For all we know, he could be a German
agent."

"You must be joking—in *those* trousers?"

Seton was almost patronizing: "Just remember why we're
here."

They bought fruit, bread, some pâté, and a bottle of Vi-
chy water. The run to Bordeaux was slower, with the traffic
from Paris more evident. They passed a French airfield. Seton
saw twelve Glenn Martin fighter bombers lined up by the
hangars.

"Why aren't they where they're needed?" she said.

"They're still waiting for parts from America."

"Jesus!"

At Bordeaux they crossed the wide bridge over the Gi-
ronde. Seton nodded toward the estuary: "Look at those vineyards. The greatest wines in the world. Guess who's going to
be collecting the 1940 vintage."

"Maybe it will be a bad year."

The bulk of the cars were pouring into the city. They
took the orbital road to the last leg of the N10. Leaving behind the vineyards and peach orchards north of Bordeaux, the
road now cut through the endless pine forests of the Landes,
flat sandy country offering no break in the tree line. The forest shaded the road as the sun disappeared to their right. It
was dark when they reached Bayonne and Seton turned off to
the coast road; already there was a change in the air marking
the presence of ocean. Ahead, in moonlight, they saw the
spine of the Pyrenees.

* * *

As he always did when receiving an underling, Joachim von Ribbentrop stood behind his desk, arms folded across his chest. Walther Schellenberg had always disliked the man, had never quite understood why he had risen so far, and saw now that pretension had left this victim unaware of his own absurdity. But here at the Foreign Ministry in Berlin Ribbentrop was unchallenged, and Schellenberg knew of Hitler's trust in him. Ribbentrop's salesman's eyes ran over Schellenberg, as though judging a hock by its color.

"The Führer has asked me to take up your report on the Dunsinnan group," said Ribbentrop, invoking the supreme power with an air of intimacy. "You are now under my direct orders. Make that plain to Heydrich." He waved Schellenberg to a seat and walked to the front of the desk to stand over him.

"This Lord Dunsinnan, I do not know him, which is odd since I am known to the best of the British aristocracy. Tell me about him."

"He studied mathematics under Hilbert at Göttingen, made contact with the party there, then—"

Ribbentrop waved him silent. "I don't want his life story. Can we trust him?"

"He has been of great help to us in the past. Yes. I can rely on him."

"Just as well. This whole scheme is very risky. The Führer does not want any mistakes. The repercussions could be of great embarrassment. However, it comes at a fortunate time. On my advice the Führer is prepared to give the English one more chance. He will make a speech, carefully phrased, to encourage those in England who are still sensible enough to want to avoid the destruction of their country."

Ribbentrop finally walked back behind the desk and sat down. "My sources in London are excellent. They are still looking for a way of saving face, of finding peace. Lord Halifax is looking. The American ambassador, Kennedy, he is urging them to make terms. Lord Lothian, the British ambassador in Washington, he suggests the same. The Duke of Westminster. You see, my dear Schellenberg, the aristocracy know what is right. You see the significance?"

"The Duke of Windsor?"

Ribbentrop leaned across the desk. "An invasion of England would be costly. It is some centuries since it was done, successfully." The trace of humor surprised Schellenberg.

"The Duke could be the way of avoiding it. His voice could count for much as the mediator. I know his regard for Germany, he still retains that." He picked up a file. "The Duke is very annoyed at the way he has been treated. You can exploit that. You can suggest that he is in danger from his own secret service."

"What is the objective?"

"The Führer wants the Duke taken to a neutral country of his choice, to be ready when we need him. If need be, use force."

Schellenberg's eyebrows rose.

"The Duke and his wife are not to be harmed, but the Führer orders that if the Duke should prove hesitant, you can use an attractive form of persuasion . . . fifty million Swiss francs."

Schellenberg gaped. "Fifty million . . . ?"

"If need be, the Führer will go to a higher sum."

"What about Dunsinnan?"

"Use him. But say nothing of the money, that might give *him* exaggerated ideas of his own worth. Be careful. The British may be watching him. This is why it needs a man of your experience and rank. The responsibility is considerable."

Schellenberg was still openly uneasy. "Where do I begin?"

"We are preparing papers, for France. It will be easy— we will arrange for you to join the refugees, the checks are very slack, you can get to Paris before the Wehrmacht! A one-man advance party!"

"Paris?"

"You can rendezvous with Dunsinnan there."

Biarritz had its Boulevard du Prince-de-Galles, the Edouard VII gardens, and a Hotel Windsor. Seton explained that these associations were rooted in patronage. "The old Prince of Wales, the chap who became Edward VII, he put this place on the map. It was one of his favorite watering holes. In those days the Riviera was just a collection of fishing villages. It was the British who created the playgrounds of Europe."

"You mean, to escape the awful climate."

They were parked by the municipal casino, alongside the beach.

"It's like being in an empty ballroom," she said. "Why would *they* come here?"

"The Simpsons came here in the summer of '34, as his guests. When the flame was kindling."

"What a *quaint* way of putting it."

His fingers drummed on the steering wheel. "So how do we find them?" Silently he answered his own question. They went to the Hotel Windsor and, with light innocence, remarked to the desk clerk on the fitness of such a name for English visitors.

As intended, the clerk leaned toward Seton and confided, "They are here, now, monsieur, in Biarritz—the Duke and Duchess."

"Oh, really?" said Seton, signing the register.

"Yes, in the Palais." He shrugged, splaying his hands. "They will find it very different. You have come from Paris?"

Seton grunted.

"Will the Boches take Paris?" Waiting for the answer, he looked at the register, suspicious of the age difference.

"It seems so."

"Your passports, monsieur?"

In the morning the beach chairs and parasols were out as usual. Several people swam in the ocean. A few families settled on the beach. Shrimp boats returned from the night fishing, and the tuna boats went out. Two cars heavily laden with luggage crawled along the promenade. The smell of fresh coffee and bread came up the stairwell. There were five people in the restaurant. The only evidence of France *in extremis* was that the Bordeaux newspaper had shrunk to four pages. Its news was sparse. The censor kept his grip. There was no mention of Churchill's visit, nor any evidence of the British military presence. The ennui of Biarritz already dulled him. He poured more coffee and drank it black. "We'd better walk up to the Palais and check. The important thing is, keep out of sight in case our friends turn up."

"Do you mean—they came here without any escort?"

"Only Ladbroke, the driver, and a maid. It was very impulsive."

But at the Palais events had overtaken them. The Duke had left for Paris before dawn, with the driver, leaving the Duchess with the maid.

"I didn't expect this," said Seton, exasperated. "It's very dangerous—God knows what he's up to."

"She's rather vulnerable, on her own, isn't she?"

He nodded. "And so is he. Look—I think I'm going to

have to go back to Paris too. Would you mind, staying on here? Just to keep her in sight?"

"Of course I mind." She frowned. "I mind a lot—about you going back. But there's no choice really, is there?"

"No."

Piekenbrock had seldom seen Canaris more furious. It was not a demonstrative fury but a quiet, contained anger evident in a lower voice and a rapping of the desk with his knuckles. What made it even more unnerving for Piekenbrock was that Canaris appeared in uniform—a rare occurrence. It was clammily hot in the Abwehr building; the window facing the canal was open, but there was no relieving breath of wind, only the stench of traffic. Canaris loosened his tie. "Heydrich is behind this, it's clear," he said.

"But he wasn't there?"

"No. Just the Führer and Ribbentrop, a pretty pair. Ribbentrop looked like a cat that had been at the cream."

Piekenbrock risked a joke: "And was ready to lick boots."

The levity did not appeal to Canaris. He began delivering a monologue: "The Führer stood there, you know that strange habit he has, rising up and down on the balls of his feet, grunting. He listened to Ribbentrop, then turned on me. He said, 'The Abwehr is useless to me in England, you never have anything from there, you never have . . . Ribbentrop is right, we know only what comes from the Foreign Ministry, now we discover these messages between Roosevelt and Churchill, Churchill is telling Roosevelt that the threat of defeat could force him out of office and bring in people who want to make peace, but *who* are these pepole, Admiral?' He went on and on in this vein. Then it came out, this wild scheme of Ribbentrop's."

"To kidnap the Duke of Windsor?"

"They've put Schellenberg in charge. *His* star is rising fast."

"Yes," said Piekenbrock, then grudgingly added, "He *is* good. And if Schellenberg pulls this one off, it would be very dangerous for us. What Heydrich is waiting for, to finish us."

"On the other hand," said Canaris, his interest suddenly reviving, "if it went wrong. . . ."

Each day for three days Ruth went to the beach by the Palais and rented a chair and parasol. She bought a swimsuit with a plunging back and slowly turned to a shade of mahogany. In the afternoon the band still played on the terrace, though its male membership had been diminished to only geriatrics; they were supplemented by two skeletal women fiddlers who took a sadistic joy in accelerating the music beyond the arthritic pace of their colleagues, until each tune broke down into two distinct tempos. English tea was served—a touch of nostalgic chic.

The Duchess seemed to be living like a recluse. On the afternoon of the third day Ruth rented a heavy cycle and rode south, leaving the main road for a smaller one that followed the cliffs. But an hour of this idyll was unsettling, not calming. She freewheeled down into the town and was returning the cycle when, reflected in the shop window, she saw a green Renault going toward the Palais. Bedaux was at the wheel and his stately wife in the rear. It was too early for her regular call to Seton. She went back to the Windsor and changed, then sat in the lobby of the Palais, behind a pillar. There was no evidence of Bedaux, except his car parked outside.

Each night it took longer to get a connection to Paris. The hotel operator was graphic in her knowledge of the battlefront and its intrusions: "They have taken *Arras*—it is terrible! *Boulogne, Calais,* they are next! We cannot get a line to *Bordeaux,* madame! *Bordeaux-Paris* has priority! Your husband, he is in *Paris*? You must tell him to leave . . . !" Finally Seton's voice was faintly audible, the faintness perversely amplifying his anxiety. Using a prearranged code, she said, "The grocer is here, with his wife."

"Just them? What about their friend?"

"I don't think so."

She knew the equivocal answer bothered him, but he didn't question it. She asked, "How is the Rolls-Royce?" The primitive code made her feel foolish.

"It is not ready to be moved yet. Are you all right?" The line seemed overlapped by two or three others.

When he put down the phone, Seton was disturbed. The arrival of Bedaux in Biarritz seemed to confirm that some kind of contact was being made with the Windsors—but where was Dunsinnan? In Paris, as the French armies fell back, the Duke of Windsor was overheard complaining that military defeat was the inevitable result of social decadence.

Seton, out of patience with his assignment, defied his orders. Early one morning he left Paris driving north on the N16. Progress was impeded by frequent military road blocks, but he was struck by the absence of large troop movements. It was not until nearly noon that he found what he was looking for, south of Arras—a telltale line of bellshaped tents on the fringe of a field. The grass was deeply rutted by the tracks of fuel bowsers. All the men around the tents wore steel helmets. As he stopped the Citroën six Hurricanes came in low over the hedge, one of them trailing a thin line of smoke. All the faces around him showed extreme fatigue.

The wing commander recognized him, looking up from a map table improvised from wine crates and a door. Seton felt the man's eyes on his own too-neat suit, on his buffed shoes. "We don't expect people like you around here anymore," he said, not quite managing to disguise the sarcastic inference.

"Nothing at Vincennes makes any sense," said Seton gently. "I thought I'd get a better picture here."

"Yes. I can give you the picture all right. It's a shambles."

Behind the wing commander a young French Air Force officer materialized, his eyes raw from the lack of sleep. "Vincennes?" he said. "You have come from there? The old men have lost the battle."

Tactfully Seton evaded the statement. He looked at the grease-pencil marks on the map. "*That* close?"

"We're moving tonight," said the wing commander. "Third time in four days. Amiens is getting too hot. The Luftwaffe are softening up for the Panzers, but they'll get around to us anytime now. My spares have run out. There are planes here I can't take with me, unserviceable. I'll have to destroy them."

"The depots still close on Sundays," said the Frenchman hopelessly.

The Hurricane pilots came in. Seton was shocked to see how young they were. The wing commander followed Seton's thoughts: "These were our reserve pilots." The field telephone perched on the edge of the upturned door rang. The wing commander picked it up and frowned. "*Now?* I can't, now. I have six more Hurricanes committed, not back yet. Yes. When we can refuel."

He looked across to Seton: "That's it. We have to pull out now."

"Where now—Abbeville?" said the Frenchman.

"Tangmere," said the wing commander. "Home."

The Frenchman went to speak, then stopped himself.

Slowly he put down a pencil on the map and walked out of the tent.

"A good man, that," said the wing commander, watching him go. "They don't have many."

After lunching from a field canteen, Seton watched the remnants of three squadrons load their trucks and prepare the planes. The tents were left behind. Finally Seton stood with only the French officer as the last of the Hurricanes came bouncing toward them, weatherworn and with improvised patches on their fabric fuselages. Something in the engine note suggested deep fatigue. Untidily they crabbed into the air and folded their landing gear.

"We won't see them again," said the Frenchman.

Seton said nothing, watching the most slovenly formation takeoff he could remember.

The Frenchman turned to him: "You know what broke us. Munich. When honor goes—the spirit is gone."

"*We* went to Munich too."

"Ah, yes! But you have the Channel." He fanned his palms from his shoulders. "*La Manche.*"

The Hurricanes wobbled and then bunched together like sheep scenting a fox. Seton sighed. "It's going to be very medieval, the next battle. No more than a thousand men. That's all we have. I hope to God it's enough."

The Frenchman had walked away.

33

Guy Burgess and sunlight were unfamiliar partners: in the brightness of St. James's Park he blinked like a surfaced mole, looked too flaccid, felt out of place. He leaned against the parapet of the bridge, left elbow resting over it, right foot folded over left, paunch forward—no part of him was gainly, or settled. He didn't hear or see the man approach.

"Ah. Burgess . . . !"

Burgess, still uncoordinated, swivelled round, keeping his elbow on the bridge. He was always irritated by this man's sudden materializations, and a bit unnerved. This time, though, some of the details were untypical: The jacket was unbuttoned, a gas-mask case hung on rough string from one shoulder, and the usually grave face was whimsical, almost playful.

"I do apologize for the abruptness of the summons. The pace of things has rather quickened." The silver-tipped umbrella tapped the parapet. "Yes. Things are uncommonly decisive these days." He turned away from Burgess to the lake. "I wanted to say . . . I don't think it will be wise, for some time, for us to make contact." He turned back slowly to Burgess and gave him a searching look—rather, Burgess thought, like the scrutiny of a doctor, judging interior debilities by exterior blemishes. "You will understand, as things now are, we must be devoted to the cause of the war." He looked at Burgess's hands. "Time to settle down, establish a record of reliability." The last words conveyed skepticism, even censure.

Burgess slipped his right hand out of view, into a trouser pocket, and looked up at a sky marked with arabesques of vapor trails. "You mean we are all patriots now."

"There is no need to make it sound a novelty." The umbrella stopped tapping. "Philby is nicely placed. An unusual fellow, that. I'm not quite sure of his intellect yet, but he's personable enough." He gave Burgess another dubious glance and turned again to the lake. "I just wanted to make it absolutely clear, since we won't be meeting again for some considerable time, that the more useful you make yourself now, the better it will be later—if you follow me."

34

The agile Feisler Storch dropped its speed to fifty miles per hour, its nose tilting up as its large wing flaps drooped. With its antlike landing gear it looked like a hovering insect, skating around below the tree line looking for a landing spot. It was difficult, unlikely country: wooded and dotted with sudden crests. They had flown in from the east, keeping to the profile of the land at around two hundred feet, over a part of France taken by the Tenth Panzer Division. The pilot kept

the river Oise well to his left, having been warned that a
French colonel called de Gaulle was irritating the German
flank with unseemly resistance. Schellenberg had expected to
see something like the line in the First World War—a clear
delineation. Instead he found no visible front line at all: The
Panzers outran the German infantry who were only now
catching up as they straggled across the country roads with
mostly horsedrawn supplies. Of the French Seventh Army,
supposedly holding this region, there was no sign. But the pilot was wary, alternately scanning the sky above and the land
below. He pointed to a road rising to a bald crest between the
woods, and Schellenberg nodded.

The road was empty. To the south it disappeared into a
forest, and beyond that lay the Oise and the small town of
Ribecourt. Schellenberg kept a gloved finger on the map to
memorize the location; the map would be left behind with the
plane. The Storch nosed up to an even sharper angle and
dropped onto the road, sending up a swirl of dust before it
came to a stop. The pilot kept the engine ready to be gunned
for a quick takeoff, and Schellenberg jumped down, throwing
the gloves in the cabin at the last moment.

The noise of the departing Storch was swallowed by the
first band of trees. Only the indigenous sounds of the wood-
land remained: birds settling after the intrusion, a dog somewhere, a wasp in the weeds at the fringe of the road. Down
the road the reflected heat produced the mirage of black water. Schellenberg felt the paradox of this tranquillity: He was
more vulnerable now as a lone figure than he would be once
absorbed into the drifting groups on the main roads. His papers were those of an engineer from Lille, a place chosen because his French accent was imperfect and might be explained as being the harsher dialect of the Belgian border.
The disarray of flight made his wandering plausible.

It was dusk before he reached the high green ridge over
Compiègne. The sound of the town carried upwards—trucks,
trains, and, intermittently, tanks. His first use of the French
patois was the worst. At a road junction opposite the station a
French army sergeant watched him and then challenged him.
Schellenberg knew that the French phobia about the fifth column was indiscriminate. The soldier, made curious by the unfamiliar accent, thumbed through the papers—they were authentic, taken from a corpse, but whether the switch of
photographs would be discernible rested on a quarter of the
embossed circle on the photograph, which had to match the

original on the page. In the blacked-out street the soldier held a pencil flashlight to the papers, squinting at the picture and then at Schellenberg. The Abwehr's forgery was accepted. For his own reasons Schellenberg relished the poignancy of the situation: Heydrich had wanted his own people to provide the papers, but Ribbentrop insisted that Canaris's men were the specialists, and even Canaris himself had taken an interest. The grim joke dissipated the tension of the encounter.

He waited five hours for a place on a train. As trains were now terminating at Compiègne, and were requisitioned for military evacuation, there was chaos at the station. Getting out of the town before dawn was essential now that the Luft-waffe were bombing the line. They had already severed the line farther to the east. Even as Schellenberg finally got on a train the sirens went, and the tracks emptied of people. Those on the train were torn between the fear of bombs and the anxiety to keep their seats. There was a period of panic, and some left while the rest looked uselessly for refuge. All move-ment in the town stopped. Inexorably the line of bombs ad-vanced diagonally toward the station. Schellenberg first heard the inimitable whistle, saw the yellow flash, and then heard the explosion. For a second there was a lag, an onrush of air from the blast lifted dust from the seats in the train, and then one blast overlapped another. Schellenberg sat frozen in the seat watching the window bow outwards in the suction. But the train remained intact; the bombs had straddled the line behind them. There was a sudden lurch, and they moved off, people racing along the tracks trying to leap on.

As they reached the suburbs of Paris the passengers stood at the windows, unbelieving. The Luftwaffe had still spared the city, and Compiègne seemed a world away. At the station Shellenberg had the sensation of being watched—and then re-alized that to the station staff each train was a harbinger of the approaching disaster, each passenger's face a mirror of the expected future. There were no taxis, and buses were scarce. He felt safer walking.

The apartment in the Avenue Wagram was one of ten in a building compressed between two much larger mansions. A young girl sat in the concierge's kiosk off the hall, sucking a dry straw. Two bicycles stood against the wall behind her. Somewhere in a ground-floor room a radio gave out bromidic news reports. Schellenberg nodded at the girl, mentioned a name, and walked up three flights of stairs.

Drummond responded to Schellenberg's knock and stood

back in the manner of a man trained to move quickly. For a second he failed to recognize Schellenberg in the soiled clothes, smelling the stench of the train. Schellenberg grinned, and then Drummond saw the duelling scar. He waved him inside without a word.

Dunsinnan was in a further room, fleshier than Schellenberg remembered, thickening under the chin. His waistline bulged over corduroy trousers. He spoke in German: "You look exhausted. Was it difficult?"

"Have a drink, dear chap. Malt whisky—you remember it?"

Schellenberg gulped down the whisky, not liking it.

Dunsinnan said, "I should think Paris will be ours in a matter of days."

The *ours* jarred with Schellenberg. He grunted assent.

"Which means that our man will be taking flight any day now. I've been wondering, why don't we move now, here? They might whisk him out of reach."

Schellenberg was alerted. "Absolutely not. For one thing, we want them together. For another, the risk in Paris is too great. The British would be on to us. The Duchess is essential to the whole plan: He will go only where she wants to go. If he goes to Biarritz, and they stay there, then perhaps we might move. The essence is to be patient."

Dunsinnan had been inclined to argue, but he yielded, knowing that for the moment Schellenberg represented German wishes. He said, "Bedaux has their total confidence. He will keep us informed."

Schellenberg had seen the suppressed impulse in Dunsinnan and realized what it was about the man that made him uneasy: zeal. The simplistic zeal that he saw all too often around him in Berlin, the zeal that could convince itself that snow would fall in August if Hitler decreed it. From the first encounter in Switzerland Schellenberg had seen this glint in Dunsinnan, and it had obviously got worse. To emphasize his own authority, Schellenberg cited a higher one: "Ribbentrop directs that we play on the Duke's worry about the British secret service."

"That's interesting." Dunsinnan took his whisky and spread himself on a chaise longue, waving Schellenberg to a seat alongside. "Actually, I don't understand what they're up to. They don't seem to be worrying about him at all. They can't face up to the possible embarrassments of shipping him home."

"I never really understood why he gave up all that for this woman."

"Ah!" said Dunsinnan, regarding the point as ingenuous. "You don't realize? It was an excuse to get rid of him. He was too sympathetic, too sensible, he believed in the essential fraternity of Britain and Germany." He saw that Schellenberg was unconvinced. "You should ask Herr Ribbentrop."

"Yes—I have. He's running this thing himself, it is so important." Schellenberg put aside the unfinished whisky. "So. Tell me, please, how you think we should work."

The Duke of Windsor walked around the house on the Boulevard Suchet for the last time, through the four interconnecting salons where the survivors of his old set and the newer social climbers in Paris had come to dinner. The rooms had been painted and repainted. A succession of decorators, furnishers, antique dealers, and jewellers had come to serve each passing whim. Almost impossible to satisfy, the Duke and the Duchess had tried to make the mansion fill an unfillable void—the space left where a throne had been.

Now all of it was to be summarily abandoned. Without telling even his doting flunkey Major "Fruity" Metcalfe. the Duke called his chauffeur and fixed his exodus for 6:30 the following morning. The advancing army was now audible in Paris, like gravel thrown at a plate-glass window.

"He just *went!* Not even the Military Mission knew. I *ask* you!" Seton's incredulity overcame the faintness of the line to Biarritz.

"I guess they don't mind too much," said Ruth.

"They do have other priorities," said Seton, "like saving our army."

"You're coming, then?"

"Right away."

He was in Biarritz just after midnight, so exhausted that she barely saw him before he was inert beside her. In the morning she got breakfast brought to the room, and he slowly revived with the draft of coffee. He pulled himself from the bed and blinked at the serene ocean beyond it. "It's hard, down here, to know. Out there, in the Bay of Biscay, there are swarms of U-boats, God knows what else. Unbelievable— like finding a shark in a swimming pool."

He looked awful. Her own deeply tanned radiance made

her feel guilty. "Where are they going to go, the Duke and his lady?" she asked, giving him another cup of coffee.

"I've no idea," he said, exasperated. "I don't bloody care. It's all crazy. When you know what's really happening."

"The news is very sketchy."

"We may lose the whole army, the expeditionary force, the lot."

The resignation in his voice shocked her. She stood over him, rubbing his hair. "I want you so much, so much. But I'm frightened. I feel you being drawn away. I know why, I do understand, but I can't stand the thought of you going." He looked up and saw that she was crying. Then she said, "I know you want to be in England."

He took her and pulled her to him.

In the evening they walked along the Boulevard du Prince-de-Galles to the promontory. The harbor light rotated over the water and the town, a sign of the imagined immunity to war. On the horizon they saw the lights of Saint-Jean-de-Luz.

"You know," she said, "the hardest thing? How all this, this awful war, began with that man I saw sitting at a table in Munich?"

He stopped and encircled her with an arm. "I sometimes have a kind of dream, a succession of faces, men with white hair, all talking. Then they taper off, and another face emerges, faintly at first and then more substantial. I still hear the other men talking, and this man says nothing. Then, suddenly, he shouts—and they all fade away."

"You have more to remember than I do. . . . I can't look back that far and I don't like looking ahead."

A dog came out of the water onto the beach below them and shook itself. It saw them and began barking, then turned and padded down the beach. Its footprints were lapped and dissolved.

With the light flashing behind him she could only see the outline of his face. He said, "You're the most precious thing to me, Ruth. Please believe that. Perhaps I haven't been very good at showing it, but it's true. Whatever I may have to do, please know that. In some things there's really no choice, but I'm not being pulled away from you. Quite the reverse."

The salt in the air made her eyes burn as she cried again.

Later that night Seton saw the royal Rolls-Royce brought

to the front of the Palais. The chauffeur began loading
trunks, strapping one to the roof. Seton discovered that the
Duke and Duchess were leaving early the next day. The green
Renault had gone.

"It's odd," he said, sitting on the bed at the Windsor, "for
Bedaux to leave now."

"And there's been no sign of Dunsinnan?"

"Not a dicky bird." He rubbed his eyes. "There's an
army major—Phillips or Gray-Phillips, I think it is—who is
on the Duke's staff and is supposed to stick with them, but he
was left stranded in Paris like the others. I have to stick to my
instructions, not to get too close, not to make them nervous."

"*Nervous?* Jesus!"

He held her hand, feeling that whenever he touched her,
some of her energy came to him. "I'll get there early, to find
out where they're going."

It was, in fact, simple. The desk clerk was vocal with his
advice to the chauffeur: "You can avoid Toulouse, monsieur—there is a route through Carcassonne, look here, I show
you." He took the Michelin map and pencilled in a route:
"Carcassonne, Béziers, Montpellier. The rest is clear, yes? You
go through Aix, avoid Marseille."

Seton went back to the Windsor.

"As unbelievable as it sounds, they're going to the Riviera."

Ruth sat up in bed. "You see—*nervous?* They think they
can sit out the war there!" She saw his own disgust. "Come
back to bed."

The radio in the Windsor bar reported that Paris had
been bombed, and two hundred and fifty people had died.
With the collapse of the French armies the censor had suddenly given up. Then came the shocking bulletin: "The government is compelled to leave the capital for imperative military reasons. The prime minister is on his way to the armies."

"That means to Tours," said Seton as they watched the
disconsolate faces in the room. "They had already planned
that—as the last stand." He finished the Pernod in one gulp.
"We'd better be on the way—they have enough of a start."

The black Citroën absorbed heat instead of reflecting it.
Even with all the windows down, driving across the scorched
valleys of the Midi in June was like driving across a cauldron.
At Carcassone the castellated medieval walls appeared before
them as a mirage seen through distorting screens of heat. By
nightfall, after a blistering afternoon, they reached the cool of

the hilltop town of Béziers. There was hardly any traffic in
its leafy, placid square. The small hotel seemed empty. The
kitchen, however, saved their spirits.

"The stomach will be the last thing to surrender in this
country," said Ruth, ravenously gutting the lobster. The waiter
poured the sharp, powerful local white wine. She saw that
Seton was preoccupied.

"What is it?"

"The Riviera. It's not as irrelevant as it might seem. In
Antibes, if that's where they're going, to their villa—they'll be
quite vulnerable. It's the perfect setting for an abduction. Remote hills at the back, and the sea. *They could use the sea.*"

"You think that's what Dunsinnan will try—an abduction, a *kidnap?*"

"Why not? This is war." His impatience with the pursuit
was disappearing. An instinct reconciled him to what had only
hours before seemed a triviality. As the meal purged the despair of the day his head cleared.

They reached the Mediterranean early the next day, running along the coast for a short distance and then turning
away inland again to cross the Rhône estuary. It was not until
late afternoon, having run through Provence, that they saw
the sea a second time, at Saint-Raphaël. It made Ruth gasp:
Ahead of them now, running northeast, was the crystal line of
the Riviera, villas drowned in flowers, each cut into the small
pine woods that fell with the rocks down to the water—and
the water was like lapis lazuli, a blue she had never seen
translated to liquid before. A few yachts and fishing boats sat
in the ocean. He pulled the car from the road to a *point de
vue.* They sat looking at it silently. The Citroën had picked up
hot tar from the sweating roads, and the smell mingled with
that of scorched rubber from the hoses in the engine. Seton
realized that the pause was needed as much to rest the car as
them. The back of his shirt was wet with sweat. He got out of
the car, pulled off the shirt, and walked to the edge of the
point. Below, wild flowers cascaded from coral rock into the
water. She went over to him, and they sat down. "No farther,"
she said. *"Ever."* She looked out over the bay. "I'll settle right
here."

She came back to earth reluctantly. As they walked back
to the car she did a light dance on her bare feet and swirled
around him as she once had at the Savoy. Her hair broke
across her face, and she took a deep, exhilarated breath. He
touched her cheek and allowed himself a brief smile. His

body, without the shirt, was incongruously white. As she got in the car she said, "I've been thinking about what you said, the idea of kidnapping them. Wouldn't that be self-defeating? I mean—would anyone take any notice of what he said, if he was known to be a prisoner?" She paused and then added, "Would they, anyway—prisoner or not?"

About to pull the starter, Seton stopped and slumped back into the seat, looking at the rim of the ocean through the windshield. "Take any notice—of him as a man suing for peace? I've been trying to decide that myself. How can one tell?" He turned and his right hand went from the wheel to her lap. "There's talk in London of thirty million being killed. Even with Winston in charge, they know it's touch and go. Who knows? I don't think there's a lot of love left for the Duke. But if disaster was staring them in the face, perhaps they'd listen. The French looked determined enough, three weeks ago. Look at them now."

The engine faltered and then shuddered into life. In the hills at the back of them they found a primitive *auberge* where all the attentions seemed to have been expended on the garden. The rank toilet arrangements were compensated by the garden's fragrance, but the toxic plumbing made them wary of the water and they rinsed their teeth in Perrier.

"We'll run through Antibes. I'm going on to Nice, to see the British consul."

As the golden coast flashed by she wondered again about his first wife and the sealed compartment she held in his mind, but she knew it no longer mattered.

"You've been here before, haven't you?" she said, keeping her eyes on the road.

"A long while ago."

Cannes was full of cars—their first sight of the last exodus from Paris. This time, he noticed, it was an exodus of the well-shod. He pointed to the promontory of Cap d'Antibes: "That's Eden Roc on the tip, one of the Duke's old haunts. They must be up there somewhere." Nice, too, was prospering from the decamped high society. The wealthy refugees seemed unconcerned: This was just one step in a continuous dance, and they had no sense that the band would stop playing.

That night Paris was declared an open city, volunteering her charms to the German Eighty-seventh Infantry Division which had made a bloodless entry. Within hours German troops were photographing each other at every landmark.

With all the courage of a vulture, Mussolini took Italy into the war. In Nice the familiar column of smoke rose from the British consulate. The consul told Seton he was phoning the Duke of Windsor to advise flight, and to offer him a convoy escort with the consulate staff who were going into Spain.

Making sure that the offer had been accepted, Seton decided to leave a day between their departure and his. He arranged papers with the Spanish consul and was glad that he had, two days later, when they passed through Perpignan to the Spanish frontier and found a long and fretful line where Spanish officials were turning many people back. There were twenty miles of slow road, half of it through hills by the ocean, before they reached the first Spanish town, Port Bou, which was hidden in a deep ravine. The railroad from France came out of a tunnel, passing through the middle of the town where all the trains had to stop because the Spanish and French lines were of a different gauge. The Citroën was on the brink of overheating. They found a small hotel on the harbor and collapsed into bed.

Ruth woke early. From the window she watched the Spanish fishing boats coming into harbor with the large oil lamps hanging over their bows. During the night other cars with French license plates had appeared alongside theirs on the quay. Among them was a black Ford.

She shook Seton awake. "Dunsinnan's car is outside."

He sat up. "Are you sure?"

"Come and look."

"That's it, all right." He frowned. "So they *do* know."

"He won't know our car."

"That's true." He looked along the quay. "Anything can be coming in and out of this place."

For two hours they stayed in the room, keeping watch on the car. Then Drummond appeared, carrying a case. He put the case on the rear seat and wound down all the windows, leaving the canopy up. Then he sat in the driving seat and lit a cigarette.

Dunsinnan appeared on the far end of the quay, coming up from a boat. His impetuous step was a distant expression of his personality, inimitable to Ruth and as revealing as a close-up. He spoke to Drummond but didn't get in the car. Leaning against the hood, he presented his face to the sun, preening. Ruth noticed the deterioration in his profile. Seton saw a man coming from the town, dressed in dungarees and an oiled sweater. When he reached the car, he stopped casually and stood with Dunsinnan looking out to sea.

"Know him?" said Seton.

"No."

The man walked off, and Dunsinnan climbed into the Ford alongside Drummond. The man in dungarees went down the steps at the end of the quay, the same steps Dunsinnan had used, and to the boat. Only their own black Citroën was left outside the hotel.

"Too close," said Seton. "He might have seen us."

The telephone was even less obliging than in France. It took Seton three hours to get Madrid. By that time Port Bou was sweltering in the heat cupped by the ravine. Ruth, going out for food for the journey, discovered the abrupt change of culture on this side of the border. The diet lost the diversity of the French *charcuterie*. The bread was poorer, and the sausage, tinted with paprika, slender and hard. It was not an appetizing pack.

When she got back, Seton reported, "They stopped one night in Barcelona and went on to Madrid. That should be much easier to keep control of." He looked dubiously at the offered sausage. "I don't think so, thanks. Not yet, at any rate."

They had no choice but to take the same route, down the coast to Barcelona and then the long drive inland, west through Saragossa to Madrid. Once they left the coast road at Barcelona, they hit the full heat of the peninsula. The mountains were shrouded in cloud, and toward evening the light went suddenly and in an instant the road was awash with rain. The first drops had turned to steam on the Citroën's hood. Seton pulled off the road. The curtain of rain was impenetrable. They ate the sausage and drank wine that tasted too much of oil. They decided to sleep out the storm, Ruth stretched out in the back and Seton, as best he could, in the front.

An hour later a light hit the rearview mirror, where it stayed, reflecting back into the car. Seton responded slowly, turning awkwardly as he woke. The rain had eased into a drizzle, but the car was now cold. He saw the headlights in the mirror and realized they were stationary, immediately behind them. He lifted his head slowly. He could hear the other car's engine still running. Somebody got out and walked toward them, stooping to look at the number plate and then coming cautiously along the driver's side. Seton saw a figure in a black-belted leather trench coat visible only from the waist to the neck, the face remaining above his line of vision. He heard Ruth's steady breathing. The man bent down and pressed his face to the window. Their eyes met. Von Klagen did a mock salute.

35

Dunsinnan's conversion was a problem for Schellenberg: he thought of Dunsinnan as a Cardinal ready to kill in order to authenticate his faith. And even the smallest mannerisms had a way of embodying this fanaticism: The left side of his upper lip lifted like the uneven hem of a curtain to show the set of teeth, indicating his tone even before he spoke:

"It was a perfect arrangement, *perfect*. I went to a great deal of trouble. Everything was right—the boat . . . the place . . . everything. You'll find it hard to explain, if this mission fails, why you lost the chance."

Schellenberg slapped his right thigh in impatience: "We cannot operate as though this is our own country. Why don't you understand that? The political background is difficult. The Führer depends on the caudillo, we cannot risk an incident. Kidnapping them on the Costa Brava road would have led to an international incident—the Spanish, the British. It would have been calamitous. It was as well I found out when I did."

Dunsinnan was stubborn, almost petulant: "They would have been in Rapallo by morning; no traces left."

"I repeat—nothing, absolutely *nothing*, is to be done in future without my authority." Schellenberg saw Drummond behind Dunsinnan, silently endorsing Dunsinnan's truculence. "The Führer is so concerned to get Spanish consent before we act that he's sending Canaris here."

Dunsinnan's brows rose. "Oh? I thought you people had a low opinion of Canaris."

"He and the caudillo are old friends." Schellenberg could not quite mask his own reservations. "In Spain, at least, there is value in Canaris."

Dunsinnan detected the ambivalence and became conciliatory. "I'm beginning to appreciate what you meant by the political background. Very well. We will keep in step, you and I. Now . . . it's been a hard, long journey. Time for some relaxation." He looked around Schellenberg's hotel room, clearly finding it unappealing. "I'm told there's an excellent German restaurant here, the Edelweiss. What could be better? It's too long since we ate decently, all this wretched dago cooking."

Schellenberg's appetite withered; his own ideas had turned to something he remembered from years before, paella à la Valenciana, a bed of yellow spiced rice with seafood stewed in garlic. A craving for Bavarian cooking in the heat of Madrid was another Dunsinnan aberration. Dunsinnan's hospitality was as unsettling as his resistance.

During the meal Dunsinnan expanded on the wisdom of France: "In years to come, my dear Schellenberg, the French people will come to realize what a debt they owe to Marshal Pétain. *That's* the real courage, to see the uselessness of resistance. It points the way for the English. Can you understand why I must make certain of the Duke? No one else could take his place. Once Churchill is got rid of, the British people will see sense." He wiped his mouth. "Fine food, eh, Schellenberg?"

Unable to sleep, Schellenberg made a phone call and then took a taxi to the Puerta del Sol. In a way the square symbolized Madrid's attractions as a center for intrigue: Ten streets converged on it from all points of the compass, and on the south side stood the large hive of the Spanish security police. Behind this building, between it and the central telegraph office, was an anonymous smaller building adorned with baroque curlicues and nymphs. The ground floor was in darkness, but the deep windows on the floor above showed rims of light around the blinds. Even a mildly curious eye could have detected the anomaly—against the classic facade—of a thick power cable running to the masts on top of the telegraph office.

Schellenberg rang the bell, setting off a chime echoing like bells in a cloister. Half a minute passed, and then the door was cautiously opened. Schellenberg spoke quietly and showed a card; he was then allowed in. He went across a bare terra-cotta floor, through an unfurnished hall, and through another door to a staircase. At the top of the staircase was a set of double doors, polished walnut with stained-glass panels.

The contrast between this eighteenth-century austerity and what lay beyond the doors was striking: Two high-ceilinged salons had been converted into three rows of cubicles. On a far wall was an armature of circuits with junction boxes, and lines led from each box to the cubicles. The whole place had the inimitable smell of hot radio equipment. There was a background level of static and several audible strains of Morse code. Along another wall Schellenberg recognized the heavy metal cipher machines he knew from the Forschungsamt building. An adjutant led him through the salons to a corridor at the far end and then into a small dimly lighted office. Behind the desk was a young, almost bald man in a civilian shirt, open at the neck. He nodded to Schellenberg to sit down, with the air of a man to whom one burden more might prove one too many.

Schellenberg knew the feeling. He tried to manifest sympathy: "Berlin told you, I hope?"

"They did. For once."

"It's quite a place you have here—I had no idea. . . ."

"We are taken for granted."

"I don't think so," Schellenberg lied. "Heydrich speaks often of your work. He says that without you the U-boats and the Luftwaffe would be wasting their time."

"He did? *Heydrich?*" The young man brightened and then relapsed. "It would be nice to hear it more often. We are wretchedly understaffed."

"Are the Spanish helpful?"

The man laughed. "We are tolerated. I can't say more than that. They make it clear that they will give us all assistance short of anything we really need. Of course, if they thought we were winning. . . ."

Schellenberg came to the point. "The ambassador here is anxious that I do not violate Spanish interests. He insists that my group work through Spanish intermediaries, for the moment. Primo de Rivera is an old friend of the Duke's, we are using him to make soundings. At all costs we do not want the British alerted. For that reason it is essential to have knowledge of the British diplomatic traffic—not a few days later, but as quickly as possible. . . ."

"You can have it straight from the machine, before even Ribbentrop sees it."

The idea of preempting Ribbentrop struck a chord of rapport. The man pulled a flask of schnapps from his desk. "You look like you need a drink—please join me." He handed

Schellenberg a glass. "I think you should see the American traffic, too. It's very instructive."

Schellenberg disguised his own oversight with flattery, profusely thanking the man for his suggestion. Then, concealing his real interest with a casual preface, he said, "I can't get used to this climate. Frying by day and freezing by night. Canaris, is he here yet?"

"No. Tomorrow, I think. He's an artful dog, yes?"

"Yes," said Schellenberg lightly.

They were now on the westward side of the Monserrat massif, the storm trap that had caught them the night before. The early sun was already so hot that any remaining water evaporated as it was exposed by the contracting shadows. The road to Madrid ran through a tunnel under the hilltop town. The three of them stood together on a south-facing balcony of a Moorish building, more caravanserai then hotel. Westwards, toward Madrid, the road followed a river, the Cervera. The irrigated valley held a fine tracery of mist. Below them, in the street, a strange ritual was in progress, a sight that delayed them. A black-shrouded family led a funeral cortege toward a church, following a crucifix borne by the priest. They stopped outside a *bodega,* where through an upper-floor window a mattress was handed down and placed on a cart at the rear of the cortege.

Von Klagen answered Ruth's preplexity: "It's a custom, to burn the mattress of the dead. A kind of purging. If they don't, they say the dead return every night to sleep."

Seton grunted. "You know Spain?"

Von Klagen tapped his flawed leg. "My Condor medal."

"I see."

They waited for the street to clear and then went down to the cars. "You'd better give us a half-hour start," said Seton.

Von Klagen grinned. "Don't worry, I'll keep my distance." He hammered the hood of the Citroën. "I hope you make it in this heap."

"When will we see you again?" said Ruth as he limped to her Mercedes. He stopped and turned round: "Who are the cats and who the mice? I wish I knew."

He watched until the Citroën was swallowed in its own dust cloud, pitching on its peculiar suspension. He knew why he envied Seton, and remained arrogantly annoyed that such a woman should be so devoted to such an undemonstrative man; he shared the Gallic concept of English sexuality—and the

German belief in American vitality. If only. . . . But Seton
need not have worried about too close a pursuit. The archaic
telegraph office in Cervera detained von Klagen for more
than an hour and exhausted his already depleted reserves of
good humor.

As Seton drove through the suburbs of Madrid they saw
for the first time the ravages of the war. It was barely a year
since Franco's triumph, and the cost of the capital's resistance
in blitzed streets seemed to have been left as some kind of
visible penance. Looking at it, Seton saw not only the recent
past but an imminent future.

Watching Seton, Ruth understood this too. She said, "I
didn't realize. . . ."

Turning into another shattered boulevard, Seton said, "So
much for those Bloomsbury poets, all the idealism of the war.
It must be hard, if you're a communist these days, to understand the allegiances. Moscow let Franco win, then made the
pact with Hitler. You'd need blind faith to follow that."

For Ruth the end of the day brought a moment that in
the simplicity of its achievement was more luxurious than anything she had experienced for days: a long submersion in a
bath. The tub stood on a marble pedestal. The taps were brass,
and at first the water came in rust-tinted surges. But it was
hot, and the hotel had provided herbal salts. Like the bath, the
bathroom combined grandeur with improvised plumbing. It
was large enough to house a family. The wall tiles were white
with dark-blue arabesques; crude inlays of flaking cement
broke the pattern in places where the pipes had been added.
The window frames were warped, and the blinds remained
firmly up. But she had no need of privacy. They overlooked
the Madrid Botanical Gardens, and the scent of almond trees
came through the gap between frame and lintel. As she lay in
the bath the mad kaleidoscope of the last week compressed
into salient moments: Seton's gauntness on his return from
Paris; the new intimacy of his words on the beach at Biarritz;
the abjection of the radio announcer in Paris; the lobster in
Béziers; the first sight of the Côte d'Azur and the impervious
faces of the rich in Nice; the final glance back to France as
they descended to Port Bou feeling a kind of severance; Dunsinnan strutting the quay; the cool scrutiny of von Klagen.

She used the towel as a toga and went into the bedroom.
Seton was asleep on the bed. She went to the dressing table
and looked herself in the face, noticing the subtle marks of the
past year: too much of a shadow under the eyes, a worry

mark as fine as a surgical cut above the bridge of the nose, a more superficial rawness in the eyes. She let the toga slip to her waist. If anything, she was thinner. She put a finger under one breast and measured the slackness of the muscle. It was imperceptible but faintly annoyed her. She raised her arms and put her hands on the back of her head. They were really not too bad. The sun of Biarritz left an almost black line between her breasts. She assured herself that minor vanities were inseparable from self-esteem. She realized how Spanish she looked, a chameleon as soon as she had crossed the border. And Goya's women were only a walk away, at the Prado. Goya's women came from inside the canvas and burned their way out through the pigment.

In a corner of the mirror she saw Seton's head move and then settle again on the pillow. Something in this movement reminded her of a child. She tried in her mind to retrieve the boy in the man, an imaginary peeling away of the years to the face set in innocence. It was not a face fleshed out by age so much as one tautened by it. She went to the bed and lay beside him, putting one hand on his brow, pushing back strands of hair. His eyes opened, and he looked up. The eyes, she realized, made his youth irretrievable. Slowly she unbuttoned his shirt, running a finger down his chest, feeling the pectoral bones. He put a hand to the back of her neck and found the junction of hair and skin.

Schellenberg looked at himself in the driving mirror of the Packard convertible and noticed with satisfaction his developing tan. Not a natural sybarite, he was being seduced into pleasure by the luxury of the car, hired on first sight. It softened the rough dirt road, floating like a boat in a light swell. Ahead of him was a single mountain protruding like an upturned breast—a simile made vulgar by the thirty-foot-high statue of Christ on its crest. The dirt road forked away to the right, down to a small river and a grove of fig trees. The wooden bridge barely accommodated the width of the Packard. He nosed up the far bank and across a flat field baked as hard as tarmac by the sun. On the other side of the field was a small farmhouse, with a clock tower and a vaulted verandah. Once smothered in trailing flowers, the walls now retained only shrivelled vines the texture of straw. Dunsinnan's black Ford convertible stood in the shade of the building.

Drummond's hairy torso was exposed to the sun, like a boar's belly on a spit. A newspaper covered his head. He raised it slightly, watched Schellenberg park the car, and, without disturbing his sun worship, muttered, "He's inside."

The house, despite all the windows being open, had the unmistakable mustiness of a place that had been long unoccupied. Dunsinnan lay on a shaded couch; he looked drawn.

"Are you sick?" said Schellenberg, getting some satisfaction from the obvious passivity.

"Gippy tummy, that's all. The bloody water."

Schellenberg grinned. "That *can* be inconvenient. Just as well we can't move."

"What's the excuse now?"

Schellenberg let the sarcasm pass. "I've seen the interior minister, Suner. He's worried about overplaying our hand, thinks our Spanish agents should be used sparingly."

"Pussyfooting. Why not get on with it?"

Dunsinnan was not sick enough, thought Schellenberg. "Von Stohrer is still very jumpy."

"That's the trouble with ambassadors. Once you involve them, they complicate things with their own vanities."

Schellenberg went to a sideboard. "Can I help myself?"

Dunsinnan grunted, and Schellenberg poured himself a Schweppes tonic water. "The quinine is good, in this climate. A little trick you British learned in India, yes? In the great days of empire."

The past tense stung Dunsinnan. "Greater days to come, eh, Schellenberg?" he said weakly. "The Anglo-German empire, the greatest the world has seen, greater even than Rome."

Schellenberg regretted the jibe; the man was becoming a bore. His visit was a pretext, anyway. He felt obliged to watch Dunsinnan, expecting another rash move. It was reassuring to see that the gastric disorder would do his job for him, for a day or two. Perhaps he should contaminate the Schweppes. He fingered the bottle. "Why did you choose this awful place, anyway? It would have been much simpler to stay in Madrid."

"You forget. I'm on the British wanted list."

Paranoia, too? wondered Schellenberg. "You're not in much danger in Madrid. The British ambassador here is a 'soft.' "

"If you mean by that term a realist, yes, he is. It's not him I'm worried about."

"Still bothered about agents?"

"It's *not* seeing any that bothers me."

When Schellenberg got back to Madrid, there was a mes-

sage for him at the hotel: "The duck is quacking." The desk
clerk gave him a curious look.

There was now sun in the young man's office, and his
bald head looked like an sweating overripe melon. The ancient
fan turned above, futile in the bottled-up heat. He gave Schellenberg a copy of a telegram.

"That's from Weddell, the American ambassador, to
Washington, last night."

Schellenberg read:

IN A CONVERSATION WITH A MEMBER OF THE EM-
BASSY STAFF THE DUKE OF WINDSOR DECLARED
THAT THE MOST IMPORTANT THING NOW TO BE DONE
WAS TO END THE WAR BEFORE THOUSANDS MORE
WERE KILLED OR MAIMED TO SAVE THE FACES OF A
FEW POLITICIANS. . . . IN THE PAST TEN YEARS
GERMANY HAD TOTALLY REORGANIZED THE ORDER
OF ITS SOCIETY IN PREPARATION FOR THIS
WAR. . . . COUNTRIES WHICH WERE UNWILLING TO
ACCEPT SUCH A REORGANIZATION OF SOCIETY
SHOULD DIRECT THEIR POLICIES ACCORDINGLY AND
THEREBY AVOID DANGEROUS ADVENTURES. . . . THE
DUCHESS PUT THE SAME THING MORE DIRECTLY BY
DECLARING THAT FRANCE HAD LOST BECAUSE IT WAS
INTERNALLY DISEASED. . . THESE OBSERVATIONS
HAVE THEIR VALUE IF ANY AS DOUBTLESS REFLECT-
ING THE VIEWS OF AN ELEMENT IN ENGLAND, POSSI-
BLY A GROWING ONE, WHO FIND IN WINDSOR AND
HIS CIRCLE A GROUP WHO ARE REALISTS IN WORLD
POLITICS AND WHO HOPE TO COME INTO THEIR OWN
IN EVENT OF PEACE.

Schellenberg handed back the telegram. "You were right
about watching the Americans. This is quite intructive." Too
instructive for Dunsinnan's eyes, he thought.

A score of lectures at Radcliffe were inadequate preparation for the Prado. Ruth found the great museum a revelation; to do it justice would take weeks and she had only hours.
She saw the essence of Spanish character in the paintings,
something that transcended the political present. And on the
ground floor she found Goya's tapestry cartoons, ecstatic with
life; then there was the shock of his *Desastres de la Guerra*,
etchings depicting people crushed in the machine of war, the

faces of 1812 identical with those of Guernica. The Maid of Saragossa, standing on corpses as she lit the fuse of the cannon, a dark resisting figure, Mother Spain.

"Velásquez is more to my taste," said a voice behind her. She turned to look into von Klagen's steady eye. He continued: "And then there are the Titians, Charles the Fifth on the field at Mühlberg, *that's* the side of war *I* like, idealized victory." He turned to the ravaging Goyas: "This is too emotional."

She was caught off balance by this new dimension to von Klagen, the language confident, the knowledge broader than she expected. He openly enjoyed her being disconcerted.

"In the Luftwaffe, war becomes impersonal. You keep above it. Things like this, you don't want to think about them."

"Are you following me?"

He smiled. "Just put it down to good fortune, and shared taste." He stood with his feet slightly apart, hands on hips, the bad leg not obvious. "May I take you to lunch? I would like that."

She chose a table in the open air as being less compromising. He made her feel prim, a novelty that was uncomfortable. He was droll and careless in spirit. They drank sangría, and slowly she laughed, the primness dissolving with each sip of the drink, a drink not as innocuous as it looked, especially when laced with Fundador.

"The group captain is a fortunate man," he said, leaning back with his arms folded across his chest. "To find brains and beauty in one person—very fortunate."

"Are you flirting with me," She was quite bold now.

His eyes turned upwards thoughtfully. "What is it that the English say: All is fair in love and war?"

"We're supposed to be on opposite sides."

"Ah—yes. I was forgetting." He was mocking. "You don't like Germans?"

She dipped her head uneasily and then looked back at him hard. "*I* know which side I'm on."

At dinner Seton unburdened some of the day's frustrations:

"Our embassy profess themselves to be at a loss to know *how* to handle it. Of course, the ambassador is not one of my favorite men."

"Hoare?"

"That's right. Slippery Sam. He deserves the label. He and his wife couldn't wait to get here, once Chamberlain went. As far as they were concerned, the Luftwaffe would wipe out London at any moment. They saw Madrid as a bolt hole. Got here within days. Now, tell me about von Klagen." He looked at her alertly.

"He seemed different, in a kind of way. More relaxed. Quite funny, really."

"*Funny?*"

"You know—funny German."

"Ahah. . . ." Seton became openly wary: "You like him?"

She hesitated. "I don't *dis*like him."

"Be careful. A Hun is a Hun is a Hun."

"*You* read Gertrude Stein? I never knew." Was this misjudging his mood? She put a pacifying hand on his. "It's okay. I am *very* careful."

At that moment the emerging irritant chose to materialize in front of them. Von Klagen appeared at the door, then limped across the restaurant purposefully, all drollery gone. He gave Ruth a chaste nod and said, "May I, please?"

Seton waved him to a seat, disliking the rigid courtesy of von Klagen's bow.

"I'm sorry to disturb you," said von Klagen, "but I have to ask you to do something that you will find difficult." He fixed Seton with a direct look: "To trust me." He paused, then said, "The time has come to repay what you did for me in Scotland."

"There was no outstanding debt," said Seton frostily.

Undeflected, von Klagen came to the point: "In the morning I want you to come with me, Group Captain, for a short journey." He turned to Ruth: "You, I am afraid, cannot come." Then to Seton he said, "A few miles out of Madrid. I want to introduce you to somebody."

Seton scoffed openly: "That's ridiculous, man. You can't expect me to fall for that."

Von Klagen was suddenly urgent. "I cannot say anything more. It is a matter of the greatest importance. I swear to you, you will be in no danger. If you really want to see an end to this matter, you will come."

Seton looked at Ruth, who said, "Set a time limit. After that, I can blow the whistle."

"When?" said Seton, turning back to von Klagen.

"Nine o'clock. Be at the front entrance here. I will come on my own with the car. You'll do it?"

"Against my better judgment." Seton looked from von Klagen to Ruth.

Von Klagen got up, scrupulously avoiding acknowledging his debt to Ruth. "Please do not arrange to be followed. If there is any sign of that, the whole arrangement is off."

Watching him limp away, Ruth said, "I think I *do* trust him—now."

Seton looked at her coolly. "Oh, really? I wish I did." There was an unsettling edge to his voice that she had not heard before.

36

Seton sat alongside von Klagen in the Mercedes. They saw gaps in the apartment blocks lining the boulevard where splintered walls had been levelled off. In places the internal anatomy of a building showed where a new end wall had been improvised to seal off a severed apartment block.

"It was bad, the bombing," said von Klagen.

"Not as bad as Warsaw."

Von Klagen rationalized Seton's hostility as a symptom of the tension and gave up trying to talk. At every turn he checked in the mirror; there seemed to be no pursuit. They passed the University City, decimated by the bombing, little restoration done. On the outskirts of Madrid they came to the Manzanares River. Von Klagen slowed down, checking again in the mirror, and stopped by the gate of a large walled garden.

"Please take a walk in the garden, turn left at the gate, and stop by the strawberry trees."

Seton got out and stood by the car.

"It used to be the royal deer park," von Klagen explained, seeing Seton's hesitance and not wanting to push him. "Quite a wall, isn't it?"

The high-pitched notes of crickets came from the park An ancient bus approached them, down on its springs and full

of peasants who waved leather flasks as they passed. When
the bus had disappeared, Seton went inside.

The gardens and trees were laid out geometrically in a
miniature scale that distorted perspective like a medieval
painting. The strawberry trees were clipped into neat rows,
their scent reminding Seton of an English summer. In a far
corner a nurse in a light-blue smock attempted to contain a
rebellion among half a dozen small children. There was nobody else in sight. He stood in the shade of the wall, shrinking
from the sun. His nose had turned pink and was slightly blis-
tered.

He had been waiting nearly five minutes when he heard
a car pull up outside. A man came through the gate and
turned toward him. Seton recognized the inimitable walk of
someone who had been at sea, the peculiar flexing of the
thighs and quick step. The man was wearing dark-blue trousers and, in spite of the heat, a white turtleneck sweater. He
was small, compact, with a high brow and white hair.

As he joined Seton he said, "Come for a walk, Group
Captain—please." He cocked his head half sideways, needing
to look up slightly to meet Seton's eye. "I'm sorry about this
method of meeting, but I have to be very careful." He paused,
and a smile flickered. "After all, we are enemies, you and I."

"I'm begining to have trouble identifying sides," said Seton.

The man pulled out a small leather pouch holding five
cigars. He offered it to Seton. "Please. Won't you try one?
Havana Greens, from Mr. Hunter of Holborn—probably the
last I will be seeing."

"No—I don't, thank you."

The man took one for himself and stopped to light it. He
studied Seton as he drew on the cigar. "Everything in war has
to be so absolute, Group Captain, yes? You can't have half-
enemies. So—we are enemies, but perhaps only *technically*."

"Technically?"

"Ethically, perhaps, we are allies."

As they began to walk again Seton said, "It is Admiral
Canaris, isn't it?"

"You are thorough." Canaris grinned. "But then, I've
known that for some time."

"What did you mean by *ethical* allies?"

"How far does war require the conscience to surrender to
duty, do you think, Group Captain?" Canaris half turned but
kept walking. "There are two wars for me, the one you and I

are engaged in, and another, a private war. It is hard for you to understand." He waved the cigar. "It is a question of defining madness. Not the kind of madness you find in big men. It reveals itself in small movements. It takes time to see it. Its signature is never traceable." Canaris looked away from Seton, as though focussing on some invisible, distant point. "We are in a world where many thousands of people can just disappear, and nothing happens. In Germany, in Russia. Every day it happens, another thousand more. *That* is the kind of madness I mean."

He edged ahead of Seton and then stopped, turning on him: "So, yes—I *am* your enemy in one sense, and I am going to give you a hard fight. But in this other war we should be collaborators. It is essential for me to stop this scheme to kidnap your Duke of Windsor. You see, if it succeeds, it would be a serious defeat for me in that private war. And it woud also be a serious defeat for you, Group Captain, as you know. So . . . in this one thing at least we appear to have the same interests."

There was a long silence. At last Seton knew that his worst suspicions were true, but it was a shock to realize the extent of the intrigue. There was no longer any question of it being a trivial assignment, and Canaris's appearance on the scene made it doubly treacherous. He said, "Admiral, I know a little about you. It has never been easy to understand."

Canaris allowed a cryptic smile.

Seton went on: "What do you want me to do—exactly?"

"Collaborate. Collaborate with von Klagen. There are heavy odds against him. There are S.S. people here, led by a man called Schellenberg."

"*Schellenberg?*"

"You know him?"

"I know his work," said Seton grimly.

"You will have to leave *him* to us. Please. It is the Lord Dunsinnan who worries me more. That is why we need you, Group Captain. As von Klagen can explain."

They walked toward the gate. Before they got to the street Canaris put out his hand and gripped Seton's. "Group Captain, God help you."

"God help us all."

"He *killed* a woman. We know that," said Seton tensely.

"Then he must have had a good reason," said Ruth. She was sitting on the floor wrapped in a towel.

"I can't think of one. Margery Taverner could hardly
have been a threat to the Third Reich."

"Maybe he knew more than we did."

Seton got up from the bed and went to a table to pour
himself another brandy. "I don't like it. The more I think
about it. I don't know which of the two Canarises I'm dealing
with. I wonder if he knows—himself." He sipped the Fundador. "Ironic, isn't it? I can get no help at all from London, but
Berlin wants me to collaborate."

"Since you need all the help you can get, I would take
the chance."

"I suppose so." He looked at her pointedly. "More for
Canaris than von Klagen. I don't like that man."

"Why not?"

"Too sweetly reasonable."

Ignoring the bait, she said, "It's crazy, really. Canaris,
Schellenberg, von Klagen, the embassies, *even* Churchill. All
worried about the Duke of Windsor."

"He has to be saved from himself."

"The worst kind," she said, getting up and letting the
towel slip to the floor. "Uxorious, too. Now, how about *you*
being a bit uxorious, for once?" She knew how to repair his
mood for the edgy dinner that was to come. She wished he
would put on more weight. He was beginning to take on the
appearance of an ascetic, reminding her of a figure in a
Velásquez portrait.

But later, when they met von Klagen at the restaurant,
she knew that Seton was still far from sure of the collaboration, worried about being compromised. Von Klagen, sensing
the same reserve, worked tactfully to break the ice: "You
know, the old man was quite flattered that you recognized
him—surprised, too." He grinned. "It didn't seem to fit with
his idea of your secret service."

"*That* I can understand," said Seton ruefully.

"I wish I'd seen him," said Ruth. She was amused by the
metamorphosis in von Klagen and wondered if it was she who
had brought out his vanities. He was in a new lightweight silk
suit, very Spanish in its sheen, a cream silk shirt, and a cerise
tie. His hands were freshly manicured, and his hair had had
the overcreative attentions of Spanish barbering and smelt too
strongly of sweet oil. He was better when he was more careless in his clothes; in this new guise of man-about-Madrid his
charms evaporated.

"His English is good. Almost as good as yours," said Seton.

"He has English, Russian, French, and Spanish."

"And a different personality for each?"

Von Klagen laughed, hoping for a feeling of rapport. "Nobody really knows him— You know, he's been in the game so long, he was an agent here in Spain in the first war, had to be picked up by U-boat. He's ridden across the Andes. There are few places he doesn't know."

"You like him?" said Ruth.

Von Klagen hesitated. "Like him? I don't think that comes into it. That would be a luxury in our work, yes? I respect him."

"And do you trust him?" snapped Seton.

"Do you?" said von Klagen.

Seton sipped his wine.

Ruth realized her mistake too late, in the middle of the meal. Her enthusiasm for the Prado had developed into a dialogue with von Klagen that excluded Seton. His touchiness was beginning to irritate her anyway, and it began to manifest itself in pertinent questions to von Klagen, clearly designed to disperse any feeling of social intimacy.

He leaned across the table. "How do you frustrate this operation of Schellenberg's without bringing the wrath of the Gestapo on your heads?"

Reluctantly von Klagen shifted his attention from Ruth. "I think you can leave that problem to the old man and his Spanish friends. We have a large bureaucracy in Germany. More people with desks than with guns. There is such a thing as bureaucratic sabotage. It will be very subtle. Nobody will quite realize what is going on, but I think Schellenberg will find obstructions."

"I wouldn't underrate Schellenberg," said Seton.

"I do not. But he has Berlin to worry about."

Ruth attempted diplomacy: "So you see Dunsinnan as more dangerous?"

Von Klagen relaxed, as though at last someone had got the point. "Exactly." His smile lingered on her a little too long. He turned back to Seton: "You see, Dunsinnan can do what Schellenberg on his own cannot. He can appeal to the Duke, as one patriot to another."

"Patriot?" said Seton, outraged.

"But of course," said Ruth. "Don't you see—in *both* their eyes, that's how they would rationalize it."

Seton looked from her to von Klagen and then back at her. "Yes . . . yes, I'm afraid I do see that. I've never liked that word, *patriot*. What was it Johnson said about it? 'Patriotism is the last refuge of the scoundrel through the ages.' "

"Johnson?" said von Klagen.

Seton was patronizing: "One of our great men of letters. More amusing than Goethe."

Ruth forgave the light in Seton's eye. She said, "I guess we had better find Dunsinnan, then."

"You'll collaborate, then?" said von Klagen.

"Another word I don't like," said Seton. "It's beginning to have unfortunate associations." He pushed his glasses to the end of his nose and turned to intercept the dessert trolley. "Figs are good for the constitution, I believe." Under the table Ruth kicked him too sharply on the shin.

The portrait of Hitler hanging behind the desk of the German ambassador in Madrid had one diagonal bar of sunlight falling across it, so sharp that the detail of the face was bleached out. All Schellenberg could see from where he sat were the eyes—disembodied, accusatory, conveying urgent command. In spite of the fans the air in the office was torpid, tainted faintly with the antiseptic odor of fly spray. Schellenberg looked away from the portrait to the ambassador, who was speaking:

"It was clever of you, Schellenberg—the idea of letting the Duchess's maid return to Paris. That has given you a little more time."

Schellenberg was impatient with the compliment. "It's taking too long to get Spanish cooperation. After all that we have done for them."

The ambassador took up a Toledo paper knife and ran a finger along its edge. "They are nervous. Franco is suspicious of anything suggesting an open commitment to any side, even ours."

"And why is Canaris here? What is he doing?"

"Here in Madrid, he has many old associations. He and the caudillo—you know they are very close. And, as I am sure you also know, Canaris goes his own way."

"You don't think—this Spanish reluctance to help with the Duke—that it could be his doing?"

The ambassador put down the knife, annoyed by the tone of the questioning. "You have a Gestapo mind, Schellenberg."

Schellenberg's eyes were drawn again, ineluctably, to the

portrait. "I have to make sure that we are all of one mind," he said, getting up.

The sharpness of Ruth's step on the marble was an index of her temper, a muscular tautness extending a psychological one. Another trace was the faint smudge under her eyes and an unfamiliar tightness in her lips. Her concentration was insecure: The pictures formed clearly and then dissolved, replaced by impositions of Seton's face of the night before, white and bitter. There was a moment of transmutation when a Velásquez portrait, a gaunt and noble face shaped by tragedy, assumed Seton's features. She felt dizzy and took a seat at the end of the gallery, holding the guidebook to steady her hands. Remorseful yet obdurate, she wanted suddenly to be out of the Prado, out of Madrid, out of Spain, to—*where?*

She walked distractedly through one more gallery and then went outside across the square to the Botanical Gardens. There was no privacy even here. Short-legged Don Juans ogled, children skipped by, and a dog sought attention, which she gave cursorily. She got up again and walked without really caring about direction. Identities were as remote to her as the streets. The noise of the city receded into monotone, losing its features as had everything else.

Without consciously willing it, she was back in the hotel room, and back with Seton's acid words like a piece of the furnishings. She knew that his misgivings over von Klagen were as much to do with an irrational sense of sexual threat as with professional care—at first an unsuspected neurosis, which she had exacerbated by arguing for collaboration into the night. At one moment it even seemed he might hit her. And then, when she woke in the morning, he had already gone.

The memory was punctured by the phone ringing, and she went to it too eagerly.

It was von Klagen. "Where is the group captain?"

"I don't know. At the embassy, probably." In the pause that followed she knew her tone had given away too much.

"I see."

"Can I do anything?"

"I know where Dunsinnan is."

"Here?"

"Not in the city, but not far."

"What are you going to do?"

He hesitated again, then said, "We must talk, quickly.

Can you meet me where we had lunch—in fifteen minutes?"

As she went out the door she already felt compromised, as though confirming Seton's absurd suspicions of assignations. Strangely, she didn't mind.

Von Klagen's silk suit had gone; in its place was a light shirt and blue gabardine trousers. His hair had also lost its Spanish gloss and was back to its raggedness. She thought he looked his old self, the one she preferred.

"Can I be frank?" he said, pouring the coffee. "The group captain does not really trust me, is that so?"

"You have it."

He stirred three tablets of coarse sugar into his coffee. "This is a problem. Of course, I understand." He looked at her knowingly. "However, the admiral thinks very well of him. It would be a pity . . . to disappoint the admiral."

"You'll have to take it easy. Don't push him too hard."

Von Klagen sighed. "I don't think we have the time for that."

"Tell me, I don't understand— Why do you *need* us?"

"You can't guess?"

"Nope."

The Americanism amused him—but only briefly. He leaned across the table, unable to suppress the attraction he felt. "I think *you* should know. The admiral *can* arrange everything. But it's important that he should be able to blame British agents. So you see, the group captain's ends and his own *are* the same."

"And the means?"

Von Klagen sat back and persisted with the undissolved sugar, saying nothing.

"You," she insisted, "you have to make sure of an alibi?"

His smile confirmed her shrewdness.

When she got back to the hotel, Seton lay on the bed and she knew, from the pitch of his glasses on the end of his nose, that the squall had passed. He was reading telegrams.

"Ah," he said, looking at her over the glasses.

"Ah what?"

"Ah—news. The caravan is about to move on yet again. They're going to Lisbon."

"Is that good?"

"It's better. Easier to get them out."

"Just as well." She trod dangerous ground again. "Von Klagen has found Dunsinnan."

Seton pulled himself up, dropping the languid pose. "Where?"

"Outside the city someplace. In a farmhouse."

"You've seen Von Klagen?"

"He called." She took no chances and lied. "He wanted you. I took the message."

"Careless—over the phone in this place."

She went over to the bed and sat beside him, picking up one of the discarded telegrams. "What's all this?"

"A remarkable correspondence. Messages from the Duke to London. He's trying to get his menservants released from the army."

"*Jesus!*" She read one of the telegrams. "You mean— *Churchill* has to bother with this? *Now?*"

"That's right." Seton pushed his glasses back up his nose and put down the papers. "In a farmhouse? How did von Klagen get on to him?"

"He didn't say."

"No—I'm sure he didn't." Seton conceded a wry smile. "The embassy still doesn't want to know about Dunsinnan, and there's no word from London."

"It must seem yet another distraction," she said, reaching out for his hand.

A hot wind cut across the plateau of Castille, and it seemed to snatch air from the lungs and give each particle of dust the burn of a cinder. Schellenberg had put up the Packard's canvas top, but the dust penetrated the car; it was like riding through the jets of a sand-blasting machine. From a crack above the windshield a fine spray forced him to hunch his head over the wheel as he navigated the wooden bridge. The leaves of the fig trees were ochre with clinging grit. As the car came up from the bridge he saw a curious halo effect: The layer of driving dust was about ten feet deep, and the sun, in the clear air above, was refracted through the particles as a distorted disc.

The shutters on the farmhouse were having no more success against the wind than the car; as he got inside the door the dust was re-forming into suspended clouds. Dunsinnan had retreated to the kitchen on the leeward side, sitting at a pine table. His convalescence was clearly over: The color was back in his face and his zeal too obvious. Schellenberg disliked Drummond's habit of always hovering just a few paces behind his master, silently suggesting blind obedience; Schellenberg felt that he should have been connected by a chain.

"There is an important change of plan," said Schellenberg, sitting uninvited at the table. "They are going on to Lisbon, by road. I have spoken to Ribbentrop—"

Dunsinnan cut in: "But that's *disastrous!* We must stop it. We must get to them while they're here in Spain. Otherwise it will be too late."

With greater emphasis Schellenberg repeated, "I have spoken to Ribbentrop. He agrees that, with things as they are here, it would be easier in Portugal. There is a new idea. Through contacts of ours in Lisbon we will arrange for the Duke to make a hunting trip near the Spanish border. It would be natural for this to be in a remote place, and from there they can be taken somewhere to await the call."

Dunsinnan began to shout: "All you ever have is new reasons for *not* taking action. If my plan with the boat had been followed—"

Schellenberg banged the table with his fist. "Ribbentrop is right! This is what we are going to do. Once they are in Lisbon, I am going to arrange for the Portuguese to put a heavy guard on them, make them feel captives."

"What good will that do?"

"He is already suspicious about the British secret service. We will aggravate that feeling. He'll be only too glad to get away to a hunt."

Dunsinnan fell silent. His hysteria seemed exhausted. To Schellenberg's surprise he simply said, "So be it. If that *is* what Herr Ribbentrop wants."

Seton leaned over the desk of the cipher clerk, visibly agitated. "You're absolutely sure—there's no answer? It's been forty-eight hours, and it was marked highest priority."

The clerk, harassed and tired of Seton, said, "Look, old chap, we're very busy here, losing the war."

Seton turned away, only just stifling a response. Perhaps the delay was a good sign; his instructions would come from the very top. A tall man in a dark suit came into the room, projecting a limp calm.

"Ahhhh. Seton. Still here?"

The banality of the question got no response.

"Look—it's not much good your hanging around, not in here. Come into my office—got some really nice oloroso, just what you need, from the look of you."

Seton was stung into a memory of another oloroso, the distant agent. He resigned himself to the offer. They went into a huge panelled room that reminded him of an English headmaster's study, and he realized that his host fitted the role.

The decanter gurgled. They stood in shade, the office a tranquil island.

"Don't understand what you're so exercised about, Seton. Everything's under control, now that he's agreed to move on, to Portugal. You know, Portugal, our oldest ally. Salazar is *much* more understanding. Can't say I'll be sorry to be rid of them. The man's turned impossibly peevish."

"I can't get any answers out of London."

"I expect they're quite happy to leave it to you. Got their hands rather full, what with Dunkirk and all that."

"How is that going—do you know?"

"Well, against all the expectations, rather well. It seems like divine intervention. We might get most of them home, if not dry. Of course, that mayn't help much, since they've left all their equipment behind. I suppose it's good for morale, though—Winston will be moved to more of his great exhortations. Not enough, if you ask me."

"You still don't think there's much hope, then?"

The man became wary. "Well—one doesn't want to be *too* defeatist, not now." He assessed Seton's own mood. "Of course, the ambassador takes a *very* grim view. Halifax says it will all depend on Roosevelt. I'm afraid Kennedy doesn't help much, there—as ever, he's urging us to come to terms with Hitler while we still can." His Adam's apple moved with the passage of sherry. "That *is* a point of view, of course." He turned again to the decanter. "Some more oloroso? Really unusually dry, don't you think? I know the chap who makes it."

The Duke's Rolls-Royce had a trailer to carry the portable remnants of the world of the Boulevard Suchet, now supplemented by the trunks brought by the maid from Paris. The trailer had been loaded and unloaded several times in its course across France and Spain. The Duchess had several large cabin trunks as well as her valises, and the Duke's own wardrobe was not modest.

Leaving the British embassy, Seton had gone to check on the Duke's activity and found in progress outside the hotel yet another struggle with the trailer. The caravan was about to leave for Portugal. There was still only one escorting car, driven by the dogged Major Gray-Phillips who had caught up with them and was now helping with the packing. Several pairs of eyes were engrossed in the spectacle, one on behalf of Schellenberg, one on behalf of Canaris, and another sent independently by the German ambassador. Seton picked out two of the three without much trouble; by now he knew all the signs and the peculiar maladroitness of men not used to being out of uniform. The Abwehr agent, on the other hand, was a woman at the hotel desk, and—under the desk—she checked Seton against a new photograph supplied by Canaris. She thought that for an Englishman he looked rather unkempt.

There was an outbreak of murmuring in the lobby, and heads turned in one direction. Seton saw the Duchess walk to the door with a maid. Queen in all but title, he thought—impressed in spite of himself. Outside, the Duchess gave her final assent to the arrangement of the trailer. She checked the valises and then the inside of the Rolls.

Seton picked out the soft American voice: "Very well, Ladbroke. We will be down in an hour."

Seton decided—in the absence of any instructions from London—that he should again shadow the caravan, but this time running closer to it. He would be glad to be rid of Spain: the heat of Madrid, the inanities of the British embassy, the ascendancy of the Germans, and the view, implicit in Spanish attitudes, of Britain's impending defeat—subtly endorsed by the dispenser of oloroso sherry and his colleagues.

37

Buckinghamshire, England, July 1940

The driver of the black Humber limousine was unfamiliar with the route, and by the time they reached the guarded lodge they were already fifteen minutes late. The driver knew his passenger was agitated and, once through the security check, accelerated up the hill to the sprawling medieval house. As the car bounced over the gravel the passenger in the rear seat reflected on how vulnerable this place must be to a well-informed air raid. But he knew that Winston Churchill carried a deep conviction about his own immunity from attack, and that this, the countryseat gifted to British prime ministers, had swiftly become an addiction of Churchill's, a nourishment of his romantic view of history: The house called Chequers had roots going back to the Norman Conquest and got its name from a corruption of a twelfth-century Clerk of the Exchequer who had lived here on the brink of the Chiltern hills.

On this Sunday evening there was no sign of sabbath rest: Uniformed men of all three services were milling in the Great Hall, attended by frenetic aides. But the visitor was propelled urgently through the mass and up a wide staircase, through a tapestried anteroom and a pannelled parlor into a long narrow gallery lined on one side by bookcases. The main source of light was peculiarly spectral, filtered through stained glass in a bay window at the far end of the gallery. Against the heraldic patterns in the glass, framed in their glazed tints, stood England's warlord. He seemed the most serene figure in the house.

A young W.A.A.F. orderly retreated, leaving the visitor with Churchill advancing toward him down the gallery.

"You know this room?" said Churchill, stopping at a screened fireplace.

"No, Prime Minister."

"No, I expect not. . . . My predecessor preferred other houses." Churchill lifted his cigar and pointed to six portraits hanging over the fireplace. "Cromwells—all of them. The Lord Protector's progeny. And these swords—these were his own."

Two swords hung over the mantelpiece.

" 'God made them as stubble to our swords,' " said Churchill resonantly. "I quote, of course, from Cromwell's despatch from the battlefield." He moved away from the fireplace into shadow by the bookcases. " 'Stubble to our swords.' At this very moment, I fear, our swords are unready. Of twenty-five divisions, only one has anything approaching its proper equipment. We have lost nearly one thousand aeroplanes in a month."

Churchill sat down in a high-backed tapestried chair and signalled the visitor to take the opposite chair. He drew on his cigar. From a pocket of his plain naval jacket he drew out a sheet of paper. "I would like to read from this note, which I received this day from Sir Robert Vansittart at the Foreign Office." He unfolded the paper and read in staccato: " 'It is now probable that we are about to be the object of an American peace-feeler . . . perhaps even of a peace offensive.' " He stopped and looked across, watching the response, and then resumed: " 'All our own loose-thinkers are on the scent. These people range from bishops and Quakers to cowards and cranks, from capitalists to communists, from peers to ordinary dyspeptics. . . .' " He looked up again, folding the paper. "He has been discreet enough not to mention my principal cause for concern in this matter." In the weakening light the cigar glowed like a cinder.

"They have now arrived in Lisbon, Prime Minister."

Churchill savored the cigar and nodded, then ruminated before speaking again: "You may tell your agent that he has carte blanche, but there must never be, *never*, any public knowledge of this affair, whatever we may feel about their personal conduct."

"I fear, Prime Minister, we may still have some trouble persuading them to depart. Every day they linger increases the danger."

"Then harsher persuasions may prevail."

38

Lisbon, July 1940

The Deuxième Bureau's black Citroën was as fatigued as its driver after the punishing ride along the road southwest through Badajoz and across the border into Portugal; one nearly bald tire had blown, and the engine was misfiring as they reached Lisbon. Fortunately it was downhill into the city. Ruth watched Seton nurse the car and knew he was near the end of his own endurance—yet he seemed strangely calm, not brittle. They pulled into the courtyard of a hotel near the waterfront. In the sudden quiet after Seton turned off the engine, he sighed and turned to Ruth: "Why do I feel like a fugitive?"

She put a hand on his shoulder. "If we go any farther, I guess we'll be in the ocean." The air was different: Atlantic-

borne, carrying salt, no longer soporific. In the light of the
hotel she saw a familiar figure. Von Klagen limped over to
the car.

"A hard journey, yes?" he said, bending to the window.

Seton looked up. "He's here, then, already?"

"Dunsinnan? Yes. I nearly overran him. They broke
down at Badajoz. He seems to have friends here."

"Yes. Yes, he would have." Seton climbed stiffly from
the car. "Your leg playing up?"

"It's the sea air," said von Klagen. He looked across the
roof of the Citroën as Ruth got out. She stretched and took
deep breaths, and gave him a cautionary glance. There had
been too little sympathy in Seton's question.

The hotel lobby had a marble floor: Seton heard his own
lassitude paced out across it as he went to the desk. Von Klagen had already reserved their room. His efficiency was another of the several irritants he provided for Seton. As they
went up in the elevator von Klagen said, "We must talk—
please, will you come to my room, when you are ready?"

The river Tagus came down from the Spanish highlands
and disgorged into a broad bay and was then forced into the
Atlantic through a narrow neck. On the north shore of this
neck Lisbon spread over steep terraces to a plateau above.
They sat on a balcony looking over the water, and once more
Ruth had the sensation of time in suspense, of a seduction
from reality.

Von Klagen poured a sharp green wine. "So," he said,
raising his glass. "To exile. The Duke and the Duchess are
going to the Bahamas, yes?"

"You seem well informed," said Seton.

"I need to be." Von Klagen put down the glass, becoming
solemn. "Do you know how things are here? I will tell you.
You realize the price of information in a place like this? Playing the role of the neutral can be highly profitable. Your embassy here is not known for its generosity. They feel there are
ties of tradition. What innocence! They have put the Duke
and Duchess in a villa at Estoril. It is owned by the banker,
Espírito Santo. You know what that name means? *Holy
Ghost!* They put their faith in the Holy Ghost, but the Holy
Ghost is talking—to Schellenberg. Then there is the director
of the Portuguese counter-espionage, he is reporting daily to
our minister. So you see, the hope that you now have things
under control is an illusion." He picked up the glass again.

"Tell me, Group Captain, why are you not given more assistance?"

"There's no particular value in numbers, in this case. It would be too conspicuous."

Von Klagen looked unconvinced. "Schellenberg is bringing in more agents from Berlin. It's quite clear that Ribbentrop wants this scheme to succeed. There are at least three agents in the villa already."

Ruth broke in: "You said *you* were taking care of Schellenberg."

"That's correct. But Schellenberg can succeed now only through Dunsinnan, this I am afraid is true. There has to be a pied piper. The Duke is not ready to follow the tune of a German, a Spaniard, or a Portuguese— But one of his own kind, that would change everything. It is Dunsinnan who has to be dealt with, *then* you can leave the rest of us."

"*Dealt* with?" said Seton.

"Group Captain. What do you imagine is the solution?"

Ruth said slowly, "I suppose . . . I suppose we've known, really, that it might have to come to this." She looked from von Klagen to Seton.

"*Might?*" said von Klagen.

Seton said sharply, "You, of course, are quite practiced in such work."

Von Klagen stood up and rubbed his bad thigh. He moved the leg and then looked hard at Seton: "Group Captain. I do not know, I cannot really explain it to myself, why it should be, but . . . sometimes I think you English are going to win this war our of moral force alone. Anyone who has so much conviction in their own superiority *should* be absolutely *invincible.*"

His voice had risen with the sarcasm but now fell again to earnestness. "I would like to believe that—perhaps that is *my* one weakness. But I know better. The trouble is that moral superiority cannot *kill* anyone."

"What do you expect me to do," said Seton, ". . . become a professional assassin?"

"Yes. Yes, that is exactly what I expect you to do."

Ruth looked at Seton: "Remember McCabe."

"*You,* too?" said Seton.

"It *is* war," she said.

"Yes, it is. It is war. And that changes a lot of things, it seems."

She got up, annoyed, and walked to the edge of the balcony, looking out over the great bay. Both men watched her silently. After a few seconds she turned back and spoke quietly: "You know, I have just realized—what's so really bad about this? It's not the hotel rooms, the plumbing, the interminable journeys. It's as though along the way we've been systematically leaving parts of us behind. The books, the music—the time. Especially the time. We've had no time."

Seton leaned forward cupping his wineglass, hair falling over his brow. "That's exactly what I meant, about being a fugitive." He looked across to von Klagen. "And now I'm supposed to become pitiless."

"Pitiless?" said von Klagen.

"That's what it needs, isn't it?"

Von Klagen looked at Ruth: "Music . . . you miss the music? That is true. You know, Heydrich listens a lot to Mozart."

Seton took another long draft of the wine and then put the glass on his knee. "How do you propose that I do it, may I ask?"

Schellenberg had declined the car offered by the Portuguese, despite the inconvenience of the city's hills. It was partly a concession to Dunsinnan's paranoia, and partly an instinct of his own after seeing the endemic duplicities of the Portuguese security service. He walked across a square and through the central railroad station. He ambled, apparently directionless, around the station concourse and then slipped from a side entrance to the funicular that ran above the ascending avenues to near the city's summit. The funicular car was full of children. As it rose it undulated on the cable in a slow motion that began to sicken him. The children's playfulness amplified his discomfort, and at the terminal Schellenberg staggered out and found a bench on a terrace to recuperate. Below him the city slowly reassembled in his vision. He thought again about the pressures of this seemingly intractable assignment, and about the telegram received that morning from Berlin; for the first time Ribbentrop had said Hitler himself was impatient. Inexorably the situation led to Dunsinnan as the last chance of success, yet Schellenberg was no happier with that thought than before. He left the bench and walked across the Boulevard de São Pedro de Alcántara to the apartment block on the other side. He remembered Paris and the first meeting there with Dunsinnan; perhaps Dunsinnan should have been given his head then, and none of this farrago would have been necessary. Now, as then, it was the minatory Drummond who opened the door.

Dunsinnan had discerned that the logic of events was in his favor; his manner had become crisply assertive. He took Schellenberg directly to a dining table where a map lay.

"It's a long way. Three hundred and twenty kilometers. I hope they can be persuaded to travel that far."

Schellenberg looked at the map, running a finger along the twisting red line indicating the route north up the Tagus valley and then into the mountains toward the Spanish border. "Yes," he said, openly dubious. "I had to accept the advice of the people here. They said it had to be remote but near the border. From Guarda to Vilar Formoso—that's the area where the hunting will be arranged."

"And the border crossing?"

"Primo de Rivera guarantees no trouble."

Dunsinnan grinned. "They have no passports. That is one of the things that, fortunately for us, has so annoyed the Duke."

Schellenberg looked up from the map, rubbing his stomach. "Do you have some water?"

"Nothing stronger—you're sure?"

"No. No, thank you." Schellenberg recalled the predilection for malt whisky.

Dunsinnan signalled to Drummond to fetch a bottle of mineral water. "Come. Come and sit down."

Schellenberg took the water and gulped it down.

"The psychological warfare seems to be going well," said Dunsinnan. "I heard about the bouquet of flowers for the Duchess, with the warning about the British secret service. It had quite an effect."

Schellenberg covered his mouth and belched. "There is another idea, which has had even better results. They have warned the Duke of the danger of a Jewish assassin, especially on a boat. He finds that only too plausible. So you see, the ground has been well prepared for you."

Dunsinnan poured himself a whisky. "Quite so. Once you get them to this hunting lodge, I think they'll be quite receptive, quite glad to see me. The question is, Schellenberg—how soon can you get them to me up there?"

It was the funicular that had nearly beaten von Klagen. He had almost missed Schellenberg's sudden exit from the concourse and, once in the street, saw the doors of the funicu-

lar car close on Schellenberg in the wake of the jostling children. He had had to wait several minutes for the next car, and
then, on arriving at the top, he nearly ran straight into Schellenberg walking up from the bench. Now, after nearly an
hour, he saw Schellenberg leave the building as Drummond
came to a balcony and watched Schellenberg cross to the funicular. Within half an hour von Klagen had studied the building and been inside to check the geography of the apartments.

Standing at the door, before ringing the bell, Ruth was
oddly calm; she had a sudden comprehension of where Dunsinnan's commitment had led him—to this final effort to
prove the validity of his faith. When he opened the door and
she saw his face in close-up for the first time in nearly two
years, there *was* a look of religious fanaticism in him, as well
as the physical decline, the fatness of the chin, the thinness in
his hair.

He didn't speak for some seconds, clearly disconcerted.
His upper lip tightened and rode up over the teeth, and he
stepped back half a pace, not opening the door fully.

"Well," he said, "you *have* got a nerve." Then a hand
went inside his jacket. "I hope you're alone."

For a split second there was a trace of fear in his eyes.

"Yes. I am."

His right hand remained inside the jacket, but he waved
with the other for her to enter. She stepped into the apartment, and he closed the door behind her, leaning against it as
she turned and regaining his composure.

"I'm sure this is no coincidence," he said, *"Mrs.* Seton.
And where *is* your gallant husband? Not far away, I'll be
bound. It's his style, is it not? To have you do the dangerous
work. It was your delicate hand that lifted the address book,
of course. Quite the Mata Hari. I trust you don't think I'm
going to be caught twice. You're out of your depth now."

"Whatever you think of me doesn't really matter." She
looked from his eyes to the hand in the jacket and then back
again. "It's what you think you can do. It's not going to work.
It's going to be stopped. You have a choice. Quit now . . . or
face the consequences."

"Consequences?" He moved slowly away from the door,
walking around her, catching the familiar scent, offensively
appraising. "No. Quite clearly this is not a coincidence. Oh,
dear. That's what they've asked you to do, is it? Talk me
round? How generous. I suppose there's a place already re-

served for me in one of those camps. You know who invented
concentration camps, do you? The British. In the Boer War.
Can you really see me, in some squalid compound on the Isle
of Man? Surely, *you* know me better than that? Just at the
moment when I can help stop this whole futile war?"

"Don't you realize—it's too late?"

There seemed something narcotic in his eyes. He
laughed. "That's a surprisingly pragmatic objection, coming
from you. *Too late?* I would have thought your objections
would be far more fundamental. You used to be quite moving,
in your way. I think you had better sit down." He nodded to a
sofa.

She realized when she moved how near she was to openly
trembling. She had to fight to keep herself steady as she sat
down. He stood over her, more paunchy than she remembered, shirt strained at the waist.

"I don't think you understand," he said, his voice acquiring an oddly metallic quality. "You seem to have been misled.
I am not alone. There are many who still see things my way.
For me this isn't a last-minute capitulation. I'm not running
away from anything. I'm not even interested in last-minute
converts, those who are taking to the lifeboats. *I've* wanted
this, all along."

"Yes—you have, haven't you." Her voice had an unam-
biguous damning edge.

He sighed. "It's a pity about you, really. There was a
time— My mother, of course, had high hopes of us. But there
was always *something* about you. Something *not quite*—"

"So you're not going to stop."

"The devil I will."

The room had a wide parquet floor. The sofa was against
the wall. Dunsinnan stood on a small Persian carpet. The
space in the room and the delicacy of the furniture gave it a
bare, eighteenth-century feeling. Thirty feet from the sofa
there was one deep window looking out over the city, and behind Dunsinnan she saw the light beginning to go. To their
left another door led to a bedroom. She felt a light draft at her
ankles. He was looking at her silently, observing the thin line
of gold at her neck.

"Get up," he said, and then, harshly insistent: *"Get up!"*
He half pulled her to her feet and spun her round so that her
back was to him; then he drew her toward him, in the same
movement bringing the gun from inside his jacket.

He looked toward the bedroom and called out, "I think you had better come out, Group Captain."

Seton stepped through the door and saw Ruth held as a shield, and Dunsinnan's gun. He lowered his own gun.

"What on earth made you think this little ambush would work?" said Dunsinnan. "How very pathetic."

"And you're heroic, I suppose?" said Seton.

"The gun," said Dunsinnan, "throw it down, please." He watched it slide across the parquet.

Quietly Seton said, "It's treason of course—what you're doing, what you have already done. Whatever gloss you put on it."

Dunsinnan coughed, and then the cough tapered into a hoarse laugh. *"Treason?* By *whose* judgment? I'm the greatest patriot in this room. You know, Seton—what I really can't stand about your kind? You're so sanctimonious. So *bloody* sanctimonious. This belief of yours in justifiable war. *You* are old enough not to need telling, what was achieved last time, by all that carnage?"

A key turned in the main door. Dunsinnan kept the gun on Seton, but looked toward the door as it opened.

Drummond appeared and stopped abruptly, arrested by the sight of the tableau, and then Dunsinnan said, "Pick up that gun—from the floor." He looked back to Seton: "I suppose he came back sooner than you reckoned?" He relaxed his grip on Ruth, but still holding her by an arm. "You see, Drummond? Both of them now. And still trying to preach." He looked sideways at Ruth: "I have no taste for this kind of thing, I really don't—the guns—whatever you may imagine. But I'm sure you realize I have to have an insurance against further interference. I'm going to take you with me, since I cannot remain here." He turned again to Seton: "No harm will come to her just as long as you make sure that we are not bothered again. As it is, it is annoying enough—having to leave now." He gripped Ruth and took her to the door, leading her out. Drummond, behind them, turned the key on Seton. Ruth had caught one agonized look from Seton as the door closed.

Dunsinnan held the gun inside his jacket pocket. "Don't be rash when we get outside."

Drummond walked ahead of them, down one flight of stone steps and through a vaulted hall into the boulevard. The Ford convertible stood outside. He opened the rear door. His hand was still on the handle when the first shot came, entering his head cleanly above the bridge of the nose. He collapsed, slowly swinging outward to the pavement with the door still in his grip.

Dunsinnan pulled Ruth against his body again and swung round, drawing out his pistol and searching for the origin of the shot. He looked up and tried to get Ruth more in front of him, but she pulled away, kicking. The second shot caught Dunsinnan in the throat. His gun went off involuntarily, the bullet embedding itself in a balcony above. He tried to speak, but his mouth filled wth blood, and he fell back into the car. Ruth fell with him, awkwardly. She lay across his chest, and his blood seeped into her dress.

In the boulevard, against the noise of the traffic, the shots had been indistinct. A handful of people passing near the Ford had not yet, in the twilight, comprehended clearly what was happening: They saw the three bodies collapsed against the car but not yet the source of the chaos. A boy on a bicycle swerved onto the sidewalk and stopped just short of Drummond as he sank to the curb behind the open door. Ruth rolled from Dunsinnan to the pavement, traumatized.

Von Klagen entered from the balcony above just as Seton came bursting through the bedroom. Von Klagen blocked the way through the balcony windows. "It's all right—she isn't hit."

Exasperated, Seton pushed against him. "Let me see—"

"Not yet," said von Klagen. "First, take this." He pushed the gun into Seton's hand. "You see, it's a Webley. Very accurate, fortunately." He took off his gloves. "You will, of course, accept responsibility."

Seton pushed past von Klagen to the balcony, emerging just as the boy with the bicycle looked up. He saw the gun and shouted.

The Mercedes came slowly down the hill toward the British embassy.

"You'd better pull up well short," said Ruth.

"Of course," said von Klagen, pulling into the curb a hundred yards from the gates. "They gave him a bad time, those Portuguese security people," he said. "No doubt Schellenberg had something to do with that."

"I don't think the British ambassador is going to give him a tea party," said Ruth.

Von Klagen grinned. "No. I expect not. They do not like this kind of thing, ambassadors. What is the phrase . . . ?"

"A diplomatic incident."

"Yes, that's it, so." He wound down his window for air. "It was fortunate that I found those telegrams of Schellenberg's in the apartment. That should help him. I took great care over the translations so that there should be no doubts."

"I wish I was in there with him," she said, looking down the road.

"Sit down. Sit down, will you please?" The ambassador took a walnut-backed chair and moved it to face a corner of his desk, overanxious to bring Seton to rest. He remained standing himself until Seton was in the seat, and then, reassured, moved back and sat behind the desk. "I've had the Portuguese security people here for two days," he said. "Very awkward questions. It was very difficult to get you out. We've enough on our plate here, as it is."

Seton pulled the sheaf of papers from his pocket and handed them across the desk. "Read those."

The absence of courtesies annoyed the ambassador. He put the papers before him and pulled out pince-nez, picking up the first sheet only after looking again at Seton.

He read through two of the translations, checking each against the original German telegrams. Then he looked up and removed the glasses. "Where did you get these?"

"They're quite authentic."

"I have no doubt." A hand drummed on the table. "Some tea?"

Seton nodded and got up, walking over to the window, trying to get a view of the street, but the wall was too high.

Von Klagen tilted his head back over the top of the driver's seat, staring at the roof of the car. "How well did you know Dunsinnan?"

Ruth was glad that he was not looking directly at her—and then realized the averted gaze was a sign of discretion. She affected blandness. "Well . . . I'd known him awhile before. . . ."

Still looking at the car roof, he said, "At the castle, when I was there, in Scotland—I couldn't quite understand the relationship."

"His mother was a close family friend." She heard the falseness in her own words.

"It seemed to me—" He turned his head sideways, still resting on the back of the seat, and looked at her steadily, then completed the thought: "—it seemed to me that he knew you rather well."

She kicked off her shoes and stretched out her legs, looking out of the car to the embassy again. "He'd gotten a little crazy, even then."

"Mmmmm." Von Klagen sat up and pulled out a pack of miniature Spanish cigars, offering one to her. She shook her head. "You don't mind?" He lit the cigar and drew on it and wound down his window still further. Then he turned to her again: "What's going to happen to *you*, in this war?" He saw the skirt risen slightly up her thigh and the long dark legs. "Will you go home—to America?"

"Home is England."

"England may not be England for much longer."

"That's a possibility."

"You think they'll follow Churchill into the hills?"

She shrugged. "I don't know. I guess some of them will still try to settle for peace."

"At what price?"

"You could judge that better than I could."

"Yes," he said, lying back again on the seat and exhaling to the roof. "I hope the group captain appreciates your loyalty."

"One lump or two?" said the ambassador, silver tong in hand.

"None."

The cup was passed across the desk, and the ambassador hesitated before pouring his own tea. "Of course, the Germans could be misinterpreting the Duke's remarks—for their own purposes."

"You know the German minister, Huene, surely? Is he likely to do that?"

The Ambassador sat down and stirred the sugar into his tea. "No, as a matter of fact, to be frank, he isn't. He's not a party man. The legation here has been something of a haven for heretics." He sipped the tea. "Of course, this man Schellenberg, being here—that could be a source of pressure."

"Then it's pretty clear, isn't it? The Duke is already more than halfway over to their way of thinking."

The ambassador moved away his cup and took up more of the telegrams. "I see they've even roped in Franco's brother, Nicolas. And, of course, Primo de Rivera, the Fascist leader in Madrid." He looked across to Seton. "The trouble is, dear chap, I can do very little to keep these people away from them. The Duchess is constantly complaining, as it is, that they live like prisoners."

Seton slipped his cup onto the desk and began speaking quietly: "I think we had better be straightforward, don't you? The evidence is damning. You might see it as subversion. I don't. The man has been behaving disgracefully, to say the least. I don't give a damn about the so-called delicacies any longer. You've got to get them out of here. Pretty damn quick. The place is crawling with Schellenberg's agents."

The ambassador shuffled the telegrams uneasily. "The prime minister has certainly been very patient. This business about the manservants—"

"Either you get them out now—or I'll make sure those telegrams get out."

"*Get out?*" repeated the ambassador, incredulous. "Get out *where*, man?"

"The American papers."

There was a protracted silence. Finally the ambassador said, "That is quite the most intolerable suggestion I've ever heard."

"I can imagine that it is," said Seton, getting up and going to the door. "But if you check with London, you'll find it's perfectly consistent with my record."

A day later Seton came down the steps from the police headquarters and entered the square. He saw a newsstand outside the Europa Hotel and asked for an English paper.

"Sorry, no more come," said the man looking at Seton with unmasked pity. "Have the New York paper, from the Clipper, only three days old." He produced a copy of the *New York Times*. Seton took it like a man finding water in a desert, half expecting it to dematerialize on touch like a mirage, but it proved substantial enough, the first fat newspaper he had seen in a year, a sign of a world still free of material shortage. Reading it, he hardly noticed the other pedestrians or anything else as he walked. The main story was an account of the Dunkirk evacuation of the British army, in prose so purple that it conveyed some measure of what the spiritual experience must have been like. Not content with the factual recital, it culminated in phrases more suitable to a sermon:

So long as the English tongue survives, the word Dunkirk will be spoken with rever-

ENCE. FOR, IN THAT HARBOR, IN SUCH A HELL AS
NEVER BLAZED ON EARTH BEFORE, AT THE END OF A
LOST BATTLE, THE RAGS AND BLEMISHES THAT HAVE
HIDDEN THE SOUL OF DEMOCRACY FELL AWAY. . .
THIS SHINING THING IN THE SOULS OF FREE MEN
HITLER CANNOT COMMAND, OR ATTAIN, OR CON-
QUER. . . . IT IS THE FUTURE . . . IT IS VICTORY.

When he reached the hotel, he saw von Klagen waiting
in the lobby.

"Group Captain."

Taking his arm, Seton led him over to the bar. He
perched on a stool, and handed von Klagen the paper. "Read
that."

Von Klagen put down the paper as the drinks were
poured. "How is it that such a defeat can be seen as a victory?" he said.

Seton took up his glass. "What was it you said the other
day—winning the war out of moral force alone?"

Von Klagen raised his glass. "*Salut.* And farewell."

"Farewell?"

"Berlin. Tonight."

Seton sipped the drink. "You must see Ruth before you
go."

Von Klagen nodded. "You are very lucky, Group Captain."

Seton looked at his watch. "They've cut it fine."

From a corner of the quay they watched the last passengers board the American Export Line steamer, painted drab
gray for the Atlantic crossing. A Rolls-Royce had just pulled
up at the foot of the companionway, followed by two black
limousines.

"Look," said Ruth.

The two familiar figures, the purposeful woman and the
hesitant man, separated from the cluster of officials and
walked up into the ship, not turning. A succession of trunks
and suitcases followed, carried in haste.

"Who is this man—Sir Walter Monckton?" said Ruth.

"Churchill's man. He was in the thick of the abdication."

"He is here only three days—and they're off. What on
earth did he say to them?" She looked at Seton carefully.

"I wonder," he said.

Postscript

The Nazi plan to kidnap the Duke of Windsor in the summer of 1940 came to nothing. Walther Schellenberg left a self-serving account in his memoirs. As an alternative source there are the offical German despatches of the time. On July 11, 1940, the German minister in Lisbon told Berlin: "The Duke is convinced that if he had remained on the throne the war would have been avoided, and he characterises himself as a firm supporter of a peaceful arrangement with Germany."

It is impossible to be definitive about the Duke's state of mind in this period (as opposed to his own later recollection of it), since the British papers that bear on it, official and personal, have been withheld: official documents because of the fifty- and one-hundred-year British embargoes, and the personal papers because of family discretion. The record of the Duke's conversation with Hitler in 1937 (and that of other conversations between Hitler and leading British figures of the time) disappeared from the German archives some time after the war.

Despite the gaps in the record it seems clear from other accounts that the duke had a simplistic and credulous respect for Hitler's transformation of Germany. He was probably quite guileless enough to believe that by his appearing as the peacemaker between Britain and Germany, the interests of both nations could have been reconciled. He believed (with others) that otherwise many millions of Britons would die in the war. And probably, that the war would be lost.

There was no Lord Dunsinnan. However, his ends (if not his means) were ardently pursued by a number of prominent people during the 1930s. It was only possible to invent Dunsinnan because, in varying degrees, his creed existed.

ABOUT THE AUTHOR

CLIVE IRVING was born the day after Hitler came to power. Growing up in wartime Britain gave him an abiding curiosity about the Hitler phenomenon. But it was only after twenty years working as a journalist in Britain and the United States that he conceived the idea for a novel dealing with the origins of the war, and *Axis* is his first work of fiction, based on extensive factual research.

Bantam Book Catalog

Here's your up-to-the-minute listing of over 1,400 titles by your favorite authors.

This illustrated, large format catalog gives a description of each title. For your convenience, it is divided into categories in fiction and non-fiction—gothics, science fiction, westerns, mysteries, cookbooks, mysticism and occult, biographies, history, family living, health, psychology, art.

So don't delay—take advantage of this special opportunity to increase your reading pleasure.

Just send us your name and address and 50¢ (to help defray postage and handling costs).